FIRST LOVE,
Second Chance

**MARIE
FERRARELLA**

**MELISSA
McCLONE**

**TINA
BECKETT**

MILLS & BOON

CONTENTS

The Fortune Most Likely To...

Marie Ferrarella

USA TODAY bestselling and RITA® Award–winning author **Marie Ferrarella** has written more than two hundred and seventy-five books for Harlequin, some under the name Marie Nicole. Her romances are beloved by fans worldwide. Visit her website, marieferrarella.com.

Books by Marie Ferrarella

Matchmaking Mamas

Engagement for Two
Christmastime Courtship
A Second Chance for the Single Dad
Meant to Be Mine
Twice a Hero, Always Her Man
Dr. Forget-Me-Not
Coming Home for Christmas
Her Red-Carpet Romance
Diamond in the Ruff
Dating for Two
Wish Upon a Matchmaker
Ten Years Later...
A Perfectly Imperfect Match
Once Upon a Matchmaker

The Montana Mavericks: The Great Family Roundup

The Maverick's Return

The Fortunes of Texas: The Secret Fortunes

Fortune's Second-Chance Cowboy

Montana Mavericks: The Baby Bonanza

A Maverick and a Half

Montana Mavericks: What Happened at the Wedding?

Do You Take This Maverick?

Visit the Author Profile page
at millsandboon.com.au for more titles.

Dear Reader,

Welcome back to the tumultuous, always exciting world of the Fortunes. One of my favorite themes to write about is former lovers who have gone their separate ways, only to have circumstances forcing them, for one reason or another, to interact with each other again. The characters always have a history to revisit, which makes the story so much richer for me to tell.

Such is the case with Lila Clark and Everett Fortunado. They were high school sweethearts, and the world was rosy and full of promise for them—until Lila became pregnant. Neither one of them felt that they were ready to be parents, so at Everett's urgings, Lila gave the baby up for adoption. It immediately changed the way that she viewed Everett. He had taken the situation in stride, but Lila couldn't, and she broke up with him shortly afterward, leaving not just Everett but the city they lived in, Houston, as well. Fast forward fourteen years. A chance encounter with Lila while Everett is visiting his younger sister in Austin resurrects that old feeling for him. Neither of them ever found anyone to replace the other. Could this be fate trying to drive them together? Everett wants to fully explore that. Read the story and see if he's right.

As always, I thank you for taking the time to read one of my stories, and from the bottom of my heart, I wish you someone to love who loves you back.

All the best,

Marie

To
Susan Litman,

with thanks

for her

patience

PROLOGUE

IT WAS TIME that he finally faced up to it. He had never gotten over her.

Sitting on the sofa in his living room, Dr. Everett Fortunado frowned as he looked into the glass of expensive whiskey he was sipping. The single glass, two fingers, was his way of winding down. Not from a hectic day spent at his successful, thriving medical practice, but from the stress of terminating yet another less-than-stellar, stillborn relationship.

How many failed relationships did that make now? Ten? Twelve? He wasn't sure.

He'd honestly lost count a number of years ago.

Admittedly, the women in those incredibly short-lived relationships had all become interchangeable. Now that he thought about it, none of them had ever stood out in his mind. And, if he was being honest about it, Everett couldn't remember half their names.

As for their faces, well, if pressed, he could give a general description, but there again, nothing about any of them had left a lasting impression on his mind. Strictly speaking, he could probably pass one or more of them on the street and not recognize them at all.

A mirthless laugh passed his lips. At thirty-three he was way too young to be on the threshold of dementia. No, that wasn't the reason behind this so-called memory loss problem. If he were being entirely honest with himself, he thought, taking another long, bracing sip of whiskey, this cavalcade of women who had been parading through his life for the last thirteen years were only poor substitutes for the one woman who had ever really mattered to him.

The only woman he had ever been in love with.

The woman he had lost.

Lila Clark, the girl he'd known since forever and had barely been aware of until he suddenly *saw* her for the first time that day in Senior English class. Though a straight A student, Everett had found himself faltering when it came to English. Lila sat next to him in class and he'd turned to her for help. She was the one responsible for getting him through Senior English.

And somewhere along the line during all that tutoring, Lila had managed to make off with his heart. He was crazy about her and really excited when he found out that she felt the same way about him. Not long after that, they began making plans for their future together.

And then it had all blown up on him.

When he'd lost her, his parents had told him that it was all for the best. They had pointed out that he was too young to think about settling down. They wanted their brightest child to focus on his future and not squander his vast potential by marrying a girl from a working-class family just because he'd gotten her pregnant. To them it had been the oldest ploy in the world: a poor girl trapping a rich boy because of his sense of obligation.

But Lila really wasn't like that. And she hadn't trapped him. She'd walked out on him.

Everett sat on the sofa now, watching the light from the lone lamp in his living room play across the amber liquid in the chunky glass in his hand. He would've given anything if he could go back those thirteen years.

If he could have, he wouldn't have talked Lila into giving up their baby for adoption.

Because that one thing had been the beginning of the end for them.

He'd been at Lila's side in the delivery room and, even then, he kept telling her that they were doing the right thing. That they were too young to get married and raise this baby. That they could always have more kids "later."

Lila changed that night. Changed from the happy, bright-eyed, full-of-life young woman he'd fallen in love with to someone he no longer even knew.

And that was the look in her eyes when she raised them to his. Like she was looking at someone she didn't recognize.

Right after she left the hospital, Lila had told him she never wanted to see him again. He'd tried to reason with her, but she just wouldn't listen.

Lila had disappeared out of his life right after that.

Crushed, he'd gone back to college, focusing every bit of energy entirely on his studies. He'd always wanted to be a doctor, ever since he was a little boy, and that became his lifeline after Lila left. He clung to it to the exclusion of everything else.

And it had paid off, he thought now, raising his almost-empty glass in a silent toast to his thriving career. He was a doctor. A highly successful, respected doctor. His career was booming.

Conversely, his personal life was in the dumpster.

Everett sighed. If he had just said, "Let's keep the baby," everything would have been different. And his life wouldn't have felt so empty every time he walked into his house.

He wouldn't have felt so empty.

Blowing out a breath, Everett rose from the sofa and walked over to the liquor cabinet. Normally, he restricted himself to just one drink, but tonight was different. It was the anniversary of the day Lila had ended their relationship. He could be forgiven a second drink.

At least, he told himself, he could fill his empty glass, if not his life.

CHAPTER ONE

"YOUR PROBLEM, BROTHER DEAR," Schuyler said after having listened to him tell her that maybe he'd made a mistake talking Lila into giving up their baby all those years ago, "is that you think too much. You're always overthinking things and making yourself crazy in the process."

"Says the woman who always led with her heart," Everett commented.

"And that seems to be working out for me, doesn't it?" Schuyler asked.

He could hear the broad smile in her voice. It all but throbbed through the phone. Everett had no response for that. All he could do at the moment was sigh. Sigh and feel just a little bit jealous because his little sister had found something that he was beginning to think he never would find again: love.

"By thinking so much back then about how everything would affect your future," Schuyler went on, "I think you blew it with Lila. You were so focused on your future, on becoming a doctor, that you just couldn't see how badly she felt about giving up her baby—*your* baby," she emphasized. "And because you didn't notice, didn't seem to feel just as badly as she did about the adoption, you broke Lila's heart. If it were me, I would have never forgiven someone for breaking my heart that way," Schuyler told him.

"Thanks for being so supportive," Everett said sarcastically.

This was *not* why he'd called his sister, why he'd lowered his guard and allowed himself to be so vulnerable. Maybe he should have known better, he thought, about to terminate the call.

"I *am* being supportive," Schuyler insisted. "I'm just calling it the way I see it. I love you, Ev, and you know I'm always on your side. But I know you. I don't want you to get your hopes up that if you just approach her, she'll fly back into your arms and everything'll be just the way it was back then. Not after thirteen years and *not* after what went down between the two of you back then. Trust me, Lila is not going to get back together with you that easily."

"I know that and I don't want to get back together with Lila," he insisted defensively. "I just want to talk to her." Everett paused because this next thing was hard for him to say, even to Schuyler, someone he had always trusted implicitly. Lowering his voice, he told his sister, "Maybe even apologize to her for the way things ended between us back then."

He could tell from Schuyler's voice that she felt for him. But she was far from optimistic about the outcome of all this. "Look, Everett, I know that your heart's in the right place, but I really don't want to see it stomped on."

"No worries," Everett assured her. "My heart is not as vulnerable as you think."

What he'd just said might have been a lie, but if it was, it was a lie he was telling himself as well as his sister.

He had a feeling that Schuyler saw it that way too because he could hear the skepticism in her voice as she said, just before she ended their call, "Well, I wish you luck with that. Maybe Lila'll listen to reason."

* * *

Maybe.

The single word seemed to throb in his head as Everett decided to find out as much as he could about Lila and what she was doing these days.

It had all started two months ago when he'd taken the day off, gotten another doctor to cover for him and had driven the 165 miles from Houston to Austin to pick up his sister, Schuyler. At the time, he was supposed to be bringing Schuyler back home.

Given to acting on impulse, his younger sister had initially gone to Austin because she had gotten it into her head to track down Nathan Fortune. The somewhat reclusive man was supposedly her cousin and the ever-inquisitive Schuyler was looking for answers about their family tree. The current thinking was that she and the rest of their brothers and sisters were all possibly related to the renowned Fortune family.

It was while Schuyler was looking for those answers that she decided to get closer to the Mendoza family whose history was intertwined with the Fortunes. She managed to get so close to one of them—Carlo Mendoza—that she wound up completely losing her heart to him.

Confused, unsure of herself for very possibly the first time in her life, Schuyler had turned to the one person she was closest to.

She'd called Everett.

Listening to his sister pouring out her heart—and citing her all uncertainties, not just about her genealogy investigation but about the direction her heart had gone in—he had decided he needed to see Schuyler and maybe convince her to come home.

But Schuyler had reconciled with her man and decided to stay in Austin after all. Everett returned home without her. But he hadn't come away completely empty-handed. What Everett had come home with was a renewed sense of having made a terrible mistake thirteen years ago. And that had come about because while he'd been in Austin, he had run into Lila.

Sort of.

He saw Lila entering a sandwich shop and it had been a jarring experience for him. It had instantly propelled him back through time and just like that, all the old feelings had come rushing back to him, saturating him like a huge tidal wave. At least they had in his case. However, he'd been struck by the aura of sadness he detected about her. A sadness that had *not* been there when they were in high school together.

He'd thought—hoped really—that when he got back to Houston, back to his practice, he'd be able to drive thoughts of Lila back into the past where they belonged. Instead, they began to haunt him, vividly pushing their way into his dreams at night, sneaking up on him during the day whenever he had an unguarded moment.

He began wondering in earnest about what had happened to her in all those years since they'd been together. And that sadness he'd detected—was *he* responsible for that? Or was there some other reason for its existence?

He felt compelled to find out.

Like everyone else of his generation, Everett turned to social media in his quest for information about Lila Clark.

He found her on Facebook.

When he saw that Lila had listed herself as "single" and that there were only a few photographs posted on her page, mainly from vacation spots she had visited, he felt somewhat heartened.

Maybe, a little voice in his head whispered, it wasn't too late to make amends after all.

Damn it, Everett, get hold of yourself. This is exactly what Schuyler warned you about. Don't get your hopes up, at least not until you talk to Lila again and exchange more than six words with her.

Who knows, she might have changed and you won't even like Lila 2.0.

Everett struggled to talk himself out of letting his imagination take flight. He tried to get himself to go slow—or maybe not go at all.

But the latter was just not an option.

He knew he felt too strongly about this, too highly invested in righting a wrong he'd committed in the past. Now that he'd made up his mind about the matter, he needed to make Lila understand that he regretted the way things had gone thirteen years ago.

Regretted not being more emotionally supportive of her.

Regretted not being able to see the daughter they had *both* lost.

Still, he continued to try to talk himself out of it for two days after he found Lila on Facebook. Tried to make himself just walk away from the whole idea: from getting in contact with her, from apologizing and making amends. All of it.

But he couldn't.

So finally, on the evening of the third day, Everett sat down in front of his computer, powered up his internet connection and pulled up Facebook. Specifically, he pulled up Lila's profile.

He'd stared at it for a full ten minutes before he finally began to type a message to her.

Hi, Lila. It's been a long time. I'm planning on being in Austin soon. Let's have lunch together and do some catching up. I'd really welcome the chance to see and talk with you.

Those four simple sentences took him close to half an hour to settle on. He must have written and deleted thirty sentences before he finally decided on those. Then it took him another ten minutes before he sent those four sweated-over sentences off into cyberspace.

For the next two hours he checked on that page close to a dozen and a half times, all without any luck. He was about to power down his computer for the night when he pulled up Lila's Facebook page one last time.

"She answered," he announced out loud even though there was no one around to hear him.

Sitting down in his chair, he read Lila's response, unconsciously savoring each word as if it was a precious jewel.

If you're going to be here Friday, I can meet you for lunch at 11:30. I just need to warn you that I only get forty-five minutes for lunch, so our meeting will be short. We're usually really swamped where I work.

Everett could hardly believe that she'd actually agreed to meet with him. He'd been half prepared to read her rejection. Whistling, he immediately posted a response.

11:30 on Friday sounds great. Since I'm unfamiliar with Austin, you pick the place and let me know.

After sleeping fitfully, he decided to get up early. He had a full slate of appointments that day. Best to get a jump on it. But the minute he passed the computer, he knew what he had to do first.

And there, buried amid approximately forty other missives—all of which were nothing short of junk mail—was Lila's response. All she'd written was the name of a popular chain of restaurants, followed by its address. But his heart soared.

Their meeting was set.

If he'd been agile enough to pull it off, Everett would have leaped up and clicked his heels together.

As it was, he got ready for work very quickly and left the house within the half hour—singing.

The second Lila hit the send button on Facebook, she immediately regretted it.

What am I thinking? she upbraided herself. Was she crazy? Did she actually *want* to meet with someone who had so carelessly broken her heart? Who was responsible for the single most heart-wrenching event to have happened in her life?

"What's wrong with you? Are you hell-bent on being miserable?" she asked herself as she walked away from her computer. It was after eleven o'clock at night and she was alone.

The way she was on most nights.

Maybe that was the problem, Lila told herself. She was tired of being alone and when she'd seen that message from Everett on her Facebook page, it had suddenly stirred up a lot of old memories.

"Memories you're better off forgetting, remember?" she demanded.

But they weren't all bad, she reminded herself. As a matter of fact, if she thought back, a lot of those memories had been good.

Very good.

For a large chunk of her Senior year and a portion of her first year at community college, Everett had been the love of her life. He'd made her happier than she could ever remember being.

But it was what had happened at the end that outweighed everything, that threw all those good recollections into the shadows, leaving her to remember that awful, awful ache in her heart as Emma was taken out of her arms and she watched her baby being carried away.

Away from her.

She'd wanted Everett to hold her then. To tell her that he was aching as much as she was. That he felt as if something had been torn away from his heart, too, the way she felt it had for her.

But all he had said was: "It's for the best." As if there was something that could be described as "best" about never being able to see your baby again. A baby that had been conceived in love and embodied the two of them in one tiny little form.

Lila felt tears welling up in her eyes even after all this time, felt them spilling out even though she'd tried hard to squeeze them back.

She wished she hadn't agreed to see Everett.

But if she'd said no to lunch, Everett would have probably put two and two together and realized that she hadn't the courage to see him again. If she'd turned him down, he would've understood just how much he still mattered to her.

No, Lila told herself, she had no way out. She *had* to see him again. Had to sit there across from him at a table, making inane conversation and proving to him that he meant nothing to her.

That would be her ultimate revenge for his having so wantonly, so carelessly, ripped out her heart without so much as a moment's pause or a word of actual genuine comfort.

"We'll have lunch, Everett," she said, addressing his response that was posted on her Facebook page. "We'll have lunch, and then you'll realize just what you lost all those years ago. Lost forever. Because I was the very best thing that could have ever happened to you," she added with finality.

Her words rang hollow to her ear.

It didn't matter, she told herself. She had a couple of days before she had to meet with him. A couple of days to practice making herself sound as if she believed every syllable she uttered.

She'd have it letter-perfect by the time they met, she promised herself.

She *had* to.

CHAPTER TWO

HALF THE CONTENTS of Lila's closet was now spread out all over her bed. She spent an extra hour going through each item slowly before finally making up her mind.

Lila dressed with great care, selecting a two-piece gray-blue outfit that flattered her curves as well as sharply bringing out the color of her eyes.

Ordinarily, putting on makeup entailed a dash of lipstick for Lila, if that. This morning she highlighted her eyes, using both mascara and a little eye shadow. She topped it off with a swish of blush to accent her high cheekbones, smoothed her long auburn hair, then sprayed just the slightest bit of perfume.

Finished, she slowly inspected herself from all angles in her wardrobe mirror before she decided that she was ready to confront a past she'd thought she'd buried—and in so doing, make Dr. Everett Fortunado eat his heart out.

Maybe, Lila thought as she left her house, if she took this much trouble getting ready for the occasional dates she went out on, she might not still be single at the age of thirty-three.

Lila sighed. She knew better. It wasn't her clothes or her makeup that were responsible for her single status.

It was her.

After breaking up with Everett, she had picked herself up and dusted herself off. In an all-out attempt to totally reinvent herself, Lila had left Houston and moved to Austin where no one knew her or anything about the past she was determined to forget and put totally behind her.

She'd gone to work at the Fortune Foundation, a nonprofit organization dedicated to providing assistance to the needy. Through hard work, she'd swiftly risen and was now manager of her department.

And because of her work, Lila's life went from intolerable to good. At least her professional life did.

Her personal life, however, was another story.

Sure, she'd dated. She'd tried blind dates as well as online dating. She'd joined clubs and had gone to local sporting events to cheer on the home team. She'd gone out with rich men as well as poor ones and those in-between.

It wasn't that Lila couldn't meet a man, she just couldn't meet *the* man.

And probably even if she could, she thought, that still wouldn't have done the trick. Because no matter who she went out with, she couldn't trust him.

Everett had destroyed her ability to trust any man she might become involved with.

Try as she might, she couldn't lower her guard. She just couldn't bear to have a repeat performance of what had happened to her with Everett.

Rather than risk that, she kept her heart firmly under lock and key. And that guaranteed a life of loneliness.

At this point in her life, Lila had decided to give up looking for Mr. Right. Instead, she forced herself to embrace being Stubbornly Single.

As she took one last look in the mirror and walked out the door, she told herself that was what she really wanted.

One day she might convince herself that was true.

Her upgraded appearance did not go unnoticed when she walked into the office at the Fortune Foundation that morning.

"Well, someone looks extra nice today," Lucie Fortune Chesterfield Parker noted the moment that Lila crossed the threshold. "Do you have a hot date tonight?" she asked as she made her way over toward Lila.

"No, I don't," Lila answered, hoping that would be the end of it.

Belatedly, she thought that maybe she should have brought this outfit with her and changed in the ladies' room before going to lunch instead of coming in dressed like this.

Lucie and she were friends and had been almost from the very first time they met at the Foundation, but Lila really didn't want to talk about the man she was having lunch with.

Initially from England, Lucie was married to Chase Parker, a Texas oil heir who had been her teenage sweetheart. Because of that, Lucie considered herself to be an expert on romance and she felt she had great radar when it came to the subject.

Her radar was apparently on red alert now as she swiftly looked Lila over.

Studying her, Lucie repeated, "Not tonight?"

"No," Lila said firmly. She never broke stride, determined to get to her office and close the door on this subject—literally as well as figuratively.

"Lunch, then?" Lucie pressed. "You certainly didn't get all dolled up like that for us."

Lila looked at her sharply over her shoulder, but her coworker didn't back off. The expression on her face indicated that she thought she was onto something.

When Lila made no response, Lucie pressed harder. "Well, *are* you going to lunch with someone?"

Lila wanted to say no and be done with it. She was, after all, a private person and no one here knew about her past. She'd never shared any of it. No about the child she'd given up for adoption or the man who had broken her heart. However, it wasn't in her to lie and even if it were, Lucie was as close to a real friend as she had in Austin. She didn't want to risk alienating her if the truth ever happened to come out—which it might, likely at the most inopportune time.

So after a moment of soul-searching, she finally answered Lucie's question.

"Yes."

Lucie looked at her more closely, obviously intrigued. "Anyone I know?" she asked.

"No," Lila answered automatically.

Not anyone I know, either. Not really, Lila silently added. After all, it had been thirteen years since she'd last been with Everett. And besides, how well had she known him back then anyway? He certainly hadn't behaved the way she'd expected him to. It made her think that maybe she had never really known Everett Fortunado at all.

"Where did you meet him?" Lucie wanted to know, apparently hungry for details about her friend's lunch date.

"Why all the questions?" Lila reached her office, but unfortunately it was situated right next to Lucie's. Both offices were enclosed in glass, allowing them to easily see one another over the course of the day.

"Because you're my friend and I'm curious," Lucie answered breezily. "You've practically become a workaholic these last couple of months, hardly coming up for air. That doesn't leave you much time for socializing."

Pausing by her doorway, Lila blew out a breath. "It's someone I knew back in high school," she answered. She stuck close to the truth. There was less chance for error that way. "He's in town on business for a couple of days. He looked me up on Facebook and he suggested having lunch to catch up, so I said yes."

Lila walked over to her desk, really hoping that would be the end of it. But apparently it wasn't because Lucie didn't retreat to her own office. Her friend remained standing in Lila's doorway, looking at her as if she was attempting to carefully dissect every word out of her mouth.

"How well did you know this guy—back in high school, I mean?" Lucie asked, tacking on the few words after a small beat.

Lila stood there feeling as if she was under a microscope.

Did it show, she wondered. Did Lucie suspect that there had been more than just high school between her and Everett?

"Why?" she asked suspiciously, wondering what Lucie was getting at. It wasn't that she didn't trust Lucie, it was just that inherently she had trouble lowering her guard around *anyone*.

"Well, if someone who I knew back in high school suddenly turned up in my life," Lucie said easily, "I don't think I'd dress up in something that would make me look like a runway model just to go out to lunch with him."

Lila shrugged, avoiding Lucie's eyes. "I'm just showing off the trappings of a successful career, I guess."

"Are you sure that's all it is?" Lucie asked, observing her closely.

Lila raised her chin, striking almost a defiant pose. "I'm sure," she answered.

Lucie inclined her head, accepting her friend's story. "Well, if I were you, I'd remember to take a handkerchief with me."

Lila stared at the other woman. What Lucie had just said made absolutely no sense to her.

"Why?"

Lucie's smile was a wide one, tinged in amusement. "Because you'll need a handkerchief to wipe up your friend's drool once he gets a load of you looking like that."

Lila looked down at herself. Granted, she'd taken a lot of time choosing what to wear, but it was still just a two-piece outfit. "I don't look any different than I usually do," Lila protested.

Lucie's smile widened a little more as she turned to leave. "Okay, if you say so," she answered agreeably, going along with Lila's version. "But between you and me, you look like a real knockout."

Good, Lila thought. That was the look she was going for.

There were mornings at work when the minutes would just seem to drag by, behaving as if lunchtime would never come. Lila would have given anything for that sort of a morning this time around because today, the minutes just seemed to race by, until suddenly, before she knew it, the clock on the wall opposite her office said it was eleven fifteen.

She'd told Everett that she would meet him at the restaurant she'd selected at eleven thirty.

That meant it was time for her to get going.

Lila took a deep breath, pushed her chair away from her desk and got up.

When she stood up, her hands braced against her desk, her legs felt as if they had suddenly lost the power of mobility.

For a moment, it was as if she was rooted in place.

This was ridiculous, Lila told herself, getting her purse from her drawer.

She closed the drawer a little too hard. The sound reverberated through the glass walls and next door Lucie immediately looked in her direction. Grinning, Lucie gave her a thumbs-up sign.

Lila forced herself to smile in response then, concentrating as hard as she could, she managed to get her frozen legs moving. She wanted to be able to leave the office before Lucie thought to stick her head in to say something.

Or ask something.

This was all going to be over with soon, Lila promised herself.

Once out of the building, she made her way to her car. An hour and she'd be back, safe and sound in the office and this so-called "lunch date" would be behind her, Lila thought, trying to think positive thoughts.

It would be behind her and she'd never have to see Everett again.

But first, she pointedly reminded herself, she *was* going to have to get through this ordeal. She was going to have to sit at a table, face Everett and pretend that everything was just fine.

She was going to have to pretend that the past was just that: the past, and that it had nothing to do with the present. Pretend that those events from thirteen years ago didn't affect her any longer and definitely didn't get in the way of her eating and enjoying her lunch. Pretend that the memory of those events didn't impede her swallowing, or threaten to make her too sick to keep her food down.

Reaching her car, Lila got in and then just sat there, willing herself to start it. Willing herself to drive over to the restaurant and get this lunch over with.

Not a good plan, Lila. This is not a good plan. You should have never agreed to have lunch with Everett. When he wrote to you on your Facebook page, asking to meet with you, you should have told him to go to hell and stay there.

You've got no one to blame but yourself for this.

Lila let out a shaky breath and then glanced up into the rearview mirror.

Lucie was right. She looked fantastic.

Go and make him eat his heart out, Lila silently ordered herself. *And then, after you've finished eating and he asks if he could see you again, you tell him No!*

You tell him no, she silently repeated.

Taking another deep breath, she turned the key in the ignition.

The car rumbled to life. After another moment and a few more words of encouragement to herself, Lila pulled out of her parking space and drove out of the parking structure and off the lot.

* * *

The restaurant she'd selected was normally barely a five-minute drive away from the Foundation. Even with the sluggish midday traffic, it only took her ten minutes to get there. Before she knew it, she was pulling into a space in the restaurant's parking lot.

Sitting there, thinking of what was ahead of her, Lila found that she had to psych herself up in order to leave the shelter of her vehicle and walk into the restaurant.

To face her past.

"No," she contradicted herself through gritted teeth. "Not to face the past. To finally shut the door on it once and for all and start your future."

Yes, she had a life and a career, a career she was quite proud of. But she also needed to cut all ties to the woman she had once been. That starry-eyed young woman who thought that love lasted forever and that she had found her true love. That woman had to, quite simply, be put to rest once and for all.

And she intended to do that by having lunch with Everett, the man who had taken her heart and made mincemeat out of it. And once lunch was done, she was going to tell him goodbye one last time. Tell him goodbye and make him realize that she meant it.

Lila slowly got out of her car and then locked it.

Squaring her shoulders, she headed for the restaurant. It was time to beard the lion in his den and finally be set free.

CHAPTER THREE

THIS WAS ABSURD, Everett thought. He was a well-respected, sought-after physician who had graduated from medical school at the top of his class. Skilled and exceedingly capable. Yet here he was, sitting in a restaurant, feeling as nervous as a teenager waiting for his first date to walk in.

This was Lila for God's sake, he lectured himself. Lila, someone he'd once believed was his soul mate. Lila, whom he'd once been closer to than anyone else in the world and had loved with his whole heart and soul. There was absolutely no reason for him to be tapping the table with his long fingers and fidgeting like some inexperienced kid.

Yet here he was, half an hour ahead of time, watching the door when he wasn't watching the clock, waiting for Lila to walk in.

Wondering if she wouldn't.

Wondering if, for some reason, she would wind up changing her mind at the last minute and call him to cancel their lunch. Or worse, not call at all.

Why am I doing this to myself? Everett silently demanded.

Why was he making himself crazy like this? So what if she didn't show? It wouldn't be the end of the world. At least, no more than it was all those years ago when Lila had told him she didn't ever want to see him again.

The words had stung back then and he hadn't known what to do with himself, how to think, what to say. In time, he'd calmed down, started to think rationally again. He had decided to stay away from her for a while, thinking that Lila would eventually come to her senses and change her mind.

Except that, when he finally went to see her, he found out that she was gone. Lila had taken off for parts unknown and no one knew where. Or, if they did know, no one was telling him no matter how much he asked.

That was when his parents had sat him down and told him that it was all for the best. They reminded him that he had a destiny to fulfill and now he was free to pursue that destiny.

Not having anything else to cling to, he threw himself into his studies and did exactly what was expected of him—and more.

He did all that only to end up here, sitting in an Austin restaurant, watching the door and praying each time it opened that it was Lila coming in and walking back into his life.

But each time, it wasn't Lila who walked in.

Until it was.

Everett felt his pulse leap up with a jolt the second he saw her. All these years and she had only gotten more beautiful.

He immediately rose in his seat, waving to catch her attention. He had to stop himself from calling out her name, instinctively knowing that would embarrass her. They weren't teenagers anymore.

Lila had almost turned around at the door just before she opened it. It was only the fact that she would have been severely disappointed in herself for acting like such a coward that forced her to come inside.

The second she did, she immediately saw Everett and then it was too late to run for cover. Too late to change her mind.

The game was moving forward.

She forced a smile to her lips despite the fact that her stomach was tied in a knot so tight she could hardly breathe. It was the sort of smile that strangers gave one another in an attempt to break the ice. Except that there was no breaking the ice that she felt in her soul as she looked at Everett.

All the old heartache came rushing back to her in spades.

"I'm sorry," she murmured to Everett when she finally reached the table. "Am I late?"

"No," he quickly assured her. "I'm early. I didn't know if there was going to be a lot of traffic, or if I'd have trouble finding this place, so I left the hotel early." A sheepish smile curved his lips. "As it turned out, there was no traffic and the restaurant was easy enough to find."

"That's good," she responded, already feeling at a loss as to what to say next.

She was about to sit down and Everett quickly came around the table to hold out her chair for her.

"Thank you," she murmured, feeling even more awkward as she took her seat.

Having pushed her chair in for her, Everett circled back to his own and sat down opposite her. He could feel his heart swelling just to look at her.

"You look really great," Everett told her with enthusiasm.

Again she forced a quick smile to her lips. "Thank you," she murmured.

At least all that time she'd spent this morning fussing with her makeup and searching for the right thing to wear had paid off, she thought. Looking good, she had once heard, was the best revenge. She wanted Everett to be aware of what he'd given up. She wanted him to feel at least a little pang over having so carelessly lost her.

The years had been kind to him, as well, she reluctantly admitted. His six-foot frame had filled in well, though he was still taut and lean, and his dark hair framed a handsome, manly face and highlighted his dark-blue eyes. Eyes that seemed to be studying her.

"But you do seem a little…different somehow," Everett said quietly a moment later.

She wasn't sure what he meant by that and it marred her triumph just a little. Was that a veiled criticism, she wondered.

"Well, it has been thirteen years," she reminded Everett stiffly. "We knew each other a long time ago. That is," she qualified, "if we ever really knew each other at all."

He looked at her, wondering if that was a dig or if he was just being extremely touchy.

It seemed there were four of them at the table. The people they were now and the ghosts of the people they had been thirteen years ago.

The moment stretched out, becoming more uncomfortable. "What's that supposed to mean?" Everett asked her.

"Just an observation," Lila answered casually. "Who really knows who they are at that young an age?" she asked philosophically. "I know that I didn't."

He sincerely doubted that. "Oh, I think you did," Everett told her.

Seeing the server approaching, she held her reply. When the server asked if he could start them out with a drink, Lila ordered a glass of sparkling water rather than anything alcoholic. Everett followed her example and asked for the same.

"And if you don't mind, I'd like to order now," Lila told the young server. "I have to be getting back to the office soon," she explained.

"Of course."

After he took their orders and left, Everett picked up the thread of their conversation. "I think you knew just what you wanted years ago," he told her. "I'm the one who got it all wrong."

Was he saying that out of pity for her, she wondered, feeling her temper beginning to rise as her stomach churned.

"On the contrary," Lila responded. "You were the only kid who was serious when he said he wanted to play 'doctor.' If you ask me, 'Dr. Fortunado' achieved everything he ever dreamed about as a kid."

Everett's eyes met hers. Longing and sadness for all the lost years filled him. For the time being, he disregarded the note of bitterness he thought he detected in her voice.

"Not everything," he told her.

This was an act. She wasn't going to fall for it, Lila thought, grateful that the server picked that moment to return with their drinks and their orders. Everett wasn't fooling her. He was just saying that so that she would forget about the past. Forget her pain.

As if that were remotely possible.

Silence stretched out between them. Everett shifted uncomfortably.

"So, tell me about you," he finally urged. "What are you doing these days?"

Lila pushed around the lettuce in her salad as if the fate of the world depended on just the right placement. She kept her eyes on her plate as she spoke, deliberately avoiding making any further eye contact with him. She had always loved Everett's dark blue eyes. When they'd been together, she felt she could easily get lost in those eyes of his and happily drown.

Now she couldn't bear to look into them.

"I'm a manager of one of the departments at the Fortune Foundation. My work involves health outreach programs for the poorer families living in the Austin area."

That sounded just like her, Everett thought. Lila was always trying to help others.

But something else she'd said caught his attention. "Did you say the Fortune Foundation?"

"Yes," she answered. Suspicion entered her voice as she eyed him closely and asked, "Why?"

"Well, it just seems funny that you should mention the Fortunes. My family just recently found out that our last name might very well be 'Fortune' rather than 'Fortunado.'" He pulled his face into a grin. "Crazy coincidence, isn't it?"

Coincidence. Lila had another word for it. Her eyes narrowed as she pinned him with a look. "Is that why you wanted to get together for lunch?" she wanted to know. "To ask me questions about the Fortunes and see how much information you could get?"

He stared at her, practically dumbstruck. What was she talking about?

"The fact that you work for the Fortune Foundation has absolutely nothing to do with my wanting to get together with you," Everett insisted. Thinking over her accusation, he shook his head. "I'm not even sure if the family *is* connected to the Fortunes. It could all just be a silly rumor or a hoax.

"And even if it *does* turn out to actually be true, my family's not positive if we want to reveal the connection. It sounds like there are a lot of skeletons in the Fortune closet. Actually," he confessed, backtracking, "maybe I spoke out of turn, talking about the possible connection. I'd appreciate it if you didn't say anything to anyone at the Foundation."

Did he think she was going to go running back after lunch and act like a human recording device, spilling every word that had been said between them? Just what sort of an image did he have of her?

Lila found herself struggling to tamp down her temper before she said anything.

"Well, obviously not everyone at the Foundation is a Fortune," she pointed out icily. "And anyway, the Fortunes are a huge family. I don't think anyone would be surprised to find out that there's another branch or two out there. There've been so many that have been uncovered already."

Everett nodded. "Makes sense," he agreed, even though he still felt a little leery about having the story spread around that the Fortunados believed that they were really Fortunes. Trying to steer the conversation in a different direction, he asked, "I'm curious—what do you think of the Fortunes?"

Lila's smile was reserved. She remembered hearing a great many unnerving rumors concerning the Fortune family before she began working at the Foundation. But most of what she'd been told turned out not to be true. For the most part, the stories were just run-of-the-mill gossip spread by people who were jealous of the family's success as well as their money.

"In my experience," she qualified in case he wanted to challenge her words, "they're a great family. A lot of people hold the fact that they're rich against them, but the family does a lot of good with that money. The Fortunes I've met aren't power hungry or self-centered. A great many of them have devoted their lives to the Foundation, to doing as much good as they can," she emphasized.

"Power-hungry and self-centered," Everett repeated the words that she had used. "Is that the way you think of most rich people?" he asked. Then, before Lila could answer, he went on to ask her another question—the question he *really* wanted the answer to. "Is that how you think of me?"

Her eyes narrowed again as she looked at Everett intently. Rather than answering his question, she turned it around and asked Everett a question of her own. "Did I say that?" she asked pointedly.

"No," he was forced to admit. She hadn't said it in so many words, but he felt that Lila had implied it by the way she'd structured her sentence.

"Then let's leave it at that, shall we?" Lila told him.

It was obvious to Everett that he was going to have one hell of a rough road ahead of him if he ever hoped to win her over. And despite what he had told his sister to the contrary, he really did want to win Lila back.

He admitted to himself that Lila was the missing ingredient in his life, the reason that every triumph he had had felt so hollow, so empty. It felt that way because Lila wasn't there to share it with him.

For now, he changed the subject to something lighter. "You know," he said as he watched Lila make short work of her Caesar salad, "as a doctor I should tell you that eating your food that fast is really not good for your digestion."

"And being late getting back from lunch isn't good for my job approval," Lila countered tersely. Finished, she retired her fork.

Was she really serious about needing to get back so quickly? Initially, he'd thought it was just an excuse, a way to terminate their meeting if she felt it wasn't going well. Now she seemed to be waving it in front of her like a flag at the end of a marathon.

"I thought you said that you were the manager of your department."

"I am. And as manager, it's up to me to set a good example," she told him.

If she really wanted to leave, Everett thought, he couldn't very well stop her. "Can't argue with that, I guess."

"No, you can't," she informed him, a stubborn look in her eyes as they met his.

He gave it one last try. "I suppose this means that you don't want to order dessert. I remember that you used to love desserts of all kinds," he recalled.

"I did," she acknowledged. "But then I grew up," she told him crisply. "And right now, I'm afraid I have no time for dessert."

He nodded. "Maybe next time, then."

Lila was about to murmur the obligatory, "It was good seeing you again," but his words stopped her cold. "Next time?" she echoed, surprised and stunned.

She sounded far from happy about the prospect. Everett did his best to ignore the coolness in her voice. Instead, he explained his comment. "I might be spending more time in Austin over the next few months."

"Oh?" She could feel the walls going up around her. Walls meant to protect her. She could feel herself struggling with the strong desire to run for the hills. She forced herself not to move a muscle. "Why?"

"Well, with Schuyler engaged to Carlo Mendoza and living here, I thought I'd be the good brother and visit her from time to time to make her transition here a little easier for her." This was harder than he thought it would be and it took him a few moments before he finally said, "I was wondering if it's all right with you if I call you the next time I'm in Austin."

His question was met with silence.

CHAPTER FOUR

DESPITE THE FACT that the restaurant was enjoying a healthy amount of business with most of the tables taken, the silence at their table seemed to wrap tightly around Everett and Lila.

Lila realized that Everett was waiting for her to answer him. And unfortunately, the floor hadn't opened up and swallowed her, so she was forced to say *something*. At a loss and wanting to stall until something came to her, Lila played dumb.

Clearing her throat she asked, "Excuse me? What did you say?"

Everett had a sinking feeling in the pit of his stomach as he repeated, "I asked if it would be all right with you if I called you the next time I was in Austin. You know, so we could get together again," he added and then watched her, waiting for an answer.

Again? Lila thought, astonished. *I'm barely surviving this time.*

She debated just shrugging her shoulders and saying, "Sure," with the hopes that if and when Everett called, she would have been able to come up with some sort of a viable excuse why she couldn't see him again.

But if she didn't put him off now, there was the very real possibility that she'd be doomed to go through another uncomfortable meeting in the near future.

Gathering her courage, Lila told him, "Um, I'm not sure if that's such a good idea."

If he were being honest with himself, Everett had half expected her to react this way. Still, actually *hearing* Lila say the words was very difficult for him.

Nodding grimly at her rebuff, he told her, "I understand."

But he really didn't understand because he didn't think it was a bad idea. He thought it was a perfectly *good* idea, one that would allow him another chance to convince her that they should try making their relationship work again after all these years.

Because they *belonged* together.

"Well, I really need to get going," she told Everett, rising to her feet. When he began to do the same, she quickly said, "Oh, don't leave on my account. Stay," she urged. "Have that dessert," she added. And then she concluded coldly, "I wish you luck with the rest of your life."

Then, turning on her heel, she quickly left the restaurant without so much as a backward glance.

Lila didn't exhale until the restaurant doors closed behind her.

Her heart was hammering hard and the brisk walk to her car had nothing to do with it. Lila didn't come anywhere close to relaxing until she reached her vehicle and got in.

Then she released her breath slowly.

She'd done it, she thought. She'd survived seeing him again.

She really hoped that Everett hadn't realized just how affected she was by his presence. With that in mind, there was just no way she could see him again, Lila thought. She was certain that she wouldn't be able to endure being face-to-face with Everett a second time, even if it was only for a couple of minutes.

But she'd done it. Lila silently congratulated herself as she started up her car. She'd sat across from Everett Fortunado and she hadn't bolted. She'd held her ground until she announced that she had to be getting back.

And now, having made it through that and gotten it out of the way, she could go on with the rest of her life.

Everett left the restaurant a couple of minutes after Lila did. There seemed to be no point in staying. He'd only mentioned having dessert because he remembered how fond of sweets she had always been. The thought of dessert had no allure for him, especially now that Lila had left. So he paid the tab and walked out.

He had barely managed to get into his car and buckle up before his cell phone rang. His first thought when he heard the phone was that it was Lila, calling to say she had changed her mind about having him call her the next time he was in Austin.

But when he answered the phone, it wasn't Lila. It was Schuyler.

"So how was it?" his sister asked in lieu of a hello.

Trying hard not to sound irritated, he asked her, "Why are you calling? I could have still been at the restaurant with Lila."

"I took a chance," she told him. "If you were still with Lila, I figured you wouldn't have answered your cell. But you did," she concluded with a resigned sigh. "So I take it that she really did have a short lunch break."

He didn't have it in him to lie or make something up, so he just said vaguely, "Something like that."

He should have known Schuyler wanted to know more. "What was it like *exactly*?" she asked him.

Everett sighed. There was no point in playing games or pretending that everything was fine. He'd been pretending that for the last thirteen years and it had just brought him to this painful moment of truth. And he knew that Schuyler would just keep after him until he told about lunch.

"I think Lila might hate me," he said to his sister. He'd said "might" because stating it flatly just hurt too much.

"Hate you?" Schuyler questioned in surprise. "Why? What happened at lunch?" Then she chuckled. "Did she try to set you on fire?"

Everett laughed dryly. "No, she stopped short of that. But when I asked if I could call her again the next time I was in Austin, she told me she didn't think that was such a good idea."

"Wait, back up," Schuyler told her brother. "You *asked* her if you could call?"

"Yes." Schuyler was making it sound like he'd done something bad, but he had just been trying to be thoughtful of Lila's feelings. He didn't want Lila thinking he just presumed things. He was proud of the fact that he was first and foremost a gentleman.

He heard his sister sigh in disbelief. "Everett, you are a brilliant, brilliant doctor and probably the smartest man I know, but what you know about women could be stuffed into a walnut shell with room for a wad of chewing gum. You don't *ask* a woman if you can call her. You just call her."

He didn't operate like that. "What if she doesn't want me to call?"

"Then you'll find that out *after* the fact," Schuyler told him. "Believe me, if she doesn't want you to call, she'll let you know when she answers the phone. But if you hold off calling because she said she doesn't want you to, then you might wind up missing out on an opportunity."

This was making his head hurt. "Nothing is straightforward with you women, is it?"

"That's where the aura of mystery comes in," Schuyler told him with a laugh. And then her voice sobered. "*Are* you planning on seeing Lila again?"

Lila had as good as told him not to—but he couldn't bring himself to go along with that. Not yet. Not while he felt that there might be the slimmest chance to change her mind.

"I'm going to try," he confessed.

"When?" Schuyler questioned. "Now?"

"No." He was still smarting from Lila's rejection. "I think I'm going to give her a little time to mull things over. I'll probably talk with her the next time I'm in Austin."

"Talk with her about what?" Schuyler wanted to know.

"I want to make things right," Everett explained simply. "Maybe even tell her—"

Schuyler cut him off before he could say anything further. "Ev, not even *you* can bring back the past, you know that, right?"

"Yes, I know that," he said impatiently, "but I just want Lila to know that I wish I'd handled things differently back them. Schuyler, you have your happy ending in the works," he pointed out, "but I wound up driving away the best thing that ever happened to me and I'll do anything to get her back."

"Oh Everett," Schuyler said, emotion in her tone, "that is deeply, deeply romantic—and deeply, deeply flawed. You're going to wind up failing and having your heart broken into a thousand little pieces, and then ground up into dust after that."

"I don't want to hear about it, Schuyler," he told his sister with finality. "I don't need you to tell me how I can fail. I need you to tell me that I'll get her back. I *need* to get her back," he emphasized.

He heard Schuyler sigh, as if she was surrendering. "Okay. Just please, *please* don't do anything stupid," his sister warned.

"I already did," Everett told her. "I let Lila go in the first place."

"Everett—"

"I'll be in touch, Schuy," he told her before he terminated the call.

Everett gave it to the count of ten, then opened his phone again. He had a call to make and then he had to get back on the road if he wanted to reach Houston before nightfall.

Lila didn't need to get back to the office that quickly. She'd just told Everett that she did so she had a way to end their lunch.

She'd estimated that half an hour in his company was about all she could take.

She had a feeling that if she came back early, the people she worked with, the ones who seemed to take such an inordinate interest in her life, would be all over her with questions.

Especially Lucie.

But if she timed it just right, she could slip into the office just as they were coming back from their own lunches. That way she stood a better chance of avoiding any questions.

She thought it was a good plan and it might have actually worked—if it hadn't been for the flowers. Two dozen long stemmed red roses in a glass vase to be precise. They were right there, in the middle of her desk, waiting for her when she walked into the office an hour after she'd left.

And there, right next to the vase, was Lucie. With a broad smile on her face.

"You just missed the delivery guy," she told Lila. "I signed for them for you."

"Um, thank you," Lila murmured, although what she was really thinking was that Lucie shouldn't have bothered doing that.

"No problem," Lucie answered cheerfully. Her eyes were practically sparkling as she looked from the flowers to her friend. It was obvious that she had barely been able to curtail her curiosity and keep from reading the card that had come with the roses. "Who are they from?"

"I have no idea," Lila murmured, eyeing the roses uneasily, as if she expected them to come to life and start taunting her.

"You know a really good way to find out?" Lucie asked her innocently. When Lila glanced in her direction, Lucie told her with great clarity: "Read the card."

Lila nearly bit off that she *knew* that. Instead, resigned, she said, "I guess I'll have to."

"Boy, if someone sent me roses, I'd sound a lot happier than that," Lucie commented.

"Want them?" Lila offered, ready to pick up the vase and hand it over to her friend.

"I'd love them," Lucie said with feeling. "But I can't take them. They're yours. Now who sent them?" Her eyes narrowed as she looked directly into Lila's.

Steeling herself, Lila reached over and plucked the small envelope stuck inside the roses. Slowly opening it, she took out the off-white rectangular card.

Till next time. Everett.

Her hand closed around the card. She was tempted to crush the small missive, but something held her back.

Damn it, why couldn't the man take a hint? Why was he determined to haunt her life this way? Why couldn't he just stay away the way he had done for the last thirteen years?

"Well?" Lucie asked, waiting. She tried to look over her friend's shoulder to read the card. "Who sent the flowers?"

"Nobody," Lila answered evasively.

"Well 'nobody' must have some pretty deep pockets," Lucie commented, eyeing the roses. "Do you know what roses are going for these days?"

"I don't know and I don't care," Lila answered defiantly. She was debating throwing the card into the trash.

"Well, 'nobody' certainly does. Care, I mean," Lucie clarified. "By any chance, are these flowers from the guy you went out to lunch with?"

Lila closed her eyes. She really did wish she could convincingly carry off a lie, but she couldn't. Absolutely no answer came to her, so she found herself having to admit the truth.

"Maybe."

Lucie gave a low whistle as she regarded the roses. "All I can say is that you must have made one hell of an impression at lunch."

"No, I didn't," Lila replied. "He asked if he could call me again and I told him I didn't think that was such a good idea."

Taking in the information, Lucie nodded. "Playing hard to

get. That really turns some guys on," she confided. "They see it as a challenge."

"I'm not playing hard to get," Lila stressed between gritted teeth. "I'm playing impossible to get."

"Same thing for some guys," Lucie responded knowingly. "What you did was just upped the ante without realizing it. Play out the line a little bit, then tell him that you've had a change of heart because he's so persistent. Then reel him in."

She felt like her back was up against the wall and Lucie was giving her fishing analogies. She looked at the other woman in disbelief. "You're telling me I should go out with him?"

"What I'm telling you is that you should give him another chance," Lucie told her.

Another chance. She knew that was what Everett wanted as well, even though he'd started out by acting as if he didn't, Lila thought. But there was no other reason why he would want to call her the next time he was in Austin *unless* he wanted another chance. It certainly wasn't because they'd had such a spectacular time today at lunch and he wanted to continue that.

They hadn't been spectacular together in a long, long time, Lila thought.

She tried to close her mind off from the memories, but they insisted on pushing their way through, punching through the fabric of the years.

Echoes from the past both softened her and squeezed her heart, reminding her of the pain she'd gone through at the end.

How could she willingly open herself up to that again? She'd barely recovered the last time.

Lila blinked. Lucie was standing in front of her, waving her hand in front of her eyes.

"Hey, Earth to Lila. Earth to Lila," Lucie called out.

"What?" Lila responded, stopping short of biting off an angry cry.

"I was talking to you and you seemed like you were a million miles away. Where were you just now?"

Lila blew out a quick breath and pulled herself together.

"You called it," she told the other woman. "I was a million miles away. And now it's time to come back and get to work," she announced. "I've got a stack of reports to review so I can make the rounds tomorrow."

Lucie inclined her head. "I can take a hint."

"I certainly hope so," Lila murmured under her breath.

Hearing her, Lucie added, "For now," as she left the room.

Lila suppressed a groan. Glaring at the roses, she moved the vase to the windowsill.

It didn't help.

CHAPTER FIVE

"HAVE YOU GIVEN 'Mr. Roses' any more thought?" Lucie asked her a few days later completely out of the blue.

They were each preparing their input to submit for their departments' monthly budget and, taking a break, Lucie had peered into her office to ask about Everett.

Surprised by the unexpected salvo—she'd thought she was out of the woods since Lucie hadn't brought the subject up for several days—Lila answered, "None whatsoever." She deliberately avoided Lucie's eyes as she said it.

"You're lying," Lucie said.

This time Lila did look up. She shot her a look that was just short of a glare, but Lucie wasn't intimidated.

"You know how I know?" Lucie asked her.

Lila braced herself inwardly. Her outward countenance didn't change. "Please, enlighten me," she requested coolly.

"You're blushing," Lila pointed out triumphantly. "Every time you say something that you're not entirely comfortable about—like a little white lie—you start to blush."

Lila drew herself up. "I do not," she protested. But even as she said it, she could feel her cheeks getting warmer.

"Got a mirror?" Lucie asked. She appeared to be serious. "I'll show you."

Lila sighed, dropping her head back. "Okay, so I've thought about him, but the answer to your next question is still 'no.' I'm not going to be seeing him again anytime soon—*or ever.*"

Lucie shook her head. It was obvious by her expression that she thought Lila was turning her back on a golden opportunity.

"I think you're making a mistake," Lucie told her in no uncertain terms.

"My mistake to make," Lila informed her cheerfully. And then, because she knew that Lucie was only looking out for her, she relented. "No offense, Lucie. I know you're a romantic at heart. I'm aware of your story," she went on. "You and Chase were teenage sweethearts who, despite a few bumps on the road—"

"Big bumps," Lucie emphasized, interjecting her own narrative.

"—were meant to be together," Lila continued, pushing on. "But not everyone is like you. Most teenage sweethearts usually outgrow each other and are meant to be apart."

"Aha," Lucie exclaimed. "So you two were teenage sweethearts."

Lila stared at her. That had been a slip. "I didn't say that," she protested.

"Not in so many words," Lucie countered. "But you definitely implied it. Lila," she said, lowering her voice as she put her hand over her friend's. "The heart wants what the heart wants and it doesn't always make perfect sense. But old loves imprint themselves on your heart and on your brain. Take it from me. They *always* stay with you."

"That might have been your experience," Lila granted. "And I know that you and Chase are extremely happy—"

"We are," Lucie assured her.

Lila forged on. "—but not everyone is like you," she concluded. "As a matter of fact, I'm pretty sure that very few people are like you."

Apparently her remark didn't satisfy Lucie, who went on. "Why don't you give this guy another chance and see if you belong to the 'very few?'" she suggested.

Lila went back to looking over her notes and figures for the budget. "Not going to happen."

Lila might have wanted to drop the subject, but Lucie obviously didn't. The subject of reunited lovers was something that was near and dear to her heart.

"Why?" Lucie asked her. "What are you so afraid of, Lila?"

Lila's eyes met her friend's. "I'm afraid of not getting my budget done in time," she said in a crisp voice.

"Seriously," Lucie coaxed.

"Seriously," Lila insisted, refusing to be distracted from the subject any further.

Just then, she saw a movement out of the corner of her eye. She looked toward the doorway. For a split second, she was afraid that Everett had found his way up to the office, but then she realized, as the man drew closer, that it was a deliveryman—and he was carrying another vase filled with flowers.

Not again!

"Oh, look, more roses," Lucie announced gleefully. "Just in time to replace the ones that are beginning to wilt," she added, grinning at Lila.

"How do you know they're for me?" Lila asked almost defensively. "There are plenty of other people who work here."

"Oh, I just have a feeling," Lucie told her, her eyes sparkling as she looked at her.

Her grin grew wider as the deliveryman came over to Lila's office where they were working.

"Ms. Clark?" the deliveryman asked, looking from one young woman to the other.

"That would be her," Lucie said, pointing toward Lila.

With a nod of his head, the deliveryman offered Lila what looked like a rectangular, brown Etch A Sketch.

"Would you sign here for the flowers, please?" the man requested.

Though she was strongly tempted to refuse the flowers, Lila didn't want to create problems for the deliveryman, so she did as he had said.

Then he indicated the flowers. "Where do you want them?" he asked her.

"Be nice, Lila," Lucie cautioned, as if she could see that her friend was tempted to tell the man exactly where she wanted him to put the roses.

Resigned, Lila told the deliveryman, "I'll take them."

When she did, she realized that this vase felt even heavier than the last one had. Looking closer, she saw that the vase appeared to be cut crystal.

"Have a nice day," the deliveryman told her cheerfully, retreating.

"With those roses, how could she do otherwise?" Lucie asked, calling after him.

"You like them so much, here, you take them," Lila said, trying to hand the vase over to the other woman.

But Lucie raised her hands up high, putting them out of reach and thus keeping the transfer from being carried out.

"You know what this means, don't you?" she asked Lila.

"That the price of roses is being driven up even higher?" Lila asked sarcastically.

Lucie shook her head. She looked very pleased with this turn of events.

"No. It means that you might think you're done with this guy from your past, but he clearly is *not* done with you."

Lila had another take on the situation. "Maybe he's just not used to taking no for an answer," she countered, frowning, then insisted, "All these flowers don't mean anything."

"You know, you still haven't answered my question," Lucie

said, watching as Lila placed the flowers on the windowsill beside the other vase.

Lila didn't bother fussing with the newest arrangement. Instead, she sat down at her desk again, still trying to focus on the budget that was due. "What question is that?"

Slowly, enunciating each word for emphasis, Lucie repeated, "What are you afraid of?"

"I thought I answered that," Lila told her. "I believe I said I was afraid of not getting my budget done in time."

Lucie's eyes met hers. "You know I'm just going to keep after you until you tell me what's up with you and this guy."

And she knew very well that Lucie would, Lila thought. This had to stop. It was bad enough she was trying to get Everett to back off and leave her alone. She did *not* need her friend championing Everett's cause as well.

"Lucie, I love you like a sister—but butt out," she told Lucie in no uncertain terms.

"Sorry," Lucie replied, looking at her innocently. "That doesn't compute."

Lila rolled her eyes. "*Make* it compute," she told Lucie and with that, she ushered the woman out and closed the door to her office because, all distractions and two dozen roses aside, she really *did* have a budget to hand in before the end of the week. Which meant that she had no time to think about Everett Fortunado and his attempts to get her to give him another chance to shatter her heart.

The roses on the windowsill were beginning to drop their petals. They fell sporadically, drifting like soft pink tears onto the industrial beige floor covering in her office.

There was something sad about watching the flowers wilt.

Or maybe she felt that way because, despite the two separate deliveries of long-stem roses, she had not heard from Everett since she'd left him in the restaurant on their one and only lunch date—if it could actually have been called that.

Lila told herself that she was relieved. If Everett didn't call, then she didn't have to come up with an excuse not to see him.

But amid all that so-called relief, she had to admit that there was just the slightest tinge of disappointment as well. She really hadn't thought that Everett would give up so easily, or so quickly.

But he obviously had.

He'd moved on and he was off her conscience—not that she'd ever done anything to feel guilty about when it came to Everett, she silently insisted. Everett, on the other hand, had a lot to atone for—

What was wrong with her? she suddenly upbraided herself. Why was she wasting time thinking about Everett or trying to figure out why he'd behaved the way he had? She didn't have time for all that, she admonished herself. Less time than usual.

She was in the middle of a very real health crisis.

Everyone at the Fortune Foundation was. They had been stricken by an unseasonable, full-fledged flu epidemic that was laying everyone low. As a result, they were understaffed, with almost a third of both the volunteers and employees alike calling in sick.

Being short-staffed when it came to the workers was one thing. But now two of the doctors who regularly volunteered their services, making the rounds and tending to the people in her district, had fallen sick and were out of commission as well.

What that meant in the short run was that there weren't enough doctors to administer the flu vaccines or to treat the people who were down with it.

This directly affected Lila, who oversaw the department that made certain poor families in her area had access to flu shots and to medical care.

She needed replacement for the sick doctors. STAT.

Lila had spent half the morning on the phones, calling every backup physician she could think of in the area. All the calls yielded the same results. The doctors were either up to their ears in patients—or they were sick themselves.

The cupboard, Lila thought, exasperated, was appallingly bare. There weren't any doctors in or around Austin left to call.

Frustrated, she closed her physicians' file on the computer. The people whose trust she had painstakingly worked to gain and whom she had gathered into the fold now needed help, and they were counting on her to come through. They weren't going to believe her when she said that she couldn't find any doctors to make house calls.

But it was true. She was totally out of doctors to call. Totally out of options…

Except for one, she suddenly realized as the thought zig-zagged through her brain.

She hated to do this. Hated to have to call him and sound as if she was begging.

But this wasn't about her, Lila reminded herself. This was about the sick people who were counting on her. People who were in desperate need of medical care. Otherwise, some of them, the very young and the very old, might not make it.

Telling herself not to think about what she was doing, Lila took out the card Everett had handed her during the less than successful lunch. The card with his phone number on it.

Not his cell phone. She didn't want this to sound personal, although *that*, she had a feeling, might get the fastest results.

Lila squared her shoulders and rejected the thought about using Everett's cell phone number. She was going to try his office phone number first—and pray that she got through that way.

Tapping out the number on her landline, Lila found herself connected to a recording with a list of menu options.

Feeling unusually short-tempered, Lila nearly hung up at that point. But she forced herself to stay on. This was about the kids, she reminded herself. The kids, not her. She needed to try every available possibility.

After dutifully listening to the selections, she pressed "Number 4 for Dr. Fortunado."

That connected her to yet another recording, which asked her to leave her name, phone number and a brief message. The recording promised her a return call within twenty-four hours. It didn't sound reassuring, but she supposed that it was better than nothing.

The second the "beep" went off, Lila began talking.

"Everett, it's Lila. I'm sorry to bother you like this, but we've been hit really hard with this flu epidemic. I'm down two doctors, not to mention a number of staff members. Every backup physician I've called is already handling too many patients— if they're not sick themselves. I'm totally out of options, otherwise I wouldn't be bothering you. I know you're an internist and not a family practitioner, but to put it quite simply, I'm desperate. A lot of the people I interact with are down with this flu and I need help.

"If you're too busy to return this call, I'll understand. However, I hope you'll consider it. You can reach me in my office, or on my cell." She proceeded to recite both numbers slowly. "I hope to hear from you soon, but like I said, if you decide you can't help, I'll understand."

With that, she hung up and desperately tried to think of some other course of action. Maybe she could try physicians' assistants in the area. The way she saw it, it was any port in a storm at this point.

But she just ran into wall after wall.

Lila was beginning to think that the situation was hopeless.

And then her phone rang.

Snatching the receiver up, she cried, "This is Lila Clark," as she literally crossed her fingers, hoping that one of the many, *many* doctors she had called today was calling back to tell her that after due consideration, they had found a way to spare a few hours to work with the needy families.

"Lila," the deep voice on the other end of the line said. "It's Everett."

CHAPTER SIX

As the sound of his voice registered, Lila felt as if everything had suddenly ground to a standstill all around her.

But maybe her imagination was playing tricks on her, or she had just heard incorrectly and *thought* it was Everett calling her. Someone else might have said that wishful thinking was to blame, but she refused to call it that.

Rousing herself, Lila asked in a small, stilted voice, "Everett?"

"Yes."

She exhaled a shaky breath before saying his name, as if to make certain that it really was him calling. "Everett."

Had he gotten her message? Lila wondered. Or was this just a coincidence and he was calling because she hadn't acknowledged the roses he'd sent her? Taking nothing for granted, Lila replied, "I called you earlier today—"

"Yes, I know," he responded. "About a flu epidemic you're having in Austin. That's the reason I'm calling back. If you still need me, I can be there by tomorrow morning."

Relief swept over her, drenching her like a huge tidal wave

and stealing her breath. Lila was certain she now understood how lottery winners felt.

"Oh, I need you," she said with feeling, and then she realized how that must have sounded to him. Mortified, Lila immediately backtracked. "That is… I mean—"

She heard Everett laugh softly. That same old laugh that used to make her skin tingle and had warm thoughts flowing all through her, fast and heavy.

"That's okay, I know what you meant," Everett assured her. "Are you really that short-handed out there?"

Looking at the mounting stack of calls on her desk, almost all requesting help, she stifled a groan. "You have no idea."

"Well, you can give me a tour and let me see what you're up against when I get there tomorrow," he told her.

She knew that Everett had his own practice and that he was going to have to make arrangements on his end in order to accommodate her, even for one day. It didn't take a genius to know that that he was really going out of his way for her.

"I can't begin to tell you how much I appreciate this, Everett," Lila began.

Everett cut her short. "I'm a doctor," he replied simply. "This is what I do." She heard papers being moved around on his end. "I should be able to get in by eight. Where should I meet you?"

This was really happening, she thought. Everett was actually coming to her rescue, despite the way everything had ended between them the last time they saw one another. Relief and gratitude mingled with a sharp twinge of guilt within her.

"Why don't we meet at the Fortune Foundation?" she suggested to him. "And we can go from there."

Lila went on to give him the address of the building, although that would have been easy enough for him to look up if he wanted to. She told him which floor she was on as well as the number of her office.

"I can wait outside the building for you if that'll be easier," Lila added.

"That won't be necessary," Everett assured her. "They taught me how to count in medical school."

Had she just insulted him somehow? Afraid of saying something wrong, Lila felt as if she was stumbling over her own tongue. "Oh, I'm sorry. I didn't mean to—"

"Lila," Everett raised his voice as he cut into her words. When she abruptly stopped talking, he told her, "Stop apologizing."

She took a deep breath, trying to center herself and regroup. None of this was easy for her. Not when it came to Everett. "Um, I guess I'm just not used to asking for favors."

Everett read between the lines. "Don't worry. I'm not going to ask you for a favor back if that's what you're thinking," he assured her. There was another moment of awkward silence on her end and then he said, "All right, if I'm going to be there tomorrow morning, I've got a few things to see about between now and then. See you tomorrow," he told her.

Everett hung up before she had a chance to thank him again.

Lila slowly returned the receiver back to its cradle. "Well," she murmured, still feeling somewhat numb as she continued to look at the receiver, "that at least solves some of my problem."

She was still one doctor down, but one out of two was a lot better in her opinion than none out of two, she told herself. She could definitely work with one.

In the meanwhile, she needed to get the list of patients prepared for the doctors who *were* coming in so that they could start making those house calls.

Lila looked down at the various names and addresses she'd already jotted down. The number of people who were just too ill to get to a local clinic on their own was astounding, and growing rapidly. Some of the people, she thought, were probably exaggerating their conditions, but she couldn't really blame them. The free clinics were always positively jammed from the moment they opened their doors in the morning. Waiting to be seen by a doctor was exceedingly challenging when you weren't running a fever. Sitting there with a fever of a hundred or more and feeling too weak to win a wrestling match against a flea was a whole different story. If she were in that position, she'd ask to have the doctor come to the house, too.

Oh, who are you kidding? You could be at death's door and you'd drag yourself in to see the doctor because you wouldn't want to inconvenience anyone.

Lila smiled to herself as she gathered her things together to meet with the physicians who were volunteering their time today.

The silent assessment rang true. She'd rather die than to surrender to her own weakness, Lila thought, going out the door.

Lila was exhausted.

Having stayed late, reorganizing supplies and hustling all over the city to beg, borrow or threaten to steal more vaccine serum as well as arranging for more lab tests to be done, she had finally dragged herself home after midnight.

Too tired to eat, she still hadn't been able to get right to sleep—most likely because part of her kept thinking about having to interact with Everett after she had summarily rejected him the last time they had been together.

But she had finally dropped off to sleep somewhere around 1:00 a.m., only to wake up at 4:30 a.m., half an hour before her alarm was set to go off.

She lay there for several minutes, staring at the ceiling, telling herself that she had half an hour before she needed to get up, which meant that she could grab a few more minutes of sleep.

She gave up after a couple more minutes, feeling that there was no point in trying to get back to sleep. She was wired and that meant she was up for the day.

With a sigh, she got up, showered and dressed. A piece of toast accompanied her to her car, along with a cup of coffee that would have been rejected by everyone except a person who felt they had no extra time to make a second, better cup of coffee.

Sticking the thick-sludge-contained-in-a-cup into a cup holder, Lila started the car.

There had to be a better way to achieve sainthood, she thought cryptically to herself as she drove to the Foundation in the dark.

The streets were fairly empty at that time in the morning. The lack of light just intensified the pervasive loneliness that seemed to be invading every space in her head.

Snap out of it, damn it, she ordered. *He's a doctor and you need a doctor in order to help out. And that's all you need.*

However, ambivalent feelings about seeing Everett again refused to leave her alone. They continued to ricochet through her with an intensity that was almost numbing.

He's not Everett, she silently insisted. *He's just an available doctor who's willing to help you. That's what you have to focus on, not anything else, understand? Don't you dare focus on anything else.* She all but threatened herself.

It helped.

A little.

Arriving in the parking lot located behind the Fortune Foundation building, she found that there were only a few vehicles that pockmarked the area at this hour. Apparently the Foundation had a few early birds who liked to come in and get a jump-start on the day and the work they had to do.

As she made her way toward the entrance, she saw that one of the cars, a navy blue high-end sedan, had someone sitting inside it in the driver's seat.

As she passed the vehicle, the driver's side door opened and Everett stepped out. A very casual-looking Everett wearing boots, jeans and a zippered sweatshirt with a hood.

She almost hadn't recognized him.

Her heart suddenly began to hammer very hard when she did.

"I got here early," he told her, nodding at Lila by way of a greeting. "Traffic from Houston wasn't too bad this time," he explained. He saw the way she was looking at what he was wearing. He looked down at his attire himself, just to be sure that he hadn't put anything on inside out. "I didn't want to look intimidating," he explained. "Someone told me that three-piece suits make some people nervous."

The way he said it, she felt as if he was implying she was the nervous person.

You've got to stop reading into things, she upbraided herself. Out loud she told him, "You look fine. We need to go in," she said, changing the subject as she turned toward the building. "I need to get a few things before we head out."

Everett nodded, gesturing toward the main doors. "You're the boss," he told her.

That almost made her wince. "This'll work better if you just think of me as your tour guide," she said, avoiding looking at him.

Holding the door open for her, Everett followed her into the building. "You told me that you manage the department," he recalled.

"I do," she answered cautiously, wondering where he was going with this.

"Then that would make you my boss for this," Everett concluded. "At least for now."

This had all the signs of degenerating into a dispute. But Everett *was* doing her a favor by coming in today and he was getting no compensation for it. She didn't want to pay him back by arguing with him.

"Whatever works for you is fine with me," Lila told him loftily.

He smiled at her as they headed toward the elevators. "I'll keep that in mind."

Was he just being agreeable, or was that some sort of a veiled warning, she wondered. This was all very exhausting and they hadn't even gotten started, Lila thought.

The next moment, as she got into the elevator, Lila told herself that any way she looked at it, this was going to be one hell of a long day.

But then, she had her doubts that Everett was going to be able to keep up. Making house calls to all the people on her list was going to turn into a marathon as well as an endurance test, at least for Everett.

And maybe her, too.

Getting what she needed from her office, Lila led the way back out of the building. "We'll use my car," she told him.

"Fair enough," Everett answered agreeably. "You know your way around here a lot better than I do."

"At least in the poor sections," she answered. They had barely gotten out on the road when she said, "Be sure to let me know when you've had enough."

He thought that was rather an odd thing to say, seeing as how they hadn't even been to see one patient yet. "And then what?" he wanted to know.

She spared him a glance as she drove through a green light. The answer, she thought, was rather obvious. "And then we'll stop."

"For the day?" he questioned.

"Well, yes." What else did he think she meant? They weren't talking about taking breaks.

"You made it sound like you needed me for the long haul," he said. And to him, that meant the entire day—with the possibility of more after that.

"I do." However, she didn't want to seem presumptuous and she definitely didn't want to totally wear him out. "But—"

"Well, then that's what you've got me for," Everett said, interrupting. "The long haul," he repeated.

Was he saying that to impress her, or did he really mean it, she wondered.

"I just wanted to warn you," she said as they drove to a rundown neighborhood. "This isn't going to be what you're used to."

He looked at her then. "No offense, Lila, but we haven't seen each other for a very long time," he reminded her. "You have no idea what I'm used to."

Everett was right, she thought, chagrined. She had no idea what he been doing in the years since they had seen one another. She knew, obviously, that he had achieved his dream and become a doctor. She had just assumed that he had set up a practice where he tended to the needs of the richer people in Houston. It never occurred to her that he might concern himself with even middle-class patients, much less those who belonged to the lower classes: the needy and the poor. And she had no idea that he ever volunteered his time to those less fortunate.

"You're right," she admitted quietly. "I don't. I just know that your parents had high hopes for you and that you weren't the rebellious type."

Everett was only half listening to her. For the most part, he was taking note of the area they were now driving through. It appeared seedy and dilapidated. It was light out now, which made the streets only a tad safer looking.

He tried to imagine what it was like, driving through here at night. "How often do you come out here?" he wanted to know.

"As often as I need to. I usually accompany the doctors who volunteer at the Foundation. It wouldn't be right to ask them to come here and not be their go-between."

"Go-between?"

She nodded. "Some of the doctors have never been to places like this before. They're uneasy, the patients they've come to treat are uneasy when they see the doctor. I'm kind of a human tranquilizer," she told him. "It's my job to keep them all calm and get them to trust each other enough so they can interact with one another," she explained.

"A human tranquilizer, huh?" he repeated with a grin, trying to envision that. "I kind of like that."

She laughed as she brought her small compact car to a stop in front of a ramshackle house that looked as if it was entering its second century.

"I had a feeling you would." Pulling up the hand brake, she turned off the ignition. "We're here," she announced needlessly. "You ready for this?" she asked, feeling somewhat uneasy for him.

Everett looked completely unfazed. "Let's do it," he told her, getting out on his side.

Lila climbed out on the driver's side, rounded the hood of her car and then led the way up a set of wooden stairs that creaked rather loudly with each step she took. Like the house, the stairs had seen better years and were desperately in need of repair.

Reaching the top step, she approached the front door with its peeling paint and knocked.

"The doorbell's out," she explained in case Everett was wondering why she hadn't rung it. "I've been here before," she added.

"That was my guess," Everett responded.

A moment later, the front door opened rather slowly. Instead of an adult standing on the other side, there was a small, wide-eyed little boy looking up at them. He was holding onto the doorknob with both hands.

In Everett's estimation, the boy couldn't have been any older than four.

CHAPTER SEVEN

LILA THOUGHT THAT Everett had dropped something when she saw him crouching down at the door of their first house call—single mother Mrs. Quinn. The next moment, she saw that what he was doing was trying to get down to the level of the little boy who stood across the threshold.

"Does your mom know you open the door to strangers?" Everett asked the boy.

The little boy shook his head from side to side, sending some of his baby-fine, soft blond hair moving back and forth about his face. "No. Mama's asleep next to my little brother."

"You're very articulate," Everett told the little boy. "How old are you?"

"Four," the boy answered, holding up four fingers so that there would be no mistaking what he said. "What's ar-tic—, ar-tic—" Giving up trying to pronounce the word, he approached it from another angle. "What you said," he asked, apparently untroubled by his inability to say the word.

"It means that you talk very well," Everett explained. Then he rose back to his feet. Glancing toward Lila so that the boy would know she was included, he requested, "Why don't you take us to see them? I'm a doctor," he added.

That seemed to do the trick. The little boy opened the door further, allowing them to come in. "Good, 'cause Mama said they need a doctor—her and Bobby," the four-year-old tacked on.

Impressed at how well Everett was interacting with the boy, Lila let him go on talking as she and Everett followed him through the cluttered house.

"Is Bobby your brother?" Everett asked.

This time the blond head bobbed up and down. "Uh-huh."

"And what's your name?" Everett asked, wanting to be able to address their precocious guide properly.

"Andy," the boy answered just as he reached the entrance to a minuscule bedroom. "We're here," he announced like the leader of an expedition at journey's end.

There was a thin, frail-looking dark-haired woman lying on top of the bed, her eyes closed, her arm wrapped around a little boy who was tucked inside the bed. The woman looked as if the years had been hard on her.

Andy tiptoed over to her and tried to wake her up by shaking her arm.

"Mama, people are here. Mama?" he repeated, peering into her face. He looked worried because her eyes weren't opening.

Lila finally spoke up. "Mrs. Quinn?" she said, addressing the boys' mother. "It's Lila. I brought a doctor with me."

The young woman's eyelashes fluttered as if she was trying to open them, but the effort was too much for her. She moaned something unintelligible in response to Lila's announcement.

Before Lila could say anything either to the woman or to Everett, he took over.

Moving Lila aside, he felt for the woman's pulse. Frowning, he went on to take her temperature next, placing a small, clear strip across her forehead.

"No thermometer?" Lila asked.

"This works just as well," he assured her. Looking at the strip, he nodded. "She's running a low-grade fever." Checking the boys' mother out quickly, he told Lila, "I can't give her a flu shot because she already seems to have it. But I can lower her fever with a strong shot of acetaminophen."

As Everett spoke, he took out a syringe and prepared it.

Andy's eyes followed his every move, growing steadily wider. "Is my Mama gonna die?" he asked, fear throbbing in his voice.

"No, Andy. I'm going to make your mom all better. But you're going to have to be brave for all three of you," Everett told him. "Think you can do that?" he asked, talking to him the way he would to any adult.

The boy solemnly nodded his head. He held his breath as he watched his mother getting the injection.

"Good boy." Everett moved on to the woman's other son. "Looks like he's got it, too," he said to Lila. Turning to Andy, he asked him, "Andy, do you know how long your mom and brother have been sick?"

Andy made a face as he tried to remember. He never took his eyes off the syringe, watching as the doctor gave his brother an injection next.

"Not long," Andy answered. "We were watching *Captain Jack* yesterday when Bobby said he didn't feel so good. Mama carried him to bed and she laid down, too."

Everett turned to look at Lila. *"Captain Jack?"* he questioned.

"It's a syndicated cartoon," Lila told him. "I think it airs around eight or so in the morning. One of the women in the office has a little boy who likes to watch it," she explained in case he wondered why she would know something like that.

"So Mrs. Quinn could have been sick for a couple of days?" Everett questioned, attempting to get a handle on how long mother and son had been down with the illness.

Lila was about to narrow it down a little more. "Mrs. Quinn called my office yesterday, but I didn't have anyone I could send."

Everett nodded, taking the information in. "You can only do as much as you can do," he told her. He knew Lila would beat herself up but it wasn't her fault. She couldn't make doctors appear out of thin air.

He performed a few tests on Mrs. Quinn and Bobby, and then he turned in Andy's direction. "It's your turn, Andy."

Andy looked totally leery as he slanted a long glance in the doctor's direction. "My turn for what?" he asked in a small voice.

"You get to be the one in your family to get a flu shot," Everett told him.

"But I don't want a shot. I'm not sick," Andy cried, his voice rising in panic.

"No, you're not," Everett agreed. "And if you let me give you a flu shot, you'll stay that way. Otherwise…" His voice trailed off dramatically.

Andy tried to enlist Lila to help him. She was just returning into the bedroom, bringing bottles of drinking water she'd brought with her in her car.

"But won't a flu shot give me the flu?" the boy asked, anticipatory tears of pain already gathering in his eyes.

"No, it acts like a soldier that keeps the flu away," Everett told him. "You don't want to get sick like your mom and your brother, do you?" Everett asked. "Someone's got to stay well to take care of them."

Andy looked torn, and then he sighed. "I guess you're right."

"Good man," Everett congratulated the little boy with hearty approval.

Lila set down the bottles of water as well as several pudding cups and bananas she'd brought in. "Attaboy," she said to Andy. "If you like, I'll hold you on my lap while Dr. Everett gives you that shot."

She didn't wait for the boy to answer. She gathered him up in her arms and held him on her lap.

"Okay, Dr. Everett. Andy's ready." She felt the little boy dig his fingers into her arm as Everett gave him the flu injection. She heard Andy breathe in sharply. "You were very brave," she commended the boy.

"I'll say," Everett said, adding his voice to praise the boy. As he packed up his bag, he looked around, concerned. "Is there anyone who can stay with the kids until Mrs. Quinn is well enough to take care of them?" he asked Lila in a low voice. "I don't like the idea of just leaving them this way."

"Mrs. Rooney comes by to stay with us sometimes whenever Mama has to go out," Andy said, looking from the doctor to Lila as if to see if they thought that was good enough.

"Do you know where Mrs. Rooney lives?" Everett asked Lila.

"I think that's the woman next door," she told him before Andy could respond. Shifting Andy off her lap, she rose to her feet. "I can go and knock on her door," she volunteered.

"We'll go together," Everett told her. When she looked at him quizzically, he said, "You shouldn't be out there alone."

In a low voice, she told Everett, "I've been dealing with people in this neighborhood and places *like* this neighborhood for several years now. You don't have to worry about me."

"No," Everett agreed. "I don't 'have to.' But since I'm here, I'd feel better going with you," he told her, adding, "Humor me."

Instead of answering him, she looked at Andy, who was rubbing his arm where he had received his vaccination. "Andy, do you know if Mrs. Rooney does live next door?" she asked.

Sniffing as he blinked to keep big tears from falling, Andy nodded. "Uh-huh, she does."

Lila smiled at Everett. "Problem solved. I'll just pop in next door and ask the woman to keep an eye on this family."

She glanced at her watch. They had spent more time here than she'd anticipated. She was glad that it had gone so well for Everett, but they did need to speed things up.

"And then we're going to have to get a move on," she told Everett. "Otherwise, we're not going to get to see all the people on my list unless we work through the night and possibly into the next morning."

He hadn't thought that there were going to be *that* many houses to visit. But as far as he knew, Lila had never been one to exaggerate.

"Then you'd better find out if Mrs. Rooney is willing to stay with Andy and his family," he urged.

That went off without a hitch.

After getting the woman to stay with the Quinn family, Lila drove herself and Everett to the second name on her list.

Again she was treated to observing Everett's bedside manner. She was completely amazed by how easily he seemed to get along with children. Not only get along with them but get them to trust him and rather quickly.

She smiled to herself as she recalled worrying that he might frighten the children because he'd be too stiff or too cold with them, but that definitely didn't turn out to be the case. Right from the very beginning, she saw that Everett knew exactly how to talk to the children.

Moreover, he acted as if he actually *belonged* in this sort of a setting.

Talk about being surprised, she mused.

As they drove from one house to another, Lila found herself wondering what these people who had so little would think if they knew that the man who was administering their vaccinations, writing out their prescriptions and listening so intently to them as they described their symptoms was actually a millionaire's son with a thriving, fancy practice back in Houston.

She laughed quietly to herself. They'd probably think that she was making it up because Everett seemed so down-to-earth, not to mention so focused on making them feel better.

As she continued observing Everett in setting after setting, Lila could feel her heart growing softer and softer.

MARIE FERRARELLA 71

It became harder for her to regard Everett in any sort of a cold light and practically impossible for her to keep the good memories at bay any longer.

Everett had grown into the good, decent man she had, in her heart, always felt that he was destined to become.

"How many more?" Everett asked her as they drove away from yet another house.

He and Lila had been at it for a straight twelve hours, stopping only to pick up a couple of hamburgers to go at a drive-through. They ate the burgers while driving from one patient to the next.

Keeping her eyes on the road as she drove, Lila smiled at his question. She didn't have to pull out her list to answer him. "That was the last house on my list."

"No more left?" Everett questioned, thinking that she might have accidentally overlooked one or two more patients.

"Nope, no more left," Lila told him. She flashed him a relieved grin to underscore her words.

"Wow." Everett leaned his head back against his headrest. "I was beginning to feel like we were going to go on with these house calls forever."

She laughed. "Does feel that way, doesn't it?" She spared him a glance as she came to a stop at a light. "Bet you're sorry now that you returned my call yesterday."

"No," Everett responded quite seriously. "I'm not."

After twelve hours of work on very little sleep, all she should be thinking about was getting some rest, nothing else. So why in heaven's name did she suddenly feel what amounted to an all-consuming hot tingle passing over the length of her body just because Everett had said that he wasn't sorry he'd called her back?

What was wrong with her?

Punchy, she was punchy. That had to be it, Lila decided.

Talk, damn it. Say something! she ordered herself. The silence was getting deafening.

Clearing her throat, Lila said, "Well, I have to admit that you surprised me today."

"Oh?" Everett responded. "How so?"

Lila was honest with him. She felt it was the best way. "I didn't think you had it in you to just keep going like this. And I really didn't think you knew how to talk to children."

"Why?" he asked. "Children are just short adults."

Lila laughed, shaking her head. "You would be surprised how many doctors don't really know how to talk to fully grown adults, much less to little children," she told him.

"That's right," Everett recalled. "When we started out today you told me that you were there to act as the go-between." He continued to look at her profile, curious. "So I guess I passed the test?"

The light turned green and Lila pressed down on the accelerator. Once they were moving again, she answered, "With flying colors." Again she felt she had to tell him how surprised she was by his performance. "I didn't think that you'd keep at it long enough to see all the people on the list." She struggled to stifle a yawn. The long day was catching up to her. "But it's kind of late now," she told him needlessly.

"It is," he agreed.

She glanced at the clock on the dashboard, even though she already knew what time it was. "Too late for you to be driving back to Houston tonight," she told him.

"Are you offering to put me up?" he asked, doing his best to keep a straight face.

That startled her. "What? No, I just—"

"Take it easy," he laughed. "You don't have to worry. I've already talked to Schuyler. She's expecting me. I'm spending the night at her place."

"So that means that you're not going back until sometime tomorrow?" Lila asked.

He laughed again. "I can see the wheels turning in your head. No, I'm not going back to Houston until the day after tomorrow. So, if you want me to make a few more house calls with you tomorrow, I'm available."

That would be a huge help. She was still down a few volunteer doctors and she still hadn't found any more replacements.

"Don't toy with me, Everett," she told him, casting a glance his way.

His eyes were smiling at her. "I wouldn't dream of it."

Her heart fluttered. She forced herself to face forward. "All right. If you don't mind putting in some more time, then yes, absolutely. I could *really* use you for however much time you can spare."

"All right, then, same time tomorrow?" he asked as she pulled into the Foundation's parking lot.

"Make it eight-thirty," she told him.

"I'll be there," he promised, getting out of her car.

"If you decide to change your mind," she began, feeling obligated to give him a way out. After the day he had put in today, she didn't want to force him to come in tomorrow.

But Everett cut her off. "I won't," he told her just before he walked over to his own car.

Lila caught herself smiling. She knew he meant it.

CHAPTER EIGHT

WHEN LILA GOT up the next morning, she felt absolutely wiped out. If possible, she was even more tired than the day before. It was as if her get-up-and-go had physically gotten up and left.

"You're just burning the candle at both ends," she told the tired-looking reflection staring back at her in the bathroom mirror. "And maybe a little in the middle as well."

The shower did not invigorate her the way it usually did.

Dragging herself over to her closet after her shower, Lila pulled out the first things she found and got dressed. She was staring down the barrel of another grueling day, but at least she had a doctor for part of it, she thought. And after Everett left for Houston, maybe she would get lucky and be able to scrounge up another volunteer physician to conduct the house calls that were left on the list.

Determined to make herself look a little more human than what she saw in her mirror, Lila patiently applied her makeup. She succeeded in making herself look a little less exhausted—or at least less like someone who had recently been run over by a truck. The last thing she wanted was to have Everett take one look at her this morning and breathe a sigh of relief that he had dodged a bullet thirteen years ago.

Lila was still struggling to pull herself out of what was for her an atypical funk when she drove to the Foundation. This just wasn't like her, she thought. No matter how tired she felt, she never dragged like this, as if there was lead in her limbs.

C'mon, snap out of it! she silently ordered.

Just like the day before, when she drove into the parking lot, she found Everett sitting in his car, waiting for her.

When Everett saw her car approaching, he quickly got out of his vehicle. The cheery greeting on his lips didn't get a chance to materialize because he took a closer look at her as she got out of her car.

"Are you feeling all right, Lila?" he asked her.

So much for makeup saving the day, Lila thought. "I'm just running a little behind," she answered, deliberately being vague. Changing the subject, she asked, "Do I have you for half a day—or less?"

Rather than give Lila a direct answer, Everett told her, "Why don't we play it by ear and see?"

Lila put her own spin on his words. Everett was setting the stage so he could bail whenever he felt as if he'd had enough. Not that she blamed him, she thought. The man had already given a hundred and fifty percent of his time yesterday, far more than she had the right to expect, and she couldn't be greedy.

The hell she couldn't, Lila caught herself thinking. After all, this wasn't about her. This was about all those people who were counting on her to find a way to keep them healthy—or get them healthy—and at the very least, that involved having a doctor pay them a house call.

"Okay," Lila said with all the pseudo enthusiasm she could muster as she opened the passenger door for Everett. "Let's get started."

* * *

"How do you do this every day?" Everett wanted to know after they had made more than half a dozen house calls.

"Doctors used to do this all the time," she told Everett.

It took him a moment to understand what Lila was referring to. He realized that they weren't on the same page.

"I'm not talking about the house calls," Everett told her. "I'm talking about seeing this much poverty and still acting so cheerful when you talk to the people."

"I'm being cheerful *for* their sake. An upbeat attitude brings hope with it," she told him. "And hope and perseverance are practically the only way out of these neighborhoods," Lila maintained.

Everett was more than willing to concede the point. "You probably have something there." And then he blew out a breath, as if mentally bracing himself for round two. "How many more people are on that famous list of yours for today?" he wanted to know.

It was already closer to one than to noon. Did he know that, she wondered. They'd been at this for hours and she'd assumed that no matter what he'd said on the outset, she just had him for half a day.

"Don't you have a plane to catch or a car to drive?" she asked.

"Trying to get rid of me?" he asked her, an amused expression on his face.

"No, on the contrary, trying not to take you for granted and start relying on you too much," Lila corrected. And in a way, that was true. That had been her downfall all those years ago. She'd just expected to be able to rely on Everett forever. And look how that had turned out, she thought. Determined to pin him down, she asked, "How long did you say you could work today?"

"I didn't, remember?" he reminded her.

"Right. You said, quote, 'why don't we play it by ear and see,'" Lila recalled.

"Well, it still seems to be going, doesn't it?" he observed, his expression giving nothing away. "Who's next on the list?" he asked, redirecting her attention back to the immediate present.

Eyes on the road, Lila put one hand into the purse she kept butted up next to her and pulled out the list of patients that she'd put right on top. All she needed was a quick glance at the page.

"Joey Garcia's next," she answered. "Joey's the baby of the family," she added, giving Everett an encapsulated summary of his next patient. "He's got two big sisters and two big brothers and he always gets everything after the rest of the family's gotten over it.

"However, according to my records," she said, trying to recall what she had entered on her tablet, "I don't think anyone in the family has had the flu *or* gotten the vaccine this year."

"Well, I guess we're about to find out, aren't we?" Everett speculated as she pulled the car up before another house that looked as if it might have been new over fifty years ago.

Lila got out on her side and immediately found that she had to pause for a moment. She held onto the car door for support. Everything around her had suddenly opted to wobble just a little, making her head swim and the rest of her extremely unsteady.

Realizing that she wasn't with him as he approached the house, Everett looked back over his shoulder. "Something wrong?"

"No." Lila refused to tell him she'd felt dizzy, especially since the feeling had already passed. She didn't want to sound whiny or helpless and she definitely didn't want him fussing over her. "Just trying to remember if I forgot something."

Everett thought that sounded rather odd. What could she have forgotten? "Did you?"

"No," she answered rather abruptly. "I've got everything."

He played along for her sake. She didn't look as if she was herself today.

"I don't know how you manage to keep track of everything," he told her as they approached the Garcias' front door.

"It's a gift," Lila told him wryly. She forced a wide smile to her lips as she fervently wished that she'd stop feeling these odd little waves of weakness that kept sweeping over her.

Taking a deep breath, she knocked on the front door. It swung open immediately. The next moment, she was introducing Everett to a big, burly man who appeared to be almost as wide as he was tall.

"Mr. Garcia, this is Dr. Everett Fortunado. He'll be giving you and your family your flu vaccinations," Lila told Juan Garcia and the diminutive wife standing next to him.

The couple went from regarding Everett suspiciously to guardedly welcoming him into their home.

"The children are in the living room," Mrs. Garcia said, leading the way through what amounted to almost railroad-style rooms to the back of the house.

As he walked into the living room, Everett was immediately aware of five pairs of eyes warily watching his every move.

Everett did his best to set the children at ease, talking to them first and asking their names. He explained exactly what he was about to do and what they could expect, including how the vaccine felt going into their arms.

When he was done, he surprised Lila by handing out small candy bars to each child. "For being brave," he told them.

"That was nice of you," Lila said as they left the Garcias' house twenty minutes later.

Everett shrugged. "Candy makes everything better." He got into the car. "I thought you said they called you."

"Well, sometimes I call them," Lila replied. She could feel Everett regarding her quizzically as she pulled back onto the street. "Mr. Garcia is very proud. He doesn't like accepting help. He's also out of work. I thought he and his family could do with a little preventative medicine so that if a job *does* come up, he won't be too sick to take it. He's a day laborer when he's not driving a truck," she explained. When Everett didn't say anything, she elaborated on her statement. "The man has five kids. If they all came down with the flu, it would be guaranteed pure chaos. This was a pre-emptive strike."

That was one way to look at it, Everett thought. Obviously Lila was focused on doing good deeds. "So when did you get fitted for the wings and halo?" Everett asked her.

"I didn't," she answered crisply. "They were left behind by the last department manager." She kept her eyes on the road, not trusting herself to look at him. Sudden movements made her dizzy. "I just try them on for size occasionally."

"Oh." He pretended as if what she'd just said made perfect sense. "So, how many more house calls do we have left?" he asked, getting serious again.

This time Lila didn't have to consult her list. "We've got two more."

"Just two more?" he questioned. Yes, they'd been at this for a long time, but he'd just expected to keep going until almost nightfall again, the way they had yesterday.

"Just two more," Lila repeated. "And then you're free."

"Free, eh?" he echoed. He studied her profile. "How about you?"

"How about me what?" she asked. Had she missed a question? Her brain felt a little fuzzy and she was having trouble following him.

"Are you free?" Everett asked, enunciating each word clearly.

"Free for what?" she asked. She was still having trouble following him.

"Free for dinner," he asked, then quickly added, "I thought that maybe, since we've developed this decent working relationship, you wouldn't mind grabbing some dinner together."

Lila pressed her lips together. All she'd been thinking about the last few hours was going home and crawling into bed. But she was not about to tell Everett that. She didn't want to have to listen to a lot of questions.

So instead, sounding as cheerful as possible, she said, "I guess I do owe you that."

"I don't want you to have dinner with me because you 'owe' me," he told her. "I want you to have dinner with me because you want to."

Potato, po-tah-to, she thought. He'd come through for her, so she supposed that she could humor him. "I want to," she answered quietly.

"Great," he said. "Let's go see these last two patients."

The visits took a little longer than he'd come to anticipate, mainly because the second one involved more than just dispensing flu vaccinations to the two older children and their parents. Everett found himself tending to a pint-size patient with a sprained wrist that he didn't even know he had.

Afraid of being laughed at by his brothers for being clumsy, when it was his turn for the vaccine, little Alan had tried to hide his swollen wrist.

Drawing him over to Everett, Lila had accidentally brushed against the boy's wrist and saw him wince, then try to pretend he was just playing a game with her. The truth came out rather quickly.

"Never try to hide something like that," Lila told him as Everett bandaged the boy's wrist and then fashioned a makeshift sling for him. "They just get worse if you ignore them," she told him.

Alan solemnly nodded his head.

"He's been moping all day," Alan's mother told them as they were packing up their supplies. "Now I know why. Here," she said handing Lila a pie, which, by its aroma, had just recently left the oven. "This is my way of saying thank-you."

Lila declined. "As a Foundation worker, I can't accept payment," she told the other woman.

"Then take it as a friend," Alan's mother told her. "One friend to another. You will be insulting me if you don't accept it," the woman insisted.

The way she felt, Lila was not up to arguing. Pulling her lips back into a thin smile, she expressed her thanks, saying, "Dr. Everett will take it home with him. Maybe your gift will encourage him to return to Austin again soon."

The woman was obviously pleased to play her part in coaxing the good-looking doctor back.

"Maybe," she agreed, flashing a bright, hopeful smile at Everett.

"I wouldn't have thought of that," Everett told Lila when they were back in her car again. "That was quick thinking," he complimented her.

Lila was hardly aware of shrugging. "I didn't want to hurt her feelings, but I didn't want to set a precedent, either. Having you take it seemed like the only logical way out."

"Still wouldn't have thought of it," he told her.

"Sure you would have," she countered. "You're the smartest man I know."

No I'm not, he thought. He could cite a time when he'd been downright stupid.

Like thirteen years ago.

Everett studied her quietly as she drove. In his opinion, Lila had blossomed in the intervening years. She was no longer that stricken young girl who'd told him she never wanted to see him again. She'd become a self-assured woman who obviously had a mission in life. A mission she was passionate about, and that passion made her particularly compelling and exciting.

He found himself being attracted to Lila all over again and even more strongly this time than he had the first time around.

"Can you clock out once we get back to the Foundation?" he asked suddenly, breaking the heavy silence in the car.

"This actually is the official end of my day, so yes, I can clock out."

"And we're still on for dinner?" he asked, not wanting to come across as if he was taking anything for granted. He knew that winning Lila back was going to take time and patience—and he very much intended to win her back.

"If you still want to have dinner with me, then yes, we're still on," she answered cautiously. She made a right turn, pulling into the parking lot. "Are you sure this won't interfere with you getting back to Houston? I feel guilty about keeping you away from your practice for so long."

"Nothing to feel guilty about," he assured her. "The choice was mine. And my practice is part of a group. We all pitch in and cover for one another if something comes up."

"And this qualifies as 'something?'" she asked him, a touch of amusement entering her voice.

"Oh, most definitely 'something,'" Everett assured her.

My lord, she was flirting with him, Lila realized. She really wasn't herself.

The next moment, there was further proof. "Lila, you're passing my car," Everett pointed out.

Preoccupied and trying to get a grip on herself, she hadn't realized that she had driven right by the navy blue sedan.

"Sorry," she murmured. "Just double-checking the schedule in my head."

"Schedule?" he questioned. But she'd said there was no one left on today's list, didn't she? Was there some secondary list he didn't know about?

"The list of patients," she clarified.

"Did we miss anyone?" he asked, wondering if she was going to find some excuse to turn him down at the last minute.

She wished she didn't feel as if her brain had a fog machine operating right inside her head. It was getting harder and harder for her to think straight.

"Lila?"

She realized that Everett was waiting for her to answer him.

"Oh, no, we didn't. We saw everyone on the list. I was just thinking about tomorrow," she lied. "Let's go have dinner."

"Sounds good to me," he replied, silently adding, *Anything that has to do with you sounds good to me.*

CHAPTER NINE

"On second thought, maybe I should drive," Everett said to her just as Lila started her car up again.

Putting her foot on the brake now, Lila looked at Everett, confused.

"Why?" she wanted to know. "I know the city better than you do. You said so yourself."

"True, but I've been able to find my way around without much trouble and I don't mind driving. To be honest, you look like you're rather tired and you don't want to push yourself too hard," Everett stressed.

He was right. She *was* tired, Lila thought, but her pride kept her from admitting it. Her self-image dictated that she was supposed to be untiring, with boundless energy.

"Is that your professional opinion?" she asked.

"Professional and personal," Everett replied quietly.

There was that calming bedside manner of his again, Lila thought. But she wasn't a patient, she reminded herself.

"Tough to argue with that," she responded. "But you'll have to drive me back here after dinner so I can pick up my car."

Everett had already taken that into account. "No problem," he assured her. Getting out of her car, he took a few steps, then stood waiting for her to follow suit.

After a moment, Lila sighed, surrendering. Since she hadn't pulled out of the parking space yet, she left her car as it was and got out.

Crossing to his car, Everett unlocked it and then held the passenger side door open for her. After Lila got in, he closed the door and got in behind the wheel. He looked at her and smiled just before he started his car.

Was that smug satisfaction she saw, or something else? Lila wondered. "What?" she asked him.

"I thought you'd put up more of a fight," he confessed as he started up his vehicle. Within moments, they were on the road.

Lila lifted one shoulder in a careless shrug. She realized that her shoulder felt heavy for some reason, like someone was pushing down on it. After dinner, she was heading straight for bed, she promised herself.

"I guess I'm more tired than I thought," she told Everett.

He accepted her excuse. "You in the mood for Chinese or Italian?" he asked, offering her a choice of the first two restaurants he thought of. He favored both.

"The Italian place is closer," Lila told him.

And in this case, he thought, closer seemed to mean better, otherwise she would have cited a different criterion first.

"Italian it is." He spared her one quick glance, coupled with a grin. "Now all you have to do is give me the address."

Lila dug in just for a second. "I thought you said you knew your way around."

"I do," he assured her, then added, "Once I have an address." She laughed shortly. "That's cheating," Lila accused.

"I'd rather think of it as being creative," he told her, then asked again, "The address?"

She was much too tired to engage in any sort of a war of resistance. With a sigh, she rattled off the address to the Italian restaurant.

Everett immediately knew where it was. "You're right, that is close," he acknowledged.

They were there in less than ten minutes. As luck would have it, someone in the first row of the parking lot was just pulling out and Everett smoothly slipped right into the spot.

Shutting off his engine, he quickly came around to Lila's side.

Aware that Everett had opened the door for her, she felt a little woozy and it took her a moment to focus and swing her legs out. She really would have rathered that Everett wasn't holding the door open for her so he wouldn't see just how unsteady she was.

"You know, I have learned how to open my own door," she told him defensively.

If she was trying to antagonize him, Everett thought, he wasn't taking the bait.

"I know," he responded cheerfully. "I've seen you. But I like doing this," he told her, putting out his hand to her. "It makes me feel like a gentleman."

The wooziness retreated. Lila wrapped her fingers around his hand with confidence. Maybe she was worrying for no reason.

"Then I guess I'll humor you," she said, "seeing what an asset you were yesterday and today."

His smile sank deep into her very soul as he helped her out of the vehicle. "Whatever works."

Closing the door behind her, they crossed to the restaurant.

The homey, family-style restaurant was beginning to fill up, but there were still a number of empty tables available. The hostess seated them immediately and gave them menus.

"Do you come here often?" Everett asked Lila when they were alone.

"Often enough to know that they have good food," Lila answered.

Everett nodded. "Good, then I'll let you do the ordering," he told her, placing his menu on the table.

That surprised her. "Well, you certainly have changed," she couldn't help observing. When he raised an inquisitive eyebrow, she said, "There was a time when you took charge of everything."

He couldn't very well argue the point. He remembered that all too well.

"I've learned to relax and take things light," he explained. "Somebody once told me I'd live a lot longer that way—or maybe it would just seem longer," he added with a laugh.

As their server approached the table Lila asked, "Were you serious about my doing the ordering for you?"

"Very."

Lila proceeded to order. "We'll have two servings of chicken Alfredo," she told the young woman. "And he'll have a side dish of stuffed mushrooms."

"And you?" the young woman asked, her finger hovering over her tablet.

"No mushrooms for me," Lila answered.

"And what would you like to drink?" the server asked, looking from Lila to the man she was sitting with.

"I'll have a glass of water," Lila answered, then looked at Everett, waiting for him to make a choice himself. She remembered he liked having wine with his meals, but maybe that had changed, too, along with his attitude.

"Make that two," Everett told the server, then handed over his unopened menu to her.

Lila surrendered hers after a beat.

"I'll be back with your bread and waters," the server told them.

"Sounds more like a prison diet than something from a homey-looking restaurant," Everett commented.

"That's probably what she thought, too," Lila said. "She looked like she was trying not to laugh." She looked around the large room. More patrons had come in moments after they did. "Certainly filled up fast," she observed, saying the words more to herself than to Everett.

"Worried about my being seen with you?" Everett asked, amused.

"No." She was actually thinking about how all those bodies were generating heat. "Does it seem rather warm in here to you?"

"Well, when you have this many bodies occupy a relatively small space, it's bound to feel somewhat warm," he speculated. And then he smiled. "You remembered I liked mushrooms," he said, clearly surprised.

"I remember a lot of things," she said, and then the next moment regretted it. "Like quadratic equations," she added glibly.

Everett laughed. And then he looked at her more closely. There was a line of perspiration on her forehead, seeping through her auburn bangs and pasting them to her forehead. "It's not warm enough in here to cause you to perspire," Everett observed.

"Maybe you make me nervous," Lila said flippantly.

"If that were the case, then you wouldn't have agreed to dinner," he pointed out. The woman he knew wouldn't do anything she didn't want to.

Lila shifted in her chair, growing progressively more uncomfortable. "It seemed impolite to turn you down after you went out of your way to be my white knight."

Her terminology intrigued him. "Is that what I am? Your white knight?" he asked.

"Did I say white knight?" she asked, as if she hadn't heard herself call Everett that. "I meant Don Quixote, not white knight. I always manage to get those two mixed up," she said.

"I've been called worse," he said with a tolerant laugh.

Their server returned with their glasses of water and a basket of garlic breadsticks. "I'll be back with your dinners soon," she told them, placing the items on the table and withdrawing.

Everett noticed that Lila immediately picked up her glass of water. Drinking, she practically drained the entire contents in one long swallow.

Seeing that Everett was watching her, Lila shrugged self-consciously. "I guess I was thirstier than I thought."

"I guess you were," he agreed good-naturedly. Something was up, but he wasn't about to press. He didn't want to ruin their dinner. Spending time with Lila like this was far too precious to him. Having taken a breadstick, he pushed the basket toward her. "Have one. They're still warm."

He watched her take a breadstick, but instead of taking a bite, she just put it on her plate and left it there, untouched.

"What's wrong?" he asked. "You always loved breadsticks, especially garlic breadsticks."

"I still do," she answered defensively. And then she relented. "I guess I'm just not hungry."

Something was definitely off. "I've been with you all day. You haven't eaten since you came in—that's assuming that you *did* eat before you came in this morning."

Lila shrugged, then grew annoyed with herself for doing it. She wished that he'd stop asking questions. Most of all, she wished that she was home in bed.

"I'm not hungry," she snapped. "What do you want me to say?"

This was *not* like her. His eyes met hers. "The truth," Everett told her simply.

"I don't know what you're talking about," Lila retorted, irritated. "I'm just not hungry. That's not a crime," she protested.

It felt as if her emotions were going every which way at the same time.

"Look, maybe we should—"

Without thinking, Lila started to get up—which was when the world decided to launch itself into a tailspin all around her. She grabbed the edge of the table, afraid that she would suddenly go down and find herself unceremoniously sitting on the floor. The table wobbled as she grabbed it and she stifled a cry, sitting down again.

Everett reached across the table and put the back of his hand against her forehead. Lila pulled her head away. She regretted the movement immediately because the spinning in her head just intensified.

Her forehead was hot, Everett thought. That and the sharp intake of breath he'd just heard her make gave him all the input he needed.

"Dinner is canceled," he told her. "I'm taking you home and putting you to bed."

"If that's your idea of a seductive proposition, you just washed out," she informed him, struggling very hard to keep the world in focus.

"No, that's my idea of putting a sick woman to bed where she belongs." He looked around and signaled to the server. The latter was just approaching them with their orders. "Change of plans," he told her. "We have to leave."

Without missing a beat, the young woman told him, "I can have these wrapped to go in a few minutes."

Everett was about to tell the woman that they wouldn't be taking the meals home with them, but then he had a change of heart. Lila was going to need something to eat once she was feeling better. As for him, he *was* hungry and he could always take the food to eat later once he had Lila situated.

"There's an extra tip in it for you if you can get it back here in two minutes," Everett told her.

Taking his words to heart, the server was gone before he finished his sentence.

"You're making a scene," Lila protested weakly.

"No," he retorted. "I'm trying to prevent making a scene. You're sick, Lila. I should have seen the signs. But I was so eager just to have dinner with you, I missed the fact that you were steadily growing paler all day."

Just then, the server returned. She had their dinners and breadsticks packed in two rather large paper sacks.

"Your salad is packed on top," she told him.

"Great." Taking out his wallet, Everett handed the young woman a twenty, then put a hundred-dollar bill on the table. "This should cover it," he told the server. When he turned to look at Lila, his concern grew. She was almost pasty. "Can you walk?"

"Of course I can," Lila retorted just before she stood up— and pitched forward.

Thanks to his quick reflexes, Everett managed to catch her just in time. Had he hesitated even for just half a second, Lila's head would have had an unfortunate meeting with the floor.

The server stared at them, wide-eyed. "Is she all right?" she asked, clearly concerned.

"She will be," Everett told her. He had perfected sounding confident, even when he wasn't. "I think she just has the flu," he added. In one clean, swift movement, he picked Lila up in his arms as if she was weightless. Turning toward the server, he requested, "If you could hand me her purse."

The woman had already gathered Lila's purse. "Don't worry, I'll take it and your dinners and follow you to your car," she volunteered. Looking at Lila, who was unconscious, she asked again, "You're sure she'll be all right?"

Reading between the lines, Everett told her, "Don't worry, it wasn't anything she had here." Then he made his way to the front entrance.

Seeing them, the hostess at the reservation desk hurried to open the front door for them, holding it open with her back. "Is everything all right?" she asked Everett.

"She has the flu. She'll be fine," he answered crisply. "You do know how to make an exit," he whispered to Lila in a hushed voice. Speaking up, he said, "The car's right in front," directing the server who was hurrying alongside of him.

Still holding Lila in his arms, Everett managed to reach into his pocket and press the key fob to open the car doors.

The server moved quickly to open the passenger door for him, and Everett flashed a grateful smile at her. "Thank you."

The server waited until he buckled Lila into her seat, then handed the purse and the dinners she was holding to him.

"Are you sure you don't want me to call the paramedics for you?" she asked one last time, eyeing Lila.

"Very sure," Everett answered. "I'm a doctor. She's been out in the field, visiting sick people for the last two days and it looks like she came down with the flu for her trouble." Closing the door, he looked at the young woman and tried to set her mind at ease one last time. "Thanks for all your trouble—" he paused to read her name tag "—Ruth."

The young woman grinned broadly when he addressed her by her name. "My pleasure, Doctor." With that, she quickly hurried back into the restaurant.

Everett's attention was already focused on Lila. She was still unconscious. How the hell could he have missed all those signs? he thought, upbraiding himself again.

"I'm sorry, Lila. I should have realized what was wrong this morning in the parking lot."

And then it suddenly occurred to him that he had no idea where Lila lived. Getting her purse, he went through it until he found her wallet with her driver's license in it. Looking at it, he repeated her address out loud in order to memorize it.

"Let's get you home, Cinderella."

CHAPTER TEN

EVERETT WAS ABLE to locate the development where Lila lived with only a minimum of difficulty.

Finding her house was a little trickier. Driving slowly and trying to make out the addresses painted on the curb, he finally drove up toward her house.

Pulling up into her driveway, he turned off his engine and then sat in the car, looking at Lila. She hadn't come to once during the entire trip from the restaurant to her house.

"Okay, I got you here. Now what?" he wondered out loud. "The logical step would be to get you *into* the house, wouldn't it?" Everett said as if he was carrying on a conversation with the unconscious woman sitting next to him. "But for that to happen, I'm going to need either a roommate who's living in your house or a key to the front door."

He looked back toward the house. There weren't any lights on, which meant that either Lila lived alone, or if she did have a roommate—which she hadn't mentioned—the roommate was out.

He opened her purse again. This time he was rummaging

through the purse looking for her keys. He found a set of keys at the very bottom of her purse. There were five keys on the ring.

"You sure don't make things easy, do you, Lila?" he asked.

He decided he needed to find the right key and open the front door before carrying her out of his car. If he was lucky, she might even wake up by the time he discovered which of the keys fit the front door lock. And awake, she might be able to walk—with some help—to the house. That would eliminate some complications, like nosy neighbors, he thought.

Everett went up the front walk to her door and patiently started trying out keys.

The very last key turned out to be the one to open her front door.

"It figures," he murmured.

Everett went inside the house and flipped on the first light switch he found. The darkness receded.

At least he could find his way around, he thought.

Leaving the front door standing open, he pocketed the key ring and went back to the car.

Lila was still unconscious.

Unbuckling her seat belt, Everett found that the clothes she was wearing were all practically soaked.

"You're sweating this flu out," he told her. "As a doctor, I know that's a good thing. But I'd still feel a lot better if you opened your eyes." He looked at her, half hoping that the sound of his voice would somehow make her come around. But it didn't. "Nothing, huh?" He sighed.

The next moment, Everett took her purse and slung the straps onto his shoulder. Then he lifted her up carefully and carried her to her front door.

"If any of your neighbors are watching this, Lila, we should be hearing the sound of police sirens approaching very shortly. For both our sakes, I hope you have the kind of neighbors who keep their curtains drawn and mind their own business, at least this one time."

The wind had caused the door to close a little but he managed to shoulder it open.

Like a groom carrying his bride over the threshold, he carried Lila into the house. Once inside, he closed the door with his back, making a mental note to lock it as soon as he found some place to put Lila down.

Looking around, Everett found himself standing in a small, sparsely decorated living room.

"You never were one for a lot of possessions," he commented, scanning the room.

He saw a tan sectional sofa facing a medium-size flat-screen TV mounted on the opposite wall. Crossing over to it, Everett gently placed Lila on the sofa, leaving her there for the moment. Going back, he locked the front door and then walked around the single-story house, orienting himself. Like the living room, everything was in place and neatly arranged.

"Anyone here?" Everett called out, although he took the darkened state of the house to indicate that it was empty.

He continued to make his way through the house, looking into each room. There were two bedrooms located in the back across from one another. One was larger than the other. He took the smaller one to be a guest bedroom. Looking into it, he found that it was empty. There were no clothes in the closet.

Apparently, Lila did live alone.

His smile vanished after a moment. This wasn't good, he thought. She was sick and she needed someone here to take care of her.

With a sigh, he went back to the living room. She was right where he'd left her—and still unconscious. He thought of his medical bag in his trunk.

"First things first," he told himself. Picking Lila up again, he said to her, "I need to get you out of these wet clothes and into bed." He caught himself smiling as he carried her to what he had determined to be her bedroom. "There was a time that would have meant something entirely different. But don't worry, I've got my 'doctor hat' on and you have nothing to worry about."

As attracted as he still was to her, his first thought was about her health. He wanted to get Lila well again.

Bringing Lila into the larger bedroom, he managed to move aside the comforter and put her down on the queen-size bed. He took off her shoes and then began going through the drawers of her bureau, looking for a nightgown or something that looked as if she wore it to bed.

Moving a few things aside, he froze when he came across an old college jersey.

His old college jersey.

He remembered when he'd given it to her. He'd told her that when she wore it, she'd be close to him. Taking it out now, he looked at the jersey for a long moment, then at her.

"You actually kept it," he said in disbelief. "And judging by how faded it is, you've been wearing it. Maybe this isn't as hopeless as I thought," he murmured under his breath, referring to his plan to get back together with her.

Moving quickly, Everett removed the rest of her clothes and slipped the college jersey on her. Done, he tucked Lila into bed as if he was tucking in a child. He refused to allow himself to become distracted. Right now, Lila was his patient, not the only woman he had ever loved.

"I'll be right back," he told her even though she was still unconscious and couldn't hear him. "I'm going to bring in the food and get my medical bag out of the trunk."

He was back in a few minutes, leaving the to-go bags on the kitchen table for the time being. He had something far more important on his mind than food, despite the fact that his stomach kept rumbling in protest over being neglected.

Opening up his medical bag, Everett took out his stethoscope and several other basic instruments he never went anywhere without. Then he gave Lila a quick but thorough exam to confirm what he pretty much already suspected.

Her pulse was rapid, her temperature was high and, at one point, as he conducted his examination, she began to shiver.

"Chills," he noted. "And you were already displaying signs of fatigue this morning. You, Lila Clark, are a regular poster child for the flu," he concluded. Setting aside his stethoscope, he frowned. "I bet with all that running around you were doing, you forgot to get yourself immunized for the flu, didn't you?"

Mentally crossing his fingers, he looked through his bag and found that he had thought to pack some extra acetaminophen. Taking out a fresh syringe, he removed the plastic casing and gave her an injection.

"That should help lower your fever," he told Lila. He frowned thoughtfully. "But you still can't be left alone, not like this."

There was a chair over in the corner by the window and he dragged it over to her bed. Sitting down, Everett studied her for a few minutes, reviewing his options. He was due back in Houston tomorrow, but there was no way he was about to leave her in this condition.

The injection he gave her should lower her fever, but things didn't always go the way they were supposed to. If Lila took a turn for the worse, there was no one here to take her to the hospital. Or do anything else for her, for that matter.

Even if he didn't feel the way he did about her, he couldn't just abandon her.

Everett made up his mind. He might not have been there for Lila thirteen years ago, but he could be here for her now.

Stepping out into the hallway, he took out his cell phone and placed a call to one of the doctors he worked with. He found himself listening to an answering machine telling him to leave a message. He'd hoped to talk to the other man directly, but that wasn't an option right now.

"Ryan, it's Everett. I'm in the middle of some sort of flu epidemic here in Austin and I'm going to be staying here a few more days. I'm going to need you and Blake to cover for me at the office. I appreciate it and I owe you—big time. Any questions, you have my cell."

With that, he terminated the call.

Coming back into the room to check on Lila, Everett called Schuyler next. His sister answered on the second ring.

"Schuy, it's Everett. I'm going to be staying in Austin a few more days."

"Oh?" Schuyler really didn't sound all that surprised, he thought. "Did you and Lila manage to patch things up?" she asked.

He wasn't about to get into that right now. That was a personal matter and it was officially on the back burner until Lila got well.

"It's not what you think," Everett was quick to tell his sister.

"Okay, if you're not trying to romance Lila into taking you back, then why are you going to be staying in Austin a few more days?" Schuyler wanted to know.

"You know that flu epidemic I came here to help treat?"

"Yes, I got my vaccination, Ev," she told him, thinking that was what her brother was going to ask her.

"Good, but that wasn't what I was about to tell you," Everett said.

"Okay, then what were you going to tell me?" Schuyler asked gamely.

"Lila came down with the flu," he told his sister simply. "She lives by herself and there's no one to take care of her."

"My Lord," Schuyler cried. "If I saw this story on one of those movie-of-the-week channels I'd shut off the TV."

"I didn't ask for your evaluation," Everett told her impatiently. "I just wanted you to know that I was still in town—and why."

After a moment, Schuyler said, "You're serious. Then she's really sick?"

Did Schuyler think that Lila would pretend to be ill—and that he'd just blindly fall for it?

"Schuy, I'm a doctor. I know what 'sick' looks like. Right

now, Lila's not only displaying all the signs of the flu, she's unconscious."

Schuyler's tone of voice changed immediately. "Anything I can do?"

He thought of Lila's car. It was still at the Foundation's parking lot where Lila had left it. He knew that Lila would undoubtedly prefer to have the car close by when she regained consciousness—if for no other reason than there might be something in it that she needed.

"As a matter of fact, there is," Everett told her. "If you and one of your friends could swing by here tomorrow morning to get the keys, could you pick up Lila's car from the Foundation's parking lot and drive it over to her house?"

"I think I liked you better when you didn't feel it was seemly to ask for favors," Schuyler told him.

He knew she was kidding. He also knew he could count on his sister.

"I'm growing as a person," Everett quipped.

"That's not how I see it," she told him. "All right, where's 'here'?" his sister asked.

He thought he heard her shuffling papers on the other end and then he heard Schuler say, "Okay, give me Lila's address."

He did, and then he said, "I assume you know where the Fortune Foundation is located."

"You know, you can be very insulting, big brother," Schuyler told him.

"Not intentionally," he told her, then added, "Thanks for this, Schuy."

"Yeah. I just hope you're not going to wind up regretting this, that's all," she told him, sounding concerned.

She was worried and he appreciated that. But there was no need for his sister to feel that way. "Schuy, Lila's sick. I'm a doctor. I'm supposed to take care of sick people."

Schuyler barely stifled a laugh. "You don't think this a little above and beyond?" she questioned.

"I'm an 'above and beyond' kind of doctor," Everett answered, doing his best to make light of the concerns his sister was displaying.

"Not funny, Ev," Schuyler informed him. "I worry about you," she stressed.

"And I said I appreciate that. I also appreciate you picking up that car and bringing it back to Lila's house for me," he said, bringing the conversation back to what he was asking her to do.

Schuyler sighed. "What time do you want me to come by?"

There was no reason to push. "Whenever it's convenient." He glanced toward Lila's room. "It doesn't look as if I'm going to be going anywhere for at least a while."

"I'll still call you first," she told Everett. It was obvious that she wasn't going to take a chance on walking in on something.

Everett was just about to end the call when he heard his sister say his name. Bringing the cell phone closer again so he could hear her, he asked, "Did you just say something?"

"I just had a last-minute thought," she told him.

"And that is?"

His sister hesitated for a moment. "I don't suppose I can talk you into hiring someone to look after Lila, can I?"

He knew she was just thinking of him, but he wished she would stop. He wanted to do this and his mind was made up.

"I'll see you in the morning, Schuyler," he said just before he terminated the call.

Putting the phone back into his pocket, he returned to Lila's bedside.

When he touched her forehead, it seemed a little cooler to him. Taking out the thermometer he'd used earlier, he laid the strip across her forehead and watched the numbers registering.

He removed the strip and put it back into his medical bag.

"You still have a fever," he told her. "But at least it's a little lower. Although not low enough," he stressed with a frown. "You can't go out and do your angel-of-mercy bit until that fever is gone and you're back to your old self again."

Lila moaned.

He knew it wasn't in response to what he'd just said, but he pretended that there was a semblance of an exchange going on between the two of them.

Lila had a small TV in her bedroom. Nothing like the one in the living room, but at least it would be something to fill the silence and distract him, he thought.

Turning on the TV, he put the volume on low, sat down in the chair next to Lila's bed and made himself as comfortable as possible.

He knew he could make use of the guest room and lie down on the bed there, but he preferred proximity over comfort. He wanted to be there for her if Lila woke up in the middle of the night and needed him. One night in a chair wouldn't kill him.

Besides, how many nights had he gone without sleep when he was an intern at the hospital? That certainly hadn't done him any harm, Everett reminded himself—and neither would spending a night sitting up and keeping vigil in a chair.

Everett doubted that he would get any sleep in the guest room anyway. He knew himself. He'd be too busy straining his ears, listening for any strange noises that would indicate that Lila was awake.

No, he decided, trying to make himself as comfortable as possible in the chair. Staying in Lila's room this way was better. He'd be right here, able to hear her make the slightest sound when she woke up. And he figured she *had* to wake up soon.

"I know you need your rest so I'm not going to worry about this yet. But I'd take it as a personal favor if you opened those big blue eyes of yours soon, Lila. *Very* soon."

The only response he heard was the sound of Lila breathing.

CHAPTER ELEVEN

"WHAT ARE YOU doing in my house?"

The raspy voice was hardly louder than a hoarse whisper, but it was definitely unnerving and accusatory in nature. Catching Everett off guard, it made him jump in his chair and almost caused him to knock it over.

Coming to, Everett realized that he must have finally dozed off for a few minutes.

It took him a moment longer before it hit him that it was Lila who'd asked the question.

Fully awake now, he got up and stood over Lila's bed. Her eyes were open and she looked bewildered. Relief washed over him as he took her hand in his. "You're awake!"

"And you didn't answer my question," Lila responded, annoyed with herself because she couldn't seem to speak any louder. "What are you doing in my house?" she asked again.

Bits and pieces were slowly beginning to dawn on her. She looked down at herself. "And where are my clothes?" Her eyes narrowed as she looked up at Everett angrily. "You undressed me," Lila choked out. It was not a question.

Everett wasn't about to deny the obvious, but she needed to understand why he'd removed her clothes. "You had a high fever and you were sweating. Your clothes were soaked straight through."

Frustration robbed her of the little voice she had so she couldn't immediately respond. She struggled to sit up.

All Everett had to do was put his hand gently on her shoulder to keep her down, which he did. "Don't exert yourself," he told her.

Who the hell did he think he was? He couldn't tell her what to do, Lila thought angrily. Her head was throbbing and she couldn't remember anything. But one thing was obvious.

"You took off my clothes," she accused again.

"I already explained why," Everett told her patiently.

She couldn't make any sense out of what he'd told her. "But we were in the restaurant," she protested, desperately trying to piece things together. It felt as if there was a huge gaping hole in her brain and facts were just falling through it, disappearing without a trace.

Maybe if he gave her a summary of the events, Everett thought, it might calm her down.

"You passed out in the restaurant," he told her. "I brought you to your house and carried you to your room. Your clothes were all wet, so I got you out of them and into that jersey."

She looked down again, doing her best to focus on what she was looking at. The jersey seemed to swim in front of her eyes. "You went through my things," she accused.

"Just in order to find something to put on you," he answered simply. Maybe he should have let it go at that, but he couldn't help saying, "You kept my jersey."

She wasn't about to get into that—and she wouldn't have had to if he hadn't gone rummaging through her drawers, she thought angrily.

"You had no right to go through my things," she said defensively.

This was going nowhere. He wasn't about to get sucked into a circular debate about what he'd done and why he'd done it.

"Lila, you have the flu. The best thing for you right now is to rest and drink plenty of fluids. Arguing is not part of that formula. Now I'll get you some water—or tea if you'd prefer. Your job in this is to take care of the 'rest' part."

Lila made a disgruntled face. "I don't like tea," she told him.

"Water it is," he responded, heading out to the kitchen.

A couple of minutes later Everett came back with a large glass of water. He propped her up with one hand beneath her pillows while he held out the glass to her with the other.

Lila took the glass with both hands and began to drink with gusto.

"Sip, don't gulp," he cautioned.

"I know how to drink water," she informed him, her voice still raspy. However, she grudgingly complied with his instructions. Getting her fill, she surrendered the glass.

Taking it from her, Everett slowly lowered her back down on the bed.

Lila's head felt as if it was floating and there were half thoughts darting in and out of her brain. Her eyes shifted in his direction.

"Did you enjoy it?" she asked.

His back was to her as he put the glass down on the bureau. Turning around, Everett looked at her quizzically. He had no idea what she was referring to. "Did I enjoy what?"

"Undressing me."

Her voice was even lower than it had been before and he could hardly make out what she was saying. He filled in the blanks.

"I did it in my capacity as a doctor," Everett answered.

Confusion furrowed her brow. Nothing was making sense. "Meaning you didn't look?"

Everett had deliberately divorced himself from his feelings while he'd gotten her out of the wet clothes and into the jersey.

But not enough to be completely unaffected by what he was doing. However, he wasn't about to tell her that. That would have been deliberately buying trouble in his opinion.

Instead, he said, "Only to make sure I didn't rip anything."

Her eyes narrowed further as she tried to look into his. "I don't think I believe you," she whispered.

The next moment, her eyes had closed and within a few seconds, she was asleep again.

"That's okay," he whispered back, gently pushing her hair away from her face and tucking her back under the covers. "I wouldn't believe me either if I were you."

He'd gotten her out of her clothes and into the jersey as quickly as he could, but that didn't mean that doing so hadn't stirred something within him even though he had tried his damnedest to block out those thoughts and feelings.

He *had* been functioning as a doctor, but he was remembering as her lover and that image was really difficult to shake.

The next time Lila opened her eyes and looked around, she saw that she was alone.

It had all been a dream, she thought with a twinge of disappointment.

She struggled into an upright position, her body aching and protesting every movement she made.

She stifled a groan. She felt as if she'd been run over by a truck. A truck that had deliberately backed up over her then taken off after running her over again.

She struggled to focus, her head throbbing, impeding her thoughts.

How did she get here? The last thing she actually remembered was being in the restaurant—sitting opposite Everett.

Everett had been part of her dream, she realized.

All these years and she was still having dreams about Everett. Strange dreams.

She needed to get up, she thought.

Just as she was about to throw back her covers, Everett walked into the room carrying a tray.

He smiled, pleased to see her up. "You're awake."

Lila's mouth dropped open as she stared at him. "I didn't dream you."

He set the tray down on the bureau for the moment.

"You dreamt about me?" he asked. He was practically beaming.

She became instantly defensive. "What are you doing here?"

"We went through this last night," he reminded her patiently. "Don't you remember?"

"I thought that was a dream." She was repeating herself, Lila thought. She held her head. It was really throbbing. "I feel awful."

"Well, if it makes you feel any better, you don't look awful," he told her. "But you are sick."

"No, I'm not," she protested. She tried to throw the covers off again and found that the single movement was exceedingly taxing to her strength. What the hell had happened to her? "I have to get ready for work," she told Everett defiantly, wanting him to leave.

Everett carefully drew her covers back up. "No work for you until you get well," he told her, leaving no room for argument.

Didn't he understand? "I've got people counting on me," she told him.

"And if you turn up, you'll be *infecting* those people." She tried to get up again and this time, he held down her hands just enough to keep her where she was. "Are you familiar with the story of Typhoid Mary?"

Was that what Everett thought she was? A woman who wantonly infected people? "That's not funny."

"I'm not trying to be funny, Lila," he told her. "But I am trying to get through to you. You're sick." Everett told her, enunciating every word slowly. "You have the flu."

She felt like hell warmed over, but she still protested, "No, I don't."

His eyes met hers. "Which one of us went to medical school?" he asked her in a quiet, tolerant voice that only served to infuriate her.

She blew out an angry breath. "You did," she said grudgingly.

Everett smiled. She had made his point for him. "You have the flu," he repeated.

"I can't have the flu," she insisted. She looked up at Everett, her eyes pleading with him.

This had to be good, he thought. "Why?"

Exasperation throbbed in every syllable. "Because I just can't."

Everett decided to play along as if she had a valid argument that needed exploration. "Did you get vaccinated?"

"No," Lila admitted, mumbling the word under her breath.

A triumphant look slipped over his face. "Okay, all together now: You have the flu."

Defeated, Lila sank back onto her pillow as if all the air had been suddenly pumped out of her.

"I really have the flu?" Lila asked him, silently begging him to come up with another explanation.

Rather than answer her immediately, Everett decided to back himself up with evidence. "What's your throat feel like?"

She didn't have to think before answering. "Sandpaper."

"And your head?" he asked, giving her a chance to contradict his diagnosis.

It was getting harder and harder for her to focus because of the pain. "Like there're twelve angry elves with steel hammers in it trying to beat their way out."

"Add that to the chills I observed last night and the high

fever—which by the way is going down—and you have more than your fair share of flu symptoms."

"The flu," Lila repeated in despair, saying it as if it was the mark of Cain on her forehead. "Isn't there anything you can do for me?" she asked, almost pleading with him.

"I'm doing it," he told her. "I'm nursing you back to health with bed rest, liquids and I have here a bowl of chicken soup that's guaranteed to cure what ails you," he quipped.

He'd found a folding TV tray tucked away in one of the closets and he set it up now next to her bed. When he was satisfied that it was stable, he put the bowl of soup on it along with a large soupspoon.

"See if you can hold that down," he told her.

Lila looked down into the bowl of soup as if she was trying to make up her mind about it. "Chicken soup?" she repeated.

"Highly underrated, by the way," he told her. "Apparently, our grandmothers knew something about its healing powers that we didn't. Seriously," he told Lila. "Try taking a few spoonfuls," he urged, helping her sit up and placing two pillows at her back to keep her upright.

The spoon was in her hand, but it remained motionless for now. "Where did you get the soup?" she asked. She knew she didn't have any canned soups in her kitchen cabinets.

"I had Schuyler bring it," he answered. He'd called his sister this morning and added that to his first request. "Along with your car," Everett said.

"My car?" Lila repeated. And then it suddenly came back to her. "My car's at the Foundation." Panic had entered her voice.

"Not anymore. Schuyler and her fiancé swung by this morning to pick up the keys to your car. They already drove it over. It's right outside in your driveway," he told her.

Lila looked at him in wonder. "You took care of everything," she marveled.

Everett grinned. "What can I say? I'm an overachiever."

Lila smiled at his choice of words. "I remember that about you," she said with almost a fond note in her voice.

When she sounded like that, he could feel himself melting. Now wasn't the time. "Eat your soup before it gets cold," he urged.

"And loses its magic healing powers?" she asked in an amused voice that was finally beginning to sound more like her.

"Something like that."

Lila nodded. "All right, I'll eat—if you tell me exactly what happened last night," she bargained.

"I already told you," he said. Seeing that she wasn't about to budge until he'd told her the whole story without skipping anything, Everett sighed. "But I'll tell you again," he said, resigned. "We were at the restaurant and you suddenly passed out."

She visualized that now and became horrified. "In front of everybody?"

"Just the people looking our way," he quipped. "I didn't take a head count," he said, doing his best not to get her agitated.

"Nobody called the paramedics, did they?" Lila asked. The last thing she wanted was for this to get around. She wanted to be able to do her job when she got back, not have to constantly be answering a lot of questions because there were rumors circulating about her. Rumors always had a way of escalating and becoming exaggerated.

The thought of having to deal with that made her feel more ill.

"Well, you frightened the server, but I told her I was a doctor and that seemed to satisfy her. So I picked you up and carried you to my car. Our waitress followed us with your purse and the dinners she packed up to go—which, by the way, are in the refrigerator waiting for you once you get your appetite back."

"How did you know where I lived?" Lila asked suddenly. She hadn't told him her address.

"I got it from your driver's license in your purse," he told her. "Which, before you ask, is where I found the keys to your house. And the car," he added, "so that Schuyler could drive it here. Okay," he informed her, "that about catches us up."

Turning, he was about to return to the kitchen when she cried, "Wait."

Now what? He did his best not to sound impatient. "I told you everything," he stressed.

"Weren't you supposed to go back to your practice in Houston today?" she asked, remembering he'd said something to that effect.

He looked at her pointedly. Was she trying to get him to make some sort of a declaration about the way he felt about her, or was this just an innocent question? "My plans changed."

"You don't have to stay here on my account," she protested.

"Lila, right now a pregnant cat could beat you at arm wrestling with one paw tied behind her back. You have the strength of an overcooked noodle. You need to rest and you need someone to take care of you while you're resting. I'm volunteering."

She shook her head and almost instantly regretted it. Her head started swimming and she waited for it to steady itself again. "I can't let you do that."

"I don't recall asking for permission," he told her. "I've got more vacation time coming to me than any two people in my office combined and I'm electing to take some of it now. Now don't argue with me. Eat your soup and lie back, watch some mindless TV and rest. Doctor's orders," he added when she opened her mouth to protest. "Understood?"

Looking somewhat subdued, which both surprised and worried him, Lila repeated, "Understood."

CHAPTER TWELVE

SHE REMEMBERED.

Although Lila tried very hard not to, over the course of the next few days she began to remember why she had fallen in love with Everett to begin with. Not because he was so devastatingly handsome—which he still was, perhaps even more so—but because he was so kind.

Kind and thoughtful and caring.

She'd witnessed those traits in action while accompanying Everett on the house calls they'd paid together before she'd gotten ill, and now she was witnessing it up close and personal while he was taking care of her and nursing her back to health.

In essence, Everett was very quietly waiting on her hand and foot. He made sure she drank plenty of fluids. He prepared a soft, bland diet for her, then slowly substituted food with more substance when he felt she could handle it. The progression took close to a week because he told her he didn't want to rush things and risk her having a setback.

By the end of the fourth day of her convalescence, Lila had gotten comfortable enough with him to allow herself to share a few old stories about people they had known back in high school.

Since she had left Houston thirteen years ago, he was in a far better position to tell her what some of the people they had grown up with were doing these days.

"Remember Jack Logan?" Everett asked, bringing up another name as they were sharing a lunch of soup and sandwiches in her room.

It took Lila a moment to put a face to the name. "Oh, you mean the guy who expected every woman to faint at his feet just because he looked their way?" She remembered that Jack was always telling everyone he had big plans for himself. "Whatever happened to him?"

Everett smiled, remembering how brash and abrasive Logan had been. "He still lives in Houston and works at the airport as a baggage checker."

As she recalled, that didn't exactly match up to Logan's lofty goals. "Is he still a lady-killer?"

He looked at Lila and answered her with a straight face. "Only if he fell on top of one. I saw him recently. He must have gained over a hundred pounds since graduation."

Lila tried to stifle a laugh, but she couldn't help herself. Somehow, that seemed like poetic justice. Logan had always been cruelly critical of anyone he felt wasn't as good-looking as he was. His remarks were always particularly hurtful about women he viewed to be overweight, even if they were carrying only a few extra pounds.

"He was always such an egotist," she said when she stopped laughing.

"That part hasn't changed," Everett told her. Finishing his meal, he wiped his mouth and put down his napkin. "I think he just sees his expanding weight as there being more of him to be impressed with." He looked at Lila's plate. "Are you finished?" he asked, nodding at her tray.

"Yes." As Everett removed the tray, she told him, "You know, you really don't have to wait on me hand and foot like this."

For the time being, Everett placed the tray aside on the bureau. He could take both trays to the kitchen the next time he left the room.

"Well, I'm here and there's not that much else to do," he reasoned. "So, to my way of thinking, I might as well make myself useful."

"That's another thing," she said, picking up on the fact that he was still in Austin. "I'm keeping you from your practice."

His eyes met hers for a long moment. And then he said, "Maybe I like being kept."

Lila felt herself growing warm and she didn't think that she was having any sort of a relapse. At least not the kind that involved the flu.

She did her best to steer the conversation in the initial direction she'd intended.

"What I'm saying is that you don't need to take care of me anymore. I'm getting better all the time."

"That's because of all the excellent care you've been getting."

Lila smiled, shaking her head. Everett had always had a way with words. "I won't argue with that."

"Good," Everett said with finality. He had brought her that day's TV schedule earlier for her to look through. He picked it up now and thumbed through it. "Now what would you like to watch this afternoon?" he asked. Watching TV after lunch had become a ritual for them the last few days, something he felt that they both looked forward to. "There're some pretty good old movies on the Classic Channel and I found a station that's streaming a lot of those old sitcoms you used to like watching." He named a couple of specific programs.

Hearing them cited, Lila looked at him in surprise. "You remember that?" she marveled.

"I remember a lot of things," he told her. He had committed a great many things to memory about her, Everett thought.

Lila could feel her heart racing even though she fiercely ordered it not to. She'd been this route before and she knew exactly where it ended. Nowhere, leaving her with an ache in her heart. She did *not* want to go there, not again.

But somehow, she just couldn't seem to convince herself to turn away, to choose a different path. She tried to assuage her conscience by telling herself that this was only for a little while.

Lila shrugged in response to his question. "I don't know, you pick something," she told him. The next moment, she threw back her covers and swung her legs down. "I'll be right back."

"Where are you going?"

"I need to use the bathroom," she informed him with as much dignity as she could muster.

All the other times she'd felt the need to go, Everett had taken her arm and walked her to the bathroom as if they were out for an evening stroll. It was obvious to him that this time around, Lila was attempting to assert her independence. Not that he could blame her. In her place, he'd try to do the same thing.

Everett took a step back, allowing her space so she could get out of bed. However, he still kept a watchful eye on her.

On her feet now, he could see that Lila was still rather unstable. She took a single step and her right knee buckled.

Everett's arms were around her instantly, keeping her from landing on the floor. When he drew her back up, her body slid ever so slightly against his.

It was only for a second, but it was enough. Enough to send sparks flying between them and throwing old longings into high gear.

Everett caught his breath, silently ordering himself to remain steady instead of pulling her closer to him and kissing her the way he wanted to.

Instead of making love with her the way he desperately wanted to.

Only extreme self-control kept him from acting on the impulses that were urgently telegraphing themselves throughout his whole body.

"I know you wanted to do this alone, but maybe I should just walk with you to the bathroom this one more time," he suggested.

"To keep me from doing a pratfall?" she asked ruefully.

Her ego stood as much of a chance of being hurt as her body, so he tactfully rephrased what she'd just asked. "So you don't risk bruising anything if you do happen to fall," he told her. "So, is it okay?" he asked, waiting for her to give him the go-ahead on this.

She sighed and then smiled at him. She realized Everett was trying to spare her feelings. "Well, the old saying is that pride always goes before a fall and I don't want to fall, so I guess I'll have to just tuck away my pride and let you walk me to the bathroom one more time."

Everett laughed softly. "Good call," he congratulated her. "You'll be doing solo runs again before you know it," he promised.

Sitting on the edge of Lila's bed, Everett set aside his stethoscope. He'd just finished giving Lila her latest examination.

"Well, your fever's gone," he told her. "You're keeping your food down and your color's definitely back. And when you talk, you no longer sound like someone who starts their mornings with a shot of scotch and a cigarette. Although I have to say that I was getting kind of used to hearing that sexy voice. I might actually miss it," he admitted, smiling fondly at her.

"Well, I won't," Lila assured him with feeling. "I thought I sounded like some kidnapper placing a ransom call." She looked at him hopefully. "Does this mean that I'm being cleared for work?"

Everett nodded. He closed his medical bag and set it on the floor.

"Our little unofficial holiday is over," he told her, then in case there was any doubt, he added, "Yes, I'm clearing you for work."

Lila didn't take her eyes off him. "And you'll be going back to Houston?"

"I will," Everett confirmed. He knew he had to be getting back, but there was a part of him that didn't want to leave.

If he were honest with himself, he'd admit that he'd used nursing Lila back to health as an excuse to spend more time with her.

The last thirteen years had been filled with work, at times almost nonstop. He knew now that he had been trying to fill the emptiness—the gaping void that losing her had created—with work. Work and the occasional woman. None of them ever measured up to Lila simply because no one had ever even come close to making him feel the way Lila had.

The way she still did.

"But I'll still be coming back to Austin a lot," he told her, never breaking eye contact. "To see Schuyler and help her out with some things," he added, not wanting to scare Lila off. He paused for a moment, then, despite the advice Schuyler had given him, he asked, "Is it all right if I call you when I'm in town?"

After the way that he had put himself out for her, she hadn't expected Everett to ask permission to call her. She assumed he'd think he'd earned the right to call her any time he wanted to.

"How can I say no to the man who nursed me back to health?" she asked, trying to sound as if she was amused by his question.

"I'm not asking you to see me as the man who nursed you back to health," Everett pointed out. "I'm asking you to see me—" he paused for a moment, looking for the right phrasing "—as an old friend."

The silence between them grew until she finally said to him, "I couldn't say no to that, either."

"Glad to hear it," he told her.

He let out the breath he'd been holding. Honestly, he really hadn't known what Lila would say in response to his question. He wouldn't have put it past her feelings of self-preservation to tell him that seeing each other again wouldn't be a good idea.

But now that she had agreed, he saw that there was something far greater than self-preservation going on between them.

He could feel it.

And it was not just on his end. Nor was it just wishful thinking.

There was something tangible and real pulsating between them, ready to spring to life at the slightest bit of encouragement.

But even with all that, Everett knew he had to tread lightly. One wrong step and it could all crumble right beneath him, sending him plummeting head first into an abyss.

"Hi, are you free for dinner tonight?"

"Everett?" Lila was immediately alert. She'd answered her cell phone just as she'd walked in her front door, thinking it was someone at the Foundation working late, calling with a question.

But it wasn't.

"I didn't expect to hear from you this soon," she said.

It had been six days since she had gone back to work and he had returned to Houston.

"Well, I'm only in Austin for a few hours," he explained, "so I thought, if you're free, you might want to get together."

There it was, she thought. Her way out. He was handing it to her.

If you're free.

That was all she had to say to him. That she wasn't free. That her evening was already spoken for and she had somewhere else to be. And knowing Everett, he would accept that, murmur his regrets and that would be that.

The problem was, she didn't want to take this way out that he was handing her on a silver platter. She *wanted* to see him.

The truth of it was, after seeing him every day for almost a week, she missed him.

She knew that she shouldn't feel this way. Knew that she needed to cut Everett out of her life before he became a habit. But then on the other hand, this *was* only going to be dinner. And dinner would last for a few hours at most, nothing more. She knew that Everett was far too conscientious to lie to her, especially for some ulterior motive. If he said he was only here for a few hours, then he *was* in Austin only for that time.

Those few hours might as well be spent with her, she thought in a moment of weakness.

"I am free," she heard herself saying, sealing her fate, at least for the next few hours. "We can do dinner if you like. And I promise not to pass out this time," she added with amusement, remembering the last time they were in a restaurant together.

"Oh." He pretended to sound as if he was sorry to hear that. "Too bad," he told her. "I was looking forward to playing the hero, sweeping you into my arms and carrying you to my car."

"I think being the hero once would be enough for any guy."

"Oh, I don't know," Everett speculated. "It's kind of addictive if the hero has the right damsel in distress to save."

That definitely conjured up an image, Lila thought. "I never envisioned myself as a damsel in distress," she told Everett.

"I wouldn't have thought of you as one, either," he admitted. "I guess the world is full of surprises." Then he changed topics. "Well, like I said, I'm only in Austin for a bit, so where would you like to go?"

"Seeing what happened the last time when we went to the Italian restaurant, how about Chinese food?" Lila suggested.

"Sounds good to me," he told her. He would have said the same thing if she had suggested strolling through the park, eating ice cream cones. He just wanted to see her. It had been six long days during which time he had forced himself not to call her just to see how she was doing. Or to hear the sound of her voice. He didn't want Lila to feel as if he was crowding her, or worse, as if he was stalking her.

But it hadn't been easy.

He had spent six days *with* her when she'd been ill with the flu and he had quickly gotten used to seeing her everyday. *Not* seeing her was hell now, but he couldn't behave like some privileged adolescent who was accustomed to having his every whim indulged—no matter how much he wished.

This was too important for him to risk messing up again. So he treaded lightly.

"If it's okay, I can be at your place in half an hour. Or is that too soon? Do you need more time?"

"Actually, I need less if you're close by. I just got home from work and I still look very businesslike, so I don't need to change."

He preferred the temptress look he'd seen on her, but to remain safe, he thought that it was best to go along with the business suit.

"You always look good no matter what you have on." *And sometimes even better the less you have on*, he added silently. "I'll be there in fifteen minutes."

CHAPTER THIRTEEN

LILA FELT AS if she had suddenly blinked and just like that, found herself going back to square one all over again. She was experiencing feelings of excitement and wariness and that in turn had created knots in her stomach.

Big ones.

But not quite big enough for her to call Everett and tell him that she'd changed her mind about having dinner with him.

Despite saying that she didn't need any extra time to get ready because she was still dressed for work, Lila impulsively flew into her bedroom for a quick change of clothes. She didn't want to look as if she was going to a business meeting. She wanted to look as good as she could possibly look.

Like a woman who was going out to dinner with a man who had once owned her heart.

Not that she planned on letting him own it again, she maintained as she quickly pulled the pins out of her hair. Instantly, the changed hairstyle made her appear more carefree. Her auburn hair cascaded around her face instead of being neatly pulled back, out of the way.

Her practical attire gave way to an attractive, form-flattering dress. She had just slipped on a pair of high heels that could have never, by any stretch of the imagination, been called sensible, when she heard the doorbell ring.

The sound instantly had her heart accelerating.

Showtime, she thought.

Hurrying to the front of the house, she stopped just short of the front door in order to catch her breath. She pulled herself together, doing her best to look as if she was totally nonchalant about the evening that lay ahead of her.

Everett would probably see right through her, she thought. Even so, she felt that she still had to keep up the charade.

Taking in one more deep breath and then slowly releasing it, she opened the door.

"When you say fifteen minutes, you really mean fifteen minutes," she said as she smiled up into Everett's handsome face.

"A man's only as good as his word," he responded. "You know, we don't have to leave right away if you're not ready yet."

"Do I look like I'm not ready yet?" she asked.

Despite her coy bravado, Lila couldn't help wondering what it was that Everett saw when he looked at her. Had he been hoping she'd be wearing something more appealing? Sexier?

Don't borrow trouble, she warned herself.

Everett's eyes slowly washed over the length of her. There was nothing but approval evident in his eyes. "You look, in a word, perfect," he pronounced.

Lila smiled at the compliment, secretly pleased although she tried her best to appear indifferent. "Then I guess I'm ready." Taking her purse, she walked out of the house, then paused to lock up.

Everett's Mercedes was waiting in her driveway.

"By the way," Everett said as he held the passenger door open for her, "I know you said we were going to a Chinese restaurant, but if I'm driving, you need to tell me the address."

She waited for Everett to get in on his side. Once he buckled up, she gave him the address, adding, "It's about half a mile past the Foundation. A lot of people from work like grabbing lunch at Gin Ling's."

Everett thought for a second. "I think I know which restaurant you mean," he told her. He remembered seeing it when he'd driven to the Foundation. "That's the one that's built to look like a pagoda, right?"

"Right."

Gin Ling's was doing brisk business when they arrived. They had to wait a few minutes to be seated.

Thinking that Everett might grow impatient, Lila told him, "We can go somewhere else if you don't want to wait."

Everett made no move to take her up on the suggestion. "Do you like eating here?" he asked her.

She wouldn't have suggested coming here if she hadn't. That wasn't the point. "Yes, but—"

"Then we'll wait," he told her, adding, "I'm not in any hurry. I like making the most of the little downtime I get."

There was a reason why she had mentioned the idea of going to another restaurant. "I just don't want to make you late."

Everett looked at her as if he wasn't quite following her. "For what? I don't have a plane to catch," he reminded Lila. "I'm driving back to Houston."

"Doesn't all that driving make you tired?" In his place, she'd find driving back and forth between Austin and Houston exhausting after a while.

However, Everett shook his head. "On the contrary. Driving relaxes me."

Relaxing made her think about falling asleep at the wheel—not that Everett would ever admit that he was in danger of doing that. But she didn't want to think that he ran the risk of having something happen to him because of her.

"Still," she told him, "I don't want you so relaxed that you just slide right out of your seat."

"Never happen," Everett assured her. Still, her comment made his heart lighter.

She was clearly worried about him, he thought, and that felt particularly encouraging. Because that meant that there were still feelings there. Feelings he intended to stoke and encourage.

"Don't worry," he said. "I like staying in one piece as much as the next man. If I ever feel too tired to drive back, I'll rent a motel room and sleep until I feel up to driving. And, don't forget, there's always Schuyler," he reminded her.

A hostess came to show them to their table. Lila fell into place behind the woman with Everett following right behind her.

"Sorry, I was just remembering how stubborn you could be," Lila told him as they were being shown to a cozy booth.

"Not stubborn," Everett corrected, waiting for her to slide in before taking his own seat opposite her. "Determined."

Lila smiled. "Right. Determined," she repeated, humoring him.

"So how was going back to work?" Everett asked her after their server had brought them a pot of tea and then departed after taking each of their orders.

"Wonderfully hectic as always," she told him.

But Everett was more interested in the state of her health. "You didn't have any relapses or feel any ill effects from the flu?"

"No. I didn't expect that there would be," she told him honestly, smiling at Everett. "I always knew that you would be a fantastic doctor."

Everett maintained a straight face as he nodded. "I haven't mastered walking on water yet," he deadpanned, "but I'm working on it."

About to bring the small cup of tea to her lips, Lila stopped just short of completing the action, staring at him.

Everett laughed. "Well, you were making it sound as if I'd done something extraordinary," he told her. "I just took it a step further."

"You went out of your way for a patient—which was what I was," she reminded him. "Not every doctor would have stayed with a patient for almost a week because there was no one to take care of her."

"Not just any patient," Everett pointed out, "but a patient I was once nearly engaged to."

"And that near-engagement ended badly," she reminded him. Before he could say anything in response, she went on to tell him, "You had every right in the world to call the paramedics, then have them take me to the hospital while you walked away."

He inclined his head like a man conceding a point. "Okay. You got me. I'm a magnificent doctor—who was hoping for a second chance at dinner," he added as if that had been his sole motive behind seeing to it that she got well. "In order to do that, I had to make sure that you stayed alive. The best way to do that was to see to it myself." He shrugged. "I don't delegate very well."

She paused to sample the egg roll appetizer that had been brought to the table and then laughed.

"When did you get so good at twisting around words to make them back you up?" she wanted to know.

"It comes with the medical degree," Everett responded.

"No, it doesn't," Lila countered. She felt herself verging on impatience at the way he was so dismissive of his own abilities.

"Okay, then let's just say it's an inherent talent. A gift," he emphasized. "Born out of necessity," he added. "Satisfied?" He studied her across the table.

"No," Lila answered honestly. "But I guess that it'll have to do for now."

She was rewarded with a smile that seemed to come from deep inside of Everett. She could feel her heart flutter in response.

They talked for another hour, long after the main course and the fortune cookies had come and gone and the pot of tea had been refilled.

"I think we'd better get going. It looks like our server wants the table." She looked toward the reception area and saw why. "There's a line going all out the door now."

Everett found himself reluctant to leave. "I'm sure I can find a way to make it up to him if you want to stay a little longer. Would you like a few more appetizers?" he asked.

Lila laughed. "If I so much as look at another one, I'll explode."

"Okay, that's a no," he acknowledged. "So I guess you're ready to go?"

Lila nodded. "I've got another day at work tomorrow and you, you've got a long drive ahead of you," she reminded him. "I can call a cab for myself if you'd like to get started on that drive home," Lila offered, watching Everett's expression for any indication that he did want to leave.

Everett regarded her thoughtfully. "If I didn't know any better, I would venture to say that you were trying to get rid of me."

"No," Lila denied, saying the word with feeling. "I'm not."

He grinned at her. "Good, because it's not working. I'm going to be taking you home. The few extra minutes that it'll take me isn't going to make a difference as far as my trip is concerned," he assured her. Raising his hand, he signaled to the server.

True to his word, Everett left an extra large tip on the table for the man. Large enough to prompt their server to call after them as they left, saying, "Please come again!"

Lila and Everett exchanged looks and grinned at one another just before they walked out of the increasingly crowded restaurant.

"I had a really nice time tonight," she told Everett once she was at her door.

Everett nodded, doing his best to look solemn as he reviewed their evening.

"Well, you made it all the way back home without passing

out, so the way I see it, it was a successful evening," he said dryly.

Lila shook her head. "You're not going to let me live that down, are you?" she asked.

"In time, maybe," he conceded.

Key in hand, Lila stopped just short of putting it into the lock. She knew she was stalling, but she couldn't help herself.

"Does that mean you want to do this again?" she asked Everett.

"Absolutely," Everett answered with certainly. He paused for a moment, debating whether or not to say what was on his mind or quit while he was ahead. After a beat, he made up his mind to continue. "Lila, I just want you to know that I intend to rebuild what we once had," he told her. He saw the wary look that came over her face even though he could tell she was trying to appear unaffected by his words. "I didn't say that to scare you, Lila. I want to be fair about this. I'm not going to go behind your back, or spring something on you. This is all going to be aboveboard and honest. I just really want to make the most of this second chance."

"Second chance?" Lila repeated.

The fact that she wasn't immediately dismissing what he'd just said told Everett that at least to some extent, she felt the same way he did. This *was* their second chance. Or more accurately, *his* second chance.

"I think that Fate threw us together like this for a reason, Lila, and I'm not about to ignore that," he told her.

He could see that she still looked wary.

"Don't worry," he reassured her quickly. "I don't plan on throwing a sack over your head and running off with you to some isolated cabin in order to wear you down until you see things my way. I told you that I'm patient and that's not just when it comes to getting a table in a restaurant. I will go as slow as you want me to go, but I have a feeling that in the end, you'll agree with me that we were meant to be together."

As he talked, standing so close to Lila, he was overwhelmed by an urge to kiss her. But he instinctively knew that doing so at this moment would spook her and he couldn't afford the setback that would create. Kissing Lila might satisfy the need he had just to feel her lips against his, but it very well might cost him in the end. He'd be winning the battle but losing the war, so to speak.

So, difficult as it was, he was determined to hold himself in check and wait.

He had no other choice. He had told Lila the truth. Patience was at the very core of his psychological makeup. He intended to wait as long as he had to in order to win Lila back.

"Are you sure that you're up to driving all that distance?" Lila asked him, breaking into his thoughts.

The fact that she worried about him touched Everett again. It proved to him that he was right. In the long run, they were going to wind up together. Fate wouldn't be that cruel to him, to bring her back into his life like this only to ultimately have him lose her a second time. He just had to stay strong and keep his wits about him.

"I'm fine," he told her. "And I'm going to be back sometime next week for a day. I'll see you then," he promised. "Now go inside and lock the door so I can get going."

Lila was about to point out that she got inside her house on her own every night without supervision, or having anything happen to her, but she let it go. She didn't want to ruin the evening. Everett was being protective and there was something to be said for that, she told herself. Besides, being this close to him was practically setting her on fire, which she could not afford.

So she unlocked her door under his watchful eye and then went in, closing the door behind her.

"Now lock it," he told her after a beat, raising his voice to be heard.

"Yes, sir," Lila called back, humoring him. She turned the lock. "It's locked," she announced.

"Good night, Lila."

"Good night, Everett."

And then, after a couple of beats, she heard Everett's car starting up. He was leaving.

Why did that have such a mournful sound to her, she asked herself. After all, she *wanted* him to leave. Everett might be confident about their future together, but she wasn't.

He'd also been confident about their future when they were younger. *Very* confident. And look how that had ultimately turned out, she reminded herself. That big, wonderful future he had been so sure stretched out before them had shriveled up and died before it had ever had a chance to actually take root and thrive.

And history, she reminded herself as she went into her bedroom to change out of her dress, had a terrible habit of repeating itself.

Lila closed her eyes and shivered. She couldn't bear to go though that kind of heartbreak a second time.

She wasn't strong enough.

CHAPTER FOURTEEN

LILA HAD VACILLATED about whether or not to invite Everett to the Fortune Foundation fund-raiser for the better part of a week. And now the event was tonight. That meant it was too late for her to change her mind again and invite him.

Just as well, Lila told herself. She'd attend the black-tie gala solo, just as she had initially planned when she'd first gotten the invitation.

Before Everett had popped up back in her life.

The only problem was, she felt conflicted.

Ever since Everett had gone out of his way and nursed her through that bout with the flu, she'd been sorely tempted to invite him—just as a show of gratitude, of course. However, she felt that if they attended the function together, that would be like practically announcing to the world at large that they were a couple—again.

And it was much too premature for that sort of speculation to make the rounds.

Because they weren't a couple anymore and they might never *be* a couple.

So, as she wavered back and forth, Lila fell back on her old stand-by: Why borrow trouble?

Consequently, she was going alone.

It wouldn't be the first time, she thought. And given what her life was like, it undoubtedly wouldn't be the last.

The way she felt at the moment, Lila had a premonition that she was destined to be alone for the rest of her life. Her dreams about Everett had been just that: dreams. And sooner or later, people were destined to wake up from dreams.

To boost her spirits, Lila bought herself a brand-new dress. It was a gown really, she thought, looking herself over from all angles in her wardrobe mirror as she prepared to leave.

The floor-length baby-blue silk gown swirled around softly as she moved and made her feel like she was a princess.

A princess without a kingdom—or a prince, Lila added ruefully—but a princess nonetheless.

"At least for one night," Lila whispered to her reflection.

Taking a deep breath, she gathered up her wrap and her purse. She checked her purse one last time to make sure she had her invitation. It was right where it had been the last four times she'd checked, tucked against her wallet.

She was ready.

"Nothing left to do but drive Cinderella over to the ball," Lila murmured to her reflection.

She smiled to herself as she locked the door and got into her car.

Where are the singing mice when you need them? she wondered wryly, starting up her vehicle.

The Fortune Foundation's fund-raiser was being held on the ground floor ballroom of Austin's finest hotel. Everything about the evening promised to be of the highest, most expensive quality.

After slipping into her purse the ticket that the valet who'd taken her car had given her, Lila went into the hotel.

She didn't need to look at the signs to know which ballroom the fund-raiser was being held in. All she had to do was follow the sound of music and laughter. It was evident that the crowd was having a good time.

The sound quadrupled in volume the second she opened one of the doors to the Golden Room.

She stood there just inside the doors, acclimating herself and looking around what seemed like a cavernous ballroom. There were people absolutely everywhere.

"You made it!"

Surprised, Lila turned to her right and found herself looking at Lucie. Her friend easily hooked her arm through hers.

"I was beginning to think you'd decided to take a pass on this," Lucie said as she began to gently steer Lila in what seemed to be a predetermined direction.

"I didn't think the Foundation allowed us to take a pass," Lila answered honestly. Not that she would have. Her sense of duty and loyalty was just too strong.

"Well, I don't know about 'allowed,'" Lucie replied, considering the matter, "but I do think that there would have been a lot of disappointed people here if you hadn't shown up."

Lila laughed. "I really doubt that," she told Lucie.

"I don't," Lucie retorted. Her eyes were sparkling with humor as she added, "Especially one someone in particular."

Lila stared at her. Lucie had managed to completely lose her. Her brow furrowed as Lila asked, "What are you talking about?"

"Come." The woman tugged a little more insistently on Lila's arm. "I'll show you. By the way, I like the gown. Light blue's a good color for you. It brings out your eyes," she added with approval.

"It's new," Lila confessed, having second thoughts and thinking that maybe she shouldn't have indulged herself like this.

Glancing at the gown one more time, Lucie nodded. "I had a feeling."

"Why? Did I forget to remove a tag?" Lila asked nervously,

looking down at her gown and then trying to look over her shoulder to see if there were any telltale tags hanging from the back.

"No, you didn't forget to remove a tag, silly. It just has that first-time-off-a-hanger look." Looking past Lila, Lucie raised her hand and waved.

"Who are you waving at? Chase?" Lila asked, referring to her friend's husband. Scanning the immediate area, Lila tried to get a glimpse of the rancher.

"Chase is off talking to Graham about that pet project of theirs, the center for military equine therapy," Lucie said. She was talking about Graham Fortune, the man who not only had taken over Fortune Cosmetics but also owned the successful Peter's Place, a home where troubled teens were helped to put their lives together. "No," Lucie told her, a very satisfied smile playing on her lips, "I was waving at the person I said would have been disappointed if you'd decided not to attend tonight."

Before Lila could ask any more questions, she suddenly found herself looking up at someone she'd never expected to see.

Everett. In an obligatory tuxedo.

At that moment Lila realized Everett in a tuxedo was even more irresistible than Everett in jeans.

Face it, the man would be irresistible even wearing a kilt.

"What are you doing here?" Lila asked when she finally located her tongue and remembered how to use it.

"You know, we're going to have to work on getting you a new opening line to say every time you see me," Everett told her with a laugh. "But to answer your question, I was invited."

Lucie stepped up with a slightly more detailed explanation to her friend's question. "The invitation was the Foundation's way of saying thank-you to Everett for his volunteer work."

"Disappointed to see me?" he asked Lila. There was a touch of humor in his voice, although he wasn't quite sure just what to make of the stunned expression on Lila's face.

"No, of course not," Lila denied quickly. "I'm just surprised, that's all. I thought you were still back in Houston."

"I was," Everett confirmed. "The invitation was express-mailed to me yesterday. I thought it would be rude to ignore it, so here I am," he told her simply, as if all he had to do was teleport himself from one location to another instead of drive nearly one hundred and seventy miles.

"Here you are," Lila echoed.

Everything inside her was smiling and she knew that was a dangerous thing. Because when she was in that sort of frame of mind, she tended not to be careful. And that was when mistakes were made.

Mistakes with consequences.

She was going to have to be on her guard, Lila silently warned herself. And it wasn't going to be easy being vigilant, not when Everett looked absolutely, bone-meltingly gorgeous.

As if his dark looks weren't already enough, Lila thought, the tuxedo made Everett look particularly dashing.

You're not eighteen anymore, remember? Lila reminded herself. *You're a woman. A woman who has to be very, very careful.*

She just hoped she could remember that.

"Since your last name practically sounds like Fortune," Lucie was saying to Everett, flanking him on the other side, "maybe you'd like to meet a Fortune or two—or twelve," she teased.

He turned to look at Lila. "Is that all right with you?"

The fact that he asked surprised her. "Why would I object?" she asked, puzzled.

Bending over, he whispered into her ear. "I thought, looking like that," he paused to allow his eyes to skim over her from top to bottom, "maybe you'd want me all to yourself."

She wasn't sure if it was what he said, or his warm breath in her ear that caused the shiver to run rampant up and down her spine.

Whatever it was, it took everything Lila had not to let it get the better of her. She knew where that sort of thing led her. To heaven and then, eventually, to hell as a consequence.

That wasn't going to happen again, she silently swore.

Clearing her throat, Lila ignored the last part of what he'd said and crisply answered, "Yes, it's fine with me."

Lucie smiled. "Then let the introductions begin," she announced, taking charge.

Lucie led off with her husband, Chase. The latter was a genial man who struck Everett as being very down-to-earth, considering the fact that he was an extremely wealthy man.

It was while Everett was talking to Chase that he was introduced to Graham Fortune Robinson. Graham, Everett was told, was one of Jerome Fortune/Gerald Robinson's eight legitimate offspring. Again, rather than behaving as if he was spoiled or indifferent, or extremely entitled—all traits that Everett had seen displayed by many of the wealthy people he'd grown up with—Graham Fortune came across as only interested in the amount of good he could do with the money he had.

The man, like so many of the other Fortunes who were there that evening, had a keen interest in philanthropy, Everett concluded.

While he was being introduced to and talking with various members of the Fortune clan, Everett found himself exploring the subject that was so near and dear to Schuyler's heart: that perhaps there was some sort of a family connection between the Fortune family and his own. Was "Fortunado" just a poor attempt by someone in the previous generation to either connect to the Fortunes, or to clumsily try to hide that connection?

Everett's radar went up even higher when, after Lucie said that her connection to Graham went beyond just bloodlines, Graham joked that it seemed like everyone was related to him these days.

Everett forced himself to bite his tongue in order to refrain from asking Graham if, by that comment, he was referring to the Fortunados.

The next moment, Graham cleared up the possible confusion by saying that he was referring to the fact that numerous illegitimate Fortune offspring had been located over the past couple of years. Apparently, many years ago the prodigious patriarch Jerome Fortune had deliberately disappeared. When he had resurfaced, he had changed his name, calling himself Gerald Robinson. And, in addition to going on to amass a wealthy portfolio of his own, Gerald/Jerome had amassed a sizeable number of offspring, both legitimately with his wife, Charlotte, and illegitimately with a whole host of women whose paths the man had crossed.

"How did he manage to keep track of all those kids?" Everett marveled, still trying to wrap his mind around the fact that one man had wound up fathering a legion of children.

"Quite simply, he didn't," Graham answered. "But according to one story I've heard, his wife—and my mother—did. She got it into her head to look up every one of her husband's progeny. Some of my siblings think she wanted to be prepared for any eventuality," Graham explained. "Supposedly, she has everything she found written down in a big binder or something along those lines."

Graham smiled. "My personal theory is that when she collected enough data to make that binder really heavy, she was going to use it to hit my father upside the head and teach him a lesson for tomcatting around like that."

Lila nodded, saying in all seriousness, "If you ask me, the man certainly had it coming, spreading his seed around like that without any thought of how this was affecting anyone else in his family—especially those children."

"Yes, but then on the other hand, if he hadn't done it, there would be a lot less Fortunes in the world and so far, all the ones I've met have been really decent people whose hearts are in the right place," Everett pointed out.

Graham smiled his approval at Everett's comment. "I couldn't have put it better myself. I've come to like every one of my siblings." He shrugged and held up his wineglass as if in a silent toast to them. "It's not everyone who has a family big enough to populate a medium-size town."

Everett touched his glass to Graham's. He felt as if he could go on talking about the various members of the Fortune family all night. But suddenly, everyone in the ballroom was being asked to stop what they were doing.

"Can I have everyone's attention for a moment?" a tall, imposing man with a booming voice said into a microphone. He was standing before a podium at the front of the ballroom. "This is the time in our evening where we all temporarily suspend the festivities and are asked to dig deep into our hearts—and our pockets," the MC added with a laugh. "In other words, it's time for us to donate to the Fortune Foundation so it can go on doing all those good works and helping all those people who are not nearly as fortunate—no pun intended—as we all are."

The man's piercing blue eyes seemed to sweep around the entire ballroom. No easy feat, Lila thought, watching from the sidelines.

"Now don't be shy," the MC continued. "Give as much as you're able. No donation is too small, although bigger is always better. But even a little is better than nothing. So, like I said, open your hearts and get those checkbooks out. Remember, it feels good to give. And when you do, you'll find that you'll get back in ways you never even suspected were possible."

Listening, Lila opened up her purse and took out her checkbook. She was about to start writing out what she viewed to be a modest amount—although it was all she could afford—when Everett put his hand on hers, stopping her.

She looked at him, puzzled. Why wasn't he letting her write the check?

"I'll take care of it for both of us," he told her. The next moment, as she watched, she saw Everett write out a check for the sum of one hundred thousand dollars.

At the last second, she remembered to keep her mouth from dropping open.

CHAPTER FIFTEEN

THE MC, DAVID DAVENPORT, looked at the check that had just been passed to him by one of the aides collecting donations from the guests. Holding the check aloft, Davenport scanned the crowd until he made eye contact with Everett.

"Is this right?" the MC asked Everett, astonished. "Your pen didn't slip?"

Everett's mouth curved slightly as he smiled at the man in front of the room. "My pen didn't slip," he assured the MC.

Davenport, a distinguished-looking, gray-haired man in his fifties, instantly brightened. "Ladies and gentlemen, I'm proud to announce that we have a new record," he told the gathering. "Dr. Everett Fortunado has generously donated the sum of one hundred thousand dollars to the Fortune Foundation."

A hush fell over the entire ballroom. It lasted for almost a full minute and then people began clapping. The sound swelled until the entire ballroom was engulfed in appreciative applause.

Everett wasn't really sure just how to react to the applause. He hadn't made the donation because he wanted to garner any sort of attention. He'd written the check because he felt it was his obligation to share the good fortune he had always felt so privileged to grow up experiencing.

When the applause finally died down, Davenport proceeded to try to utilize the moment to the Foundation's advantage.

"All right, people, let's see if Dr. Fortunado's generosity can motivate some of you to do your fair share as well." The MC looked around. It seemed as if he was making eye contact with everyone there. "Remember, this is for those deserving mothers and fathers and children who so badly need our help in order to make it through the hard times."

Everett stood back and watched as more of the fund-raiser's attendees began writing out checks. There seemed to be chatter going on all around him.

Except at his side.

From the moment he had written out the check, Everett noticed that Lila had fallen completely silent. She hadn't said a single word to him during the entire time that the checks were being written and collected on all sides of them.

Nor, he observed, did Lila say anything during the buffet dinner that followed, despite the fact that he had intentionally stayed close to her during the whole time. He had broached a number of topics in an effort to engage her in conversation and had only received single-word replies.

Finally, unable to take the silence any longer, he drew Lila aside to a little alcove, away from the rest of the ballroom, and asked her point-blank: "Is something wrong?"

Lila had been trying to reconcile the mixed feelings she'd been having ever since she'd watched Everett writing out a check for such an exorbitant amount. Because she didn't want to cause a scene or start an uproar, she'd been doing her best just to squelch the suspicions that had been growing in her head. That involved keeping her mouth shut and not saying anything, although it wasn't easy.

But her doubts weren't going away, and rather than taking

a hint and keeping quiet, Everett was pressuring her for an explanation.

Finally blowing out a frustrated breath, Lila asked him bluntly, "Are you trying to buy me?"

Dumbfounded and more than a little confused, Everett could only stare at her. He wasn't even sure if he had actually heard Lila correctly.

"What?"

Lila pressed her lips together, then ground out, "Are you trying to buy my love by giving that huge sum of money to the Foundation?"

Stunned, he told her, "I made that donation because the Foundation is a worthy cause that does a great deal of good work. I thought you'd be happy about my contribution." He looked at her, not knowing where this had come from. Not for the first time, he felt as if he was walking on eggshells around her.

"Why do you have to dissect every single move I make and search for an ulterior motive?" he wanted to know. "Can't I just be generous because I want to be? Because it makes me feel good to do something decent for people who weren't born as lucky as I was?" He saw tears suddenly shimmering in her eyes and immediately felt a pang of guilt because he knew he was responsible for those tears. "Hey, I didn't mean to make you cry—"

Lila shook her head, halting his apology. Taking a deep breath to center herself, she said, "You didn't. You're right. You did something selfless and I just took it apart, looking for hidden reasons behind your donation when you were just being a decent guy." She blew out a shaky breath. "I guess I've just gotten to be really mistrustful."

And that was on him, Everett thought. He'd done this to her—taken a sweet, optimistic young woman and crushed something inside of her all those years ago. He had to find a way to fix this, he told himself.

But how?

How did he convince Lila that his feelings for her were genuine? That all he wanted was to be able to show her that he loved her and that he was willing to make things up to her for the rest of his life?

Desperation had him making the next move in his desire to reach her, to communicate to her just how sincere he was.

Since he had taken her away from the rest of the guests in the ballroom by drawing her into a recessed alcove to talk to her, he knew they'd be safe from any prying eyes.

Framing Lila's face with his hands, Everett bent his head and did what he had been longing to do since he had first seen her in that sandwich shop in Austin.

He kissed her.

The moment his lips touched Lila's, Everett realized just how much he had missed her.

How much he really wanted Lila.

A little voice in his head told him he should stop kissing her, but he couldn't. Instead, Everett deepened the kiss.

And just like that, the captor became the captive.

At that moment, he knew that he would have walked through fire just to have Lila back in his life the way she had been all those years ago: loving and untainted by uncertainties and doubts.

Lila's breath caught in her throat. A split second before Everett had kissed her, she suddenly knew that he would. Knew too that with all her heart she wanted him to kiss her.

And then he did.

Just like that, all those years they'd spent apart melted away. She was instantly responding to Everett just as she had back then.

Except that now Lila was responding as a woman, not as a starry-eyed young girl.

Lila could feel every inch of her body heating as she fell deeper into the kiss. She wrapped her arms around Everett, savoring the taste of his lips urgently pressed against hers.

Longings, locked away for so long, came charging out, demanding attention as they carelessly trampled reason into the dust.

Her heart was pounding wildly when he drew his lips away. She found herself struggling in order to pull air into her lungs.

She looked up at Everett in wonder, desire mounting within her.

He hadn't meant to get this carried away, to let the moment get out of hand like this. He'd only wanted to kiss Lila again, to silently communicate to her that his feelings for her were as strong as ever.

Stronger.

"I'm sorry, Lila," Everett began. "I didn't mean to get—"

But Lila quickly cut short his apology. She didn't want Everett to be sorry for kissing her. Didn't want to have him withdrawing from her. Not when she was suddenly having all these unresolved feelings ricocheting throughout every inch of her being.

She wanted more.

Needed more.

"Let's get out of here," Lila breathed.

She didn't mean that, Everett thought, even as he asked, "Now?"

"Now," she echoed adamantly.

Everett stood there for a moment arguing with himself, trying very hard to convince himself to do the right thing.

Another man would have talked her out of it, pointing out what it might look like if someone saw them leaving before the fund-raiser was over. Another man would have taken her by the hand and led her back into the ballroom proper.

But another man hadn't spent every day of the last thirteen years missing Lila so much that there were times he literally ached.

Now that there was a glimmer of hope that they could get back together, that he could win her back, he could admit that to himself. Admit that the reason that every possible relationship that had loomed before him over the years had fallen through was because all the women in those would-be relationships hadn't been able to hold a candle to Lila.

So instead of doing the noble thing and trying to talk Lila out of what she'd just suggested, Everett took her hand in his. And together they made their way out of the ballroom. And then out of the hotel.

Once outside, as the cooler evening air slipped over them, Everett looked at Lila for some sign that she'd had a change of heart about leaving. He didn't detect any, but because he absolutely wanted her to have no regrets, he asked, "You're sure?"

"I'm sure," Lila answered breathlessly. All she wanted was to be alone with him. To be with him in every way possible.

"We both drove here separately," Everett reminded her.

While he feared that if she drove herself she might change her mind, he knew that if Lila left her car here at the hotel, someone from the fund-raiser would take note of that.

Questions would be asked and gossip would spread. He didn't want Lila subjected to any sort of talk or speculation as to why her car was still in the parking structure while she herself was nowhere to be found. He wanted to protect her from that sort of thing at all costs.

Although she didn't want to be more than a foot away from him right now, Lila didn't see any actual problem. "So? We can both drive our cars to my house. My driveway can accommodate two vehicles," she told him.

Lila could feel her heart hammering with every word she uttered as a tiny voice in her head, barely audible above the beating of her heart, was telling her to take her car and make good her escape.

But she didn't want to escape. One taste of Everett's lips and it was all she could do not to beg for more right here, right now.

When the valet came up to them, they both handed him their tickets.

"Bring the lady her car first," Everett told him.

The valet nodded. "Be right back," he promised, heading into the parking structure quickly.

"Think anyone noticed you left?" Everett asked her as they waited.

"If they notice anyone's gone, it would most likely be you," Lila told him. "After all, you're the man of the hour after that huge donation."

When the valet brought her car up and held the door open for her, she handed him a tip and then slid into the driver's seat.

She looked up at Everett, said, "I'll see you," and then drove off.

I'll see you.

Her words echoed in his brain. She hadn't said "I'll see you *later*." Just "I'll see you." Did that mean she'd had a change of heart and decided that she'd almost made a terrible mistake?

Now who's overthinking everything? Everett admonished himself.

He put the original question on hold when the valet brought up his car.

"You car handles like a dream," the valet told him enthusiastically and a bit enviously as he got out of the vehicle. Backing away, he left the driver's door open for him.

Everett inclined his head, a grin curving his mouth. "She likes to be babied," he told the valet as he handed him a ten-dollar bill and got in.

The valet's eyes widened as he looked at the bill. "Thanks!"

Everett pulled away, eager to catch up to Lila's car. But it felt like he was catching every single red light between the hotel and her house.

He really hoped that by the time he got there Lila hadn't reflected on her impulsive decision and changed her mind about the night ahead.

If she did, he would have no choice but to go along with her decision. He would never force himself on her, but he decided that he was going to do everything in his power to convince her that they were meant to be together.

Because they were.

It was hard to stay focused on the road. All he could see in his mind's eye was Lila. Lila, offering herself to him. Lila, making love with him.

Lila, who was and always had been the center of his universe.

How had he allowed himself to let her go? Everett silently asked himself. He wouldn't have tied her up in the attic, but he could have tried to talk her out of breaking up with him, could have tried his damnedest to convince her to give him another chance.

Well, this is your chance, Everett, he thought as he turned onto Lila's block. *Don't blow it.*

CHAPTER SIXTEEN

WHAT IF EVERETT didn't come?

What if he did?

Lila pressed her hand against her stomach, trying to quiet the butterflies that seemed to be wildly crashing into one another in her stomach. She'd never felt so confused before.

Back in the ballroom alcove, when Everett had kissed her, awakening all those old feelings, she'd wanted him right then and there. But now she'd had a little time to distance herself from that kiss, doubts had begun creeping in. It was as if she was playing a tennis match with herself in her brain.

Where *was* he?

Granted she'd flown through every light and gotten home in record time, moving as if her car was being propelled by a gale, but she hadn't left *that* much ahead of Everett.

He should have been here by now.

Unless he'd changed his mind and decided to go straight to his sister's house instead.

Or maybe he'd just decided to head back to Houston from the fund-raiser instead of coming over to her house.

To her.

Had she come on too strong?

But after he kissed her like that, unearthing all those old memories, she just couldn't help herself. Any thoughts of hanging back or taking it slow had just incinerated right on the spot. All she could think of was how much she'd missed being in Everett's arms, of having him hold her as if she was something very precious.

She felt as if she was losing her mind.

Lila looked out her window and saw only her car in the driveway.

He'd had a change of heart, she thought, letting the curtain drop back into place.

With a gut-wrenching sigh, she turned away. Served her right for giving in to her emotions like some silly schoolgirl and—

She jerked her head up, listening. Was that—?

Yes, it was. It was the sound of a car pulling up in her driveway.

All those doubts that were surfacing took a nosedive and she threw open the door before he had a chance to ring the doorbell.

"There are way too many red lights in this city," Everett told her.

Grabbing hold of his shirt, Lila pulled him over the threshold and into her house, slamming the door shut right behind him.

"I don't want to talk about red lights," she said just before she rose up on her tiptoes and sealed her mouth to his.

It was more than a couple of minutes later that they managed to come up for air—temporarily.

"Right," Everett breathlessly agreed, devouring her with his eyes. "No talking about red lights."

"No talking at all," Lila countered.

As she sought out his lips again, sealing hers to them, she began to systematically remove Everett's tuxedo, separating it from his body so quickly she worried that she'd wind up ripping something.

If she did, she could fix it, she assured herself. She knew her way around a needle. But right now, she wanted to relearn her way around his body.

It had been a long, long time since she'd been intimate with him. Since she'd been intimate with *anyone*, because after she had left Everett, she'd never met anyone to take his place, or even come close to qualifying as a candidate for that position. Without love as an ingredient in the mix, lovemaking just didn't seem right to her.

As she was eagerly removing his clothing, Everett was doing the same with hers.

Lila could feel his hands moving along her body. Locating her zipper, he pulled it down her back in one swift movement, then peeled away the silky gown from her skin.

It fell to the floor like a sinking blue cloud, pooling about her high heels.

Lila caught her breath as she felt his strong hands tugging away her bikini underwear, then gliding over her bare skin, swiftly reducing her to a pulsating mass of desire.

With urgent movements, she hurried to return the compliment until they were both standing there in her living room, nude—except for one thing.

She was still wearing her high heels.

Lila quickly remedied that, kicking the shoes off and instantly becoming petite.

"Damn," Everett whispered against the sensitive skin of her throat as he pressed kiss after kiss along it, "I can't tell you how many times I've dreamed about doing this."

The feel of his warm breath sliding along her skin caused all her desires to intensify. Her mushrooming needs almost engulfed her as they seized control over every single facet of her being.

Her mind in a haze, Lila felt her back being pressed against the sofa. She didn't even remember how they got there.

Everett was taking inventory of every single inch of her body with his mouth, creating wonderful sensations as he moved.

Doing wonderful things.

She was eager to return the favor, but for the moment, she couldn't find the strength to do anything but absorb every nuance of what was happening. She was utterly immersed in the deliciously wicked feelings that were erupting all over her as his lips and tongue left their mark everywhere, branding her.

Making her his.

Lila twisted and arched, savoring and absorbing every wondrous salvo wildly echoing throughout her body.

And still he continued, moving lower and lower by pulsating increments.

Anticipation rippled through her like shockwaves as she felt first his breath, and then his mouth moving down to the very center of her core.

His tongue teased her ever so lightly, skimming along the delicate, sensitive area, all the while raising her response higher and higher, creating a fever pitch within her until finally, delicious explosions erupted simultaneously all through her, undulating over her like a series of earthquakes.

Lila cried out his name, pulling him to her until he was right above her, melting her soul with the intense look of desire and passion in his eyes.

She felt him coaxing open her legs with his knee. What there was left of her shallow breath caught in her throat.

The next moment, he entered her and they were sealed to one another, creating a single heated entity.

Everett began to move his hips so slowly at first, she thought she had only imagined it. But then the movements began to increase, growing stronger. Taking her with them.

And then they were no longer on her sofa, no longer in her house. They were somewhere else, completely isolated from the world. A place where only the two of them existed.

The only thing that mattered was Everett and this insanely

wondrous sensation that they were sharing. Their bodies danced to music that only the two of them could hear.

The tempo increased, going faster and faster until suddenly they found themselves racing to the top of the world, to a place that was both new and familiar at the same time.

Lila could feel her heart slamming against his. Could feel Everett's heart echoing hers to the point that she thought their two hearts would forever be sealed together as one.

And then she felt the fireworks exploding, showering a profusion of stars all around her until that was all there was.

A world filed with stars.

She clung to Everett then, clung to the sensation that they had created together. She clung to it for as long as she could and bathed in the euphoria that came in its wake.

She held onto the sensation—and Everett—for as long as possible. But even so, it receded no matter how hard she fought to hang onto it.

Sorrow began to wiggle its way into the spaces the euphoria had left behind.

Everett shifted his weight off her, moving so that he was lying beside her.

He tightened his arm around her, exulting in the feeling of warmth generated by holding onto her. He glanced down at his chest and was mildly surprised that he wasn't glowing or giving out some sort of light like a beacon that guided the ships through the night at sea.

She was back, he thought. He'd won Lila back. And the lovemaking between them was so much better now than it had been before. The sex might have been familiar at its roots, but it had also felt wonderfully brand-new.

The woman in his arms was so much more now than she had been all those years ago.

How did he get so lucky? Everett silently marveled. Lying here next to Lila, reliving the lovemaking they had just shared, he found himself wanting to take her all over again.

Wanting her with a renewed fierceness that was impossible to ignore.

Propping himself up slightly, Everett leaned over her face and kissed one eyelid, then her other eyelid.

Then her mouth.

He lingered there, deepening the kiss until it all but consumed both of them, feeding something in his soul.

And then hers.

She looked up at him with wonder. "Again?" she questioned.

Lila saw laughter entering his eyes as Everett told her, "Honey, I am just getting started."

Something came over her.

Lila seized the moment and just like that, turned the tables on him. It was her turn to be the seducer rather than the seduced. This relationship didn't have a prayer of working if only one of them gave while the other received, she thought.

So, just as he had done before, Lila began to prime his body, ever so lightly gliding both her lips and her tongue along all the sensitive, seducible areas of his body.

Priming him until he verged on the edge of full readiness.

She moved with purpose along Everett's chest, gliding the tip of her tongue along his nipples just as he had done to her.

And then she slid her tongue along the hard contours of his chest, moving steadily down to his belly, teasing it until it quivered beneath her hot, probing mouth.

Raising her eyes, she met his. A wicked look entered them as she proceeded to work her way lower along his anatomy until she had reached his hardening desire.

With an air of triumph, she went on to make him hers by branding him.

She did it, once, then twice—then suddenly, she felt his hands on her forearms, stopping her. He drew her away and brought her back up to his level by pulling her body along his.

Arousing both of them even more.

The next second, he raised his head and captured her mouth

with his own, kissing her over and over again until he had reduced her to the consistency of a rain puddle that was about to go up in the steam of a hot summer sun. At that moment, he deftly switched their places. He was above her and she was back under him.

And just as before, they united, forming one whole.

This time he moved urgently right from the start. There was no gentle increase in tempo. There were just the swift, direct movements that were intended to bring them swirling up to journey's end.

And it did.

So quickly that it stole away their breath, leaving them gasping and panting in the aftermath of the crescendo that had brought all the stars raining down on them.

As before, the euphoria that sealed around them in the aftermath was wondrous. And, also as before, it slipped away much too soon, leaving Lila exhausted and slowly making her way back to reality.

With painstakingly slow movements, Lila shifted her head so that she was looking at the man next to her without alerting him to the fact that she was.

It was happening. Happening just as she had been afraid that it would.

She could feel it.

She was falling in love with Everett all over again. And she was totally powerless to prevent it, she thought with a sliver of panic that was beginning to grow inside of her.

Why had she done this?

Why had she allowed it to happen? She could have stopped it from ever taking place—*should* have stopped it from taking place not once, but twice, she ruefully reminded herself. She had allowed the evening—and herself—to spin completely out of control and now she had consequences to face.

She didn't like this feeling, this feeling of being unable to stop her life from spinning out of control.

Lila could feel herself growing more and more afraid. Afraid of what she'd done. Afraid of where she just *knew* it was going to lead—to the same unhappiness she'd experienced thirteen years ago.

How could something that had felt so right in the moment be so very wrong in the long run?

But it was, she thought.

It was.

What made her think that just because they'd managed to recapture the rapturous happiness of lovemaking it was destined to end any other way for them than it already had once before?

Those that do not learn from history are doomed to repeat it.

And that was her, she thought ruefully. She was doomed to repeat the mistakes she'd made once. In fact, she already had repeated those mistakes.

Well, she *could* learn from her mistakes, Lila silently insisted. And she intended to start right now, before it was too late and things spun further out of control, setting the stage for Everett to break her heart all over again.

Summoning her resolve, not to mention her courage, Lila turned toward the man lying next to her on the sectional sofa.

She struggled into an upright position.

Everett shift toward her. "Want to take this to your bedroom and do it again?" he asked her with a warm, inviting smile.

"No," she said with such finality that it froze Everett in place. "I want you to leave."

The blissful happiness he'd just been experiencing broke up into tiny slivered shards. He felt as if he'd just been blindsided.

Everett stared at her. "Did I do something wrong?" he asked, trying to understand why she had made this unexpected U-turn.

"Things are moving too fast, Everett," she told him. Her tone left no room for any sort of attempts to change her mind. "You need to go."

CHAPTER SEVENTEEN

EVERETT SAT UP. "You're really serious?" he asked, unable to believe that Lila actually meant what she'd just said to him.

He'd been with a number of women since he and Lila had broken up and although he'd never gotten to the serious relationship stage with any of those women, none of them had ever kicked him out of bed, either, figuratively *or* literally.

His confidence shaken, Everett had no idea how to react to this totally unfamiliar situation.

Lila had already gotten up off the sofa, wrapping a crocheted throw around herself in lieu of clothing. Her insides were quaking, but she held her ground.

"Yes, I'm serious," she insisted, her voice rising in pitch. "*Very* serious."

Well, he'd tried his best and for a little while there, he thought that he'd succeeded in winning Lila over. But obviously, he'd miscalculated, Everett told himself. He was willing to do anything to win Lila back except for one thing: he was not about to beg. A man had to have some pride, he thought fiercely.

Nodding his head, he quickly pulled on his discarded tuxedo

slacks. Securing them, he grabbed the rest of his things and held the clothes against his chest in a rumpled ball of material. He didn't even bother putting on his shoes. Instead, he just picked them up and held them in his other hand.

"All right then," he told her, heading for the door. "I'd better go."

Lila stood like a statue, saying nothing.

Everett let himself out the door, leaving it wide open. As he walked to his car in the driveway, he heard the front door close with finality behind him, obliterating any hope that at the last minute Lila would change her mind and either come running after him or at least call him back into the house.

Forcing himself not to look back, Everett opened his car door and got into his vehicle. He felt so totally stunned and deflated that he could hardly breathe as he started up his car and pulled out of Lila's driveway.

He stopped at the first all-night gas station he came to. Ignoring the convenience store clerk's curious looks, he asked for the restroom key. Taking it from the man, he let himself into the single stall bathroom.

The conditions in the restroom were far from ideal, but he managed to put on the rest of his clothes. He wanted to avoid having Schuyler ask him a barrage of questions if he walked in wearing only the tuxedo slacks.

He loved his sister dearly, but he just wasn't up to fielding any of her questions, however well intentioned they might be. He just wanted to quietly get his things from her guest room and drive back to Houston.

But as luck would have it, a swift, clean getaway was just not in the cards for him.

Despite the hour, Schuyler was up and heard him coming in. Everett had barely closed the front door and walked in before his sister walked out of the kitchen and managed to waylay him at the foot of the stairs.

"What are you doing back so soon?" she asked him in surprise. "I wasn't expecting you back until around midmorning."

He offered her a careless shrug in response. "Fund-raiser ended so I came back."

Schuyler furrowed her brow, as if something didn't sound right to her. "Why didn't you go get a nightcap with Lila?"

"I didn't want to drink and drive," Everett answered. He looked longingly up the stairs. So near and yet so far, he couldn't help thinking.

Schuyler's furrowed brow gave way to an all-out, impatient frown.

"Damn it, Ev, I'm trying to politely tiptoe around the subject but you're making me have to come flat out and ask." She paused, waiting for her brother to jump in and say what she was waiting for him to tell her. But he remained silent. Huffing, Schuyler asked, "Why aren't you over at Lila's place, picking things up where the two of you left off back in college?"

"It's complicated, Schuy," Everett told her.

"That's what people say when they don't want to deal with something," she insisted. She pinned her brother with a penetrating look that went clear down to the bone. "Do you care about this woman?" she asked him point-blank.

Still smarting from his rejection, he *really* didn't want to get into this with his sister. "Schuyler, go to bed."

They had always talked things out before and Schuyler apparently refused to back off now that she had broached the subject. "Do you care about this woman?" she repeated, enunciating each word slowly with intentional emphasis.

He could see that Schuyler wasn't about to let this go until she had an answer from him. So he gave her one. A short one. "No."

Schuyler's eyes narrowed, looking deep into his. "You're lying."

Everett did his best to separate himself from any emotion. He really didn't want to shout at his sister. "No, I'm not."

"Yes, you are," Schuyler retorted. When he tried to turn away, she grabbed hold of his shoulder, making him face her. "You have this 'tell' when you lie. There's a tiny nerve right under your left eye that jumps every time you don't tell the truth."

"Then why even bother asking me?" He came close to biting off his question.

"So you can hear the words out loud for yourself," she told him. "Ev, when you first told me you were going to win Lila back, I didn't think you had a chance in hell of doing it. I thought you'd eventually come to your senses and forget the whole thing."

She shook her head, amused by her preconceived notion. "But you're not the type to forget the whole thing and you managed to bring me around to your way of thinking. A guy like that doesn't just give up out of the blue."

Taking his hand, Schuyler tugged on it, making him sit down on the bottom step. She sat down beside him, just the way they used to do as kids whenever they wanted to talk about things.

"What happened?" she asked him.

After a short internal debate, Everett gave her an abbreviated version, mentioning his donation to the Foundation in passing, but not the amount.

He told his sister about going back with Lila to her place, but left it for her imagination to fill in the details of what transpired there. He ended by telling his sister that Lila had suddenly pulled back, saying that things were going too fast and that she needed to go home.

"And…?" Schuyler asked, waiting for him to tell her more.

"And I came home," Everett said with a shrug. "Or to your house," he corrected. "I wanted to change out of this monkey suit, get my suitcase and go back to Houston."

"And nothing else happened?" she questioned, studying his face closely.

"Nothing else happened," he echoed flatly. He just wanted to get his things and hit the road, putting this night—and Lila—behind him.

Schuyler's mouth curved in a tolerant, loving smile. "You do realize that your shirt is inside out, don't you?" his sister asked. "Did you wear it that way at the fund-raiser?"

He glanced down. Damn it, leave it to Schuyler to catch that, he thought, annoyed. "Yup. The whole fund-raiser," he told her stubbornly.

"I see," Schuyler replied, watching the nerve just beneath his eye flutter. "Well, maybe nobody noticed," she said loftily. "Or maybe Lila did and that's why she told you things were moving too fast and sent you away." Schuyler's smile widened. "She didn't want to be associated with someone who couldn't dress himself properly."

"Schuyler—" There was a warning note in Everett's voice.

Schuyler held up her hands, warding off what he was about to say.

"I'm just teasing you," she told him. And then her tone changed. "Why don't you stay here for what's left of the night and then go talk to Lila in the morning?" she suggested. "Things always look better in the morning," she added kindly.

"No," he told his sister, his mind made up. "I need to be getting back. I've let a lot of things slide lately and I need to do some catching up."

"That's not the Dr. Everett Fortunado I know," Schuyler told him, rising to her feet when he did. "You can juggle more balls in the air than any two people I know."

"Not this time," he answered as he started up the steps. "This time those balls are all falling right through my hands."

"Want me to help you pack?" she offered, calling up the stairs.

"No, I've got this," he told her, glancing over his shoulder.

Schuyler stood there, arms akimbo, and murmured loud enough for him to hear, "No, I don't think that you do."

* * *

"That was some hefty donation that your boyfriend made on Friday," Lucie said the following Monday morning as Lila passed her open door.

Lila made no answer, merely shrugging in response as she stepped into her office.

Lucie didn't take the hint. Instead, she followed her friend into Lila's office. When Lila sat down at her desk, Lucie peered at her a little more closely.

"You look awful," she observed. Then a small smile lit her eyes. "Didn't get any sleep all weekend, huh?"

"No," Lila answered, deliberately not taking Lucie's bait. Her tone flatly denied any further dialogue between them.

But Lucie wasn't about to take the hint. "So how was it?" she asked with a grin.

Lila spared her friend a glance. Lucie was now firmly planted on the edge of her desk. "How was what?"

"You know..." But since Lila gave no indication that she did, Lucie further elaborated. "Getting back together with Everett."

"We're not back together," Lila answered, biting off each word. They all had a bitter taste, but that would pass, she told herself. It *had* to.

"Why the hell not?" Lucie cried. When Lila looked at her sharply, Lucie said, "Anyone at the fund-raiser could see he was crazy about you. When you two left early, I was sure you were going back to your place—if you made it that far," Lucie added.

This time Lila's head shot up. She was really hoping that no one had noticed them leaving the fund-raiser. So much for hoping.

"What's that supposed to mean?" she wanted to know.

Lucie sighed.

"Lila, there were so many sparks flying between the two of you that you'd make an electrical storm seem like an afternoon at the library in comparison." She gave Lila a deep, penetrating look, as if willing the truth out of her. "You can't tell me that you two didn't get together after you left the fund-raiser."

"All right," Lila replied grudgingly. It wasn't in her to lie. "We did."

Getting up off the desk, Lucie closed Lila's door, then crossed back to her desk, coming closer. "And?" she coaxed.

Lila shifted uncomfortably in her chair, but it was clear that Lucie wasn't going anywhere until she heard all the details.

"And then I sent him away," she said, jumping to the end without elaborating anything in between.

Lucie stared at her. "You're joking."

"No, I'm not," Lila replied firmly. "I sent him away."

"Why in heaven's name would you do that?" Lucie cried incredulously.

"Because things were moving much too fast between us," Lila blurted out, frustration bubbling beneath her statement.

Leaning forward, Lucie took her friend's hands into hers. "Lila, honey," she began gently, "it's been thirteen years. After all that time, things were not moving fast. They were barely crawling by at a turtle's pace." She squeezed Lila's hands as she looked deeper into her eyes, as if trying to understand, to read Lila's thoughts. And then it must have hit her, because she sharply drew a breath. "You got scared, didn't you? He made you have all those feelings again and it scared you."

Lila looked away. Lucie had homed in on the truth.

But there was no running from the truth. She knew that now.

With a sigh, she nodded. And then she looked up at Lucie. "How did you do it?" she asked, silently begging the other woman for guidance.

"Do what?" Lucie asked.

"With Chase," Lila said, hoping that Lucie had some sage, magical knowledge to impart. Some words of wisdom that could somehow guide her through this densely wooded area she found herself stumbling through. "How were you able to pick up where you left off with Chase?" The two hadn't just been high school sweethearts, they'd eloped and had been married—for all of five minutes.

"Very easy," Lucie answered her nonchalantly. "I didn't."

Lila stared at her. She didn't understand. "But you two were just recently married."

"Actually, we'd been secretly married as teenagers and never had it annulled, but didn't find out until recently. We had to get to know each other as adults, not as the impulsive kids we once were. And that's what you have to do," Lucie told her in all honesty. "You and Everett have to do the work and get to know each other all over again—from scratch," she insisted. "You have to take into consideration that Everett, in all likelihood, may very well *not* be the person he was at sixteen or eighteen or twenty."

Lucie circled to the back of the desk and put her arm on Lila's shoulder.

"And while we're at it, why do you assume that history has to repeat itself?" she questioned gently. "What if Everett really means what he says and wants to get back together with you not for a romp or a weekend of lovemaking, but for good?"

Lila rose from her chair and paced about the small office. She couldn't come to grips with the desperate feeling she was experiencing in her gut.

"Even if Everett's serious, even if he wants things to be different this time around, the past is still standing between us like a giant roadblock," Lila insisted.

"By the past you mean the little girl that you gave up." It wasn't a question. Lucie was reading between the lines. She knew the truth about Lila's past. In a moment of weakness, Lila had entrusted her with her deepest secret.

"Yes," Lila cried, struggling not to cry. "It still haunts me," she admitted. "Holding her in my arms and then giving her up—some nights I still wake up in a cold sweat, remembering how that felt. To have her and then not have her, all in the blink of an eye," Lila confessed sadly.

"Does Everett realize how you feel?" Lucie asked.

Lila pressed her lips together and shook her head. "I don't know," she answered. "I never said anything about it."

"Did you *ask* him if he knew?" Lucie pressed. "Or say anything at all about what giving her up did to you?"

"No," Lila admitted in a low voice, avoiding Lucie's eyes.

"Then for heaven sakes, *talk* to him about it," Lucie urged. "Tell him how you felt giving up your baby. How you *still* feel."

"I can't," Lila said. "I just can't. Lucie, I know you mean well, but just please, please leave me alone right now. It'll work out."

It will, Lila told herself as Lucie walked out of her office. It had to.

CHAPTER EIGHTEEN

"ALL RIGHT, I'M HERE," Everett declared when his sister opened her front door to admit him into her house several days later. "I got Blake to take over a few of my patients, had the rest of them rescheduled and drove right out because you sounded as if this was urgent." His eyes swept over her and she certainly didn't look as if she was in the throes of some sort of an emergency. "Now what's this all about?"

Instead of answering his question, Schuyler said, "I can't tell you here." Getting her purse, she took out her car keys. "In order to explain, I need to take you some place first."

Everett looked at his sister suspiciously. This wasn't making any sense to him. "Where?" he wanted to know.

Again she avoided giving him a direct answer. "You'll understand everything once we're there," Schuyler told him, hurrying toward her spacious garage.

Fetching her red BMW, she pulled up next to her brother. "Get in," she told him, leaning over and throwing open the passenger door.

Since he'd all but raced out of Houston, driving at top speed until he'd reached Austin because he was extremely concerned about Schuyler, he went along with her instructions.

"You're being awfully mysterious about all this," he accused.

"The mystery will be cleared up before you know it, big brother," Schuyler promised, mentally crossing her fingers.

Everett suddenly sat up a little straighter in the passenger seat as a thought occurred to him.

Looking at her now, he asked, "Hey, Schuy, you're not pregnant, are you?" As the question came out of his mouth, he began grinning so widely, his lips almost hurt. He'd thought his sister would get married first before starting a family, but that didn't negate his happiness for her. "Wow, that's terrific. How far along are you?" he asked excitedly. "What does Carlo think about this? Have you picked a godfather yet?"

Apparently overwhelmed, Schuyler took a second to speak. "Hey, slow down," she said then. She slanted a look in his direction before turning back to the road. "So you like the idea of babies," she said, obviously referring to his exuberant reaction.

"Of course I do. How far along are you?" he asked her again.

"I'm not," Schuyler told him.

Everett looked as if his bubble had been pierced, sending him twisting in the wind. "Wait, I don't understand. Then you're not pregnant?" he asked, more confused than ever.

"No," Schuyler answered. "I never said I was. *You* jumped to that conclusion," she pointed out. "Let me have my wedding first, then we'll see about babies."

Everett slumped back against his seat. "Okay, then I don't understand," he said, confused. "What's this all about?"

Schuyler bit her lower lip, stalling. "I already told you—"

"No, you didn't," he insisted, trying to keep his voice even. He didn't like games, especially not at his expense.

"Just hang on a little longer and you'll see what this is all about."

Everett sighed. "Well, since you've kidnapped me, I guess I don't have a choice."

"I didn't kidnap you," Schuyler informed him. "You got into the car of your own free will."

That's not how he saw it. "You just keep telling yourself that," he said. Laying his head back against the headrest, Everett closed his eyes. Running around and not getting much sleep was finally beginning to catch up with him. "Wake me whenever we get to wherever it is that we're going," he told her.

"We're here," Schuyler announced not five minutes later.

"Well, that didn't take long," Everett commented. Sitting up, he looked around as his sister got out of the car.

Schuyler had driven them to the Fortune Foundation.

Alert, not to mention annoyed, Everett glared at his sister when he got out. "Hey, why are we here?"

"You'll find out," she said cheerfully.

Neither his mood nor the look that he was giving her over the hood of her car improved.

"Schuyler, just what the hell are you up to?" he demanded.

"You'll find out," his sister repeated. She gave him what she no doubt hoped was an encouraging look. "Just give it a few more minutes."

But Everett didn't move an inch. "And if I don't?"

"Then you'll never know how things might have turned out." When he still didn't move, Schuyler looked at him plaintively. "Do it for me, Everett. Please," she implored.

"Damn it, Schuyler, you owe me," Everett snapped, finally coming around the sporty red vehicle.

Schuyler inclined her head and gave him a wink. "We'll see."

Lila was engrossed in drawing up the following week's schedule for the volunteer doctors when Lucie walked into her office.

"Save whatever you're working on, Lila," Lucie told her. "I need your full, undivided attention right now."

Surprised by Lucie's serious tone, Lila looked up. "What's going on?"

Instead of answering her, Lucie looked over her shoulder and beckoned to someone. Just who was she summoning to Lila's office?

Totally stunned, Lila was immediately on her feet when she saw him.

Everett was the last person she'd expected to see here. After practically throwing him out of her house, she'd never thought she would see him again.

She fisted her hands, digging her knuckles into her desk to keep her knees from giving way.

She shot an angry look at her friend. "Lucie, what have you done?" she demanded.

"Saved two really nice people from a lifetime of loneliness and heartache," Lucie answered. Then she stepped out of the way, allowing a bewildered-looking Everett to enter Lila's office. But not before she gave a big grin and a high five to a well-dressed woman behind him.

Schuyler, Lila recognized.

Peering into the office around her brother, Schuyler declared, "I hereby officially call this intervention in session."

With that, she stepped away from the doorway.

Following her out, Lucie told the two people who were left in the room, "And don't come out until you've resolved this properly." And then she closed the door behind her.

"This your idea?" Lila asked Everett.

"Hell, no," he denied. "I think Schuyler cooked this up."

"Not without Lucie's help," Lila said accusingly. Furious, she let out a shaky breath. And then she turned toward Everett. She was furious. "You know you can leave," she told him.

"I know." Lord, but he had missed her, he thought now, looking at Lila. "But since I'm here…maybe we should talk."

"About what?" Lila wanted to know. "What is there left to say?" Restless, uneasy, she began to pace within the limited space. "I trusted you once and got my heart broken for my trouble."

Her accusation hurt. But this wasn't one-sided. "I could say the same thing," Everett countered.

Her eyes narrowed as she looked at Everett, stunned. "You?" she questioned. What was he talking about?

"Yes," he informed Lila. "I'd trusted you, too. Trusted that you'd be with me forever—and then you walked out. It wasn't easy for me after we broke up. I might have gone on with my studies—because that was what I was supposed to do—but there was this huge, empty, jagged hole in my chest where you used to be."

His dry laugh was totally mirthless as he continued. "I think I must have picked up the phone a hundred times that first year, wanting to call you and tell you about something that had happened in class or at the hospital, before I realized that I couldn't. That you wouldn't be there to answer the phone." His eyes met hers. "Nothing meant anything without you," he told her.

Lila stood there looking at him. The inside of her mouth felt like cotton and she struggled not to cry. She'd held her feelings in too long. For thirteen years, to be exact. Now she could hold them in no longer.

"I still think about our baby all the time," she admitted.

Everett felt her words like a knife to his heart. More than anything, he wished he could go back in time to make things right. To do things differently. "Do you regret giving her up?"

"Yes," she answered so quietly, he had to strain to hear her. And then Lila took a deep breath. "No."

She blinked hard, telling herself she wasn't going to cry. Forbidding herself to shed a single tear. Tears were for the weak and she wasn't weak. She'd proven that over and over again.

"I know that our daughter has had a good life. The people who adopted her send me letters and photographs every once in a while, to let me know how she's doing." Lila smiled sadly. "Emma's a beautiful girl and she's doing really, really well in school."

Everett looked at her in surprise. He'd had no idea this was going on. "Her name is Emma? And you've stayed in contact with the family?" he asked.

Lila nodded. "Yes. Not knowing what was going on with Emma was killing me so it took a bit of doing but I managed to get in contact with the family that adopted her. Emma's parents are good people. They understood how hard it was for me to give up the baby. As a matter of fact, they're grateful to us for giving them what they call 'the most precious gift of all,'" Lila said. "Over the years, I've kept track of her through emails and pictures from her parents."

It was a lot for Everett to take in. Numerous questions rose in his head.

"How is she doing? What grade is she in now?" Everett asked.

"You actually want to know?" Lila asked him, astonished. "I mean, after the baby was born, you seemed really eager to put the whole incident behind you and forget about it. About her."

Her words stung, but he knew they were true. He'd been young and he'd just wanted to pretend that none of it had happened because it was easier to erase the guilt that way.

"I was," he admitted. "I'm not proud of it now, but it was the only way I could deal with it at the time, to just bury it and put it all totally out of my mind." Everett put his hands on her shoulders now, looking into Lila's eyes. "I'm sorry I wasn't more understanding, Lila. I didn't realize that you were hurting. I only knew that I was."

Lila struggled to wrap her mind around what he was telling her. She'd never suspected any of this. "You were hurting?"

Everett nodded. "She was my little girl, too," he told Lila.

"Oh, Everett, I wish you had told me," she cried.

So much time had been lost because of a failure to communicate. So much heartache could have been avoided if he had only verbalized his feelings to her.

If he'd just given her a clue…

"I wish I had told you, too," Everett said with all sincerity.

And then he looked at her hopefully. "You wouldn't have a picture of Emma with you, would you?" he asked.

Lila opened up a drawer, took out her purse and pulled out her cell phone. She pressed the photo app and scrolled through a few photos until she came to the one she was looking for.

"This is Emma," she told Everett, holding out her phone to him.

Everett looked at the young girl on the screen. He could feel his heart swell as he stared at the image. Emma looked to be on the verge of her teen years and she had a mouth full of braces.

She was the most beautiful girl he had ever seen.

"She has your smile," he said, taking in every detail of the photo. And then he looked up at Lila. "I can't believe how beautiful our daughter is." With a sigh, he handed the phone back to Lila.

Lila closed her phone and put it back in her purse. "Emma's not our daughter anymore, Everett," she told him quietly.

Everett nodded. "Right. Have you ever seen her in person?"

Lila shook her head. "No. I wanted to, but I don't want to confuse Emma. One mother and father is enough for her right now at her age. Besides, her parents know how to get in contact with me. They have my cell number. Someday, when she's older, if Emma wants to meet me, they'll let me know and I'll be there in a heartbeat. But for right now, all I want is for Emma to grow up happy and well adjusted."

"You're a strong, brave woman, Lila," Everett told her with admiration. He hadn't realized until this moment just how strong and brave she really was.

Lila shrugged. "You do what you have to do in order to survive. And you make the best of the situation," she added. "The alternative is much too dark."

He nodded. "You're right. It is." He paused for a moment before looking at her and saying, "Would it surprise you if I told you that I think about Emma, too? That over the last few years, I've found myself thinking about her a lot. Wondering where

she was, what she's doing. If she was happy. If she ever wondered about her birth parents and thought they—we—gave her
up because we didn't love her."

"She knows we gave her up to give her a better life," Lila
told him.

"You're just speculating," he said.

"No, I know that Emma knows that because her adoptive
parents told me they told her that when she was old enough to
begin asking questions."

Everett was quiet for a long moment. And when he finally
spoke, what he said really surprised her. "I really wish I could
meet our daughter."

It took Lila a moment to fully absorb what he had just said.

"Do you really mean that?" she asked Everett, astonished to
hear him voice the same feelings that had been haunting her
for years.

"Yes," he told her honestly. "I do."

She pressed her lips together, thinking over the feasibility
of what he had just told her. "Well, I'm not sure how Emma's
parents would feel about that, but I could certainly let them
know that you're back in the picture and that you would like to
meet Emma whenever it's convenient for them—and for her."

He nodded. It was a difficult situation all around and he fully
understood that.

"I'd really appreciate that," he told her. He paused, trying to
find the right words to convey what he wanted to say to her.
"Lila…" Everett started, then stopped, his brain freezing up on
him. This was a great deal harder than he'd anticipated.

"Yes?" she asked, wondering what else there was left for him
to say. He'd already gladdened her heart by telling her that he
not only thought about Emma, but actually wanted to meet her.
That meant a great deal to her.

His eyes met hers. "Can you ever forgive me for not being
there for you?" he asked softly.

Lila blinked. She could have been knocked over with the proverbial feather. Staring at Everett, she realized that he was being sincere.

"Oh Everett, I really wish I had known that you were hurting, too and that you felt the way you did. It would have helped me deal with everything that happened so much better." She smiled at him, fighting back tears again. "We really should have communicated more honestly with one another."

Everett stepped closer, letting himself do what he'd wanted to since he'd walked into this office. He enfolded Lila in his arms. "You're absolutely right. I should have talked with you, told you what I was feeling. But I just closed myself off, trying to deal with what was going on. I was blind and didn't realize that you were going through the same thing, too, and could have used my support." He'd been such a fool, Everett thought, regret riddling him. "Can you find it in your heart to forgive me?" he asked again.

Now that she knew that Everett had experienced the same doubts and emotions about their daughter that had haunted her, all of Lila's old feelings of anger and resentment vanished as if they had never existed. All Everett ever had to do was tell her what he'd gone through.

Forgiveness flooded her. "Yes, of course I can," she told him.

Relief mingled with love, all but overwhelming Everett. He kissed Lila, temporarily disregarding where they were and the fact that the people she worked with could easily look over and see what was happening.

And she kissed him back.

Everett forced himself to draw back. Still holding her in his arms, he looked down into her eyes. "From now on," he promised, "I'm putting all my cards on the table."

"Are you planning on playing solitaire or poker?" she asked Everett, a smile curving the corners of her mouth.

"Definitely not solitaire," he answered. "But any other game that you want. Oh, Lila, we've wasted much too much time and we'll never get any of that time back," he told her. His arms tightened around her. It felt so good to hold her against him like this. He felt he'd never let her go. "But we can have the future."

"And by that you mean...?" Her voice trailed off.

She wanted him to spell everything out so that there would be no more mix-ups, no more misunderstandings to haunt either one of them. She wanted to be absolutely certain that Everett was talking about what she *thought* he was talking about.

"I mean that I'm planning on being very clear about my intentions this time around. I know what I want," he told her, looking deep into her eyes. "All you need to do is say yes."

But she wasn't the same person she'd been thirteen years ago. She knew how to stand up for herself, how not to allow herself to be swept away.

She surprised him by telling Everett, "I never say 'yes' unless I know exactly what it is that I'm saying yes to."

"To this," Everett told her, pulling something out of his pocket. When he opened his hand, there was a big, beautiful heart-shaped diamond ring mounted on a wishbone setting in the center of his palm. He'd brought it with him for luck—and just in case.

Lila stared at it, momentarily speechless. When she raised her eyes to his face, she could barely speak. "Is that—?"

She couldn't bring herself to ask the question, because the moment she did—and he said no—a little of the magic would be gone. And she really couldn't believe that the ring she was looking at was the one she'd fallen in love with so many years ago.

But Lila discovered that she needn't have anticipated disappointment, because Everett nodded.

"Yes," he told her, pleased by her reaction, "it is. It's the one you saw through the window in that little out-of-the-way shop that day when we were back in college. You made me stand there while you made a wish and just stared at it, like it was the most beautiful thing you'd ever seen."

She smiled, remembering every detail. "I was being silly and frivolous," she admitted.

"No, you were being honest about your reaction," he corrected.

She continued looking at the sparkling diamond in his hand, completely mesmerized. "But how did you...?"

Everett anticipated her question and was way ahead of her. "After I dropped you off home, I doubled back to the store to buy the ring. The store was closed for the night by then, but I kept knocking on the door until the owner finally came down and opened it. Turns out that he lived above the store," he told her. "Anyway, I made him sell me the ring right then and there. I hung onto it, confident that I would give it to you someday." He smiled ruefully. "I just never thought it was going to take quite this long," he confessed.

Taking a deep breath, he held the ring up to her and said in a voice filled with emotion, "Lila Clark, will you marry me? I promise if you say yes, I will never leave you again."

Lila could feel her heart beating so hard in her chest, she was certain it was going to break right through her ribs. The wish she'd made that day in front of the shop window was finally coming true.

"I don't plan to keep you on a leash," she told him, so filled with love she thought she was going to burst. "But yes, I will marry you."

Thrilled, dazed, relieved and experiencing a whole host of other emotions, Everett slipped the engagement ring on her finger.

The second he did, he swept her into his arms and kissed her again, longer this time even though he could see that they had attracted an audience. It didn't matter to him.

Lila's colleagues were watching them through the glass walls of her office and cheering them on, his sister and her cohort in front of the pack.

He looked down into Lila's eyes. "We can have more kids,"

he told her. "An entire army of kids if that's what you want. And they'll never want for anything. We can have that wonderful life that we used to just talk about having."

"A better one," she interjected.

"Absolutely," he agreed, hugging her to him again. "The sky's the limit," he promised. "But there's just one more thing."

"Oh?" Lila refused to be concerned. She'd been down that route and this was a brand-new route she was embarking on— with Everett beside her. She knew that she could face anything as long as he was with her. "What's that?"

"I don't want any more secrets between us," Everett said.

"Neither do I," Lila agreed wholeheartedly. "Is there something you need to tell me?"

"More than just you," Everett answered. "If we're going to start with a clean slate, there is something else I need to do."

Now he was beginning to really make her wonder, but she wasn't about to shrink away from his revelation. Because whatever it was, they would face it together. Conquer it together.

"Go ahead," Lila said, thinking that he was going to confess something serious to her.

Instead, Everett opened her office door and called out, "Schuyler, Lucie, would you mind stepping back in here?"

The two women obligingly filed back into Lila's office.

"Okay," Schuyler said to her brother, "make your announcement, although we both saw you put that huge rock on Lila's finger so this is going to be a little anticlimatic."

"It's not what you think," Everett told his sister.

Schuyler exchanged looks with Lucie, obviously confused. "All right, enlighten us then," she said.

"I'm through sneaking around," he told his sister. "This is what we talked about when I first came to Austin, thinking I was picking you up to bring you home."

"What is he talking about?" Lucie asked, looking at Everett's sister.

Everett turned toward Lucie. "Lucie, I think it's time I told you who we really are. Or at least who we *think* we are."

Lucie looked from Everett to Lila, her brows furrowed. "Lila?"

But Lila shrugged, as mystified as Lucie was. "I have no idea what he's talking about," she admitted.

Everett laced the fingers of one hand through Lila's hand as he went on to make his revelation. Nodding toward his sister, he told Lucie, "As you know, our last name is Fortunado."

Lucie waited for more. "Yes?"

"What you might not know, and I've recently come to find out—thanks to Schuyler's detective work—is that the Fortunado family might actually be descendants of Julius Fortune, Jerome Fortune's father," he added for clarity.

"You know," Lucie told Everett, a smile spreading across her face, "I'm not half surprised. With all of Jerome's illegitimate offspring coming to light lately, it stands to reason he learned the art of seduction from his father." She reached out and placed a hand on Everett's shoulder. "In that case, I have some people I would *really* love for you to meet."

"People who could substantiate my suspicions?" Everett wanted to know.

"Oh, more than substantiate, I think," Lucie said with emphasis.

Instead of eagerly asking her friend to make the meeting happen, the way Lila thought he would, Everett turned to look at her. She saw a wicked sparkle in his eyes. Her pulse instantly began to accelerate.

"That really sounds wonderful, Lucie, and I'd appreciate the introduction," he told her without so much as a glance her way. His eyes were solely on Lila. "But I'm afraid the meeting is going to have to wait for now."

"Oh? Why?" Lucie asked.

"Because," Everett began, raising Lila's hand to his lips and brushing a kiss lightly against her knuckles, "my fiancée and

I have plans for this afternoon. Plans," he said, "starting right now. So if you'll please excuse us…"

The request was merely a formality. Everett was already leading Lila out of the office and toward the hallway and the elevator beyond. He was vaguely aware of Schuyler's squeal of joy behind them and the sound of Lucie's laughter as she applauded.

All that and more blended into the background and then faded away as he stepped into the elevator car with Lila. They had a lot of catching up to do. And he planned to start this minute by taking her into his arms and kissing her as the elevator doors closed, locking the rest of the world out.

* * * * *

It Started With A Crush...

Melissa McClone

With a degree in mechanical engineering from Stanford University, the last thing **Melissa McClone** ever thought she would be doing was writing romance novels. But analyzing engines for a major U.S. airline just couldn't compete with her "happily-ever-afters." When she isn't writing, caring for her three young children or doing laundry, Melissa loves to curl up on the couch with a cup of tea, her cats and a good book. She enjoys watching home decorating shows to get ideas for her house—a 1939 cottage that is *slowly* being renovated. Melissa lives in Lake Oswego, Oregon, with her own real-life hero husband, two daughters, a son, two loveable but oh-so-spoiled indoor cats and a no-longer-stray outdoor kitty that decided to call the garage home.

Melissa loves to her from her readers. You can write to her at P.O. Box 63, Lake Oswego, OR 97034, or contact her via her website, www.melissamcclone.com.

Dear Reader,

For the past eight years my fall and spring Dedication weekends have been full of soccer games. All three of my children have played and my husband has coached recreational teams for years.

Soccer isn't something I grew up with. I attended my first game in 1984, but wasn't really sure what was going on. Friends kept telling me how big soccer—they called it football—was outside the U.S., but I never realized how big until June 26th 1994, when I attended a match between Colombia and Switzerland at Stanford Stadium. Not even the two Super Bowls I'd gone to came close to matching the excitement and passion of these soccer fans.

Ever since then I've wanted to write a romance with soccer as the background, but it wasn't until my son started playing competitive soccer for an Oregon club in spring 2010 that the story ideas started flowing. After speaking with one of my son's coaches, who also played for the Portland Timbers, a professional soccer player named Ryland James came to life.

Having access to people who can help with research adds realism to a story. I was fortunate in the soccer assistance I received, but when it came to my heroine, Lucy, who'd had a liver transplant as a teen, I wasn't sure where to turn for help.

A friend had been a living donor for her daughter's successful liver transplant in 2007, but I happened to mention my work-in-progress to another mom during our kids' swimming practice. Turned out she was a two-time liver and kidney transplant recipient. Talking with her helped me understand and fill in Lucy's backstory of her having liver failure. It also made me understand the importance of organ donation and the lives being saved by transplants.

To all those who have signed up to be donors: thank you!

Melissa

For all the people who generously volunteer their time to coach kids—especially those who have made such a difference in my children's lives. Thank you!

Special thanks to Josh Cameron, Brian Verrinder, Ian Burgess, Bernice Conrad and Terri Reed.

CHAPTER ONE

EVERY DAY FOR the past four weeks, Connor's school bus had arrived at the corner across the street no later than three-thirty. Every day, except today. Lucy Martin glanced at the clock hanging on the living-room wall.

3:47 p.m.

Anxiety knotted her stomach making her feel jittery. Her nephew should be home by now.

Was it time to call the school to find out where the bus might be or was she overreacting? This parenting—okay, surrogate parenting—thing was too new to know for certain.

She stared out the window, hoping the bus would appear. The street corner remained empty. That wasn't surprising. Only residents drove through this neighborhood on the outskirts of town.

What to do? She tapped her foot.

Most contingencies and emergencies had been listed in the three-ring binder Lucy called the survival guide. Her sister-in-law, Dana, had put it together before she left. But a late school bus hadn't been one of the scenarios. Lucy had checked. Twice.

No need to panic. Wicksburg was surrounded by farmland,

a small town with a low crime rate and zero excitement except for harvests in the summer, Friday-night football games in the fall and basketball games in the winter. A number of things could have delayed the bus. A traffic jam due to slow-moving farm equipment, road construction, a car accident...

A chill shivered down Lucy's spine.

Don't freak out. Okay, she wasn't used to taking care of anyone but herself. This overwhelming need to see her nephew right this moment was brand-new to her. But she'd better get used to it. For the next year she wasn't only Connor's aunt, she was also his guardian while his parents, both army reservists, were deployed overseas. Her older brother, Aaron, was counting on Lucy to take care of his only child. If something happened to Connor on her watch...

Her muscles tensed.

"Meow."

The family's cat, an overweight Maine Coon with a tail that looked more like a raccoon's than a feline's, rubbed against the front door. His green-eyed gaze met Lucy's.

"I know, Manny." The cat's concern matched her own. "I want Connor home, too."

Something caught the corner of her eye. Something yellow. She stared out the window once again.

The school bus idled at the corner. Red lights flashed.

Relief flowed through her. "Thank goodness."

Lucy took a step toward the front door then stopped. Connor had asked her not to meet him at the bus stop. She understood the need to be independent and wanted to make him happy. But not even following his request these past two and a half weeks had erased the sadness from his eyes. She knew better than to take it personally. Smiles had become rare commodities around here since his parents deployed.

Peering through the slit in the curtains gave her a clear view of the bus and the short walk to the house. Connor could assert his independence while she made sure he was safe.

Lucy hated seeing him moping around like a lost puppy, but she understood. He missed his parents. She'd tried to make him feel better. Nothing, not even his favorite desserts, fast-food restaurants or video games, had made a difference. Now that his spring soccer team was without a coach, things had gone from bad to worse.

The door of the bus opened. The Bowman twins exited. The seven-year-old girls wore matching pink polka-dot dresses, white shoes and purple backpacks.

Connor stood on the bus's bottom step with a huge smile on his face. He leaped to the ground and skipped away.

Her heart swelled with excitement. Something good must have happened at school.

As her nephew approached the house, Lucy stepped away from the window. She wanted to make sure his smile remained. No matter what it took.

Manny rubbed against her leg. Birdlike chirping sounds came from his mouth. Strange, but not unexpected from a cat that barked when annoyed.

"Don't worry, Manny." She touched the cat's back. "Connor will be home in three…two…one…"

The front door flung open. Manny dashed for the outside, but Connor closed the door to stop his escape.

"Aunt Lucy." His blue eyes twinkled. So much like Aaron. Same eyes, same hair color, same freckles. "I found someone who can coach the Defeeters."

She should have known Connor's change of attitude had to do with soccer. Her nephew loved the sport. Aaron had coached his son's team, the Defeeters, since Connor started playing organized soccer when he was five. A dad had offered to coach in Aaron's place, but then had to back out after his work schedule changed. No other parent could do it for a variety of reasons. That left the team without a coach. Well, unless you counted her, which was pretty much like being coachless.

The thought of asking her ex-husband to help entered her

mind for about a nanosecond before she banished it into the far recesses of her brain where really bad ideas belonged. Being back in the same town as Jeff was hard enough with all the not-so-pleasant memories resurfacing. Lucy hadn't seen him yet nor did she want to.

"Fantastic," she said. "Who is it?"

Connor's grin widened, making him look as if he'd found a million-dollar bill or calorie-free chocolate. He shrugged off his backpack. "Ryland James."

Her heart plummeted to her feet. Splat! "*The* Ryland James?"

Connor nodded enthusiastically. "He's not only best player in the MLS, but my favorite. He'll be the perfect coach. He played on the same team with my dad. They won district and a bunch of tournaments. Ryland's a nice guy. My dad said so."

She had to tread carefully here. For Connor's sake.

Ryland *had* been a nice guy and one of her brother's closest friends. But she hadn't seen him since he left high school to attend the U.S. Soccer Residency Program in Florida. According to Aaron, Ryland had done well, playing overseas and now for the Phoenix Fuego, a Major League Soccer (MLS) team in the U.S. Coaching a recreational soccer team comprised of nine-year-olds probably wasn't on his bucket list.

Lucy bit the inside of her cheek, hoping to think of something—anything—that wouldn't make this blow up in her face and turn Connor's smile upside down.

"Wow," she said finally. "Ryland James would be an amazing coach, but don't you think he's getting ready to start training for his season?"

"MLS teams have been working out in Florida and Arizona since January. The season opener isn't until April." Connor spoke as if this was common knowledge she should know. Given soccer had always been "the sport" in the Martin household, she probably should. "But Ryland James got hurt playing with the U.S. Men's Team in a friendly against Mexico. He's out for a while."

Friendly meant an exhibition game. Lucy knew that much. But the news surprised her. Aaron usually kept her up-to-date on Ryland. Her brother would never let Lucy forget her school-girl crush on the boy from the wrong side of town who was now a famous soccer star. "Hurt as in injured?"

"He had surgery and can't play for a couple of months. He's staying with his parents while he recovers." Connor's eyes brightened more. "Isn't that great?"

"I wouldn't call having surgery and being injured great."

"Not him being hurt, but his being in town and able to coach us." Connor made it sound like this was a done deal. "I bet Ryland James will be almost as good a coach as my dad."

"Did someone ask Ryland if he would coach the Defeeters?"

"No," Connor admitted, undaunted. "I came up with the idea during recess after Luke told me Ryland James was at the fire station's spaghetti feed signing autographs. But the whole team thinks it's a good idea. If I'd been there last night…"

The annual Wicksburg Fire Department Spaghetti Feed was one of the biggest events in town. She and Connor had decided not to go to the fundraiser because Dana was calling home. "Don't forget, you got to talk to your mom."

"I know," Connor said. "But I'd like Ryland James's auto-graph. If he coaches us, he can sign my ball."

Signing a few balls, mugging for the camera and smiling at soccer moms didn't come close to the time it would take to coach a team of boys. The spring season was shorter and more casual than fall league, but still…

She didn't want Connor to be disappointed. "It's a great idea, but Ryland might not have time."

"Will you ask him if he'll coach us, Aunt Lucy? He might just say yes."

The sound of Connor's voice, full of excitement and antic-ipation, tugged at her heart. "Might" likely equaled "yes" in his young mind. She'd do anything for her nephew. She'd re-turned to the same town where her ex, now married to her former best friend, lived in order to care for Connor but going to see Ryland...

She blew out a puff of air. "He could say no."

The last time Lucy had seen him had been before her liver transplant. She'd been in eighth grade, jaundiced and bloated, carrying close to a hundred pounds of extra water weight. Not to mention totally exhausted and head over heels in love with the high-school soccer star. She'd spent much of her time alone in her room due to liver failure. Ryland James had fueled her adolescent fantasies. She'd dreamed about him letting her wear his jersey, asking her out to see a movie at the Liberty Theater and inviting her to be his date at prom.

Of course, none of those things had ever happened. She'd hated being known as the sick girl. She'd rarely been able to get up the nerve to say a word to Ryland. And then...

The high-school soccer team had put on two fundraisers—a summer camp for kids and a goal-a-thon—to help with Lucy's medical expenses. She remembered when Ryland handed her the large cardboard check. She'd tried to push her embarrassment and awkwardness aside by smiling at him and meeting his gaze. He'd surprised her by smiling back and sending her heart rate into overdrive. She'd never forgot his kindness or the flash of pity in his eyes. She'd been devastated.

Lucy's stomach churned at the memory. She wasn't that same girl. Still, she didn't want to see him again.

"Ryland is older than me." No one could ever imagine what she'd gone through and how she'd felt being so sick and tired all the time. Or how badly she'd wanted to be normal and healthy. "He was your dad's friend, not mine. I really didn't know him."

"But you've met him."

"He used to come to our house, but the chances of him remembering me..."

"Please, Aunt Lucy." Connor's eyes implored her. "We'll never know unless you ask."

Darn. He sounded like Aaron. Never willing to give up no

matter what the odds. Her brother wouldn't let her give up, either. Not when she would have died without a liver transplant or when Jeff had trampled upon her heart.

Lucy's chest tightened. She should do this for Aaron as much as Connor. But she had no idea how she could get close enough to someone as rich and famous as Ryland James.

Connor stared up at her with big, round eyes.

A lump formed in her throat. Whether she wanted to see Ryland James or could see him didn't matter. This wasn't about her. "Okay. I'll ask him."

Connor wrapped his arms around her. "I knew I could count on you."

Lucy hugged him tight. "You can always count on me, kiddo."

Even if she knew going into this things wouldn't work out the way her nephew wanted. But she could keep him smiling a little while longer. At least until Ryland said no.

Connor squirmed out of her arms. "Let's go see him now."

"Not so fast. This is something I'm doing on my own." She didn't want her nephew's image of his favorite soccer player destroyed in case Ryland was no longer a nice guy. Fame or fortune could change people. "And I can't show up empty-handed."

But what could she give to a man who could afford whatever he wanted? Flowers might be appropriate given his injury, but maybe a little too feminine. Chocolate, perhaps? Hershey Kisses might give him the wrong idea. Not that he'd ever known about her crush.

"Cookies," Connor suggested. "Everyone likes cookies."

"Yes, they do." Though Lucy doubted anything would convince Ryland to accept the coaching position. But what was the worst he could say besides no? "Does chocolate chip sound good?"

"Those are my favorite." Connor's smile faltered. "It's too bad my mom isn't here. She makes the best chocolate-chip cookies."

Lucy mussed his hair to keep him from getting too caught

up in missing his mom. "It is too bad, but remember she's doing important stuff right now. Like your dad."

Connor nodded.

"How about we use your mom's recipe?" Lucy asked. "You can show me how she makes them."

His smile returned. "Okay."

Lucy wanted to believe everything would turn out okay, but she knew better. As with marriage, the chance of a happy ending here was extremely low. Best to prepare accordingly. She would make a double batch of cookies—one to give to Ryland and one for them to keep. She and Connor were going to need something to make them feel better after Ryland James said no.

The dog's whimpering almost drowned out the pulse-pounding rock music playing in his parents' home gym.

Ryland didn't glance at Cupcake. The dog could wait. He needed to finish his workout.

Lying on the weight machine's bench, he raised the bar overhead, doing the number of reps recommended by the team's trainer. He used free weights when he trained in Phoenix, but his parents wanted him using the machine when he worked out alone.

Sweat beaded on his forehead. He'd ditched his T-shirt twenty minutes ago. His bare back stuck to the vinyl.

Ryland tightened his grip on the handles.

He wanted to return to the team in top form, to show them he still deserved the captaincy as well as their respect. He'd already lost one major endorsement deal due to his bad-boy behavior. For all he knew, he might not even have a spot on the Fuego roster come opening day. And that...sucked.

On the final rep, his muscles ached and his arms trembled. He clenched his jaw, pushing the weight overhead one last time.

"Yes!"

He'd increased the amount of weight this morning. His trainer would be pleased with the improvements in upper-body strength. That and his core were the only things he could work on.

Ryland sat up, breathing hard. Not good. He needed to keep up his endurance while he healed from the surgery.

Damn foot. He stared at his right leg encased in a black walking-cast boot.

His fault. Each of Ryland's muscles tensed in frustration. He should have known better than to be showboating during the friendly with Mexico. Now he was sidelined, unable to run or kick.

The media had accused him of being hungover or drunk when he hurt himself. They'd been wrong. Again. But dealing with the press was as much a part of his job as what happened for ninety minutes out on the pitch.

He'd appeared on camera, admitted the reason for his injury—goofing off for the fans and the cameras—and apologized to both fans and teammates. But the truth had made him look more like a bad boy than ever given his red cards during matches the last couple of seasons, the trouble he'd gotten into off the field and the endless "reports" on his dating habits.

The dog whined louder.

From soccer superstar to dog sitter. Ryland half laughed.

Cupcake barked, as if tired of being put off any longer.

"Come here," Ryland said.

His parents' small dog pranced across the padded gym floor, acting more like a pedigreed champion show dog than a full-blooded mutt. Ryland had wanted to buy his mom and dad a purebred, but they adopted a dog from the local animal shelter, instead.

Cupcake stared up at him with sad, pitiful brown eyes. She had mangy gray fur, short legs and a long, bushy tail. Only his parents could love an animal this ugly and pathetic.

"Come on, girl." Ryland scooped her up into his arms. "I know you miss Mom and Dad. I do, too. But you need to stop crying. They deserve a vacation without having to worry about you or me."

He'd given his parents a cruise for their thirty-second wedding anniversary. Even though he'd bought them this mansion on the opposite side of town, far away from the two-bedroom apartment where he'd grown up, and deposited money into a checking account for them each month, both continued to work in the same low-paying jobs they'd had for as long as their marriage. They also drove the same old vehicles even though newer ones, Christmas presents from him, were parked in the four-car garage.

His parents' sole indulgence was Cupcake. They spoiled the dog rotten. They hadn't wanted to leave her in a kennel or in the care of a stranger while away so after his injury they asked Ryland if he would dog sit. His parents never asked him for anything so he'd jumped at the opportunity to do this.

Ryland hated being back in Wicksburg. There were too many bad memories from when he was a kid. Even small towns had bullies and not-so-nice cliques.

He missed the fun and excitement of a big city, but he needed time to get away to repair the damage he'd done to his foot and his reputation. No one was happy with him at the moment, especially himself. Until getting hurt, he hadn't realized he'd been so restless, unfocused, careless.

Cupcake pawed at his hands. Her sign she wanted rubs.

"Mom and Dad will be home before you know it." Ryland petted the top of her head. "Okay?"

The dog licked him.

He placed her on the floor then stood. "I'm getting some water. Then it's shower time. If I don't shave, I'm going to start looking mangy like you."

Cupcake barked.

His cell phone, sitting on the countertop next to his water bottle, rang. He read the name on the screen. Blake Cochrane. His agent.

Ryland glanced at the clock. Ten o'clock here meant seven o'clock in Los Angeles. "An early morning for you."

"I'm here by six to beat the traffic," Blake said. "According to Twitter, you made a public appearance the other night. I thought we agreed you were going to lay low."

"I was hungry. The fire station was having their annual spaghetti feed so I thought I could eat and support a good cause. They asked if I'd sign autographs and pose for pictures. I couldn't say no."

"Any press?"

"The local weekly paper." With the phone in one hand and a water bottle in the other, Ryland walked to the living room with Cupcake tagging alongside him. He tried hard not to favor his right foot. He'd only been off crutches a few days. "But I told them no interview because I wanted the focus to be on the event. The photographer took a few pictures of the crowd so I might be in one."

"Let's hope whatever is published is positive," Blake said.

"I was talking with people I grew up with." Some of the same people who'd treated him like garbage until he'd joined a soccer team. Most accepted him after he became a starter on the high-school varsity team as a freshman. He'd shown them all by becoming a professional athlete. "I was surrounded by a bunch of happy kids."

"That sounds safe enough," Blake admitted. "But be careful. Another endorsement deal fell through. They're nervous about your injury. The concerns over your image didn't help."

Ryland dragged his hand through his hair. "Let me guess. They want a clean-cut American, not a bad boy who thinks red cards are better than goals."

"You got it," Blake said. "I haven't heard anything official, but rumors are swirling that Mr. McElroy wants to loan you out to a Premier League team."

McElroy was the new owner of the Phoenix Fuego, who took more interest in players and team than any other head honcho in the MLS. He'd fired the coach/manager who'd wanted to run things his way and hired a new coach, Elliot Fritz, who didn't mind the owner being so hands-on. "Seriously?"

"I've heard it from more than one source."

Damn. As two teams were mentioned, Ryland plopped into his dad's easy chair. Cupcake jumped onto his lap.

"I took my eye off the ball," he said. "I made some mistakes. I apologized. I'm recovering and keeping my name out of the news. I don't see why we all can't move on."

"It's not that easy. You're one of the best soccer players in the world. Before your foot surgery, you were a first-team player who could have started for any team here or abroad. Not many American footballers can say that," Blake said. "But McElroy believes your bad-boy image isn't a draw in the stands or with the kids. Merchandising is important these days."

"Yeah, I know. Being injured and getting older isn't helping my cause." As if twenty-nine made Ryland an old man. He remembered what the team owner had said in an interview. "McElroy called me an overpaid liability. But if that's the case, why would an overseas team want to take me on?"

"The transfer period doesn't start until June. None have said they want the loan yet."

Ouch. Ryland knew he had only himself to blame for the mess he found himself in.

"The good news is the MLS doesn't want to lose a home-grown player as talented as you. McElroy's feathers got ruffled," Blake continued. "He's asserting his authority and reminding you that he controls your contract."

"You mean, my future."

"That's how billionaires are."

"I'll stick to being a millionaire, then."

Blake sighed.

"Look, I get why McElroy's upset. Coach Fritz, too. I haven't done a good job handling stuff," Ryland admitted. "I'll be the first to admit I've never been an angel. But I'm not the devil, either. There's no way I could do everything the press says I do. The media exaggerates everything."

"True, but people's concerns are real. This time at your parents' house is critical. Watch yourself."

"I'm going to fix this. I want to play in the MLS." Ryland had already done an eleven-year stint in the U.K. "My folks are doing fine, but they're not getting any younger. I don't want to be an ocean away from them. If McElroy doesn't want me, see if the Indianapolis Rage or another club does."

"McElroy isn't going to let a franchise player like you go to another MLS team," Blake said matter-of-factly. "If you want to play stateside, it'll be with Fuego."

Ryland petted Cupcake. "Then I'll have to keep laying low and polishing my image so it shines."

"Blind me, Ry."

"Will do." Everyone always wanted something from him. This was no different. But it sucked he had to prove himself all over again with Mr. McElroy and the Phoenix fans. "At least I can't get into trouble dog sitting. Wicksburg is the definition of boring."

"Women—"

"Not here," Ryland interrupted. "I know what's expected of me. I also know it's hard on my mom to read the gossip about me on the internet. She doesn't need to hear it firsthand from women in town."

"You should bring your mom back with you to Phoenix."

"Dude. Keeping it quiet and on the down low is fine while I'm here, but let's not go crazy," Ryland said. "In spite of the reports of me hooking up with every starlet in Hollywood, I've been more than discreet and discriminate with whom I see. But beautiful women coming on to me are one of the perks of the sport."

Blake sighed. "I remember when you were this scrappy, young kid who cared about nothing but soccer. It used to be all about the game for you."

"It's still about the game." Ryland was the small-town kid from the Midwest who hit the big-time overseas, playing with the best in the world. Football, as they called it everywhere but in the U.S., meant everything to him. Without it... "Soccer is my life. That's why I'm trying to get back on track."

A beat passed and another. "Just remember, actions speak louder than words."

After a quick goodbye, Blake disconnected from the call.

Ryland stared at his phone. He'd signed with Blake when he was eighteen. The older Ryland got, the smarter his agent's advice sounded.

Actions speak louder than words.

Lately his actions hadn't been any more effective than his words. He looked at Cupcake. "I've put myself in the doghouse. Now I've got to get myself out of it."

The doorbell rang.

Cupcake jumped off his lap and ran to the front door barking ferociously, as if she weighed ninety pounds, not nineteen.

Who could that be? He wasn't expecting anyone.

The dog kept barking. He remained seated.

Let Cupcake deal with whomever was at the door. If he ignored them, maybe they would go away. The last thing Ryland wanted right now was company.

CHAPTER TWO

LUCY'S HAND HOVERED over the mansion's doorbell. She fought the urge to press the button a third time. She didn't want to annoy Mr. and Mrs. James. Yes, she wanted to get this fool's errand over with, but appearing overeager or worse, rude, wouldn't help her find a coach for Connor's team.

"Come on," she muttered. "Open the door."

The constant high-pitch yapping of a dog suggested the doorbell worked. But that didn't explain why no one had answered yet. Maybe the house was so big it took them a long time to reach the front door. Lucy gripped the container of cookies with both hands.

The dog continued barking.

Maybe no one was home. She rose up on her tiptoes and peeked through the four-inch strip of small leaded-glass squares on the ornate wood door.

Lights shone inside.

Someone had to be home. Leaving the lights on when away wasted electricity. Her dad used to tell her that. Aaron said the same thing to Connor. But she supposed if a person could afford to live in an Architectural Digest–worthy home with its Georgian-inspired columns, circular drive and manicured lawn that looked like a green carpet, they probably didn't worry about paying the electricity bill.

Lucy didn't see anyone coming toward the door. She couldn't see the dog, either. She lowered her heels to the welcome mat.

Darn it. She didn't want to come back later and try again. A chill shivered down her spine. She needed to calm down.

She imagined Connor with a smile on his face and soccer cleats on his feet. Her anxiety level dropped.

If no one answered, she would return. She would keep coming back until she spoke with Ryland James.

The dog's barking became more agitated.

A sign? Probably not, but she might as well ring the bell once more before calling it quits.

She pressed the doorbell. A symphony of chimes erupted into a Mozart tune. At least the song sounded like Mozart the third time hearing it.

The door opened slightly. A little gray dog darted out and sniffed her shoes. The pup placed its stubby front paws against her jean-covered calves.

"Off, Cupcake." The dog ran to the grass in the front yard. A man in navy athletic shorts with a black walking-cast on his right leg stood in the doorway. "She's harmless."

The dog might be, but not him.

Ryland James.

Hot. Sexy. Oh, my.

He looked like a total bad boy with his short, brown hair damp and mussed, as if he hadn't taken time to comb it after he crawled out of bed. Shaving didn't seem to be part of his morning routine, either. He used to be so clean-cut and all-American, but the dark stubble covering his chin and cheeks gave him an edge. His bare muscular chest glistened as if he'd just finished a workout. He had a tattoo on his right biceps and another on the backside of his left wrist. His tight, underwear model–worthy abs drew her gaze lower. Her mouth went dry.

Lucy forced her gaze up and stared into the hazel eyes that had once fueled her teenage daydreams. His dark lashes seemed even thicker. How was that possible?

The years had been good, very good to him. The guy was more gorgeous than ever with his classically handsome features, ones that had become more defined, almost refined, with age. His nose, however, looked as if it had been broken at least once. Rather than detract from his looks, his nose gave him character, made him appear more…rugged. Manly. Dangerous.

Lucy's heart thudded against her ribs. "It's you."

"I'm me." His lips curved into a charming smile, sending her already-racing pulse into a mad sprint. "You're not what I expected to find on my doorstep, but my day's looking a whole lot better now."

Her turn. But Lucy found herself tongue-tied. The same way she'd been whenever he was over at her house years ago. Her gaze strayed once again to his amazing abs. Wowza.

"You okay?" he asked.

Remember Connor. She raised her chin. "I was expecting—"

"One of my parents."

She nodded.

"I was hoping you were here to see me," he said.

"I am." The words rushed from her lips like water from Connor's Super Soaker gun. She couldn't let nerves get the best of her now that she'd accomplished the first part of her mission and was standing face-to-face with Ryland. "But I thought one of them would answer the door since you're injured."

"They would have if they'd been home." His rich, deep voice, as smooth and warm as a mug of hot cocoa, flowed over her. "I'm Ryland James."

"I know."

"That puts me at a disadvantage because I don't know who you are."

"I meant, I know you. But it was a long time ago," she clarified.

His gaze raked over her. "I would remember meeting you."

Lucy was used to guys hitting on her. She hadn't expected that from Ryland, but she liked it. Other men's attention annoyed her. His flirting made her feel attractive and desired.

"Let me take a closer look to see if I can jog my memory," he said.

The approval in his eyes gave her goose bumps. The good kind, ones she hadn't felt in a while. She hadn't wanted to jump back into the dating scene after her divorce two years ago.

"I *have* seen that pretty smile of yours before," he continued. "Those sparkling blue eyes, too."

Oh, boy. Her knees felt wobbly. Tingles filled her stomach. *Stop.* She wasn't back in middle school.

Lucy straightened. The guy hadn't a clue who she was. Ryland James was a professional athlete. Knowing what to say to women was probably part of their training camp.

"I'm Lucy." For some odd reason, she sounded husky. She cleared her throat. "Lucy Martin."

"Lucy." Lines creased Ryland's forehead. "Aaron Martin's little sister?"

She nodded.

"Same smile and blue eyes, but everything else has changed." Ryland's gaze ran the length of her again. "Just look at you now."

She braced herself, waiting to hear how sick she'd been and how ugly she'd looked before her liver transplant.

He grinned. "Little Lucy is all grown up now."

Little Lucy? She stiffened. His words confused her. She hadn't been little. Okay, maybe when they first met back in elementary school. But she'd been huge, a bloated whale, and yellow due to jaundice the last time he'd seen her. "It's been what? Thirteen years since we last saw each other."

"Thirteen years too long," he said.

What was going on? Old crushes were supposed to get fat and lose their hair, not get even hotter and appear interested in you. He sounded interested. Unless her imagination was getting the best of her.

No, she knew better when it came to men. "It looks as if life is treating you well. Except for your leg—"

"Foot. Nothing serious."

"You had surgery."

"A minor inconvenience, that's all. Nothing like what you suffered through," he said. "The liver transplant seems to have done what Aaron hoped it would do. All he ever wanted was for you to be healthy."

"I am." She wondered why Aaron would have talked about her illness to Ryland. All they'd cared about were soccer and girls. Well, every other girl in Wicksburg except her. "I take medicine each day and have a monthly blood test, but otherwise I'm the same as everybody else."

"No, you're not." Ryland's gaze softened. "There's nothing ordinary about you. Never has been. It sucked that you were sick, but you were always so brave."

Heat stole up her neck toward her cheeks. Butterflies flapped in her tummy. Her heart...

Whoa-whoa-whoa. Don't get carried away by a few nice words from a good-looking guy, even if that guy happened to be the former man of her dreams. She'd been a naive kid back then. She'd learned the hard way that people said things they didn't mean. They lied, even after saying how much they loved you. Lucy squared her shoulders.

Time to get this over with. She handed Ryland the cookies. "These are for you."

He removed the container's lid. His brows furrowed. "Cookies?"

Ryland sounded surprised. She bit the inside of her mouth, hoping he liked them. "Chocolate chip."

"My favorite. Thanks."

He seemed pleased. Good. "Aaron's son, Connor, helped me

make them. He's nine and loves soccer. That's why I'm here. To ask a favor."

Ryland looked at the cookies, then at her. "I appreciate your honesty. Not many people are so up-front when they want something. Let's talk inside."

She hesitated, unsure of the wisdom of going into the house. Once upon a time she'd believed in happily ever after and one true love. But life had taught her those things belonged only in fairy tales. Love and romance were overrated. But Ryland was making her feel things she tried hard not to think about too much—attraction, desire, hope.

But the other part of her, the part that tended to be impulsive and had gotten her into trouble more than once, was curious. She wanted to know if his parents' house was as nice on the inside as the exterior and front yard. Heaven knew she would never live in an exclusive neighborhood like this one. This might be her only chance to find out.

Ryland leaned against the doorway. The casual pose took weight off his right foot. He might need to sit down.

"Sure." She didn't want him hurting. "That would be nice."

He whistled for the dog.

Cupcake ran inside.

Lucy entered the house. The air was cooler than outside and smelled lemony. Wood floors gleamed. A giant chandelier hung from the twenty-foot ceiling in the foyer. She clamped her lips together so her mouth wouldn't gape. Original watercolor paintings in gilded frames decorated the textured walls. Tasteful and expensive.

She stepped through a wide-arched doorway into the living room. Talk about beautiful. The yellow and green décor was light, bright and inviting. The colors, fabrics and accessories coordinated perfectly. What she liked most was how comfortable the room looked, not at all like some of those unlivable magazine layouts or model homes.

Family pictures sat on the wooden fireplace mantle. A framed poster-size portrait of Ryland, wearing a U.S. National team uniform, hung on the wall. An open paperback novel rested cover-side up on an end table. "Your parents' house is lovely."

"Thanks."

He sounded proud, making her wonder about his part in his parents' house. She'd guess a big part, given his solid relationship with his mom and dad when he'd been a teen.

"My mom thought the house was too big, but I convinced her she deserved it after so many years of apartment living." Ryland motioned to a sofa. "Have a seat."

Lucy sat, sinking into the overstuffed cushions. More comfortable than the futon she'd sold before leaving Chicago. She'd gotten rid of her few pieces of furniture so she wouldn't have to pay for storage while living at Aaron and Dana's house.

Cupcake hopped up next to her.

"Is she allowed on the couch?" Lucy asked.

"The dog is allowed everywhere except the dining-room table and kitchen counters. She belongs to my parents. They've spoiled her rotten." Ryland sounded more amused than angry. He sat on a wingback chair to her right. "Mind if I have a cookie?"

"Please do."

He offered her the container. "Would you like one?"

The chocolate chips smelled good, but she would be eating cookies with Connor later. Better not overdo the sweets. The trips to the ice-cream parlor and Rocket Burger with her nephew were already adding up. "No, thanks."

Ryland took one. "I can't remember the last time someone baked anything for me."

"What about your mom?"

"I don't spend as much time with my parents as I'd like due to soccer. Right now I'm dog sitting while they're away." Cupcake circled around as if chasing her own tail, then plopped against the cushion and placed her head on Lucy's thigh. "She likes you."

Lucy ran her fingers through the soft gray fur. She'd never had a dog. "She's sweet."

"When she wants to be." Ryland bit into the cookie. He took his time eating it. "Delicious."

The cookies were a hit. Lucy hoped they worked as a bribe. She mustered her courage. Not that she could back out now even if she wanted to. "So my nephew…"

"Does he want an autograph?" Ryland placed the cookie container on the coffee table. "Maybe a team jersey or ball?"

"Connor would love it if you signed his ball, but what he really wants is a coach for his spring under-9 rec. team." She didn't want to waste any more of Ryland's time. Or hers. "He wanted me to ask if you could coach his team, the Defeeters."

Ryland flinched. "Me? Coach?"

"I know that's a big request and likely impossible for you to do right now."

He looked at his injured foot. "Yeah, this isn't a good time. I hope to be back with my team in another month or so."

"I'm sure you will be. Aaron says you're one of the best players in the world."

"Thanks. It's just… I'm supposed to be laying low while I'm here. Staying out of the press. The media could turn my coaching your nephew's team into a circus." Ryland stared at the dog. "I'm really sorry I can't help you out."

"No worries. I told Connor you probably couldn't coach." Lucy knew Ryland would never say yes. He'd left his small-town roots behind and become famous, traveling all over the U.S. and the world. The exotic lifestyle was as foreign to her as the game of soccer itself. But maybe she could get him to agree to something else that wouldn't take so much of his time. "But if you happen to have an hour to spare sometime, Connor and his teammates would be thrilled if you could give them a pep talk."

Silence stretched between them. She'd put him on the spot with that request, too. But she'd had no choice if she wanted to help her nephew.

"I can do that," Ryland said finally.

Lucy released the breath she hadn't realized she was holding. "Thanks."

"I'm happy to talk to them, sign balls, pose for pictures, whatever the boys want."

She hoped the visit would appease Connor. "That will be great. Thanks."

Ryland's eyes darkened, more brown than hazel now. "Who will you get to coach?"

"I don't know," she admitted. "Practices don't start until next week so I still have a little time left to find someone. I can always coach, if need be."

Surprise flashed across his face. "You play soccer?"

Lucy hadn't been allowed to do anything physical when she was younger. Even though she no longer had any physical limitations, she preferred art to athletics. "No, but I've been reading up on the game and watching video clips on the internet, just in case."

His lips narrowed. "Aaron was great with those kids when we put on that camp back in high school. Why doesn't he coach the team?"

"Aaron's coached the Defeeters for years, but he's overseas right now with the army. Both he and his wife were deployed with their Reserve unit last month. I'm taking care of Connor until they return next year."

"Aaron talked about using the military to pay for college," Ryland said thoughtfully. "But I lost track of him, of everyone, when I left Wicksburg."

"He joined the army right after high school." Lucy's medical expenses had drained their college funds, her parents' saving account and the equity in their house. Sometimes it felt as if she was still paying for the transplant years later. Aaron, too. "That's where he met his wife, Dana. After they completed their Active Duty, they joined the Reserves."

"A year away from home. Away from their son." Ryland dragged his hand through his hair. "That has to be rough."

Lucy's chest tightened. "You do what you have to do."

"Still..."

"You left home to go to Florida and then England."

"To play soccer. Not protect my country," Ryland said. "I had the time of my life. I doubt Aaron and his wife can say the same thing right now."

Lucy remembered the tears glistening in Connor's eyes as he told her his mom sounded like she was crying on the phone. "You're right about that."

"I respect what Aaron and his wife, what all of the military, are doing. The sacrifices they make. True heroes. Every one of them."

Ryland sounded earnest. She wanted to believe he was sincere. Maybe he was still a small-town guy at heart. "They are."

Cupcake rolled over on her back. She waved her front paws in the air.

Lucy took the not-so-subtle hint and rubbed the dog's stomach.

"So you've stuck around Wicksburg," Ryland said.

"I left for a while. College. I also lived in Chicago." Aaron had accused her of running away when her marriage failed. Maybe he'd been right. But she'd had to do something when her life crumbled around her. "I moved back last month."

"To care for your nephew."

She nodded. "Saying no never entered into my mind. Not after everything Aaron has done for me."

"He was so protective of you."

"He still is."

"That doesn't surprise me." Ryland rubbed his thigh above the brace he wore. He rested his foot on an ottoman. "Did you leave your boyfriend behind in Chi-town or did he come with you?"

She drew back, surprised by the question. "I, uh, don't have a boyfriend."

He grinned wryly. "So you need a soccer coach and a boyfriend. I hope your brother told you the right qualities to look for in each."

Aaron always gave her advice, but she hadn't always listened to him. Lucy should have done so before eloping. She couldn't change the past. But she wouldn't make that same mistake again.

"A soccer coach is all I need." Lucy figured Ryland had to be teasing her, but this wasn't a joking matter. She needed a boyfriend as much as she needed another ex-husband. She shifted positions. "I have my hands full with Connor. He's my priority. A kid should be happy and carefree, not frowning and down all the time."

"Maybe we should get him together with Cupcake," Ryland said. "She goes from being happy to sad. I'm a poor substitute for my parents."

Lucy's insecurities rushed to the surface. She never thought she would have something in common with him. "That's how I feel with Connor. Nothing I do seems to be...enough."

Ryland leaned forward. His large hand engulfed hers. His touch was light. His skin was warm. "Hey. You're here to see me about his team. That says a lot. Aaron and his family, especially Connor, are lucky to have you."

Ryland's words wrapped around Lucy like a big hug. But his touch disturbed her more than it comforted. Heat emanated from the point of contact and spread up her arm. She tried not to think about it. "I'm the lucky one."

"Maybe some of that luck will rub off on me."

"Your injury?" she asked.

"Yeah, and a few other things."

His hand still rested upon hers. Lucy hadn't been touched by a man in over two years. It felt...good.

Better not get used to it. Reluctantly, she pulled her hand from beneath his and reached for her purse.

"If you need some luck, I've got just the thing for you." Lucy removed a penny from her change pocket and gave it to Ryland. "My grammy told me this is all a person needs to get lucky."

Wicked laughter lit his eyes. "Here I thought it took a killer opening line, oodles of charm and an expensive bottle of champagne."

Oh, no. Lucy realized what she'd said. Her cheeks burned. "I meant to change their luck."

He winked. "I know, but you gave me the opening. I had to take the shot."

At least he hadn't scored. Not yet, anyway. Lucy swallowed.

"Aaron would have done the same." She needed to be careful, though. Ryland was charming, but he wasn't her big brother. Being near him short-circuited her brain. She couldn't think straight. That was bad. The last time she allowed herself to be charmed by a man she'd ended up with a wedding ring on her finger.

"You said your nephew loves soccer," Ryland said.

She nodded, thankful for the change in subject. "Yes. Connor and Aaron are crazy about the sport. They wear matching jerseys. It's cute, though Dana says it's annoying when they get up at some crazy hour to watch a game in Europe. But I don't think she minds that much."

Lucy cringed at her rambling. Ryland didn't care about Aaron's family's infatuation with soccer. She needed to shut up. Now.

"That's great they're so into the game." A thoughtful expression crossed Ryland's face. "I haven't been back in town for a while, but I bet some of the same people are still involved in soccer. I'll ask around to see if there's someone who can coach your nephew's team."

Her mouth parted in surprise. She liked being self-reliant and hated asking for help, but in this case Ryland had offered. She'd be stupid to say no when this meant so much to Connor. "I'd appreciate that. If it's not too much trouble."

"No trouble. I'm happy to do it. Anything for…"

You, she thought.

"…Aaron."

Of course, this was for her brother. Ryland's childhood and high-school friend and teammate. She ignored the twinge of disappointment. "Thanks."

Ryland held the penny between the pads of his thumb and index finger. "You've made me cookies, given me a lucky penny. What do I get if I find a coach?"

Lucy wondered if he was serious or teasing her. His smile suggested the latter. "My undying gratitude?"

"That's a good start."

"More cookies?"

"Always appreciated, especially if they're chocolate chip," he said. "What else?"

His lighthearted and flirty tone sounded warning bells in her head. Ryland *was* teasing her, but Lucy no longer wanted to play along. His charm, pretty much everything about him, unsettled her. "I'm not sure what else you might want."

He gave her the once-over, only this time his gaze lingered a second too long on her lips. "I can think of a couple things."

So could Lucy. The man was smokin' hot. His lips looked as if they could melt her insides with one kiss. Sex appeal oozed from him.

A good thing she'd sworn off men because she could tell the soccer pitch wasn't the only place where Ryland James played. Best not to even start that game. She'd only lose. Again.

Not. Going. To. Happen.

Time to steer this conversation back to where it needed to be so she could get out of here.

"How about you make a list?" Lucy kept a smile on her face and her tone light and friendly. After all, he was going to try to find Connor's team a coach. But if Ryland thought she was going to swoon at his feet in adoration and awe, he had another think coming. "If you find the team a coach, we'll go from there."

Ryland's smile crinkled the corners of his eyes, taking her breath away. "I always thought you were a cool kid, Lucy Martin, but I really like who you are now."

Okay, she was attracted to him. Any breathing female with a pulse would be. The guy was appealing with a capital *A*.

But Lucy wasn't stupid. She knew the type. His type.

Ryland James spelled T-R-O-U-B-L-E.

Once he visited the Defeeters, she never wanted to see him again. And she wouldn't.

It was so good to see Lucy Martin again.

Ryland sat in the living room waiting for her to return with Cupcake, who needed to go outside. Lucy had offered to take the dog to the backyard so he wouldn't have to get up. He'd agreed if only to keep her here a little while longer.

He couldn't get over the difference in her.

She'd been a shy, sweet girl with freckles, long braids and yellowish whites surrounding her huge blue eyes. Now she was a confident, sweet woman with a glowing complexion, strawberry-blond hair worn in a short and sassy style, and mesmerizing sky-blue eyes.

Ryland had been wrong about not wanting company this morning. Sure she'd shown up because she wanted something. But she'd brought him cookies—a bribe, no doubt—and been straightforward asking him for a favor.

He appreciated and respected that.

Some women were devious and played up to him to get what they wanted. Lucy hadn't even wanted something for herself, but for her nephew. That was...refreshing.

Cupcake ran into the living room and hopped onto the couch.

Lucy took her same spot next to the dog. "Sorry that took so long, the dog wanted to run around before she got down to business."

"Thanks for taking her out." Lucy had brightened Ryland's mood, making him smile and laugh. He wanted her to stick around. "You must be thirsty. I'll get you something to drink. Coffee? Water? A soda?"

Lucy shifted on the couch. "No, thanks."

Years ago, Aaron had told Ryland that his sister had a crush on him so to be nice to her. He had been. Now he was curious to know if any of her crush remained. "It's no trouble."

But he could get in trouble wondering if she were still interested in him. He was supposed to be avoiding women.

Not that he was pursuing her. Though he was…curious.

She grabbed her purse. "Thanks, but I should be going."

Lucy was different than other women he knew. Most would kill for that kind of invitation from him, but she didn't seem impressed or want to hang out with him. She'd eagerly taken Cupcake outside while he stayed inside. Almost as if she'd wanted some distance from him.

Interesting. His charm and fame usually melted whatever feminine resistance he faced. Not with Lucy. He kind of liked the idea of a challenge. Not that it could go anywhere, he reminded himself. "I'd like to hear more about Aaron."

"Perhaps another time."

"You have somewhere to be?"

Her fingers curled around the leather strap. "I have work to do before Connor gets home from school."

Ryland would have liked it if she stayed longer, but he would see her again. No doubt about that. He rose. "I'll see you out."

She stood. Her purse swung like a pendulum. "That's not necessary. Stay off your foot. I know where the door is."

"My foot can handle it."

Lucy's gaze met his. "I can see myself out."

He found the unwavering strength in her eyes a big turn-on. "I know, but I want to show you out."

After what felt like forever, she looked away with a shrug. "It's your foot."

He bit back a smile. She would be a challenge all right. A fun one. "Yes, it is."

Ryland accompanied Lucy to her car, a practical looking white, four-door subcompact. "Thanks for coming by and bringing me cookies. I'll give you a call about a coach and talking to the team."

She removed something from an outside pocket of her purse and handed it to him. "My cell-phone number is on my business card. Aaron has a landline, but this is the best way to reach me."

He stared at the purple card with white and light blue lettering and a swirly border. That looked more like Lucy. "Freelance graphic designer. So you're still into art."

"You remember that?"

She sounded incredulous, but the way her eyes danced told him she was also pleased.

"You'd be surprised what I remember."

Her lips parted once again.

He'd piqued her interest. Good, because she'd done the same to him. "But don't worry, it's all good."

A charming blush crept into Lucy's cheeks.

"We'll talk later." Ryland didn't want to make her uncomfortable, but flirting with her came so easily. "You have work to do now."

"Yes, I do." She dug around the inside of her purse. As she pulled out her keys, metal clanged against metal. "Thanks. I'm... I look forward to hearing from you."

"It won't be long." And it wouldn't. Ryland couldn't wait to talk to her again. "I promise."

CHAPTER THREE

THAT AFTERNOON, the front door burst open with so much force Lucy thought a tornado had touched down in Wicksburg. She stood her ground in the living room, knowing this burst of energy wasn't due to Mother Nature—the warning siren hadn't gone off—but was man, er, boy-made.

Manny usually couldn't wait for Connor to get home and make another escape attempt, but the cat hightailed it into the kitchen. A ball of dark fur slid across the linoleum before disappearing from sight.

Connor flew into the house, strands of his strawberry-blond hair going every which way. He was lanky, the way his dad had been at that age, all limbs with not an ounce of fat on him. The set of his jaw and the steely determination in his eyes made him seem more superhero than a four-and-a-half-foot third grader. All he needed was a cape to wear over his jersey and jeans.

"Hey." Lucy knew he wanted to know about her visit to Ryland, but the sexy soccer player had been on her mind since she'd left him. Much to her dismay. She didn't want to start her time with Connor focused on the guy, too. "Did you have a good day at school? You had a spelling quiz, right?"

He slammed the front door closed. The entire house shook. His backpack hung precariously off one thin shoulder, but he didn't seem to care. "Did you talk to Ryland James?"

Connor had the same one-track mind as her brother. When Aaron had something he wanted to do, like joining the military, he defined tunnel vision.

Lucy might as well get this over with. "I went to Mr. and Mrs. James's house this morning. Ryland liked the cookies we baked."

The backpack thudded against the entryway's tile floor. Anticipation filled Connor's blue eyes. "Is he going to coach the Defeeters?"

This was the part she hadn't been looking forward to since leaving the Jameses' house. "No, but Ryland offered to see if he can find the team a coach. He's also going to come out and talk to the team."

Different emotions crossed Connor's face. Sadness, anger, surprise. A thoughtful expression settled on his features. "I guess he must be really busy."

"Ryland's trying to heal and stay in shape." Her temperature rose remembering how he looked in only a pair of shorts and gleam of sweat. "He doesn't plan on being in town long. Maybe a month or so. He wants to rejoin his team as soon as he can."

Manny peered around the doorway to the kitchen, saw Connor and ran to him.

Connor picked up the cat. "I guess I would want to do that, too."

Poor kid. He was trying to put on a brave face. She wished things could be different for him. "There's still time to find the Defeeters a coach."

He stared over the cat's head. "That's what you said last week. And the week before that."

"True, but now I have help looking for a coach." Lucy hoped Ryland had been serious about his offer and came through for... the boys. "A good thing, otherwise, you'll be stuck with me."

Connor nodded.

She ruffled his hair. "Gee, thanks."

"You're the one who said it." He flashed her a lopsided grin. "But no matter what happens, having you for a coach is better than not playing at all."

Lucy hoped he was right. "I'll do my best if it comes down to that."

"It won't." Connor sounded so confident.

"How do you know?"

"If Ryland James said he'd find us a coach, he will."

She'd been disappointed too many times to put that much faith into someone. Ryland had seemed sincere and enthusiastic. But so had others. Best not to raise Connor's hopes too high on the chance his favorite player didn't come through after all. "Ryland said he'd *try*. He's going to call me."

"Have you checked your voice mail yet?" Connor asked.

His eagerness made her smile. She'd been wondering when the call might come herself. They both needed to be realistic. "I just saw Ryland a couple hours ago."

"Hours? He could have found us five coaches by now."

She doubted that.

"All Ryland James has to do is snap his fingers and people will come running," Connor continued.

Lucy could imagine women running to the gorgeous Ryland. She wasn't so sure the same could be said about coaches. Not unless they were female.

"Check your cell phone," Connor encouraged.

The kid was relentless…like his dad. "Give Ryland time to snap his fingers. I mean, make calls. I know this is important to you, but a little patience here would be good."

"You could call him."

No, she couldn't. Wouldn't. "He said he'd call. Rushing him wouldn't be nice."

She also didn't want to give Ryland the wrong impression so he might think she was interested in him. A guy like him meant one thing—heartbreak. She'd had enough of that to last a lifetime.

"Let's give him at least a day, maybe two, to call us, okay?" she suggested.

"Okay," Connor agreed reluctantly.

She bit back a laugh. "How about some cookies and milk while you tell me about school?"

Maybe that would get Ryland James out of Connor's thoughts. And hers, too.

"Sure." As he walked toward the kitchen, he looked back at her. "So does Ryland James have a soccer field in his backyard?"

Lucy swallowed a sigh. And then maybe not.

After dinner, Ryland retreated with Cupcake into the media room aka his dad's man cave. He had all he needed—laptop, cell phone, chocolate-chip cookies, Lucy's business card and a seventy-inch LED television with ESPN playing. As soon as Ryland found Lucy a coach for her nephew's team, he would call her with the good news.

Forget the delicious cookies she'd made. The only dessert he wanted was to hear her sweet voice on the opposite end of the phone.

Ryland laughed. He must need some feminine attention if he felt this way.

But seeing Lucy again had made him feel good. She also had him thinking about the past. Many of his childhood memories living in Wicksburg were like bad dreams, ones he'd pushed to the far recesses of his mind and wanted to keep there. But a few others, like the ones he remembered now, brought a welcome smile to his face.

Cupcake lay on an Indianapolis Colts dog bed.

Even though Ryland played soccer, his dad preferred football, the American kind. But his dad had never once tried to change Ryland's mind about what sport to play. Instead, his father had done all he could so Ryland could succeed in the sport. He would be nowhere without his dad and his mom.

And youth soccer.

He'd learned the basic skills and the rules of the game playing in the same rec. league Aaron's son played in. When Ryland moved to a competitive club, playing up a year from his own age group, his dad's boss, Mr. Buckley, who owned a local farm, bought Ryland new cleats twice a year. Not cheap ones, but the good kind. Mr. Martin, Aaron and Lucy's dad, would drive Ryland to away games and tournaments when his parents had to work.

Lucy taking care of Aaron's son didn't surprise Ryland. The Martins had always been a loyal bunch.

In elementary school, other kids used to taunt him. Aaron stood up for Ryland even before they were teammates. Once they started playing on the same team, they became good friends. But Ryland had wanted to put Wicksburg behind him when he left.

And he had.

He'd focused all his effort and energy into being the best soccer player he could be.

Now that he was back in town, finding a soccer coach was the least he could do for his old friend Aaron. Ryland pressed the mute button on the television's remote then picked up his cell phone. This wouldn't take long.

Two hours later, he disconnected from yet another call. He couldn't believe it. No matter whom he'd spoken with, the answer was still the same—no. Only the reason for not being able to coach changed.

"Wish I could help you out, Ryland, but I'm already coaching two other teams."

"Gee, if I'd known sooner..."

"Try the high school. Maybe one of the students could do it as a class project or something."

Ryland placed his cell phone on the table. Even the suggestion to contact the high school had led to a dead end. No wonder Lucy had asked him to coach Connor's team.

Ryland looked at Cupcake. "What am I going to do?"

The dog kept her eyes closed.

"Go ahead. Pretend you don't hear me. That's what everyone else has done tonight."

Okay, not quite. His calling had resulted in four invitations to dinner and five requests to speak to soccer teams. Amazing how things and his status in town had changed. All his hard work had paid off. Though he was having to start over with Mr. McElroy and the Fuego.

"I need to find Lucy a coach."

Cupcake stretched.

Something flashed on the television screen. Highlights from a soccer match.

Yearning welled inside him. He missed the action on the field, the adrenaline pushing through him to run faster and the thrill of taking the ball toward the goal and scoring. Thinking about playing soccer was making him nostalgic for days when kids, a ball and some grass defined the game in its simplest and purest form.

Lucy's business card caught his eye.

Attraction flared to life. He wanted to talk to her. Now.

Ryland picked up his cell phone. He punched in the first three digits of her number then placed the phone back on the table.

Calling her tonight would be stupid. Saying he wanted to hear her voice might be true, but he didn't want to push too hard and scare her off. Other women might love a surprise phone call, but Lucy might not. She wasn't like the women he dated.

That, he realized, surprisingly appealed to him. Sitting in his parents' living room eating cookies and talking with a small-town girl had energized him in a way no visit to a top restaurant or trendy club with a date ever had.

Ryland stared at the cell phone. He wanted to talk to her, but if he called her he would have to admit his inability to find her a coach. That wouldn't go over well.

With him, he realized with a start. Lucy wouldn't be upset. She'd thank him for his efforts then take on the coaching role herself.

I can always coach, if need be.

You play soccer?

No, but I've been reading up on the game and watching coaching clips on the internet just in case.

He imagined her placing a whistle around her graceful neck and leading a team of boys at practice. Coaching would be nothing compared to what Lucy went through when she was sick. She would figure out the basics of what needed to be done and give the boys her all.

But she shouldn't *have* to do that. She was doing enough taking care of her nephew. The same as Aaron and his wife.

His gaze focused on Lucy's name on her business card. The script might be artistic and a touch whimsical, but it showed strength and ingenuity, too.

Ryland straightened. He couldn't let people saying no stop him. He was tougher than that. "I might have screwed up my career, but I'm not going to mess up this."

The dog stared at him.

"I'll find Lucy and those kids a coach."

No matter what he had to do.

Two days later, Lucy stood in the front yard kicking a soccer ball to Connor. The afternoon sun shone high in the sky, but the weather might as well be cloudy and gray due to the frown on her nephew's face. Practices began next week and the Defeeters still didn't have a coach. Ryland hadn't called back, either.

She tapped the ball with her left foot. It rolled too far to the left, out of Connor's reach and into the hedge separating the yard from the neighbor's. Lucy grimaced. "Sorry."

Connor didn't say a word but chased the ball. She knew what

he was thinking because his expression matched her thoughts. The team needed someone who knew soccer better than she did, someone who could teach the kids the right skills and knew rules without having to resort to a book each time.

Her efforts to find a coach had failed. That left one person who could come to her—and the team's—rescue.

It won't be long. I promise.

Ryland's words returned to her in a rush. Pathetic, how quick she'd been to believe them. As if she hadn't learned anything based on her past experiences.

Okay, it had been only a couple of days. "Long" could mean a few days, a week, even a month. But "promise" was a seven-letter word that held zero weight with most of the people in this world.

Was Ryland one of them?

Time would tell, but for Connor's sake she hoped not. He kicked the ball back to her.

She stopped the ball with her right foot the way she'd seen someone do on a video then used the inside of her foot to kick the ball back. She had better control this time. "Your teacher liked your book report."

"I guess."

"You got an A."

Connor kicked the ball her way without stopping it first. "Are you sure he hasn't called?"

"He" equaled Ryland. Connor had been asking that question nonstop, including a call during lunchtime using a classmate's cell phone.

Lucy patted her jeans pocket. "My phone's right here."

"You checked your messages?"

"I did." And rechecked them. No messages from Ryland. From anyone for that matter. She hadn't made any close friends in Chicago. The ones who lived in Wicksburg had remained friends with her ex-husband after Lucy moved away. That made things uncomfortable now that she was back. The pity in their eyes reminded her of when she'd been sick. She wanted no part of that ever again. "But it's only been a couple of days."

"It feels like forever."

"I know." Each time her cell phone rang, thinking it might be Ryland filled her stomach with tingles of anticipation. She hated that. She didn't want to feel that way about any guy calling her, even if the reason was finding a coach for her nephew's soccer team. "But good things come to those who wait."

Connor rolled the ball back and forth along the bottom of his foot. "That's what Mom and Dad say. I'm trying to be patient, but it's hard."

"I know it's hard to wait, but we have to give Ryland time."

Connor nodded.

Please come through, Ryland. Lucy didn't want Connor's favorite player letting him down at the worst possible time. She didn't want her nephew to have to face the kind of betrayal and disappointment she'd suffered due to others. Not when he was only nine, separated from his parents by oceans and continents.

He kicked the ball to her. "Maybe Ryland forgot."

Lucy didn't want to go there. The ball rolled past her toward the sidewalk. She chased after it. "Give him the benefit of the doubt."

Connor didn't say anything.

She needed him to stop focusing so much on Ryland. "Your dad wants to see videotapes of your games. He can't wait to see how the team does this spring."

She kicked the ball back. Connor touched the ball twice with his foot before kicking it to her.

"Next time only one touch," she said.

Surprise filled his blue eyes. "That's what my dad says."

"It might come as a shock, but your aunt knows a few things about the game of soccer." She'd found a book on coaching on the living-room bookcase and attended a coaching clinic put on by the league last night while Connor had dinner over at a friend's house. "How about we kick the ball a few times more, then go to the pizza parlor for dinner? You can play those video games you like so much."

"Okay."

Talk about an unenthused reaction.

An old beat-up, blue pickup truck pulled to the curb in front of the house. The engine idled loudly, as if in need of a tune-up. The engine sputtered off. The truck lurched forward a foot, maybe two.

The driver's door opened. Ryland.

Her heart thumped.

It won't be long. I promise.

Tingles filled her stomach. He hadn't let her down. He was still the same nice guy he'd been in high school.

Ryland rounded the front of the truck. He wore a white polo shirt with the Fuego logo on the left side, a pair of khaki shorts and the boot on his right foot. He wore a tennis shoe on his left. His hair was nicely styled. He'd shaved, removing the sexy stubble.

Even with his clean-cut look, she knew not to let her guard down. The guy was still dangerous. The only reason she was happy to see him was Connor.

A little voice inside her head laughed at that. She ignored it.

"It's him." Awe filled Connor's voice. "Ryland James."

"Yes, it's him," she said.

Ryland crossed the sidewalk and stood near them on the lawn. "Hello."

Lucy fought the urge to step back and put some distance between them. "Hi."

He acknowledged her with a nod, but turned his attention to the kid with the stars in his eyes. "You must be Connor."

Her nephew nodded.

Lucy's heart melted. Ryland knew how important this moment must be for her nephew.

Connor wiped his right hand against his shorts then extended his arm. "It's nice to meet you, Mr. James."

As Ryland shook his hand, he grinned. "Call me Ryland."

Connor's eyes widened. He looked almost giddy with excitement. "Okay, Ryland."

He motioned to the soccer ball. "Looks like you've been practicing. It's good to get some touches on the ball every day."

Connor nodded. The kid was totally starstruck. Lucy didn't blame him for being wowed by Ryland. She was, too.

Better be careful.

Ryland used his left foot to push the ball toward Connor. "Let's see you juggle."

Connor swooped up the ball and bounced it off his bony knees. He used his legs and feet to keep the ball from touching the ground.

"You're doing great," Ryland encouraged.

Connor beamed and kept going.

Ryland glanced at her. "He reminds me of Aaron."

"Two peas in a pod," she agreed.

The ball bounced away. Connor ran after it. "I'll try it again."

"The more you practice, the better you'll get," Ryland said.

"That's what Aunt Lucy told me."

His gaze met hers. Lucy's pulse skittered at the flirtatious gleam in Ryland's hazel eyes.

"Your aunt is a smart woman," he said.

Lucy didn't feel so smart. She wasn't sure what to make of her reaction to Ryland being here. Okay, the guy was handsome. Gorgeous, really. But she knew better than to be bowled over by a man and sweet talk.

So why was she practically swooning over the sexy soccer star? Ryland showing up and the way he was interacting with Connor had to be the reason. Nothing else made sense.

She straightened. "I thought you were going to call."

"I decided to stop by, instead."

Warning bells rang in her head. "The address isn't on my business card. How did you find this place?"

"I went into the café for a cup of coffee and asked where Aaron lived," Ryland explained. "Three people offered directions."

"That's Wicksburg for you," she said. "Friendly to a fault."

"No kidding," he agreed. "I received a friendly reminder about the difference between a tornado watch versus a tornado warning. More than one person also suggested I drop my dad's old truck off at the salvage yard before he gets home from vacation. But it's a good thing he has it. The truck is the only vehicle that has enough room so I can drive with my left foot."

"You went to so much trouble. A phone call would've been fine."

He motioned to her nephew. "Not for him."

A big grin brightened Connor's face. The heartache of the last few weeks seemed to have vanished. He looked happy and carefree, the way a nine-year-old boy should be.

Words didn't seem enough, but gratitude was all Lucy could afford to give Ryland. "Thank you."

"Watch this," Connor said.

"I'm watching," Ryland said, sounding amused.

Her nephew juggled the ball. His face, a portrait in concentration.

"Keep it going," Ryland encouraged.

"You're all he's talked about for the last two days," she said quietly. "I'm so happy you're here. I mean, Connor's happy. We're both happy."

"That makes three of us," Ryland said.

"Did you find a coach for the Defeeters?" Connor asked.

"Not a head coach, but someone who can help out for now."

"I knew it!" Connor screamed loud enough for the entire town to hear. The ball bounced into the hedge again.

Ryland had done his part, more than Lucy had expected. Warmth flowed through her. Not good. She shouldn't feel anything where he was concerned. She wanted him to give his talk to the team ASAP so she could say goodbye. "Thanks."

"So who's going to help coach us?" Connor asked eagerly.

Ryland smiled, a charming lopsided grin that made her remember the boy he used to be, the one she'd fallen head over heels for when she'd been a teenager.

"I am," he said.

CHAPTER FOUR

THE NEXT WEEK, on Monday afternoon, Ryland walked through the parking lot at Wicksburg Elementary School. Playing soccer here was one of the few good memories he had of the place.

He hoped today's soccer practice went well. He was looking forward to spending time with Lucy, and as for the boys...how hard could it be to coach a bunch of eight- and nine-year-olds?

Ryland adjusted the strap of the camp-chair bag resting on his left shoulder. He hated the idea of sitting during any portion of the practice, but standing for an entire hour wouldn't be good if his foot started hurting.

Healing was his number-one priority. He had to be smart about helping the Defeeters. Not only because of his foot. His agent and the Fuego's front office might not consider a pseudo coaching gig "laying low." He'd sent an email to all the boys' parents explaining the importance of keeping his presence with the team quiet.

A car door slammed.

He glanced in the direction of the sound. Lucy's head appeared above the roof of a car.

Ryland hoped she was happier to see him today. The uncertainty in her eyes when he'd said he would help with the Defeeters had surprised him. When he explained no one else wanted to coach, so he'd decided to do it himself, a resigned smile settled on her lips. But she hadn't looked happy or relieved about the news.

He'd wanted a challenge. It appeared he'd gotten one.

She bent over, disappearing from his sight, then reappeared. Another door shut.

Her strawberry-blond curls bounced. His fingers itched to see if the strands felt as silky as they looked.

Lucy stepped out from between two cars with a bag of equipment in one hand and a binder in the other. She was alone.

He hoped her nephew wasn't sick. At least Lucy had shown up.

That made Ryland happy. So did the spring weather. He gave a quiet thanks for the warm temperature. Lucy had ditched the baggy hoodies she'd worn at his parents' house and at Aaron's. Her sweatshirts and pants had been hiding treasures.

Her outfit today showed off her figure to perfection. A green T-shirt stretched tight across her chest. Her breasts were round and high, in proportion and natural looking. Navy shorts accentuated the length of her legs. Firm and sexy. Ryland preferred the pale skin color to the orangey fake tan some women had.

Little Lucy Martin was a total hottie. Ryland grinned. Coaching the Defeeters was looking better and better.

Her gaze caught his. She pressed her lips together in a thin, tight line.

Busted. He'd been staring at her body. Practically leering. Guilt lodged in his throat.

A twinge of disappointment ran through him, too. Her reaction made one thing clear. She no longer had a crush on him.

He wasn't surprised. Crushes came and went. Over a decade had passed since they knew each other as kids. But Ryland didn't get why Lucy looked so unhappy to see him. If not for him, she would be on her own coaching the boys. He didn't expect her to fall at his feet, but a smile—even a hint of one—would have been nice.

She glanced toward the grass field.

He half expected her to walk away from him, but instead she headed toward him. Progress? He hoped so. "Hello."

"Hi," she said.

"Where's Connor?"

"He went home from school with a boy from the team. They should be here soon."

"A playdate and the first practice of spring. Connor is a lucky kid."

"I wanted to make today special for him."

"You have." Ryland liked how Lucy did so much for her nephew, but she seemed to give, give, give. He wondered if she ever did anything for herself. Maybe that was how he could get on her good side. "The first practice is always interesting. Getting to know a new coach. Sizing up who has improved over the break. Making friends with new teammates. At least that's how I remember it."

"All I know is Connor has been looking forward to this for weeks," she said. "He's been writing letters and sending emails to Aaron and Dana counting down the days to the start of practice, but they must be somewhere without computer access. They haven't replied the past couple of days."

That didn't sound good. "Worried?"

Lucy shrugged but couldn't hide the anxiousness in her eyes. "Aaron said this could happen. Connor just wants to hear what his dad thinks about you working with the team."

She hadn't answered Ryland's question about being worried, but he let it go. "I hope I live up to Connor's expectations."

"You really don't have to do this."

"I don't mind showing up early to practice."

"I was talking about coaching."

That wasn't what he'd expected her to say, but Lucy didn't

seem to mince words. She also wore her heart on her sleeve. He didn't like seeing the tight lines around her mouth and narrowed eyes. He wanted to put her at ease. "It might be the last thing I expected to be doing while I'm in Wicksburg. But I want to do this for Aaron and his son."

For Lucy, too. But Ryland figured saying that would only upset her more.

"What if someone finds out?" she asked.

That thought had crossed his mind many times over the past few days. Someone outside the team would recognize him at some point and most likely wouldn't be able to keep quiet.

But he was a man who took chances.

Besides, how much trouble could he get into helping a bunch of kids? Community involvement was a good thing, surely? "I'll deal with that if it happens, but remember, I'm not coaching. I'm only helping."

A carefully laid out distinction that made a world of difference. At least he hoped so.

He waited for her to say something, to rattle off a list of reasons why his assisting the Defeeters was a bad idea or to tell him she'd found someone else to coach the team.

Instead, she raised the bag of equipment—balls and orange cones—in the air. "I picked up the practice gear. I also have a binder with emergency and player information."

Interesting. He'd expected her to put up more of a fight. He'd kind of been looking forward to it. When Lucy got emotional, silvery sparks flashed in her irises. He liked her blue eyes. And the rest of her, too. "Thanks."

"So what do you want to do with the cones?" she asked. "I've never been to a soccer practice before."

This was why Ryland wanted—no, needed—to help. He wouldn't be working only with the kids. He would be teaching Lucy what to do so she'd be all set when fall season rolled around. He didn't want the Defeeters split up as a team in September because they didn't have a coach for fall league. That wouldn't be good for the boys or for Aaron when he returned home. Lucy might end up feeling bad, too. "I'll show you."

With Lucy at his side, Ryland stepped from the asphalt onto the field. The smell of fresh grass filled his nostrils, the scent as intoxicating as a woman's perfume. He inhaled to take another sniff. Anticipation zinged through him, bringing all his nerve endings to life.

Neither soccer nor women had been part of his life since his foot surgery. He shot a sideward glance at Lucy. At least one of them would be now. Well, sort of.

"It's good to be back," he said, meaning it.

"In town?" she asked.

"On this field." For the last eleven years, no matter what level he played, soccer had meant packed stadiums, cheering crowds and vuvuzelas being blown. Shirtless men with painted faces and chests stood in the stands. Women with tight, tiny tops wanted body parts autographed. Smiling, he motioned to the field in front of him. "It doesn't matter whether I'm at an elementary school for a practice or at a sold-out stadium for a World Cup game. This is...home."

A dreamy expression formed on Lucy's face.

He stared captivated wondering what she was thinking about.

"I felt that way about this loft in Chicago." The tone of her voice matched the wistfulness in her eyes. "They rented studio space by the hour. The place smelled like paint and thinner, but that made it even more perfect. I couldn't afford to rent time that often, but when I did, I'd stay until the last second."

All the tension disappeared from around her mouth and forehead. Joy lit up her pretty face.

Warmth flowed though his veins. This was how Lucy should always look.

"Do you have a place to work on your art here?" he asked, his voice thick.

"No. It's just something I pursue in my spare time. I don't

have much of that right now between Connor and my graphic-design business."

He didn't like how she brushed aside her art when talking about the studio loft made her so happy. "If you enjoy it…"

"I enjoy spending time with Connor." She glanced at her watch. "We should get ready for the boys to arrive."

Ryland would have rather found out more about her art and her. But he still had time.

"So the cones?" she asked again.

Her practical, down-to-business attitude didn't surprise him, but he was amused. He couldn't wait to break through her hard shell. "How do you think they should be set up?"

She raised her chin slightly. "You tell me. You're the coach."

"Officially, you are." Lucy had listed herself as the head coach with the league, which kept Ryland's name off the coach's list and league website. Besides, he wouldn't be here for the whole season. "I'm your helper."

"I may be listed as the head coach," she said. "But unofficially, as long as you're here to help, my most important job is to put together the snack list."

"That job is almost as important as coaching. Snacks after the game were my favorite part of rec. soccer."

Though now that Ryland had seen her go-on-forever legs, he might have to rethink that. A mole on the inside of her calf just above her ankle drew his attention. He wondered what her skin would taste like.

"Ryland…"

Lucy's voice startled him. He forced his gaze onto her face.

Annoyance filled her blue eyes, but no silver sparks flashed. "The cones."

Damn. He'd been caught staring twice now, but all her skin showing kept taking him by surprise. He wondered how she'd look in a bikini or…naked. Pretty good, he imagined. Though thinking about Lucy without any clothes on wasn't a smart idea.

He needed to focus on the practice. "Two vertical lines with a horizontal connecting them at the top. Five cones on each side."

She dropped the equipment bag on the grass. "While I do that, set up your chair and take the weight off your foot. You don't want anything to slow down your recovery."

And your departure from town. The words may not have been spoken, but they were clearly implied.

Before he could say anything, she walked away, hips swaying, curls bouncing.

Too bad she was out-of-bounds.

Ryland removed his chair from the bag and opened it up. But he didn't sit. His foot didn't hurt.

He ran over the practice in his mind. His injury would keep him from teaching by example. He needed someone with two working feet to show the boys what needed to be done. Someone like…

"Lucy."

"Just a minute." She placed the last cone on the grass. "What do you need?"

You. Too bad that wasn't possible. But a brilliant albeit somewhat naughty idea formed in his mind. "I'm going to need you to show the boys what to do during warm-ups and drills."

Her eyes widened. "I've never done anything like this before. I have no idea what you want me to do."

Ryland wanted her. It was as simple as that. Or would be if circumstances were different. "I'll show you."

"O-kay."

Her lack of enthusiasm made him smile. "It's soccer not a walk down death row."

"Maybe not from your point of view," she said. "Show me."

"I want the boys to do a dynamic warm-up," he explained. "They'll break up into two groups. One half will go on the outside of the cones, the other half on the inside. Each time around they'll do something different to warm up their muscles."

"That sounds complicated."

"It's easy."

"Maybe for a pro soccer star."

Star, huh? He was surprised she thought of him that way. But he liked it. "Easy for a nine-year-old, too."

She followed him to the cones.

"The first lap I want you to jog around the outside of the cones."

"The boys know how to do that."

"I want them to see how to do it the right way."

Ryland watched her jog gracefully around the cones.

"Now what?" she asked.

"Backward."

She walked over to the starting point and went around the cones backward.

Each time he told her what to do, whether skipping and jumping at each cone or reaching down to pull up the toe of her tennis shoe. A charming pink colored her cheeks from her efforts. Her breasts jiggled from the movement.

This had to be one of his best ideas ever. Ryland grinned wickedly, pleased with himself. "Face the cones and shuffle sideward."

She did something that looked like a step from the Electric Slide or some other line dance popular at wedding receptions.

"Let me help you." He walked over, kneeled on his good leg and touched her left calf. The muscles tightened beneath his palms. But her skin felt as soft as it looked. Smooth, too. "Relax. I'm not going to hurt you."

"That's what they all say," she muttered.

Ryland had no idea what she meant or who "they all" might be, but he wanted to find out.

"Bring your foot to the other one, instead of crossing the leg behind." He raised her boot off the ground and brought it over to the other foot. "Like this."

Her cheeks reddened more. "You could have just told me."

He stood. "Yeah, but this way is more fun."

"Depends on your definition of fun."

Lucy shuffled around the cones.

Ryland enjoyed watching her. This was as close as he'd gotten to a female, next to the housecleaner his mom had hired while she was away. Mrs. Henshaw was old enough to be his mother.

"Anything else?" Lucy asked when she'd finished.

There was more, but he didn't want to do too many new things at the first practice. Both for Lucy's and the boys' sakes.

"A few drills." The sound of boys' laughter drifted on the air. "I'll show you those when the time comes. The team is here."

"Nervous?"

"They're kids," Ryland said. "No reason to be nervous."

Lucy studied him. "Ever spend much time with eight- and nine-year-olds?"

Not unless you counted signing autographs, posing for photographs and walking into stadiums holding their hands. "No, but I was a kid once."

She raised an arched brow. "Once."

He winked.

Lucy smiled.

Something passed between them. Something unexpected and unwelcome. Uh-oh.

A loud burp erupted from behind them followed by laughter.

Whatever was happening with Lucy came to an abrupt end. Good, because whatever connection Ryland had felt with her wasn't something he wanted. Flirting was one thing, but this couldn't turn into a quick roll in the sheets. He couldn't afford to let that happen while he was here in Wicksburg. "The Defeeters have arrived."

Lucy looked toward the parking lot. "Aaron told me coaching this age is a lot like herding cats," Lucy explained. "Except that cats don't talk back."

Another burp sounded. More laughter followed.

"Or burp," Ryland said.

As she nodded, boys surrounded them. He'd played in big

games in front of millions of people, but the expectant look in these kids' eyes disconcerted him, making him feel as if he was stepping onto the pitch for the very first time.

"Hey, boys. I'm Ryland." He focused on the eager faces staring up at him, not wanting to disappoint them or Lucy. "I'm going to help out for a few games. You boys ready to play some football?"

Nine—or was it ten?—heads, ranging in size and hair color, nodded enthusiastically.

Great. Ryland grinned. This wouldn't be difficult at all.

A short kid with long blond hair scrunched his nose. "This isn't football."

"Everywhere else in the world soccer is called football," Ryland explained.

The kid didn't look impressed. "It's called soccer here."

"We'll talk more about that later." Soccer in America was nothing like soccer in other parts of the world. No sport in the U.S. could compare with the passion for the game elsewhere. "I want you to tell me your name and how long you've played."

Each boy did. Justin. Jacob. Dalton. Tyler. Marco. The names ran into each other. Ryland wasn't going to be able to remember them. No worries. Calling them dude, bud and kid would work for today. "Let's get working."

"Can you teach us how to dive?" a boy with beach-blond hair that hung over his eyes asked.

Some soccer players dived—throwing themselves on the field and pretending to be hurt—to draw a penalty during the game. "No," Ryland said firmly. "Never dive."

"What if it's the World Cup?" a kid with a crew cut asked.

"If you're playing in the World Cup, you'll know what to do." Ryland clapped his hands together. "Time to warm up."

The boys stood in place.

He knew the warm-up routine, and so did his Fuego teammates, but based on these kids' puzzled looks, they hadn't a clue what he was talking about. "Get in a single-file line behind the first cone on the left side."

The boys shuffled into place, but it wasn't a straight line. Two kids elbowed each other as they jockeyed for the spot in front of Connor. A couple kids in the middle tried to trip each other. The boys in the back half didn't seem to understand the meaning of a line and spread out.

This wasn't working out the way he'd planned. Ryland dragged his hand through his hair.

"Meow," Lucy whispered.

"So where can I find a cat herder?" he asked.

Her coy smile sent his pulse racing. "Look in the mirror. Didn't you know cat herder is synonymous with coach?"

"That's what I was afraid you'd say."

The hour flew by. Lucy stood next to Ryland on a mini-field he'd had her set up using cones. She hadn't known what to expect with the boys' first practice, but she begrudgingly gave him credit. The guy could coach.

After a rocky start, he'd harnessed the boys' energy with warm-up exercises and drills. He never once raised his voice. He didn't have to. His excitement about the game mesmerized both the boys and Lucy. Out on the field, he seemed larger-than-life, sexier, despite the boot on his foot. Thank goodness practice was only sixty minutes, twice a week. That was more than enough time in his presence. Maybe even too much.

Ryland focused on the boys, but her gaze kept straying to him. The man was so hot. She tried hard to remain unaffected. But it wasn't easy, especially when she couldn't forget how it felt when he'd moved her leg earlier.

Talk about being a hands-on coach. His touch had surprised her. But his tenderness guiding her leg had made her want... more.

And when he'd stood behind her, his hard body pressed

against her backside, helping her figure out the drills so she could show the boys...

Lucy swallowed. More wasn't possible, no matter how appealing it might sound at the moment. Being physically close to a man had felt good. She'd forgotten how good that could be. But getting involved with a guy wasn't on her list of things to do. Not when she had Connor to take care of.

"Great pass, Tyler." Ryland turned to her. "Do you know if Aaron uses set plays?"

"I have no idea," she admitted. "I have his coaching notebook if you want to look through it."

"I would. Thanks."

"I should be thanking you," she said. "The boys have learned so much from you today. More than I could have taught them over an entire season."

"I appreciate that, but you'll be ready to do this when the time comes."

She doubted that.

All but two of the boys surrounded the ball.

Ryland grimaced.

Lucy appreciated how seriously he took practice, because she needed to figure out what should be happening on the field. "Something went wrong, but I have no idea what."

He pointed to the cluster of boys. "See how the players are gathered together and focused only on the ball?"

She nodded.

"They need to spread out and play their position." He pointed to the fastest kid on the team—Dalton. "All that kid wants is the ball. Instead of playing in the center, where he should be, he's back on the left side chasing down the ball and playing defender. See how that black-haired kid, Mason—"

"Marco," she corrected.

"Yeah, Marco," Ryland said. "You've got Marco and Dalton and those other players all in the same area."

Ryland's knowledge of the game impressed her. Okay, he

was a professional soccer player. But he never stopped pointing things out to her and helping the boys improve. She should have brought a notebook and pen so she could write down everything he said. It was like being enrolled at Soccer University and this was Basic Ball Skills 101. She, however, didn't feel like she had the prerequisites to attend.

"So what do you do?" she asked.

Ryland raised the silver whistle around his neck. "This."

As he blew the whistle, she wondered what his lips would feel like against her skin. Probably as good as his hands. Maybe even better.

Stop thinking about it.

The boys froze.

"This isn't bunch ball," Ryland said. "Don't chase the ball. Spread out. Play your position. Try again."

The boys did.

Ryland directed them to keep them from bunching again. He clapped when they did something right and corrected them when they made mistakes.

As she watched Ryland coach, warmth pooled inside Lucy. She forced her gaze back on the boys.

The play on the field reminded her of an accordion. Sometimes the boys were spread out. Other times they came together around the ball.

"Will telling them fix the problem?" she asked.

"No. They're still very young. But they'll start realizing what they're supposed to do," he said. "Only practice and game time will make the lesson stick."

Lucy wondered if that was what it took to become a competent coach. She had a feeling she would be doing her best just to get by.

The energy on the field intensified. Connor passed the ball to Dalton who shot the ball over the goalie's head. Goal!

"Yes!" Ryland shouted. "That's how you do it."

The boys gave each other high fives.

"That score was made possible by Connor moving to a space. He has good instincts just like his dad." Ryland's smile crinkled the corners of his eyes.

Her pulse quickened. "Wish you could be out there playing?"

He shrugged. "I always want to play, but being here sure beats sitting on my dad's easy chair with a dog on my lap."

His comment about his dad made Lucy look toward the parking lot. A line of parents waited to pick up their boys. She glanced at her watch. Uh-oh. She'd lost track of the time. "Practice ended five minutes ago."

"That was fast." Ryland blew the whistle again. "I want everyone to jog around the field to cool down. Don't run, just a nice easy pace."

The boys took off, some faster than the others.

"The team did well," Ryland said to her.

"So did you."

He straightened. "This is different from what I'm used to."

"You rose to the occasion." Lucy couldn't have worked the boys like he had. She usually preferred doing things on her own. But she needed Ryland's help with the team. Thank goodness she'd listened to Connor and taken a chance by going to see Ryland. "I learned a lot. And the boys had fun."

"Soccer is all about having fun when you're eight and nine."

"What about when you're twenty-nine?" she asked, curious about his life back in Phoenix.

"There are some added pressures and demands, but no complaints," he said. "I'm living the dream."

"Not many can say that." She sure couldn't, but maybe someday. Nah, best not to get her hopes up only to be disappointed. "Aaron says you worked hard to get where you are."

"That's nice of him. But it's amazing what being motivated can do for a kid."

"You wanted to play professionally."

"I wanted to get out of Wicksburg," he admitted. "I didn't have good grades because I liked kicking a ball more than studying so that messed up any chance of getting a football scholarship."

Football? She was about to ask when she remembered what he'd said at the beginning of practice. Soccer was called football overseas. That was where he'd spent the majority of his career. "Small-town boy who made it big."

"That was the plan from the beginning."

His wide smile sent her heart beating triple time. Lucy didn't understand her response. "I'd say you succeeded splendidly."

Whereas she... Lucy didn't want to go there. But she knew someone successful like Ryland would never be satisfied living in a small, boring town like Wicksburg. He must be counting the weeks, maybe even the days, until he could escape back to the big city. While she would remain here as long as she was needed.

As the boys jogged toward them, Ryland gave each one a high five. "Nice work out there. Practice your juggling at home. Learning to control the ball will make you a better player. Now gather up the cones and balls so we can get out of here. I don't know about you, but I'm hungry."

The boys scattered in search of balls like mice looking for bits of cheese. They dribbled the balls back. Lucy placed them inside the mesh bag. The boys picked up their water bottles then walked off the field to their parents.

Connor's megawatt smile could light up half of Indiana. "That was so much fun."

"You played hard out there," Ryland said.

Her nephew shot her a quick glance. "All that running made me hungry, too."

"I've got dinner in the slow cooker," Lucy said.

"Want to eat with us, Ryland?" Connor asked. "Aunt Lucy always makes enough food so we can have leftovers."

Spending more time with Ryland seemed like a bad idea, but she was more concerned about Connor. She couldn't always shield him from disappointment, but with him adjusting to his parents being away, she wanted to limit it. "That's nice of you to think of Ryland. We have enough food to share, but I'm sure he has somewhere else to be tonight."

There, she'd given Ryland an easy out from the dinner invitation. No one's feelings would be hurt.

"I'm free tonight," he said to her dismay. "But I wouldn't want to intrude."

"You're not." Connor looked at Lucy for verification.

She was still stuck on Ryland being free tonight. She figured he would have a date, maybe two, lined up. Unless he had a girlfriend back in Phoenix.

"Tell him it's okay, Aunt Lucy." Her nephew was using his lost puppy-dog look to his full advantage. "Ryland's coaching the team. The least we can do is feed him."

"You sound like your mom." Lucy's resolve weakened. "She's always trying to feed everyone."

Connor nodded. "That's how we ended up with Manny. Mom kept putting tuna out for him. One day he came inside and never left."

Ryland smiled. "He sounds like a smart cat."

"We call him Manny, but his full name is Manchester," Connor said.

Amusement filled Ryland's eyes. "After the Red Devils."

Connor nodded. "Man U rules."

"If Manny was a girl, I'm guessing you wouldn't have named her Chelsea."

Connor looked aghast. "Never."

Ryland grinned. "At least I know where your loyalties lie."

"I have no idea what you're talking about," Lucy admitted.

"Manchester United and Chelsea are teams in the Premier League in England," Ryland explained.

"Rivals," Connor added. "Can Ryland come over, please?"

Lucy could rattle off ten reasons not to have him over, but she had a bigger reason to say yes—Connor.

"You're welcome to join us." If Lucy didn't agree, she would never hear the end of it from her nephew. Besides, she liked how he smiled whenever Ryland was around. It was one meal. No big deal. "We have plenty of food."

"Thanks," he said. "I'm getting tired of grilling."

Connor's eyes widened. "You cook?"

"If I don't cook, I don't eat," Ryland explained. "When I moved to England, I had to cook, clean and do my own laundry. Just like my mom made me do when I was growing up."

His words surprised Lucy. She would have expected a big-shot soccer star to have a personal chef or eat out all the time, not be self-sufficient around the house. Her Jeff, her ex-husband, did nothing when it came to domestic chores.

"I'll have to learn how to do those things," Connor said with a serious expression.

"You're on your way," Ryland encouraged. "You already make great chocolate-chip cookies."

Connor's thin chest puffed slightly. "Yeah, I do."

Lucy shook her head. "You're supposed to say thank you when someone compliments you."

"Even if it's true?" Connor asked.

Ryland's smiled widened. "Especially then."

Connor shrugged. "Okay. Thank you."

Having Ryland over was exactly what Connor needed. But a part of her wondered if it was what she needed, too.

Now that was silly.

Ryland was coming over for dinner because of her nephew. Just because she might like the idea of being around him a little longer didn't mean anything at all.

CHAPTER FIVE

IN THE KITCHEN, the smell of spices, vegetables and beef simmering in the slow cooker lingered in the air. The scents brought back fond memories of family dinners with Aaron and her parents. But other than the smell, tonight wasn't going to be as comfortable as any of those dinners growing up.

Lucy checked the oven. Almost preheated to the correct temperature.

Ryland had heated her up earlier. She couldn't stop thinking about how he'd touched her at practice. His large, warm hand against her skin. Leaning against the counter, she sighed.

The guy really was...

She bolted upright.

Lucy needed to stop fantasizing and finish making dinner. She was a divorced twenty-six-year-old, not a swooning teenager. She knew better than to be crushing on any man, let alone Ryland James. The guy could charm the pants off everybody. Well, everyone except for her.

She placed the uncooked biscuits on a cookie sheet.

The sounds of laser beams from a video game and laughter

from all the fun drifted into the kitchen. Ryland's laugh was deep and rich, thick and smooth, like melted dark chocolate.

Lucy opened the oven door and slid the tray of biscuits onto the middle rack. Would he taste as good as he sounded?

The pan clattered against the back of the oven.

"Need help?" Ryland yelled from the living room.

Annoyed at herself for thinking about *him* that way when she knew better, she straightened the pan then closed the oven door. "Everything's fine."

Or would be when he was gone.

Okay, that wasn't fair. Connor was laughing and having fun. Her nephew needed Ryland, so did the team. That meant she needed him, too.

Watching a couple of videos and reading some books weren't the same as having Ryland show her what needed to be done at practice. The boys would have been the ones to suffer because of her cluelessness. Feeding Ryland dinner was the least she could do to repay him. It wasn't as if she'd had to go to any extra trouble preparing the meal.

Nor was it Ryland's fault he was gorgeous and seemed to press every single one of her buttons. Being around him reminded her that a few of the male species had redeeming qualities. Ones like killer smiles, sparkling eyes, enticing muscles, warm hands and a way with kids. But she knew better than to let herself get carried away.

"I'm going to win," Connor shouted with glee.

"Not so fast," Ryland countered. "I'm not dead yet."

"Just you wait."

The challenge in her nephew's voice loosened her tight shoulder muscles. Boys needed a male influence in their lives. Even if that influence filled her stomach with butterflies whenever he was nearby.

No worries, Lucy told herself. She hadn't been around men for a while. That had to be the reason for her reaction to Ryland.

She tossed the salad. The oven timer buzzed.

With the food on the table, she stood in the doorway to the kitchen with a container of milk in one hand and a pitcher of iced tea in the other. "Dinner's ready."

Connor took his normal seat. He pointed to a chair across, the one next to where Lucy had been sitting since she arrived a month ago. The "guest spots" at the table. "Sit there, Ryland. The other chairs are my mom's and dad's."

Ryland sat. The table seemed smaller with him there, even though it seated six.

Ignoring her unease, Lucy filled everyone's glasses. She sat, conscious of him next to her.

Her leg brushed his. Lucy stiffened. The butterflies in her stomach flapped furiously. She tucked her feet beneath her chair to keep from touching Ryland again. Next time...

There wouldn't be a next time.

Her nephew grabbed two biscuits off the plate. "These are my favorite."

Ryland took one. "Everything smells delicious."

The compliment made Lucy straighten. She hadn't cooked much after the divorce so felt out of practice. But Connor needed healthy meals so she was getting back in the habit. "Thanks."

As she dished up the stew, Ryland filled his salad plate using a pair of silver tongs. His arm brushed hers. Heat emanated from the spot of contact. "Excuse me."

"That's okay." But the tingles shooting up her arm weren't. Lucy hated the way her body reacted to even the slightest contact with him. She pressed her elbows against her sides. No more touching.

Flatware clinked against bowls and plates. Ryland and Connor discussed the upcoming MLS season. She recognized some of the team names, but nothing else.

"Who's your favorite team?" Ryland asked her.

She moved a carrot around with her fork. Stew was one of her favorite dishes, but she wasn't hungry. Her lack of appetite occurred at the same time as Ryland's arrival at the house. "The only soccer games I watch are Connor's."

"That was when you lived here with Uncle Jeff," Connor said. "After you moved away you didn't come to any."

"That's true." Curiosity gleamed in Ryland's eyes, but she ignored it. She didn't want to discuss her ex-husband over dinner or in front of Connor. No matter how badly Jeff had betrayed her and their marriage vows, he'd been a good uncle and still sent Connor birthday and Christmas presents. "But I'll get to see all your games now."

Lucy reached for the salt. Extra seasoning might make the stew more appealing. She needed to eat something or she'd find herself starving later. That had happened a lot when she moved to Chicago. She didn't want a repeat performance here.

Ryland's hand covered hers around the saltshaker.

She stiffened.

He smiled. "Great minds think alike."

Too bad she couldn't think. Not with his large, warm hand on top of hers.

Darn the man. Ryland must know he was hot stuff. But he'd better think twice before he put any moves on her. She pulled her hand away, leaving the salt for him.

Ryland handed the shaker to her. "You had it first."

Lucy added salt to her stew. "Thanks."

"I forgot to tell you, Aunt Lucy. Tyler got a puppy," Connor said, animated. "His parents took him to the animal shelter, and Tyler got to pick the dog out himself." Connor relayed the entire story, including how the dog went potty on the floor in the kitchen as soon as they arrived home. "I bet Manny would like to have a dog. That way he'd never be lonely."

Oh, no. Lucy knew exactly where her nephew was going with this. Connor had used a similar tactic to get her to buy him a new video game. But buying an inanimate object was different than a living, breathing puppy.

"Manny is rarely alone." She passed the saltshaker to Ryland. "I work from home."

Connor's forehead wrinkled, as if he were surprised she hadn't said yes right away. "But you don't chase him around the house. When I'm at school he just lays around and sleeps."

Ryland feigned shock. "You don't chase Manny?"

Lucy wanted to chase Ryland out of here. She hated how aware she was of him. Her blood simmered. She drank some iced tea, but that didn't cool her down. "Cats lay around and sleep. That's what they like to do during the day. I don't think Manny is going to be too keen on being chased by a dog. He's not a kitten anymore."

"Don't forget. Dogs make big messes outside," Ryland said. "You're going to have to clean it all up with a shovel or rake."

Connor scrunched his face. "I'm going to have to scoop up the poop?"

Okay, maybe having Ryland here wasn't so bad. She appreciated how skillfully he'd added a dose of dog-care reality to the conversation. He might make her a little hot and bothered, but he'd saved her a lot of back and forth by bringing up the mess dogs left in the yard. A fair trade-off in the grand scheme of things. At least she hoped so.

"Yes, you would have to do that." No matter how badly Connor wanted a puppy she couldn't make that decision without Aaron and Dana. Getting a pet wasn't a commitment to make lightly. "A dog is something your parents have to decide on, not me. Owning a dog is a big responsibility."

"Huge," Ryland agreed, much to Lucy's relief. "I've been taking care of my parents' dog Cupcake. I never knew something so little would take so much work. She either wants food or attention or to go outside on a walk."

"I've never taken a dog on a walk," Connor said.

"Maybe you could take Cupcake for a walk for me," Ryland suggested.

Connor nodded enthusiastically. "If it's okay with Aunt Lucy."

The longing in his blue eyes tugged at her heart. She couldn't say no to this request, even if it meant seeing Ryland outside of soccer again. "I'm sure we can figure out a time to take Cupcake for a walk."

"You can get a glimpse of what having a dog is like," Ryland said. "It might also be a good idea to see what Manny thinks of Cupcake. Cats and dogs don't always get along."

His words were exactly what a nine-year-old dog-wannabe owner needed to hear. The guy was turning into a knight in a shining soccer jersey. She would owe him dozens of chocolate-chip cookies for all he was doing for Connor.

Ryland smiled at her.

A feeling of warmth traveled from the top of her head to the tips of her toes. She'd better be careful or she was going to turn into a pile of goo. That would not be good.

"Did you ever have a dog?" Connor asked her.

"No, but we had cats and a few other animals," she replied. "Fish, a bird and reptiles."

As Ryland set his iced tea on the table, she bit into a biscuit. "Has your aunt told you about Squiggy?"

Lucy choked on the bread. She coughed and swallowed. "You remember Squiggy?"

Mischief danced in his eyes. "It's a little hard to forget being asked to dig a grave and then rob it on the same day."

Connor's mouth formed a perfect O. "You robbed a grave?"

"Your dad and I did," Ryland said. "It was Squiggy's grave."

Connor leaned forward. "Who's Squiggy?"

Ryland winked at her.

Oh, no. He wouldn't tell… Who was she kidding? The mischievous gleam in his eyes was a dead giveaway he would spill every last detail. Might as well get it over with.

"Squiggy was my turtle. He was actually a tortoise," she explained. "But Squiggy was…"

"The best turtle in the galaxy," Ryland finished for her. "The fastest, too."

Lucy stared at him in disbelief. Those were the exact words she used to say to anyone who asked about her Squiggy. Other kids wanted dogs. She loved her hard-shelled, wrinkled reptile. "I can't believe you remember that."

"I told you I remembered a lot of stuff."

He had, but she thought Ryland was talking about when she'd been a teenager and sick. Not a seven-year-old girl who'd thought the sun rose and set on a beloved turtle.

"Your aunt doted on Squiggy," Ryland said. "Even painted his shell."

Lucy grinned. "Polka dots."

He nodded. "I recall pink and purple strips."

Memories rushed back like water over Cataract Falls on Mill Creek. "I'd forgotten about those."

"Your aunt used to hand-feed him lettuce. Took him on walks, too."

She nodded. "Squiggy might have been the fastest turtle around, but those walks still took forever."

"You never went very far," Ryland said.

"No, we didn't," she admitted. "Wait a minute. How did you know that?"

His smile softened. "Your mom had us watch you."

Her mother, make that her entire family, had always been so overprotective. Lucy had no idea they'd dragged Ryland into it, too. "And you guys accused me of following you around."

"You did follow us."

"Okay, I did, but that's what little sisters do."

Connor reached for his milk glass. "I wouldn't want a little sister."

"I never had a little sister," Ryland said. "But it felt like I had one with Lucy spying on us all the time."

She stuck her tongue out at him.

He did the same back to her.

Connor giggled.

Sitting here with Ryland brought back so many memories. When she was younger, she used to talk to him whenever he was over at the house with Aaron. Puberty and her crush had changed that. The awkward, horrible time of hormones and illness were all she'd remembered. Until now.

"Why did you have to rob Squiggy's grave?" Connor asked him.

Ryland stared into her eyes. His warm hazel gaze seemed to pierce through her. Breaking contact was the smart thing to do, but Lucy didn't want to look away.

For old times' sake, she told herself.

A voice inside her head laughed at the reasoning. A part of her didn't care. Looking was safe. It was all the other stuff that was...dangerous.

"Do you want to tell him or should I?" Ryland asked.

Emotion swirled inside her. Most of it had to do with the uncertainty she felt around him, not the story about her turtle. "Go ahead. I'm curious to hear your side of the story."

"I want to hear both sides," Connor announced.

"You will, if Ryland gets it wrong," she teased.

"I have a feeling you may be surprised," Ryland said.

She had a feeling he was right.

"Your aunt came to your dad and me with big crocodile tears streaming down her cheeks," Ryland explained. "She held a shoebox and said her beloved Squiggy had died. She wanted us to dig a hole so she could bury him."

"Before you go any further, I wanted to have a funeral, not just bury him. I would also like to remind Connor that I was only seven at the time."

Amusement gleamed in Ryland's eyes. "Age duly noted."

Connor inched forward on his chair. "What happened?"

"Your dad and I dug a hole. A grave for Squiggy's coffin."

"Shoebox," Lucy clarified.

Ryland nodded. "She placed the shoebox into the hole and

tossed wilted dandelions on top of it. While your dad and I refilled the hole with dirt, your aunt Lucy played 'Taps' on a harmonica."

"Kazoo," she corrected. Still, she couldn't believe all he remembered after so many years.

"A few words were spoken."

"From my favorite book at the time, *Franklin in the Dark*," she said.

"Who is Franklin?" Connor asked.

"A turtle from a series of children's books," Lucy explained. "It was turned into a cartoon that was shown on television."

"Aaron said a brief prayer," Ryland said. "Then your aunt stuck a tombstone made of Popsicle sticks into the ground and sprinkled more dandelions over the mound of dirt."

Lucy nodded. "It was a lovely funeral."

"Yeah," Ryland said. "Until you told us that Squiggy wasn't actually dead, and we had to unbury him so he wouldn't die."

Connor stared at her as if she were a short, green extra-terrestrial with laser beams for eyes. "You think some video games are too violent and you buried a live turtle?"

She squirmed under his intense scrutiny. "Some games aren't appropriate for nine-year-olds. And nothing bad happened to Squiggy."

Fortunately. What had she been thinking? Maybe burying Barbie dolls had gotten too boring.

Ryland grinned. "But it was a race against time."

She had to laugh. "They dug so fast dirt flew everywhere."

"Aaron and I were sure we would be blamed if Squiggy died."

As her gaze collided with Ryland's again, something passed between them. A shared memory, she rationalized. That was all it could be. She looked at her untouched food. "But your dad and Ryland didn't get in trouble. They saved Squiggy."

Connor leaned over the table. "Squiggy didn't die under all that dirt?"

Ryland raised his glass. "Nope. Squiggy was alive and moving as slow as ever."

But that was the last time she'd thrown a funeral for anything living or inanimate. Her parents had made sure of that.

"So why did you bury him and have a funeral?" Connor asked.

Lucy knew this question would be coming once more of the story came out. "You know how some kids play house or restaurant?"

"Or army," Connor suggested.

She nodded. "One of the games I played was funeral."

"That's weird." Connor took another biscuit from the plate. "In school Mrs. Wilson told us turtles live longer than we do. Whatever happened to Squiggy?"

"He ran away," Lucy said. "Your dad and I grew up in a house that was near the park with that nice lake. We'd see turtles on tree trunks at the water's edge. Your dad told me Squiggy was lonely and ran away to live with the other turtles. I was sad and missed him so much, but your dad said I should be happy because Squiggy wanted to be in the park."

A beat passed. And another. Connor looked at Ryland. "So what really happened to Squiggy?"

Her mouth gaped.

A sheepish expression crossed Ryland's face.

Realization dawned. "Squiggy didn't run away."

Connor gasped. "Squiggy died!"

Ryland nodded once, but his gaze never left hers. "I thought you'd figured out what happened."

She'd been so quick to believe Aaron… Of course she'd wanted to believe it. "I never thought something bad might have happened to Squiggy."

"I'm sorry." The sincerity in Ryland's voice rang clear, but the knowledge still stung. "Aaron didn't want to put you through a real funeral because he knew how much Squiggy meant to you so we buried him one night in the park after you went to bed."

Lucy had imagined the adventures Squiggy had experienced at the pond. But the lie didn't surprise her. Few told her the truth once she'd gotten sick. It must have been the same way before she was so ill. "I should have figured that out."

"You were young," Ryland said. "There's nothing wrong with believing something if it makes us happy."

"Even if it's a lie?" she asked.

"A white lie so you wouldn't hurt so badly," he countered. "You know Aaron always watched out for you back then."

That much was true. Lucy nodded.

"My dad told me it's important to look out for others, especially girls." Connor scrunched his nose as if that last word smelled bad.

"He's right," Ryland said. "That's what your dad was doing with your aunt when Squiggy died. It's what he always did and probably still does with her and your mom."

Connor sat taller. "I'll have to do the same."

Ryland looked as proud of her nephew as she felt. "We all should," he said.

Her heart thudded. The guy was a charmer, but he sounded genuine.

But then so had Jeff, she reminded herself.

The harsh reality clarified the situation. She needed to rein in her emotions ASAP. Thinking of Ryland as anything other than the Defeeters' coaching assistant was not only dangerous but also stupid. She wasn't about to risk her heart with someone like that again.

She scooted back in her chair. "Who's ready for dessert?"

While Lucy tucked Connor back into bed, Ryland stared at the framed photographs sitting on the fireplace mantel. Each picture showed a different stage in Aaron's life—army, marriage, family, college graduation. Those things were as foreign to Ryland as a three-hundred-pound American football linebacker trying to tackle him as he ran toward the goal.

Footsteps sounded behind him. "I think Connor's down for the count this time," Lucy said.

Finally. The kid was cool and knew a lot about soccer, but he hadn't left them alone all evening. Twice now Connor had gotten out of bed after they'd said good-night. "Third time's the charm."

"I hope so."

Ryland did, too. A repeat performance of today's practice with some touching would be nice, especially if she touched back. Having a little fun wouldn't hurt anyone. No one, not Mr. McElroy or Blake or Ryland's mom, would have to know what went on here tonight.

She sat on the couch. "Looking at Aaron's pictures?"

"Yeah." Ryland ran his fingertip along the top of a black wood frame, containing a picture of Aaron and Connor fishing. That was something fathers and sons did in Wicksburg. "Aaron's looks haven't changed that much, but he seems like quite the family guy."

Many professional players had a wife, kids and pets. When Ryland first started playing overseas, he hadn't wanted to let anything get in the way of his new soccer career and making a name for himself. He'd been a young, hungry hotshot.

Wait a minute. He still was. Only maybe not quite so young...

"It's hard to believe Aaron's only thirty. He's done a lot for his age," Lucy said with a touch of envy in her voice. "You both have."

Ryland shrugged. "I'm a year younger and have four, maybe five, years left to play if I'm lucky."

"That's not long."

Teams used up and threw away players. But he wasn't ready for that to happen to him. He also didn't want to hang on past his time and be relegated to a few minutes of playing time or be on a team in a lower league. "That's why I want to make the most of the time I have left in the game."

"Soccer is your priority."

"It's my life." He stared at Aaron's wedding picture. Knowing someone was there to come home to must be nice, but he'd made the decision not to divide his focus. Soccer was it. Sometimes Ryland felt a sense of loneliness even when surrounded by people. But occasionally feeling lonely wasn't a reason to get involved in a serious relationship. "That's why I won't start thinking about settling down until my career is over with."

"Playing the field might be hard to give up," she commented.

"Is that the voice of experience talking?"

"Someone I knew," she said. "That's not my type of…game."

A picture of Aaron wearing fatigues and holding a big rifle caught Ryland's attention. His old friend might consider him a foe for putting the moves on Lucy. He nudged the frame so the photo of Aaron looking big, strong and armed didn't directly face the couch.

Ryland flashed her his most charming smile. "What kind of games do you play?"

"None."

He strode to the couch. "That doesn't sound like much fun."

She shrugged. "Fun is in the eye of the beholder."

Holding her would be fun. He sat next to her.

Lucy smelled like strawberries and sunshine. Appealing and intoxicating like sweet ambrosia. He wouldn't mind a taste. But she seemed a little tense. He wanted the lines creasing her forehead to disappear so they could get comfortable and cozy. "I see lots of family photographs. Is any of your artwork here?"

"Yes."

"Show me something."

Her eyes narrowed suspiciously. "Are you asking to see my etchings?"

"I was thinking more along the lines of sketches and paintings, but if you have etchings and they happened to be in your bedroom…" he half joked.

She glanced toward the hallway he assumed led to the bedrooms. Interest twinkled in her eyes. Her pursed lips seemed to be begging for kisses. Maybe Lucy was more game than she let on.

Anticipation buzzed through him. All he needed was a sign from her to make his move. Unless she took the initiative. Now that would be a real turn-on.

Her gaze met his. "Not tonight."

Bummer. He didn't think she was playing hard to get so he had to take her words at face value. "Another time, maybe."

"I'll...see."

Her response didn't sound promising. That...bugged him. Some women would be all over him, trying to get him to kiss, touch, undress them. Lucy wanted nothing to do with him. At least outside of soccer practice.

Calling it a night would be his best move. A challenge was one thing, but there was no sense beating his head against the goalpost. He wasn't supposed to be flirting let alone wanting to kiss her. Too bad he didn't want to leave yet. "Anything I can do to help my cause?"

Her blue-eyed gaze watched him intently. "Not tonight."

Same answer as before. At least she was consistent.

Ryland stood. "It's getting late. Cupcake's been out in the dog run since before practice. She has a cushy doghouse, but she's going to be wondering where I've been. Thanks for dinner. A home-cooked meal was the last thing I was expecting tonight."

Lucy rose. "I wasn't expecting a dinner guest."

Ryland wished tonight could be ending differently, but he liked that she was honest and up-front. "We're even."

"I'd say your helping with the team outweighs my cooking dinner."

He wasn't quite ready to give up. "You could always invite me over for more meals."

Lucy raised an eyebrow. "Taking another shot?"

"Habit." A bad one under the circumstances. Not many would call him a gentleman, but Lucy deserved his respect.

"Which means it's time for me to go. Practice is at five o'clock on Wednesday, right?"

She nodded.

He took a step toward the door. "See you then."

"Ryland…"

As he looked at her, she bit her lower lip. He would like to nibble on her lip. Yeah, right. He wanted to kiss her until she couldn't breathe and was begging for more.

Not tonight.

"Thanks," she said. "For coaching. I mean, helping out with the team. And being so nice to Connor."

Her warm eyes were as appealing as her mouth. "Your nephew is a great kid."

She nodded. "Having you here is just what we…he needed."

Ryland found her slip of the tongue interesting. Maybe she wasn't as disinterested as she claimed to be. He hoped she changed whatever opinion of him was holding her back. Earning her respect ranked right up there with tasting her kisses. "Anytime."

That was often a throwaway line, but he meant it with her.

Time to get the hell out of here before he said or did anything he might regret.

Lucy was the kind of woman you took home to meet your mother. The kind of woman who dreamed of a big wedding, a house with a white picket fence and a minivan full of kids. The kind of woman he normally avoided.

Best to leave before things got complicated. His life was far from perfect with all the demands and pressures on him, unwanted media attention and isolation, but his career was on the line. What was left of it, anyway. His reputation, too.

No woman was worth messing up his life for, not even the appealing, challenging and oh-so-enticing Lucy Martin.

CHAPTER SIX

ON WEDNESDAY AFTERNOON, Lucy shaded an area on her sketch pad. The rapid movement of her pencil matched the way she felt. Agitated. Unnerved.

She'd filled half a sketch pad with drawings these past two days. An amazing feat considering she hadn't done any art since she'd left Chicago to return to Wicksburg. But she'd had to do something to take her mind off Ryland.

She took a closer look at the sketch. It was *him.* Again. If she wasn't thinking about Ryland, she was drawing him.

Lucy moved her pencil over the paper. She lengthened a few eyelashes. Women would kill for thick, luscious lashes like his. Heaven knew a tube of mascara couldn't come close to making her eyes look like that. So not fair.

Lucy shaded under his chin then raised her pencil.

Gorgeous.

Not the drawing, the man. The strength of his jaw, the flirtatious gleam in his eyes, his kissable lips.

Attraction heated her blood. What in the world was she doing drawing Ryland this way?

And then she realized…

She had another crush. But this felt different from when she'd been a teenager crushing on Ryland, stronger even than when she'd started dating her ex-husband.

Stupid.

Lucy closed the cover of her sketch pad, but every line, curve and shadow of Ryland's face was etched on her brain. She massaged her aching temples.

Connor ran from the hallway to the living room. "I'm ready for practice."

He wore his soccer clothes—blue shirt, shorts and socks with shin guards underneath. As the shoelaces from his cleats dragged on the ground, he bounced from foot to foot with excitement.

Soccer practice was the last place she wanted to go. The less time she spent with Ryland, the better. She was too old to be feeling this way about him. About any guy. But skipping out wasn't an option. She was the head coach, after all. "Let me get my purse."

On the drive, Lucy glanced in the rearview mirror. Connor sat in the backseat, his shoulders hunched, as he played a game on his DS console. He was allowed a certain amount of video-game time each day, and he liked playing in the car. At least that kept him from talking about Ryland. Connor had a serious case of hero worship.

But that didn't mean she had to have one, too. Ryland hadn't known about her crush before. He didn't need to know about this one.

She would stay focused on soccer practice. No staring, admiring or lusting. No allowing Connor to invite him over for dinner tonight, either.

With her resolve firmly in place, Lucy parked then removed the soccer gear from her trunk. As Connor ran ahead of her, she noticed Ryland, dressed in his usual attire of shorts and a T-shirt, talking with Dalton's mom, Cheryl.

Lucy did a double take. Cheryl wore a tight, short skirt and a camisole. The clothing clung to every curve, showing lots of tanned skin and leaving little to the imagination. Not that Ryland would have to wait long to sample Cheryl's wares. She stood so close to him her large chest almost touched him.

Lucy gripped the ball bag in her hand.

Ryland didn't seem to mind. He stood his ground, not trying to put any distance between them.

Okay, maybe they weren't standing that close, but still...

Emotions swirled through her. She forced herself to look away.

No reason to be upset or jealous. She'd had her chance Monday night, but turned him down. Oh, she'd been tempted to have him stay and get comfy on the couch, but she was so thankful common sense had won over raging hormones. Especially now that he'd moved on to someone more...willing.

No worries. What two consenting adults did was none of her business. But like a moth drawn to a flame, she glanced over at them. She'd never considered herself masochistic, but she couldn't help herself.

Cheryl batted her mascara-laden eyelashes at him.

Ryland's grin widened. He'd used that same charming smile on Lucy after Connor had gone to bed.

Her stomach churned. Maybe she shouldn't have eaten the egg-salad sandwich for lunch. Maybe she needed to chill.

She quickened her pace. Not that either would notice her. They were too engrossed with each other.

No big deal. Ryland was a big boy, a professional athlete. He knew what he was getting into. He must deal with women hitting on him on a daily basis, ones who wouldn't think of telling him *not tonight*.

As she passed the two, Lucy focused on the boys. Seven of them stood in a circle and kicked the ball to one another while Marco ran around the center trying to steal the ball away.

Cheryl laughed, a nails-on-chalkboard sound that would

make Cupcake howl. Lucy grimaced. If Ryland wanted to be with that kind of woman, he'd never be satisfied with someone like her. Not that she wanted to be with him.

Stop thinking about it! About him!

But she couldn't. No doubt this was some lingering reaction to Jeff's cheating. She'd thought it was great how her husband and her best friend since junior high, Amelia, got along. Lucy hadn't even suspected the two had been having an affair.

Better off without him. Without any of them. Men and best friends.

"Lucy."

Gritting her teeth, she glanced over her shoulder. Ryland was walking toward her. She waited for him. Even with the boot on his injured right foot, he moved with the grace of a world-class athlete, but looked more like a model for a sportswear company.

She didn't want to be impressed, but she couldn't blame Cheryl for wanting to get to know Ryland better. The guy was hot.

Maybe if Lucy hadn't taken a hiatus—more like a sabbatical—from men…

No. Even if she decided to jump back into the dating scene, he wasn't the right man for her. He wasn't the kind of guy to settle down let alone stick around. A superstar like Ryland James had too many women who wanted to be with him and would do anything to get close to him. He'd admitted he wouldn't start thinking about settling down until his career was over with. Why should he? Ryland had no reason to tie himself to only one woman and fight temptation on a daily basis.

Or worse, give in to it as Jeff had.

Ryland was smart for staying single and enjoying the…benefits that came with being a professional athlete.

He stopped next to her. "You sped by so fast I thought we were late starting practice."

He'd noticed her? With sexy Cheryl right there? Lucy was

so stunned she almost missed the little thrill shooting through her. "I like being punctual."

The words sounded stupid as soon as she'd spoken them. She did like being on time, but that wasn't the reason she'd rushed by him. Telling him she'd been jealous of Cheryl wasn't happening. Not in this lifetime. She didn't need to boost his ego and decimate hers in one breath.

Ryland pulled out his cell phone and checked the time. He glanced at the boys on the field. "Practice doesn't start for ten minutes. We're still missing players."

Lucy noticed he didn't wear a watch or jewelry. She liked that he didn't flaunt his wealth by wearing bling as some athletes she'd seen on television did.

Not that she cared what he wore.

Feeling flustered, she set the equipment bag on the grass. "That'll give me plenty of time to set up."

His assessing gaze made Lucy feel as if she were an abstract piece of art that he couldn't decide was valuable or not. She didn't like it. If he was looking for a list of her faults, she could give him one. Jeff had made it clear where she didn't stack up in the wife department.

She placed her hands on her hips. "What?"

"You okay?" Ryland asked.

"Fine." The word came out quick and sharp. "Just one of those days," she added.

Two more women, Suzy and Debbie, joined Cheryl. Both wore the typical soccer-mom uniform—black track pants and T-shirts. The women waved at Ryland. He nodded in their direction before turning his attention back to Lucy.

"Anything I can do to help?" he offered.

"You've done enough." She realized how that might sound. She shouldn't be taking her feelings out on him. Like it or not, she needed his help if she was going to learn enough about soccer to be helpful to the boys. Not just for the spring season, but fall if no one else stepped up to coach. "I mean, you're doing enough with the team. And Connor."

"I'm happy to do more for the boys and for you."

She should be grateful, but his offer irritated Lucy. She liked being self-sufficient. Competent. Independent. Yet she was having to depend on Ryland to help with the team, to teach her about soccer and to keep a smile on Connor's face. She felt like a failure...again. No way could she have him do more. "Let's get set up so we can start on time."

As she removed the cones from the bag, she glanced up at him.

Ryland stood watching her. With the sun behind him, he looked almost angelic, except the look in his eyes made her feel as if he wanted to score with her, not the ball.

Lucy's heart lurched. Heat pooled within her. Common sense told her to ignore him and the hunger in his eyes. But she couldn't deny he made her feel sexy and desired. If only...

Stop. Now.

He was charming, handsome, and completely out of her league. An unexpected crush was one thing. It couldn't go any further than that.

"I can put them out," Ryland said.

No. Lucy didn't want any more help from him. She lowered her gaze to his mouth. His lips curved into a smile. Tingles filled her stomach.

And no matter how curious she might get or how flirtatious he might be, she didn't want any kisses from him, either. "Thanks, but I've got it."

A week later, Ryland gathered up the cones from the practice field. The sun had started setting a little later. Spring was his favorite time of year with the grass freshly cut, the air full of promise and the game fast and furious.

A satisfied feeling flowed through him. The boys were getting it. Slowly, but surely. And Lucy...

What was he going to do about her?

He'd had a tough time focusing during today's practice due to how cute she looked in her pink T-shirt and black shorts. Those sexy legs of hers seemed to have gotten longer. Her face glowed from running around.

Look, don't touch. Ryland had been reminding himself of that for the past hour. Okay, the last week and a half.

She held the equipment bag while he put the cones inside. Her sweet scent surrounded him. Man, she smelled good. Fresh and fruity. He took another sniff. Smelling wasn't touching.

"The boys had a good practice today," she said.

"We'll see how they put it to use in their first match."

"Connor said they've never beaten the Strikers." She tightened the pull string on the bag. "Will they be ready?"

"No, but soccer at this age is all about development."

"Scores aren't reported."

He was used to being surrounded by attractive women, but with Lucy her looks weren't her only appeal. He appreciated how she threw herself into learning about soccer, practicing the drills and studying the rules at home. "Maybe not, but the boys will know the score. And I'd be willing to bet so will the majority of the parents."

"Probably," she said, sounding rueful.

Empathy tugged at him. "You might have to deal with that. Especially toward the end of the season."

She nodded, resigned. "I can handle it."

Pride for her "can do" attitude swelled in his chest. "I know you can."

Lucy's unwavering smile during practices suggested she might be falling in love with the game. Too bad she couldn't fall for him, too.

But that wasn't going to happen. She didn't look at him as anything other than her helper.

Many women wanted to go out with a professional athlete. Lucy wasn't impressed by what he did. He could pump gas at the corner filling station for all she cared. She never asked him anything about his "job" only how his foot was doing. Her indifference to him bristled, even if he knew it was less complicated that way.

She scanned the field. "Looks like we've got everything."

Without waiting for a reply, she headed toward the parking lot. He hobbled along behind her, watching her backside and biting his lip to keep from commenting on how sexy she looked in her gym shorts.

Flirting with her came so naturally, he'd tried hard during practices to keep the conversation focused on soccer. Maybe he should try to be more personable. She was back in town, just like him. She could be...lonely.

Ryland fell into step next to Lucy. Maybe he was the one who was lonely. He'd had offers for company from one of the soccer moms and from several other women in town. None had interested him enough to say yes, but something about Lucy...

He knew all the reasons to keep away from her, but he couldn't stop thinking about her or wanting to spend time with her outside of practice.

Lines creased her forehead, the way they did when she was nervous or worried. "Uh-oh. Look how many parents stayed to watch practice today."

He'd been too busy with the boys and sneaking peeks at Lucy to notice the row of chairs along the edge of the grass. The different colors reminded him of a rainbow. Several dads sat alongside the moms who had come to the last two practices. Some of the men were the same ones who had either ignored or bullied him in elementary school. It wasn't until he'd proven his worth on the pitch that he'd became a real person in their eyes. Now they clamored to talk to him about their sons. "I thought they were too busy or working to be at practices."

"That's what they said when I asked if one of them could coach."

"At least no one can use that excuse now."

Her eyes widened. "You're leaving already?"

Interesting. Lucy sounded upset. Maybe she wasn't as indifferent to him as she appeared to be. "Not yet. But when I do you'll need a new assistant. Maybe two."

"Oh, okay," she said. "It's just the boys like having you around, especially Connor."

"What about you?"

She flinched. "Me?"

Ryland had put her on the spot. He didn't care. The way she reacted to his leaving suggested this wasn't only about the team. If that were true, he wanted to know even if it wouldn't change anything between them. Or change it that much. "Yes, you."

"You're an excellent coach. I'm learning a lot."

"And..."

"A nice guy."

"And..."

The color on her cheeks deepened. "A great soccer player."

"Yes, but you haven't seen me play."

"Modest, huh?"

He shrugged.

"Aaron and Connor told me how good you are."

Ryland wouldn't mind showing her just how good he was at a lot more than soccer.

Bad idea. Except...

He knew women. Lucy was more interested in him than she was letting on. His instincts couldn't be that off. Not with her. "You haven't answered my question."

She looked at the grass. "I appreciate you being here."

"Do you like having me around?"

"It doesn't suck," Lucy said finally.

Not a yes, but close enough. The ball had been passed to him. Time to take the shot.

"Bring Connor over tonight. He can walk Cupcake." Ryland might want to be alone with Lucy, but he knew that wasn't going to happen. A nine-year-old chaperone was a good idea, anyway. The last thing this could turn into was a date. "I'll have pizza delivered."

Her jaw tightened. "You don't have to do this."

"Do what?"

"Repay me for dinner."

"I'm not."

"So this is…"

"For Connor." That was all it could be. *For now,* a little voice whispered.

A beat passed. And another. "He'd like that."

Ryland would have preferred hearing she would like that, too. "I'll order pizza, salad and breadsticks."

"I'll bring dessert."

If he told her not to bother, she'd bring something anyway. And this wasn't a date. "Sounds great."

"Ice-cream sundaes, okay?"

"Perfect."

He could think of lots of ways to use the extra whipped cream with Lucy. The cherries, too. Ryland grinned.

But not tonight. He pressed his lips together. Maybe not any night. And that, he realized, was a total bummer.

The Jameses' kitchen was four times the size of Aaron and Dana's and more "gourmet" with granite countertops, stainless-steel top-of-the-line appliances and hi-tech lighting. The luxurious setting seemed a stark contrast to the casual menu. But no one seemed to notice that except Lucy.

She felt as if she were standing on hot coals and hadn't been able to relax all evening. The same couldn't be said about Connor. A wide grin had been lighting her nephew's face since they'd left practice. He seemed completely at home, hanging on Ryland's every word and playing with Cupcake.

That pleased her since she'd accepted Ryland's invitation for Connor's sake. And *Starry Night* hadn't been painted from within the confines of an asylum, either.

Lucy grimaced. Okay, a part of her had wanted to come over, too.

Insane.

She had to be crazy to torture herself by agreeing to spend more time with Ryland outside of practice. Hanging out with him was working about as well as it had when she'd been in middle school. Her insides quivered, making her feel all jittery. She rinsed a dinner plate, needing the mundane task to steady her nerves.

It didn't help much.

Ryland entered the kitchen. The large space seemed smaller, more…intimate.

She squared her shoulders, not about to let him get to her.

"Connor is chasing Cupcake around the backyard," Ryland said. "It's lighted and fenced so you won't have to worry about him."

She loaded the plate into the dishwasher. As long as the conversation remained on Connor she should be fine. "What makes you think I worry?"

"Nothing, except you pay closer attention to your nephew than an armored car guard does to his cargo."

Lucy rinsed another plate. "I'm supposed to watch him."

"I'm kidding." Ryland placed the box with the leftover pizza slices into the refrigerator. "Aaron has nothing to worry about with you in charge."

She thought about her brother and sister-in-law so far away. "I hope you're right. Sometimes…"

"Sometimes?" he asked.

Lucy stared into the sink, wishing she hadn't said anything. Letting her guard down was too easy when Ryland was around. Strange since that was exactly the time she should keep it up.

"Tell me," he said.

Warm water ran over her hands, but did nothing to soothe her. "Until Aaron and Dana deployed, I had no idea what having someone totally rely on you meant. It's not as easy as I thought it would be. Sometimes I don't think I'm as focused on Connor as I should be."

Especially the past week and a half with Ryland on her mind so much.

"Any more focused and you'd be obsessing." He smiled. "Don't worry. Connor is happy. All smiles."

She placed the plate in the dishwasher. "That's because of you."

"Yeah, you're right about that."

Ryland's lighthearted tone told her that he was joking. She turned and flicked her hands at him. Droplets of water flew in his direction.

He jumped back. Amusement filled his gaze.

"Gee, thanks," she joked.

"Seriously, you're doing a great job," Ryland said. "Your kids will be the envy of all their friends."

Her kids? Heat exploded through Lucy like the grand finale of Fourth of July fireworks. Jeff had said she was too independent to be a decent wife. He'd told her that she would be a bad mother. Funny, how his liking a self-reliant girlfriend when they were dating turned out to be one-hundred-and-eighty percent different from his wanting a needy wife to stroke his fragile ego after they married.

"Thanks." She placed a plate in the rack next to the other. "I suppose being a surrogate parent now will help if I ever have a family of my own."

"If?"

She shrugged. "I've got too much going on with Connor to think about the future."

"Nothing wrong with focusing on the present," he said.

Yeah, she imagined that was what he did. But his situation was different from hers. He was doing something with his life. And she...

Lucy picked up the last plate and scrubbed. Hard.

A longing ached deep inside her. She wanted to do some-thing, too. Be someone. To matter…

Uh-oh. She didn't want to end up throwing herself a pity-party. Not with Ryland here. Time to get things back on track.

She loaded the plate. "Connor has been writing his parents about soccer practices and telling them how well you coach."

"I bet Aaron sees right through that."

"Probably."

Ryland raised a brow. "Probably?"

"You said it," she teased.

He picked up the can of whipped cream with one hand and the red cap with his other. "You didn't have to agree."

"Well, Connor did say you're *almost* as good a coach as his dad."

"Almost, huh?" With a grin, Ryland walked toward her. "I thought we were on the same team, but since we're not…"

He pointed the can of whipped cream in her direction.

She stepped back. Her backside bumped into the granite counter. The lowered dishwasher door had her boxed in on the left. Ryland blocked the way on the right. Trapped. It didn't bother her as much as it should. "You wouldn't."

Challenge gleamed in his eyes. "Whipped cream would go well with your outfit."

His, too. They could have so much fun with the whipped cream. Anticipation made her smile.

What was she thinking? Forget about the whipped cream. Forget about him.

Self-preservation made her reach behind and pull the hand nozzle from the sink. She aimed it at him. The surprise in his eyes made her feel strong and competent. Her confidence surged. "I wonder how you'll look all wet."

A corner of his mouth curved and something shifted be-tween them. The air crackled with tension, with heat. His gaze smoldered.

Heaven help her. She swallowed. Thank goodness for the counter's support or she'd be a puddle on the floor.

"I'm game if you are," he said.

For the first time in a long time, Lucy was tempted to...play. But nerves threatened to get the best of her. She knew better to play with fire.

Unsure of what to do or say next, she clutched the nozzle as if it could save her. From what, she wasn't sure.

Still Lucy wasn't ready to back down. Surrendering wasn't an option, either. "What if I'm out of practice and don't remember how to play?"

He took a step toward her. "I'm an excellent coach. I can show you."

She bet he could. She could imagine all kinds of things he could show her. Her cheeks burned. "What are the rules?"

He grinned wryly. "Play fair. Don't cheat."

A little pang hit her heart. "Those sound like good rules. I don't like cheaters."

"Neither do I."

His gaze captured hers. She didn't know how long they stood there with their weapons ready. It didn't matter. Nothing did except this moment with him.

Lucy wanted...a kiss. The realization ricocheted through her, a mix of shock and anticipation. No wonder she held a water nozzle in her hand ready to squirt him. She wanted Ryland to kiss her senseless. If only...

Not possible. She didn't want to get burned. Again.

Still her lips parted slightly. An invitation or a plea of desperation, she wasn't certain.

Desire flared in his eyes.

Please.

She wasn't brave enough to say the word aloud.

"How do I know this isn't a trap?" he asked with mock seriousness.

"I could say the same thing."

"We could put our weapons down on three."

"Fair play."

He stood right in front of her. "Exactly."

She nodded, still gripping the nozzle. "One, two..."

Ryland lowered his mouth to hers. The touch of his lips sent a shock through her. He tasted warm with a hint of chocolate from the hot-fudge topping.

His tender kiss caressed. She felt cherished and important. Ways she hadn't felt in years. Her toes curled. She gripped the nozzle.

This was what had been missing, what she needed.

Bells rang. Mozart. Boy, could Ryland kiss.

She wanted more. Oh-so-much-more.

A dog barked.

Lucy leaned into Ryland, into his kiss. She brought her right arm around him and her left...

Water squirted everywhere.

Ryland jumped back, his shirt wet.

She glanced down. Hers hadn't fared much better. Thank goodness she was wearing a camisole underneath her T-shirt.

Laughter lit his eyes. "At least you got the playing fair part. We're both wet."

Lucy attempted to laugh. She couldn't. She tried to speak. She couldn't do that, either. Not after being so expertly and thoroughly kissed. Ryland's kiss had left her confused, wanting more and on fire despite the water socking her shirt and dripping down her legs.

A crush was one thing. This felt like...

No, it was nothing but some hot kisses.

Lucy straightened. Letting him kiss her had been a momentary lapse in judgment. She should have ended the kiss as soon as his mouth touched hers. But she hadn't. She...couldn't. Worse, her lips wanted more kisses.

Stupid. The word needed to be tattooed across her forehead

for the world to see. Correction, for her to see, a reminder of the mistakes she'd made when it came to men.

"Aunt Lucy." Connor ran into the kitchen with Cupcake at his heels. Her nephew stared at her and Ryland with wide eyes. "What happened?"

"An accident," Ryland answered.

Did he mean the kiss or the water? The question hammered at her. She wasn't sure she wanted to know the answer, either.

A sudden realization sent a shiver down Lucy's spine. For the few minutes she'd been kissing Ryland, she hadn't thought once about Connor. He'd been left unattended in a strange house. Okay, Cupcake had been with him and Lucy had only been in the kitchen, but still…

Ryland's kiss had made her forget everything, including her nephew. That could not happen again. She adjusted the hem of her shirt, smoothed her hair and looked at her nephew. "You okay?"

Connor nodded. "But there's a man at the front door. He said his name is Blake. He's here to see Ryland."

CHAPTER SEVEN

STANDING IN HIS parents' living room, Ryland dragged his hand through his hair. Uncomfortable didn't begin to describe the atmosphere. Blake's nostrils flared. A thoroughly kissed and embarrassed Lucy stared at Connor, who sat on the carpet playing with Cupcake, oblivious to what was going on.

Not that any of the adults had a clue.

At least Ryland didn't.

He was trying to figure out what had happened in the kitchen. He couldn't stop thinking about Lucy's kisses. About how silver sparks had flashed when she'd opened her eyes. About how right she felt in his arms.

Not good, since the last thing he needed was a woman in his life. Even one as sweet and delicious as Lucy Martin. But this wasn't the time to think about anything except damage control.

Blake hadn't seen them kissing, but Lucy's presence was going to be a problem. A big one.

"Let me introduce everyone," Ryland said.

Polite words were exchanged. Obligatory handshakes given. Thick tension hung on the air, totally different from the sizzling heat in the kitchen a few minutes ago. That was where Ryland wished he could be now—in the kitchen kissing Lucy.

Whoa. He must have taken a header with a ball too hard and not remembered. Ryland was in enough trouble with his agent. He needed to stop thinking about kisses. And her. Not even flings were in his playbook at the moment.

"What brings you to Wicksburg?" Lucy asked Blake.

Ryland wanted to know the answer to that question, too. Blake never dropped by unannounced. Something big must have happened with either Fuego or his sponsors.

Good news, Ryland hoped. But given the muscle flicking on Blake's jaw and the tense lines around his mouth, probably not.

"I was in Chicago for a meeting." That explained Blake's designer suit, silk tie and Italian-leather shoes. Not exactly comfortable traveling attire, but Blake always dressed well, even when he was straight out of law school and joining the ranks of sports agents. "I thought I'd swing by Indiana and see how Ryland was doing on his own."

Swing by? Yeah, right. No one swung by Wicksburg when the nearest airport was a two-hour drive away. Blake must have rented a car to get here. Something was up. The question was what.

The edges of Lucy's mouth curved upward in a forced smile. The pink flush that had crept up her neck after he'd kissed her hadn't disappeared yet. "That's nice of you."

Blake Cochrane and the word "nice" didn't belong in the same sentence. Of course Lucy wouldn't know that. He had the reputation of being a shark when it came to contract negotiations and pretty much anything else. His hard-nosed toughness made him a great agent. Blake eyed Lucy with suspicion. "I can see my concerns about Ryland being lonely are unfounded."

The agent's ice-blue eyes narrowed to slits. He focused first on Lucy then moved to Ryland.

The accusation in Blake's voice and gaze left no doubt what the agent thought was going on here. Ryland grimaced. He didn't like Lucy being lumped in with other women he'd gone out with. He squared his shoulders. "I invited Lucy and Connor over to take Cupcake on a walk for me and have some pizza."

"And ice-cream sundaes," Connor added with a grin.

Blake's brow slanted. His gaze lingered on Lucy's damp shirt that clung to her breasts like a second skin. "A water fight, too, I see."

Ryland tried hard not to look at her chest. Tried and failed.

The color on Lucy's face deepened. She looked like she wanted to bolt.

His jaw tensed. He didn't like seeing her so uncomfortable. "Faucet malfunction."

"Hate when that happens," Blake said.

Damn him. Blake wasn't happy finding Lucy here, but he didn't have to be such a jerk about it. Ryland's hands balled. "Nothing that can't be fixed."

His harsh tone silenced the living room. Only Connor and the dog seemed at ease.

"Well, it's been nice meeting you, Blake. It's a school night so we have to get home," Lucy said. "Thanks for having us over for dinner, Ryland."

"Yeah, thanks. I had fun with Cupcake." Connor stood, stifling a yawn. "This is a cool house. The backyard is so big we could hold our practices here."

"You play soccer?" Blake asked.

Connor nodded.

Blake studied the kid, as if sizing up his potential. Scouts could recognize talent at a young age. In the United Kingdom, the top prospects signed with football clubs in their teens. "What position do you play?"

Connor raised his chin, a gesture both his dad and Lucy made. "Wherever I'm told to play."

Blake's sudden smile softened his rugged features. "With that kind of attitude you'll go far."

Connor beamed. "I want to be just like Ryland when I grow up."

The words touched Ryland. He mussed Connor's hair. Working with the boys reminded him of the early years of playing soccer, full of fun, friendship and laughter. "Thanks, bud."

Ryland turned his attention to Lucy. He wanted to kiss her good-night. Who was he kidding? He wanted to kiss her hello, goodbye and everything in between. She was sexy and sweet, a potent, addictive combo. He should have his head examined soon. There wasn't room in his life for a serious girlfriend, especially one who lived in Wicksburg. He couldn't afford to lose his edge now. "I'll see you out."

Lucy nodded.

That surprised him. He'd expected her to say it wasn't necessary, like the first time she'd visited.

"I'll stay here," Blake said.

Ryland accompanied them to the driveway where Lucy's car was parked. Lights on either side of the garage door illuminated the area. Cupcake ran around the car barking. She didn't seem to want Connor to go. Ryland felt the same way about Lucy.

That made zero sense. They weren't playing house. Being with her wasn't cozy. More like being on a bed of hot knives. She needed to leave before he got the urge to kiss her again.

Connor climbed into the backseat. Cupcake followed, but Ryland lifted the dog out of the car and held on to her. As soon as Connor fastened his seat belt, his eyelids closed.

"He's out," Ryland said.

She glanced back at the house. "You're in trouble."

The word "no" sat on the tip of his tongue and stayed there. He didn't want to worry Lucy, but he also didn't want to lie. Blake's surprise visit concerned Ryland. "I don't know."

Lines creased Lucy's forehead. Her gaze, full of concern and compassion, met his. "Blake doesn't look happy."

Ryland was a lone wolf kind of guy. He wasn't used to people being concerned about him. It made him…uncomfortable.

Best not to think about that. Or her. "Blake's intense. No one would ever accuse him of being mild-mannered and laid-back."

"I wouldn't want to meet him in a dark alley. A good thing he's on your side."

"Blake's my biggest supporter after my folks." The agent had always been there for Ryland. One of the few people who had believed in him from the beginning. "He fights for his clients. I've been with him for eleven years. I was the second client to sign with him."

"You both must have been young then."

"Young and idealistic." Those had been the days before all the other stuff—the business stuff—became such a priority and a drag. "But we've grown up and been through a lot."

"You've probably made him a bunch of money over the years."

They were both rich men now. "Yeah."

But her words made Ryland think. Those closest to him, besides his parents, were people who made money off him. His agent, his PR spokesperson, his trainer, the list went on. His friends were plentiful when he was covering the tab at a club or throwing a party, but not so much now that he was stuck in the middle-of-nowhere Indiana. Bitterness coated his mouth.

Was that the reason Blake had dropped by? To make sure his income from "Ryland James" endorsements and licensing agreements wouldn't dry up?

Ryland hoped not. He wanted to think he was considered more than just a client after all the years.

The tip of her pink tongue darted out to moisten her lips.

He wouldn't mind another taste of her lips. He fought the urge to pull her against him and kiss her until the worry disappeared. "About what happened in the kitchen..."

The lines on her forehead deepened. She glanced at Connor who was asleep. "That shouldn't have happened. It was a...mistake."

Ryland studied her, trying to figure out what she was thinking. He couldn't. "It didn't feel like a mistake."

"I..."

He placed his finger against her lips, remembering how soft they'd felt against his own. They needed to talk, but this wasn't the time, and maybe the words needed to remain unsaid. "It's late."

"Blake's waiting for you."

"Don't let the suit and attitude fool you. He's not in charge here. I am," Ryland said. "Take Connor home. We'll talk soon."

She nodded.

"Blake's bag was in the entryway. He's staying the night."

An ache formed deep in Ryland's gut. He wanted to kiss Lucy. More than he'd wanted anything in a long time. He didn't understand why he was feeling that way. Staying away from her was the smart thing to do. Though come to think of it, no one had ever accused him of being smart. "I'll call you tomorrow. Promise."

So much for playing it safe. But something about Lucy made him forget reason and make promises.

She started to speak then stopped herself. "Good luck with Blake."

"Thanks, but I've got all the luck I need thanks to your penny."

Her eyes widened. "You kept it?"

Bet she'd be surprised to know the penny had been sitting on his nightstand for the past two weeks. "Never know when I'll need it to get lucky."

The color on her cheeks deepened again. "That's my cue to say good-night."

Sweet and smart. It was a good thing Blake was going to be his houseguest tonight and not Lucy. Ryland opened the car door for her. "Drive safe."

After the taillights of Lucy's car faded from view, he went inside. He couldn't put off his conversation with Blake any longer.

His agent stood in the entryway. He'd changed into shorts, a T-shirt and running shoes.

"Tell me what you're really doing here," Ryland said.

"I've been on airplanes or stuck at conference tables for the last two days," Blake said. "Let's work out."

In the home gym, Ryland hopped on the stationary bike. His physical therapist had increased the number of things he could do as his foot healed. He liked being able to do more exercises, but working out was the furthest thing from his mind. Thoughts about Lucy and her hot kisses as well as his agent's purpose for coming here filled his brain.

Blake stepped on the treadmill. He adjusted the settings on the computerized control panel. "I knew you couldn't go that long without a woman."

Ryland's temper flared. But after receiving more red cards these past two seasons than all the seasons before, he'd learned not to react immediately. He accelerated his pedaling, instead. "You're checking up on me."

"Sponsors are nervous." Blake's fast pace didn't affect his speech or breathing. "They aren't the only ones."

So now his agent had added babysitter to his list of duties. Great. Ryland's fingers tightened around the handlebars. "You."

"I don't get nervous." Blake accelerated his pace. "But I am...concerned. You'll be thirty soon. We need to make the most of the next few years whether you're playing with Fuego or across the pond."

His agent had stressed the need for financial planning to Ryland since he was eighteen years old. But he'd never set out to amass a fortune, just be the best soccer player he could be. "I'm set for life."

"You can never have too much money when your earning potential will drastically diminish once you stop playing."

Ryland had more money than he could ever spend, but dissatisfaction gnawed at him. He might be injured, but he wasn't about to be put out to pasture just yet.

"Don't be concerned. I'm laying low," he said. "Tonight is the first time I've had anyone over to the house other than the housekeeper, who's old enough to be my mom. I made sure Lucy and I had a chaperone."

"Nice kid," Blake said. "Is it his team you're coaching?"

Damn. Ryland slowed his pedaling. He reached for his water bottle off the nearby counter then took a long swig. The cool liquid rushing down his throat did little to refresh him. "Where'd you hear that?"

"Someone tweeted you were coaching a local rec. team." Blake kept a steady pace. "Tell me this was some sort of one-off rah-rah-isn't-soccer-great pep talk."

"I'm helping Lucy with Connor's team." Ryland placed his water bottle on the counter. "Her brother coaches the team, but he's on deployment with his Reserve unit. No other parent stepped up so she took on the role as head coach even though she knows nothing about soccer. I offered to help."

"Lucy's so hot she could get a man to do most anything," Blake said. "Those legs of hers go on forever."

The appreciative gleam in his agent's ice-blue eyes bugged Ryland. Women always swarmed around Blake. He didn't need to be checking out Lucy, too.

Ryland's jaw tensed. "I'm coaching for both her and the boys."

"Mostly Lucy, though." Blake grinned. "That's a good thing."

"It is?"

"Your coaching becomes a nonissue if you have a personal connection and aren't showing favoritism to one team."

"Favoritism?" Ryland didn't understand what Lucy had to do with this. "I'm helping the Defeeters, but I've also spoken to two other teams this week and will visit with three more next week."

"No need to get defensive," Blake said. "A guy helping out his girlfriend isn't showing favoritism."

Girlfriend? A knot formed in the pit of Ryland's stomach. Everything suddenly made sense. "So if Lucy and I aren't..."

He couldn't bring himself to say the word.

Blake nodded. "If you weren't dating Lucy, you wouldn't be able to coach the team."

Ryland's knuckles turned white. "What do you mean?"

As Blake moved from the treadmill to the stair-climber machine, he wiped the sweat from his face with a white towel. "You're public property. The face of the Phoenix Fuego. Showing favoritism to one team without a valid personal connection would be a big no-no for a player of your caliber. Especially one on shaky ground already."

Ryland gulped.

"But we don't need to worry about that," Blake added.

Emotion tightened Ryland's throat. His agent had always been overprotective. No doubt watching over his investment. Ryland understood that, but he wasn't going back on his word to help Lucy with the team. She needed him. "No worries."

If his agent believed a romance was going on between Ryland and Lucy, Blake wouldn't feel the need to play mother hen. No one would have to know the truth. Not the sponsors or the Fuego, not even Lucy…

Play fair. Don't cheat.

Not saying anything wasn't cheating, but it wasn't exactly fair, either.

"I must admit I'm a little surprised," Blake said. "Lucy's not your usual type."

Ryland wasn't sure he had a type, but the kind of women he met at clubs couldn't hold a candle to a certain fresh-faced woman with a warm smile, big heart and legs to her neck. Someone who didn't care how much he made or the club he played for or what car he drove. Someone whose kisses had rocked his world.

"I've known Lucy since she was in kindergarten," Ryland explained. "Her brother was one of my closest friends and teammates when I was growing up."

Blake's brows furrowed. "We might be able to use this to our advantage. McElroy is big on family. Childhood sweethearts reunited would make a catchy headline."

Whoa, so not going there. "Lucy was too young for me to date when we were in school. Don't try to milk this for something it's not. I'll be leaving town soon."

"The two of you seem cozy. Serious."

Ryland climbed off the bike. "I don't do serious."

"You haven't done serious. That doesn't mean you can't," Blake said. "Lucy could be a keeper."

Definitely.

The renegade thought stopped Ryland cold. Lucy might be a keeper, but not for him. Fame and adoring women hadn't always satisfied him, but things would improve now that he'd had a break. This time away was what he needed. He could concentrate on his career and get back on track with the same hunger and edge that had made him a star player.

Besides, Lucy needed a guy who would be around to help her with Connor. Someone who could make her a priority and give her the attention she deserved. He couldn't be that kind of guy, not when he played soccer all over the world, lived in Arizona and wasn't about to start thinking in the long-term until his career was over.

Ryland picked up his water bottle. "The only keeper I want in my life is a goalkeeper."

There wasn't room for any other kind. There just couldn't be.

While a tired Connor brushed his teeth, Lucy laid out his pajamas on his bed. She couldn't stop thinking about Ryland. About his kissing her. About what he might be saying to his agent right now.

Lucy wished she could turn back the clock. She would have turned down his offer to come over tonight. That way he wouldn't be in trouble and she wouldn't want more of his kisses.

Pathetic.

Crushing on Ryland didn't mean she should be kissing him.

Crushes were supposed to be fun, not leave her with swollen lips and a confused heart.

Not her heart, she corrected herself. Her mind.

Her heart was fine. Safe. She planned on keeping it that way. Keeping her distance from Ryland would be her best plan of action. She wasn't supposed to see him again until the Defeeters' game on Saturday. Though he'd promised he would call tomorrow...

He'd used the word "promise" again. He hadn't let her down the first time. She hoped he wouldn't this time, but she had no idea. She didn't trust herself when it came to men.

Lucy's fingers twitched. Touching her tingling lips for the umpteenth time would not help matters. She needed to hold a pencil and sketchbook. She needed to draw.

As soon as Connor was in bed...

He was her priority. Not her art. Definitely not Ryland.

The phone rang.

Her heart leaped. Ryland. Oh, boy, she had it bad.

Connor darted out of the bathroom as if he'd gotten his second wind. He picked up the telephone receiver. "Hello, this is Connor, may I ask who's calling... Dad!"

The excitement in that one word brought a big smile to Lucy's face. Relief, too. Aaron must have returned to a base where phone calls could be made. Her brother was safe. For now.

"I'm so glad you got my emails." Connor leaned against the wall. "Yeah. Ryland knows a lot about soccer. He's cool. But no one is as good a coach as you... We had dinner at his house tonight... Pizza... No, just me and Aunt Lucy. I got to walk his parents' dog. Her name is Cupcake... Can we get a dog?... Ryland said they were a lot of work..." Connor nodded at whatever Aaron said to him. "Yeah, he's a nice guy just like you said... Okay... I love you, too." Connor handed Lucy the phone. "Dad wants to talk to you."

That was odd. Usually she emailed Aaron and Dana so they

could spend their precious phone minutes speaking with Connor. She raised the phone to her ear. "Hey, Bro. Miss you."

"Ryland James?" Aaron asked.

Her brother's severe tone made her shoo Connor into his bedroom. "Ryland's helping with Connor's team."

"Dinner at his house has nothing to do with the *team*."

She walked down the hallway to put some distance between her and her nephew. "Connor likes spending time with him."

"And you're hanging with Ryland for the sake of Connor?"

"Yes. Connor's the reason I accepted the dinner invitation." She kept her voice low so her nephew wouldn't hear. "He misses you and Dana so much. But ever since Ryland started working with the team, Connor's been happy and all smiles."

"What about you?" Aaron asked. "You had a big crush on him."

"That was years ago," she said.

"Ryland James is a player, Luce. You don't follow soccer, but I do. The guy has a bad reputation when it comes to women. He'll break your heart if he gets the chance."

"I'll admit he's attractive," she said. "But after Jeff, I know better than to fall for a guy like Ryland James."

"I hope so."

Her brother sounded doubtful. "Don't worry. Ryland isn't going to be around much longer."

"Stay away from him."

"Hard to do when he's helping me with the team and teaching me what I need to coach."

"Limit your interaction to soccer. I hate to think he might hurt you," Aaron said. "Damn. Out of time. Love you. Be careful, Luce."

The line disconnected.

A lump of emotion formed in her throat. Aaron had tried to warn her about Jeff before she eloped, but Lucy hadn't listened. She couldn't make the same mistake again. Because she knew Aaron was right. Ryland James was dangerous. He could break her heart. Easily. She'd survived when that happened with Jeff. She wasn't sure she could survive that type of heartache again.

Lucy put away the phone receiver and made her way to Connor's bedroom. Aaron's words echoed through her head. She felt like an idiot. She'd questioned whether she could trust Ryland, yet she'd kissed him tonight and still wanted more kisses.

So not good.

But she couldn't wallow or overanalyze. She'd done enough of that when her marriage had ended. She knew what to do now—start a new project. As soon as her nephew was tucked into bed, she would gather her art supplies.

Forget a pencil and sketchbook. Time to pull out the big guns—brushes, paints and canvas. Painting was the only thing that might clear her thoughts enough so she could forget about Ryland James and his kisses.

CHAPTER EIGHT

AFTER CONNOR LEFT for school the next morning, Lucy worked. She enjoyed graphic design—creative, yet practical—but the painting she'd started last night called to her in a way her normal work never had. She emailed a proof to one client and uploaded changes to another's website. The rest of the items on her To Do list could wait until later.

Lucy stood in front of the painting. The strong, bright, vivid colors filled the canvas. The boldness surprised her.

She wasn't that into abstract art. She preferred subjects that captured a snapshot of life or told a story. But thanks to Ryland, her thoughts and emotions were a mismatched jumble. Geometric shapes, lines and arcs were about all she could manage at the moment.

Still the elements somehow worked. Not too surprising, Lucy supposed. She'd always found solace in art, when she was sick and after her marriage ended. The only difference was this time neither her health nor heart were involved.

She wouldn't allow her heart to be involved. That internal organ would only lead her astray.

Stop thinking. Just paint.

Time to lose herself in the work. Lucy dipped her brush into the paint.

She worked with almost a manic fervor. Joy and sorrow, desire and heartache appeared beneath her brush in bold strokes, bright colors, swirls and slashes.

The doorbell rang.

The sound startled her. She dripped paint onto her hand.

A quick glance at the clock showed she'd been painting for the past two hours. She'd lost track of time. A good thing she'd been interrupted or she could have stayed here all day.

Using a nearby rag, she wiped her hands then headed to the front door. Most likely the UPS man. She'd ordered some paper samples for a client.

Lucy opened the door.

Ryland stood on the porch. Her breath caught and held in her chest. He wore warm-up pants and a matching jacket with a white T-shirt underneath. The casual attire looked stylish on him. His hair was styled, but he hadn't shaved the stubble from his face this morning. Dark circles ringed his eyes, as if he hadn't slept much last night.

Like her.

Though she doubted she'd played a role in his dreams the way he'd starred in hers.

He smiled. "Good morning."

Ryland was the last person she expected to see. He'd told her he would call, not show up in person. But a part of her was happy to see him standing here.

That bothered her. She blew out a breath. Remember what Aaron had said. Ryland was the last person she should want to spend any time with. Yet...

Her gaze slid from his hazel-green eyes to his mouth. Tingles filled her stomach. Her lips ached for another kiss.

Lucy clutched the doorknob. For support or ease in slamming shut the door, she wasn't certain. "What are you doing here?"

Her tone wasn't polite. She didn't care. His presence disturbed her.

His smile faltered a moment before widening. "Let's go for coffee."

"I'm not sure that's such a good idea."

Talk about a wimpy response. She knew going out would be a very bad idea.

"We need to talk about my coaching the Defeeters," he added.

He would bring up coaching and the Defeeters. She was torn. Seeing him over something soccer-related didn't make Ryland James any less dangerous. She glanced down at her paint-splattered shirt and sweatpants. "I'm not dressed to go out."

His gaze took in her clothes and her hands with splotches of purple on them. "You've been painting."

She didn't understand why he sounded so pleased. "Yes."

"We can stay here," he said. "I'd like to see what you're working on."

Lucy didn't feel comfortable sharing her work with Ryland. No way did she want to expose such an intimate part of herself. Not after kissing him had brought up all these feelings. Speaking of kissing him, being alone in the house wasn't a good idea at all. "We can go to the coffee shop. Let me wash up and get my purse."

A few minutes later, refreshed and ready, she locked the front door. "Do you want to meet there?"

"We can ride together."

That was what she was afraid he would say. "I'll drive."

"Your car is nicer than my dad's old truck."

"My car is closer." She motioned to her car parked on the driveway. "Less walking for you."

He headed to her car. "That's thoughtful."

More like self-preservation. She would also be in control. She could determine when they left, not him.

Lucy unlocked the car and opened the door for him. "Do you need help getting in?"

He drew his brows together. "Thanks, but I can handle it."

She walked around the front of the car, slid into her seat and turned on the engine. "Buckled in?"

Ryland patted the seat belt. "All set."

The tension in the air matched her tight jaw. She backed out of the driveway. "So what did you want to talk about?"

"Let's wait until we get to the coffee shop," Ryland said.

They were only five minutes away. She turned on the radio. A pop song with lyrics about going home played. The music was better than silence, but not by much. She tapped her thumbs on the steering wheel. "Does it have anything to do with Blake?"

Ryland nodded. "But no need to worry."

Easier said then done.

Lucy turned onto Main Street. Small shops and restaurants lined the almost-empty street. A quiet morning in Wicksburg. She parked on the street right in front of the Java Bean, a narrow coffee shop with three tables inside and two out front on the sidewalk.

A bell jangled when Ryland opened the door for her. She stepped inside. The place was empty. As they walked to the counter, he placed his hand at the small of her back. His gentle touch made her wish she were back in his arms again, even if that was the last place she should be.

Lucy ordered a cappuccino. He got a double espresso. She went to remove her wallet, but he was handing the barista a twenty-dollar bill.

"You can buy the next time," he said.

Going out to coffee with Ryland was not something she planned on doing again. She'd figure out another way to repay him.

Once their order was ready, she sat at a small, round table. Jazzy instrumental music played from hidden speakers.

Ryland sat across from her. His left foot brushed hers. "Excuse me."

"Sorry." Lucy placed her feet under her chair. The sooner

they got this over with the better. She wrapped her hands around the warm mug. "So what's going on?"

Ryland took a sip of his coffee. "Somebody tweeted I was coaching a team of kids in Wicksburg."

"Blake saw the tweet?"

"A PR firm I use did."

She drank from her cup. "No wonder Blake looked so upset."

"He calmed down after you left," Ryland said. "Turns out helping my girlfriend coach a team is a perfectly acceptable thing for me to do."

Girlfriend? She stared at him confused. "Huh?"

"Blake thinks you and I are dating," Ryland explained.

Dating. The word echoed through her head. Even if the idea appealed to her a tiny, almost miniscule bit, she knew it would never happen. "How did he react when you told him we weren't dating?"

"I didn't tell him." Ryland wouldn't meet her gaze. "I didn't deny we were dating, but I didn't say we were a couple, either."

She stared in disbelief. "So Blake thinks we are—"

"I had no choice."

"There's always a choice." She knew that better than anyone. Sometimes the hard choice was the best option.

"I made my choice."

"You had to do what you thought was best for your career. I get that." He'd gotten into this mess with his agent for helping the Defeeters. She couldn't be angry. "I know how much soccer means to you."

His eyes narrowed. "It's not only about my career. If I'd told Blake we weren't dating, I wouldn't be able to help you and the team."

His words sunk in. Ryland hadn't been thinking of himself. He'd done this for her, Connor and the boys.

Her heart pounded so loudly she was sure the barista behind the counter could hear it.

"I wasn't sure if I should tell you," Ryland admitted.

"Why did you?" she asked.

"Fair play."

Play fair. Don't cheat. She remembered the rules he'd told her last night. Right before he'd kissed her senseless. "Thank you for being honest."

"If it's any consolation, I told Blake we weren't serious about each other."

She was glad they were on the same page about not getting involved, except she couldn't ignore a twinge of disappointment. Silly reaction given the circumstances. "Understatement of the year."

Amusement gleamed in his eyes. "True, but people will believe what they want if we don't deny it. And this way I can keep helping you and the team."

Her heart dropped. "You want us to pretend to be dating."

"It's not what I want, but what we have to do." Ryland's smile reached all the way to his eyes. "After those kisses last night, I'm not sure how much pretending is going to be involved."

Heat flooded her face. "We agreed kissing was a mistake."

"You said that. I didn't." His gaze held hers. "There's chemistry between us."

A highly combustible reaction, but she would never admit it. If she did, Ryland could use it to his advantage. She wouldn't stand a chance if he did.

"This is crazy." Lucy's voice sounded stronger than she felt. She tightened her grip on the coffee-cup handle to keep her hand from shaking. "No more kissing. No pretend dating, either."

"Then you'd better find yourself a new assistant before the game on Saturday."

"Seriously?"

He nodded once.

Darn. Lucy watched steam rise from her coffee cup. She didn't know what to do. She needed to protect herself, but she also had to think about Connor.

Connor.

He was the reason she'd approached Ryland in the first place. Her nephew would be the one to suffer if he couldn't continue coaching the Defeeters. She couldn't allow that to happen.

She tried to push all the other stuff out of her mind, including her own worries, doubts and fears, and to focus on Connor. "What's important here is…the team."

"Especially Connor," Ryland said.

She nodded. What was best for Connor might not be the best thing for her, but so what? She had to put her nephew first even if it put her in an awkward position. "You're leaving soon. Until then I'm willing to do whatever it takes so you can keep coaching the team. I can't imagine it'll be that big a deal to pretend to date since your agent lives in California."

"The other coaches in the rec. league have to believe it, or there could be trouble," Ryland clarified. "The parents, too."

Maybe a bigger deal than she realized. But for her nephew she would do it. "Okay."

"Right now there's no press coverage, but that could change."

This had disaster written all over it. If Aaron found out… She couldn't think about him. Connor was her priority, not her brother.

No matter what life had thrown at Lucy, she'd proven she was capable and able to handle anything. She would do the same here. "It's only for a few weeks, right?"

Ryland nodded. "It'll be fun."

There was that word again. She doubted this would be fun. But as long as he was working with the team, keeping a smile on Connor's face and teaching her how to coach, it would be… doable.

Besides they were just pretending. What could go wrong?

Pretending to date wasn't turning out to be all that great. So far "dating" had amounted to several texts being exchanged about soccer and an impromptu dinner at the pizza parlor with the entire team. He'd have to step things up as soon as this game was over.

It couldn't end quickly enough for Ryland. He forced himself to stay seated on the bench. The Defeeters were outmatched and losing. He couldn't do a single thing about it, either.

"Great job, Defeeters!" Lucy stood along the sideline in a blue T-shirt with the name of the soccer league across the front and warm-up pants. She held a clipboard with a list of when players should be substituted to ensure equal playing time and waved it in the air when she got excited during the game. "You can do it!"

The way she cheered was cute. If only the team could pull off a victory, but that would take a miracle given their competition today.

Lucy glanced back at him with a big smile on her face. "The boys have improved over the past two weeks."

Ryland nodded. They had lots of work to do at the next practice.

Lucy checked the stopwatch she wore around her neck. "There can't be much time left."

He glanced at his cell phone. "Less than four minutes."

Connor stole the ball from a small, speedy forward. He passed the ball to Marco, who ran toward the field. He dribbled around a defender and another one.

Parents cheered. Lucy waved the clipboard. Ryland shook his head. Marco needed to pass before the ball got stolen.

The kid sped across the center line.

No way could he take the ball all the way to the goal alone. Not against a skilled team like the Strikers.

"Pass," Ryland called out.

Lucy pointed to Jacob, who stood down field with no defenders around him.

"Cross, Marco," Ryland yelled. "To Jacob."

Marco continued dribbling. A tall, blond-haired defender

from the opposite team ran up, stole the ball and kicked it to a teammate. Goal.

The Defeeters parents sighed. The Striker parents cheered.

The referee blew the whistle.

Game over. The Defeeters had lost six–three. Not that the league kept score, but still…

Ryland would add some new drills and review the old ones. The boys needed to learn to pass the ball and talk to each other out on the field. This was a soccer match, not Sunday services at church.

Each of the teams shouted cheers. Great. The kids had found their voices now that the game was over.

The players lined up with the coaches at the end and shook hands with their opponents. Several of the Strikers grabbed their balls and asked Ryland to sign them. He happily obliged and posed for pictures.

By the time he finished, Lucy was seated on the grass with the boys. He walked their way, passing through a group of Defeeters parents.

Suzy, one of the moms, smiled at him. "They played well out there."

Cheryl nodded. "The last time they played the Strikers it was a shutout."

Marco's dad, Ewan, patted Ryland on the back. "This is the most competitive they've ever been. You've done a great job preparing them."

Interesting. Ryland would have thought the parents would be upset, but they sounded pleased. The boys were all smiles, too.

"Did you see?" Connor asked him. "We scored three goals."

Ryland had never seen so many happy faces after a loss. "Nice match, boys."

"Coach Lucy said if we could score one more goal than the last time we'd played the Strikers that would be a win in her book," Marco said.

Dalton pumped his fists in the air. "We needed one goal, but we scored three!"

Ryland had been so focused on winning he'd forgotten there was more to a game than the final score. Especially when skills development, not winning the game, was the goal. But Lucy, who might not have the technical knowledge, had known that.

She sat with a wide smile on her face and sun-kissed cheeks. Lovely.

A warm feeling settled over Ryland. They really needed to spend more time together.

"In the fall, we lost nine–zero," Connor explained.

Ouch. Ryland forced himself not to grimace. No wonder there was so much excitement over today's match. "You gave them a much better game today."

Dalton nodded. "We play them again at the end of the season."

"Let's not get ahead of ourselves. This is our first game," Lucy said. "We have lots to work on before that final match."

"I'll second that," Ryland agreed. "But that's what practice is for. All of you played so well today it's time for a celebration."

"Snacks!" the boys yelled in unison.

Suzy, the snack mom for today's game, passed out brown lunch bags filled with juice, string cheese, a package of trail mix and a bag of cookies. The boys attacked the food like piranhas.

Ryland walked over to Lucy, who jotted notes on her clipboard. "Snacks have improved since I played rec. soccer."

"Yes, but the game's still the same."

He didn't want things to stay the same between them.

Sitting behind her, he placed his hands on her shoulders.

Her muscles tensed beneath his palms.

Ryland didn't care. They were supposed to be dating. Might as well start pretending now. Kisses might be off-limits, but she hadn't said anything about not touching. As he placed his mouth by her ear, her sweet scent enveloped him.

"I wanted to congratulate you," he whispered, noticing curious looks from parents and the other coaches. "Excellent job, Coach."

She turned her head toward him. Her lips were mere inches from his. It would be so easy to steal a kiss. But he wasn't going to push it. At least not yet.

Wariness filled her eyes, but she smiled at him. "Thanks, but I have the best assistant coach in the league. The boys wouldn't have scored any goals without his help."

Her warm breath against his skin raised his temperature twenty degrees. He could practically taste her. His mouth watered. Pretend kisses would probably feel just as nice as real ones.

"Though you're going to have to explain the offside rule to me again," she continued. "I still don't get it."

Ryland laughed. Here he was thinking about kisses, and she was still talking soccer. "I'll keep explaining until you understand it."

Waiting until Monday afternoon to see her again was unacceptable. He doubted she'd agree to a date, not even a pretend one. But she'd agreed to the pretending because of Connor. The kid would give Ryland the perfect reason to see Lucy before the next practice.

Not cheating, he thought. Perhaps not playing one hundred percent fair, but being able to spend some time with her was worth it. Once they were alone, she might even agree.

Ryland stood. "The way you boys played today deserves a special treat." He looked each boy in the eyes. "Who's up for a slushie?"

Sitting on a picnic bench outside Rocket Burgers, Lucy placed her mouth around the straw sticking out of her cup and sipped her blue-raspberry slushie. Suzy, Cheryl, Debbie and the other moms from the team sat with her.

Ryland and the dads sat with the boys on a grassy area near a play structure.

Suzy set her cup on the table. "Ryland is so nice to treat us all to slushies."

"I'm sure he can afford it. You are so lucky Lucy to spend so much time with him." Cheryl pouted. "I thought I had a chance, but it's better he chose you since I'm not divorced."

Suzy smiled at Lucy. "I thought you guys looked a little chummier at the pizza party, but I didn't realize you were dating until today."

"He is a total catch," Debbie said. "The two of you make a cute couple."

Happiness shot all the way to the tips of Lucy's hot-pink painted toenails. Not for her, she countered. But for Connor. This charade was for him. She repositioned her straw. "Thanks."

Lucy was not going to confirm or deny anything about their "dating." The less she said, the less dishonest she would feel. She drank more of her slushie.

The men laughed. The boys, too. Through the cacophony of noise, the squeals and giggles, Lucy singled out Ryland's laughter. The rich sound curled around her heart and sent her temperature climbing. She sipped her slushie, but the icy drink did nothing to cool her down.

No biggie. She would be heading home soon and wouldn't have to see Ryland until Monday afternoon.

As the women talked about a family who'd moved to Iowa, Lucy glanced his way. Ryland sat with Connor on one side and Dalton on the other, the only two boys on the team without fathers here today.

While the other boys spoke with their fathers, Ryland talked to Connor and Dalton. The boys looked totally engaged in the conversation. Smiles lit up their faces. They laughed.

A soccer ball–size lump formed in her throat.

Ryland James might have a reputation as a womanizer, but she could tell someday he would be a great dad. The kind of dad she had. The kind of dad her brother was.

He flashed her a lopsided grin and winked.

Lucy had been caught staring. She should look away, but she didn't want to. She realized since they were pretending to date she didn't have to.

The fluttery sensations in her stomach reminded her of when she was thirteen and head over heels in love with Ryland. But she knew better than to fantasize about a happily ever after now with a guy like him. Besides, she knew happy endings were rare, almost nonexistent these days.

A dad named Chuck said something to Ryland. He looked at him, breaking the connection with her.

Lucy turned her attention to the table. The other women had gotten up except for Suzy.

"Well, this has been fun." Cheryl motioned to her son Dalton and gazed longingly at Ryland. "See you at practice on Monday."

"The boys will have their work cut out for them," he said.

Families said goodbye and headed to their cars. Several boys lagged behind, not wanting to leave their friends. Marco and Connor ran up to the picnic table. Ryland followed them.

"Can Connor spend the night?" Marco asked his mom.

"Sure. We have no plans other than to hang out and watch a DVD." Suzy glanced at Lucy. "Is it okay with you?"

Connor stared at her with an expectant look. "Please, Aunt Lucy?"

"He's had sleepovers at our house before," Suzy added.

Dana had provided Lucy with the names of acceptable sleepover and playdate friends. Marco had been at the top of the list. "Okay."

The boys gave each other high fives.

"But you're going to have to come home with me first. You need to shower and pack your things," she said.

"I have to run by the grocery store. We can pick him up on our way home," Suzy offered.

"Thanks." Lucy hugged her nephew. "This will be my first

night alone since I've been back in Wicksburg. I don't know what I'll do."

Connor slipped out of her embrace. "Ryland can keep you company tonight."

She started to speak, but Ryland beat her to it.

"I have no plans tonight," he said. "I'd be happy to make sure your aunt doesn't miss you too much."

The mischievous look on Ryland's face made her wonder if he'd planned this whole thing. She wouldn't put it past him. But a part of her was flattered he'd go to so much trouble to spend time with her.

Remember, it's pretend.

"Then we're all set." Suzy grinned. "See you in an hour or so."

As Marco and his parents headed to their SUV, Connor watched them go. "Tonight is going to be so much fun."

Maybe for him. Anxiety built inside Lucy. She had no idea if Ryland was serious about tonight. A part of her hoped he was serious about keeping her company. Not because she was going to be lonely, but because she wanted to see him.

Ridiculous. She blew out a puff of air.

"I'll see you at five," Ryland said.

Before she could say anything he walked off toward the old beat-up truck.

Okay, he was serious. But what exactly did he have in mind?

Connor bounced on his toes. "We'd better get home."

She wrapped her arm around his thin shoulders. "You have plenty of time to get ready for your sleepover."

"I'm not worried about me, but Dad says it takes Mom hours to get ready. You're going to need a lot of time."

His words and sage tone amused her. "What for?"

"Your date with Ryland."

Lucy flinched. She hadn't wanted to drag Connor into the ruse. "Date?"

"Ryland's taking you out to dinner." A smug smile settled

on Connor's freckled face. "I told him Otto's was your favorite restaurant, and you liked the cheese fondue best. I also told him it was expensive and only for special occasions, but Ryland said he could probably afford it."

"He can." He could probably afford to buy the entire town.

"If you and Ryland got married, that would make him my new uncle, right?" Connor asked.

Oh, no. The last thing she needed was Connor mentioning marriage to Aaron. "Marriage is serious business. Ryland and I are just going out to eat."

"But it would be pretty cool, don't ya think?"

Maybe if she were nine she would think it was cool. But she was twenty-six and pretending to be dating a soccer star. Marriage was the last thing on her mind while she took care of Connor for the next year. She wasn't even sure if she wanted to get married again. Not after Jeff.

"When two people love each other, marriage can be very cool," Lucy said carefully. "But love is not something you can rush. It takes time."

"My dad knew the minute he saw my mom he was going to marry her," Connor said. "They didn't date very long."

"That's true, but what happened with your mom and dad doesn't happen to many people."

Definitely not her and Jeff.

"But it could happen with you and Ryland," Connor said optimistically.

She gave him a squeeze. "I suppose anything is possible."

But in her and Ryland's case, highly unlikely.

CHAPTER NINE

STANDING ON LUCY'S front doorstep on Saturday night, Ryland held the single iris behind his back. At the flower shop, he'd headed straight for the roses because that was what he usually bought women, but the purple flower caught his eyes. The vibrant color reminded him of Lucy, so full of life. He hoped she liked it.

Anticipation for his "date" buzzed through Ryland. He hadn't gone to this much trouble for a woman before. Not unless you counted what he did for his mom on Mother's Day, her birthday in July and Christmastime. But like his mother, Lucy was worth it. Even if this wasn't a "real" date.

He wanted her to see how much fun they could have together. And it would be a memory he could take with him when he left Wicksburg. One he hoped Lucy would look back on fondly herself. Smiling, he pressed the doorbell.

A moment later, the door opened.

Lucy stood in the doorway. Mascara lengthened her eyelashes. Pink gloss covered her lips. He couldn't tell if she was wearing any other makeup. Not that she needed any with her high cheekbones and wide-set eyes.

She never wore any jewelry other than a watch, but tonight dangling crystals hung from her earlobes. A matching necklace graced her long neck.

Her purple sleeveless dress hugged all the right curves and fell just above her knees. Strappy high-heeled shoes accentuated her delicate ankles and sexy calves.

Beautiful.

Lucy was a small-town girl, but tonight she'd dressed for the big city. Whether this was a real date or not, she'd put some effort into getting ready. That pleased him.

"You look stunning."

She smiled softly. "I figured since we were going to Otto's…"

"Connor told you."

"Nine-year-olds and magpies have a lot in common," she explained. "So what did it cost you to enlist him and Marco as your partners in crime?"

Manny lumbered over toward the door. Lucy blocked his way so he couldn't get out of the house. The cat rubbed against her bare leg. Ryland wished he could do the same.

"Twenty bucks," he said, unrepentant.

Her mouth gaped. If this were a real date, he would have been tempted to take advantage of the moment and kiss her. But it wasn't, so he didn't.

"You paid the boys that much?" she asked.

He shrugged. "They earned it."

"Paying someone to do your dirty work gets expensive."

But worth every dollar. "A man does what he has to do."

"Even for a pretend date?" she said.

"A date's a date."

"That explains your clothes." Lucy's assessing gaze traveled the length of him. The brown chinos and green button-down shirt were the dressiest things he'd brought with him to

Wicksburg. Going out hadn't been on his list of things to do here. "You clean up well."

He straightened, happy he'd pulled out all the stops tonight. "You sound surprised."

A half smile formed on her lips. "Well, I've only seen you in soccer shorts, jerseys and T-shirts."

Ryland remembered the first day she'd shown up at his parents' house. He raised a brow. "And shirtless."

Her cheeks turned a charming shade of pink. "That, too."

He handed her the iris. The color matched her dress perfectly. "For you."

"Thank you." She took the flower and smelled it. "It's real."

"Not everything is pretend."

She smiled. "I've always liked irises better than roses."

Score. "It reminded me of you."

Her eyes widened. "You don't have to say stuff like that. No one is watching us."

He held his hands up, his palms facing her. "Just being honest."

She kept staring at the flower. "Let me put this in some water before we go."

With an unexpected bounce to his step, Ryland entered the house and closed the door behind him. He followed Lucy, enjoying the sway of her hips and the flow of her dress around her legs. Her heels clicked against the floor. Manny trotted along behind him.

In the kitchen, she filled a narrow glass vase with water. She studied the flower, turning it 360 degrees, then stuck the stem into the vase. "I want to paint this."

Satisfaction flowed through him. "I'd like to see your work."

"We need to get to Otto's."

"There's no rush," he said. "I called the restaurant. No reservations unless it's a party of six or more."

She tilted her chin. "You're going to a lot of trouble for a pretend date."

"Connor doesn't want you to be lonely tonight."

"Connor, huh?"

Ryland's gaze met hers. Such pretty blue eyes. "I don't, either."

And that was the truth. Which surprised him a little. Okay, a lot. This was supposed to be all make-believe, but the more time he spent with Lucy, the more he cared about her. He wanted to make her smile and laugh. He wanted to please her.

This had never happened to him with a woman before. He wasn't sure what to think or even if he liked it.

Silence stretched between them, but if anything, the quiet drew them closer together not apart.

The sounds of the house continued on. Ice cubes dropped inside the freezer. A motor on the refrigerator whirred. Manny drank water from his bowl.

Funny, but Ryland had never felt this comfortable around anyone except his parents. He needed to figure out what was going on here. "So your paintings…"

"I'm really hungry."

So was Ryland. But what he wanted wasn't on any menu. She was standing right next to him. "Then let's go."

As Ryland held open the door to Otto's, Lucy walked into the restaurant. The din of customers talking and laughing rose above the accordion music playing. She inhaled the tantalizing aromas of roasting pork and herbs lingering in the air.

Her stomach rumbled. She'd been too nervous about the soccer game to eat lunch. Big mistake because now she was starving.

For food and for…

She glanced over her shoulder at Ryland. The green shirt lightened his hazel eyes. He looked as comfortable in dressier clothes as casual ones. He'd gone out of his way to make tonight special. She appreciated that even if none of this was for real. "Thanks for taking me out tonight."

"Thanks for going out with me."

Otto's was packed. Not surprising given it was a Saturday night and the best place in town. The last time she'd been here was right before Aaron and Dana deployed—a going-away dinner for them.

Customers crammed into booths and tables. Servers carried heavy trays of German food and large steins full of beer. People waited to be seated. Some stood near the hostess stand. Others sat on benches.

Ryland approached the hostess, who was busy marking the seating chart. The woman in her early twenties looked up with a frown. But as soon as she saw him, a dazzling smile broke across her young, pretty face.

Lucy was beginning to realize wherever Ryland went female attention was sure to follow. But she saw he did nothing to make women come on to him. Well, except for being an extremely good-looking and all-around good guy. She stepped closer to him, feeling territorial. Silly considering this wasn't a real date.

"Hello. I'm Emily. Welcome to Otto's." She smoothed her hair. "How many in your party?"

"Two," he said.

She fluttered her eyelashes coquettishly. "Your name, please?"

"James."

The hostess wrote the information on her list. "You're looking at a thirty-minute wait, but I'll see what I can do."

Lucy was surprised the woman didn't ask for Ryland's phone number or hand him hers. More women, both staff and customers, stared at him.

He shot Lucy a sideward glance. "Half hour okay?"

"The cheese fondue is worth the wait."

Ryland raised a brow. "Even when you're hungry?"

"Especially then."

Other customers made their way out of the restaurant while more entered. He moved closer to her to make room in the small, crowded lobby area. "Connor told me how much you love the cheese fondue here."

"It's my favorite."

"Not chocolate?"

"Chocolate, cheese. I'm not that particular as long as it's warm and…"

"Gooey."

"Lucy?" a familiar male voice asked.

No. No. No. Every muscle in her body tensed. She squeezed her eyes shut in hopes she was dreaming, but when she opened them she was still standing in Otto's. Her ex-husband, Jeff Swanson, and his wife, Amelia, weaved through the crowd toward her. Jeff's receding hairline had gotten worse. And Amelia. She looked different…

Lucy narrowed her gaze for a better look.

Pregnant.

Pain gripped her chest. Life wasn't fair. She sighed.

Ryland stiffened. "You okay?"

"No." Not unless aliens were about to beam her up to the mother ship would she be okay. Being probed and prodded by extraterrestrials would be better than having to speak with the two people who had hurt her most. "But I'll survive."

At least she hoped so.

Jeff crowded in next to them. "I almost didn't recognize you."

The smell of his aftershave brought a rush of memories she'd rather forget. The bad times had overshadowed any good ones that might have existed at the beginning. "It's me."

"I see that now." Jeff's gaze raked over her. "But you cut your hair short. And you must have lost what? Twenty-five pounds or more?"

Stress had made eating difficult after the divorce. Going out solo or fixing a meal for one wasn't much fun, either. She'd also discovered Zumba classes at a nearby gym when she moved to Chicago. "Fifteen."

"Good for you," Amelia said. "It seems like we never stopped dieting when we were in high school. Remember that soup diet? I still can't stand the sight or smell of cabbage."

Until finding out about the affair, Lucy had been thankful to have Amelia for a best friend. Lucy had always felt inadequate, an ugly duckling compared to pretty Amelia with her jade-green eyes and shoulder-length blond hair. Amelia's hair now fell to her mid-back. Jeff liked long hair. That was why Lucy had chopped hers off.

Jeff extended his arm to shake hands. "Ryland James. I'm surprised to see you back in town."

His jaw tensed. "My parents still live here."

"Amelia, do you remember Ryland?" Jeff asked. "Soccer player extraordinaire."

"Of course." Amelia smiled sweetly. "Lucy had the biggest crush on you when we were in middle school."

"I know," Ryland said.

Lucy's heart went splat against the restaurant's hardwood floor. "You did?"

He nodded.

Aaron must have told Ryland. But why would her brother have done that? Her crush was supposed to be a secret.

"I didn't know," Jeff announced.

"Husbands." Amelia shook her head. "I mean, ex-husbands are always the last to know."

Ignore her. Ignore her. Ignore her.

Lucy repeated the mantra in her head so she didn't say anything aloud. The words wanting to come out of her mouth were neither ladylike nor appropriate for a public setting.

So what if she would have rather told Ryland about her failed marriage? Amelia was not worth causing a scene over.

Ryland put his arm around Lucy and pulled her against him. He toyed with her hair, wrapping a curl around his finger.

Her heart swelled with gratitude. She hated needing anyone. She'd been so weak when she'd been younger she wanted to be strong now that she was healthy. But she needed him at this moment.

She sunk against Ryland, soaking up his warmth and his strength, feeling his heart beat. The constant rhythm, the sound of life, comforted her.

Lucy smiled up at him.

He smiled back.

Both Jeff and Amelia stared with dumbfounded expressions on their faces.

Ryland had been right. Words weren't always necessary. People believed what they wanted, even if their assumptions might be incorrect.

Amelia's eyes darkened. She pressed her lips into a thin line.

Jeff's gaze bounced between Lucy and Ryland. "The two of you are...together?"

Lucy understood the disbelief in his voice. She and Ryland made an unlikely pair, but still she nodded. She didn't like dishonesty after all the lies people had told her, but this didn't bother her so much. They were having dinner together tonight. Not the "together" Jeff had been talking about, but "together" nonetheless.

"I'd heard you were back in town taking care of Connor, but I had no idea about the two of you," Jeff said, not sounding pleased at all.

Good. Let him stew in his own cheating, miserable, arrogant juices.

Biting back a cutting retort, she glanced up at Ryland.

He kept playing with her hair with one hand while the other kept a possessive hold around her. His gaze held Lucy's for a long moment, the kind that elicited envious sighs from movie audiences. She'd owe him big-time for pretending like this, but she would gladly pay up.

"Soccer isn't that big in the U.S.," Ryland said. "But I played in the U.K. where the media coverage is insane so I try to keep a low profile with my personal life."

Amelia's face scrunched so much it looked painful. "But you're not staying here, are you? I thought you played on the West Coast somewhere."

"Phoenix." Ryland's gaze never wavered from Lucy's, making her insides feel all warm and gooey. "Though I wouldn't mind playing for Indianapolis so I could be closer to Wicksburg."

A thrill rushed through her. That was only a couple of hours away.

"We're having a baby," Amelia blurted as if no one had noticed her protruding belly. "It's a boy."

"Congratulations," both Lucy and Ryland said at the same time.

"I know how badly you wanted children when you were with Jeff," Amelia said to her. "Maybe something happened because of your liver. All those medicines you took and the transplant. But adoption is always an option."

After two years of trying to conceive, she hadn't been able to get pregnant. The doctors said there was no medical reason why she shouldn't be able to have a baby. Amelia knew that. So did Jeff. And it wasn't as if the two of them had gotten pregnant right away. Still feelings of inadequacy pummeled Lucy. Her shoulders slumped.

Ryland cuddled her close, making her feel accepted and special. "Kids aren't easy to handle. But you should see how great Lucy is with Connor."

Amelia patted her stomach. "Jeff and my best friend, Madison, are throwing me a baby shower. They've been planning it for weeks. I can't wait."

The words reminded Lucy of something she'd buried in the far recesses of her mind. Pain sliced through her, sharp and unyielding, at the betrayal of trust by Jeff and Amelia.

"I remember when the two of you spent all that time planning my birthday party." The words tasted bitter on Lucy's tongue. "That's when your affair started, right?"

Amelia gasped. She glared at a contrite-looking Jeff then stormed out of the restaurant.

"Damn." Jeff ran after her calling, "It's not what you think."

Lucy looked toward the door. "I almost feel sorry for her."

"Don't. She knew who and what she was marrying. Swanson is a complete moron." Ryland kept his arm around her. Lucy felt safe and secure in his embrace. His presence took the sting out of the past. "Any guy who would choose that woman over you doesn't have a brain cell in his head."

"Thanks," she said, grateful for his support in the face of her bad judgment. "But the truth is, I should have never married a guy like him."

"Why did you?" Ryland asked.

At a small table for two in the corner of the restaurant, candlelight glowed from a glass votive holder, creating a dancing circle against the white linen tablecloth. Ryland sat across from Lucy, their knees brushing against each other. A bowl of cheese fondue, a basket of bread cubes and a plate with two Bavarian Pretzels were between them.

As Lucy talked about Jeff Swanson, Ryland wished he could change the past and erase the pain she'd experienced from her disastrous marriage.

"People warned me about Jeff." Lucy kept her chin up, her gaze forward, not downcast. But the hurt in her voice was unmistakable. "Told me to break up with him while we were dating. Aaron. Even Amelia. But I thought I knew better than all of them. I thought I could trust Jeff, but he had me so fooled."

"I doubt you're the only one he fooled."

She nodded. "After we eloped, I discovered Jeff hadn't been honest with me. He didn't like how independent and self-reliant I'd been while we were dating. He expected me to turn into his needy little wife. One who stayed home, cooked, cleaned and doted upon him. I admit I was far from the ideal spouse he expected. Amelia is more the doting type he wanted." Lucy stabbed her fork into a piece of bread. "But that didn't give him a reason to cheat."

"Jeff treated girls badly in high school, but they still wanted to go out with him."

She poked the bread again. "I don't think he knew I existed in high school. But when we bumped into each other in college, he laid on the charm. He knew what girls wanted to hear. At least what this girl needed to hear."

Her piece of bread had been stabbed so many times it was falling apart. He didn't think Lucy realized what she was doing with her appetizer fork. "There's not much left of that piece of bread. You might want to try another cube."

"Sorry." She stuck her fork into another piece and dipped the bread into the cheese. It fell into the pot. "I know I played a part in the breakup. It takes two people to make a marriage. But I wish Jeff had been more up-front and honest about what he wanted from me."

Ryland respected how she took responsibility, not laying all the blame on a cheating spouse. "If you could do it over..."

"I wouldn't," she said firmly. "I'm better off without him, but I'll admit it's hard being back in town. So many people know what happened. I'm sure they're pitying me the way they did when I was sick and talking behind my back."

"What people say doesn't matter." He wanted to see her smile, not look so sad. "Forget about them. Don't let it get to you. You're strong enough to do that."

"Strong?" Her voice cracked. "I'm a wimp."

"You came back to Wicksburg."

"Only because Aaron asked me," she admitted. "I couldn't have taken this leap on my own."

Damn Jeff Swanson. He'd not only destroyed Lucy's trust in others, but also in herself. "Give it time. Go slow."

She winced. "I'm trying. It's just when we were dating, Jeff made me feel..."

Ryland didn't want to push, but curiosity got the best of him. "What?"

Her gaze met his. The depth of betrayal in her eyes slammed into him, as if he'd run headfirst into the left goalpost. He reached across the table and laced his fingers with hers.

She took a deep breath and exhaled slowly. "You know about my liver transplant."

Ryland nodded.

"Someone died so I could live." Her tone stressed the awfulness of the situation and made him wondered if she somehow felt guilty. "I always wondered—I still wonder—whether that person's family would think I was living up to their expectations. I mean, their child's death is what enabled me to have the transplant. Given that ultimate sacrifice, would they be disappointed with what I've done with my life? What I'm doing or not doing now?"

Ryland's heart ached for her. That was a heavy load for anyone to carry. Especially someone as sensitive and sweet as Lucy. He squeezed her hand.

"Jeff's real appeal, I think, was that he made me believe we could achieve something big, something important together. With his help, I could prove I deserved a second chance with a new liver." Her mouth turned down at the corner. Angst clouded her eyes. "But we didn't. It was all talk. He no longer cared about that once we were married."

The sorrow in her voice squeezed Ryland's heart like a vice grip.

"I wanted to make a difference because of the gift I was given." Her mouth twisted with regret. "But I didn't do that when I was married to Jeff. I haven't done anything on my own, either. I doubt I ever will."

Her disappointment clawed at Ryland. "You're making a huge difference for Connor. For Aaron and his wife, too."

She shrugged. "But it's not something big, world changing."

"For your family it is." Did Lucy not know how special she

was? "Look at yourself. You graduated college. You run your own business. That's a lot for someone your age."

"I'm twenty-six," she said with wry sarcasm. "Divorced. In debt with college loans and a car payment. I'm living at my brother's house, and all my possessions fit inside my car."

"You beat liver disease," Ryland countered. "Your being here—alive—is more than enough."

She stared at him as if she was trying to figure him out. A soft smile teased the corners of her mouth. "Where have you been all my life? Well, these past two years?"

Ryland was wondering the same thing. The realization should bother him more than it did.

"Thank you." Gratitude filled her eyes. Her appreciation wasn't superficial or calculated, but from her heart and made him feel valued. She squeezed his hand. "For tonight. For listening to me."

He stroked Lucy's hand with his thumb. "Thanks aren't necessary. I asked you to tell me. I've also been there myself."

Oops. Ryland hadn't meant to say that. He pulled his hand away and took a sip from his water glass.

She pinned him with a questioning gaze. "You?"

He tightened his grip on the glass, wanting to backpedal. "It's not the same. Not even close."

"I've spilled my guts," Lucy said. "It's your turn."

Ryland never opened up the way she had with him. People only valued him for what he could give them. If they knew him, the real him, they would think he wasn't worth much off the pitch. He took another sip of water then placed the glass on the table.

The tilt of her chin told him she wasn't going to let this drop. Of all the people in his life, Lucy didn't care about his fortune or fame. She had never asked him for anything for herself. She was always thinking of others. That included him. If he could tell anyone the truth, it was Lucy.

He swallowed around the emotion clogging his throat. "When I was in elementary school, I was bullied."

"Verbally?"

He nodded. "Sometimes…a lot of times…physically."

Lucy gasped. She placed her hand on top of his, the way he'd done with hers only moments before. "Oh, Ryland. I'm so sorry. That had to be horrible."

"Some days I felt invisible. As if kids were looking right through me." He'd never told anyone about this. Not even his parents. He thought telling Lucy would be hard, but the compassion in her eyes kept him going. "Those were the good days. Otherwise I would get pushed around, even beat up."

He'd felt like such a loser, a nobody, but he'd soon realized bullies were the real losers. Bullies like Jeff Swanson. Ryland would never tell Lucy her ex-husband had been one of the kids who terrorized students like him at Wicksburg Elementary School. That would only upset her more.

Concern knotted her brow. "I had no idea that went on."

"You were a little girl." He remembered her with ponytails and freckles playing hopscotch or swinging at recess. Seemingly without a care in the world. He hadn't known until later that she was so sick. "Some older kids like Aaron knew, but if they stood up to the bullies, they got beat up, too."

Her mouth formed a perfect O. "The time Aaron said he'd fallen off the monkey bars and gotten a black eye."

"One kid couldn't do much. Even a cool guy like your brother." Ryland remembered telling Aaron not to interfere but the guy wouldn't listen. "I hated going to school so much. I hated most everything back then. Except football. Soccer."

Lucy's smile filled him with warmth, a way he'd never felt when thinking about this part of his past. "You found your passion at a young age."

"I liked being part of a team," he admitted. "It didn't matter that I lived in a dumpy apartment on the wrong side of town or was poor or got beat up all the time. When I put on that jersey, I fit in."

She squeezed his hand. "Thank goodness for soccer."

"It was my escape. My salvation." He took a sip of water. "With my teammates alongside me, the bullies had to leave me alone."

She smiled softly. "Your teammates took care of their star player."

He nodded. "Football gave me hope. A way out of Wicksburg so I could make something of myself. Be someone other than the scrawny kid who people picked on."

Kindness and affection reflected in her eyes. "You've done that. You've accomplished so much."

His chest tightened. She was one of a kind. "So have you."

Her hand still rested on his, making everything feel comfortable and natural. Right.

Ryland was in no hurry to have her stop touching him. He had no idea what was going on between them. Pretend, real... He didn't care.

Slowly, almost reluctantly, Lucy pulled her hand away. "Wicksburg holds some bad memories for both of us."

He missed her softness and her warmth. "Some good ones, too."

Like the memories they were creating right now.

She tried to pull the lost bread cube out of the fondue bowl. "At first I wasn't sure about us pretending to date. I don't like being dishonest. But after seeing Jeff and Amelia, I'm thankful you were with me tonight. I know this is what's best for Connor. And the only way for you to help the team."

"And help you."

"And me."

"We're not being that dishonest," he said. "If you think about it, what we're doing is kind of like the funeral."

Her eyes widened. "Funeral?"

Lucy reminded him of Connor. "Playacting at Squiggy's funeral."

She laughed. "You mean his first funeral. Not the top-secret one I wasn't supposed to know about."

Ryland smiled at her lighthearted tone. "Now this is more like it. No more being upset over an idiot like Jeff. It's time for laughter and fun."

"That's exactly what I need."

She raised the piece of fondue-covered bread to her mouth. Her lips closed around it.

So sexy. Ryland's temperature soared. He took another sip of water. Too bad she also didn't need some kisses.

A drop of cheese remained at the corner of her mouth. Ryland wished he could lick it off. "You have a little cheese on your mouth."

She wiped with a napkin, but missed the spot.

Reaching across the table, he used his thumb to remove the cheese, ignoring how soft her lips looked or how badly he wanted to taste their sweetness again. "It's gone."

Her eyes twinkled with silver sparks. "Thanks."

Lucy wouldn't be thanking him if she knew what he was thinking. "You're welcome."

The server arrived with their main courses. Sauerbraten, spatzle noodles and braised red cabbage for Lucy. Jagerschnitzel with mashed potatoes for him. The food smelled mouthwateringly delicious.

As they ate, Ryland couldn't stop thinking about what would happen after dinner and dessert were finished. When it was the two of them back at her house. Alone. This might be a pretend date, but he wanted to kiss her good-night.

For real.

CHAPTER TEN

RIDING IN THE OLD, blue truck, Lucy glanced at Ryland, who sat next to her on the bench seat. With his chiseled good looks, his handsome profile looked as if it had been sculpted, especially with the random headlights casting shadows on his face. But there was nothing hard and cold about the man. He was generous, caring and funny. He might be portrayed as being a bad boy in the press, but she'd glimpsed the man underneath the façade and liked what she saw.

He turned onto the street where she lived.

After spilling secrets, she and Ryland had spent the rest of dinner laughing over jokes, stories and memories. Too bad the evening had to end.

"I can't believe we ate that entire apple strudel after all the fondue and dinner," she said.

"We," he teased. "I only had two bites."

"More like twenty-two."

He parked at the curb and set the gear. "Math's never been a strong point. Which is why soccer is the perfect sport for me. Scores rarely reach two digits."

She grinned. "That's why they invented calculators. For all us right-brained people who can't tell the difference between Algebra and Calculus."

"What about addition and subtraction?" With a wink, he removed the key from the ignition. "Stay there. I'll get the door for you."

His manners impressed Lucy. Okay, she may have assumed athletes had more in common with Neanderthals than gentlemen, but Ryland was proving her wrong. About many things tonight.

The passenger door opened. He extended his arm. "Milady?"

Lucy didn't need Ryland's help, but accepted it anyway. He wasn't offering because she was incapable or unhealthy. He was doing this to be polite. She would gladly play along. "Thank you, kind sir."

The touch of her fingers against his skin caused a spark. Static electricity from the truck's carpet? Whatever it was, heat traveled through her, igniting a fire she hadn't felt in a long time and wasn't sure what to do with.

As soon as she was out of the truck and standing on the sidewalk, Ryland let go of her. A relief, given her reaction, but she missed his touch.

"You must be cold," he said.

Even with the cool night air and her sleeveless dress, she wasn't chilly. Not with Ryland next to her.

"I'm fine." Thousands of stars twinkled overhead. She'd forgotten what the night sky looked like in the country compared to that in a city. "It's a beautiful night."

"Very beautiful."

She glanced his way.

He was looking at her, not the sky. Her body buzzed with awareness. She could stand out here with him all night.

His smile crinkled the corners of his eyes and did funny things to her heart rate.

Tearing her gaze away, Lucy headed up the paved walkway

toward the front porch. Ryland followed her, his steps sounding against the concrete.

Uncertainty coursed through Lucy. Ryland made her feel so special tonight, listening in a way Jeff never had and sharing a part of himself with her.

This wasn't a real date. Except at some point this evening, she hadn't been pretending. Ryland hadn't seemed to be, either. That…worried her.

Lucy didn't trust herself when it came to men, especially Ryland. Best to say a quick good-night and make a hasty retreat inside. Alone. So she could figure this out.

On the porch, she reached into her purse with a shaking hand and pulled out her keys. "I had a great time. Thanks."

"The night's still young."

Anticipation revved her blood. She wanted to invite him in. Who was she kidding? She wanted to throw herself into his arms and kiss him until they ran out of air. Or the sun came up.

Lucy couldn't deny the flush of desire, but if they started something would she be able to stop? Would she want to stop? To go too far would be disastrous. "I'm thinking we should call it a night."

He ran his finger along her jawline. "You think?"

Lucy gulped. "I'm not ready for taking any big leaps."

"What about a small one?"

His lips beckoned. Hers ached. Maybe just a little kiss…

She lifted her chin and kissed him on the mouth. Hard.

Ryland pressed his mouth against Lucy's with a hunger that matched her own. He wrapped his arms around her, pulling her closer. She went eagerly, arching against him. This was what she wanted…needed.

The keys dropped from her fingers and clattered on the step. She placed her hands on his shoulders, feeling the ridges of his muscles beneath her fingertips.

His lips moved over hers. She parted her lips, allowing their tongues to explore and dance.

Pleasurable sensations shot through her. She clung to him and his kiss. Longing pooled low in her belly. A moan escaped her lips.

Ryland drew the kiss to an end. "Wow."

That pretty much summed it up. She took a breath and another. It didn't help. Her breathing was still ragged. And her throbbing lips...

She fought the urge to touch them to see that what she'd experienced hadn't been a dream. "I've been trying to curb my impulsive side. Looks like I failed."

"I'd give you an A+ and recommend letting yourself be more impulsive." Wicked laughter lit his eyes. He kept his arms around her. "We could go inside and see where our impulses take us."

Most likely straight into the bedroom. Lucy's heart slammed against her chest.

A sudden fear dampened her desire. She'd been hurt too badly, didn't trust her judgment or the feelings coursing through her right now. Especially with a man who had more opportunity to cheat than her ex-husband ever had.

Ryland James is a player, Luce. He'll break your heart if he gets the chance.

Aaron's words echoed through her head. "We can't. I mean, I can't."

Ryland combed his fingers through her hair. "If you think I'm pretending, I'm not."

"Me, either." Her resolve weakened. "But I have to think of Connor."

"He's spending the night with Marco."

Her mouth went dry with the possibilities. "You're leaving town soon."

"True, but we can make the most of the time I have left," Ryland said, his voice husky and oh-so tempting. "You said you didn't want a boyfriend. I'm not looking for a girlfriend."

"Not a real one at least."

"Touché."

"This has nowhere to go. I'm not up for a fling. Aaron thinks if we get involved, you'll break my heart."

Ryland stiffened. "Your brother said that?"

"The other night when he called."

His mouth quirked. "So let's just keep doing what we've been doing."

"Pretending."

"We'll date, but keep it light," he said. "No promises. No guarantees."

"No sex."

"You've made that clear." He sounded amused, not upset. "Except how do you feel about pretend sex?"

"Huh?"

"Never mind," he said. "We'll just have fun and enjoy each other's company until it's time for me to go back to Phoenix."

Lucy wasn't one to play with fire. She'd done everything in her power these past two years to keep from getting burned again. But this was different. She knew where she stood with Ryland. He'd been honest with her. They could make this work. But she would keep a fire extinguisher handy in case the flames got out of control. Getting burned was one thing. She didn't want to wind up a pile of ash. "Okay. We can keep doing what we've been doing."

On Sunday afternoon, Ryland knocked on Lucy's front door. He'd done the same thing less than twenty-four hours ago. But he felt more anticipation today.

She'd been on his mind since last night. Her kisses had fueled his fantasies, making him want more.

But she wasn't ready to give more. At least not the more he wanted.

I don't sleep around.

I'm not up for a fling.

No sex.

She hadn't said anything about no kisses. He'd settle for those. Maybe Lucy would change her mind about the physical part of their...not relationship...hanging out.

The front door opened. Connor smiled up at him with a toothy grin. "Fuego plays in an hour."

This was the second game of the season for his team. They were in L.A. to play against the Galaxy. Ryland had missed not being at the season opener earlier this week when the team lost to the Portland Timbers. He'd felt like he was letting down his teammates and fans down being unable to play. He looked at his foot.

The orthopedist had told Ryland he might get the boot off in another week or two. That meant he would be able to return to the team, but in order to do that he would have to leave Wicksburg.

Wait a minute. Leaving town would be a good thing. Nothing was holding him here. Well, except his parents who would be returning home this week.

And Lucy. But he couldn't let himself go there. When he could play again, soccer would have to be his total focus. He couldn't afford any distractions. She would be a big one.

"Aunt Lucy told me to cheer loudly." Connor grabbed Manny who was darting between his legs, trying get out of the house. "I have to finish my math homework first. Aunt Lucy said so."

"Better get to it, bud." Ryland entered the house. He closed the door behind him. "I don't want to watch the game without you."

Connor ran off to his bedroom to finish his homework. Ryland walked to the kitchen.

The scents of cheese and bacon filled the air. His mouth watered, as much for whatever was baking as the woman unloading the dishwasher. Lucy wore a pair of jean shorts. Her T-shirt inched up in the back showing him a flash of ivory skin in the back as she bent over to grab silverware. Her lime V-neck T-shirt gaped revealing the edge of her white-lace bra.

Beautiful.

He stepped behind and wrapped his arms around Lucy. Her soft-in-all-the-right-places body fit perfectly against his. Knowing they were alone while Connor did his math, Ryland showered kisses along her jawline.

She faced him. Silver sparks flashed in her eyes. "Is this how you normally say hello?"

"No, I prefer this way."

He lowered his mouth to hers. His lips soaked in her warmth and sweetness. His heart rate tripled. The blood rushed from his head.

She arched against him, taking the kiss deeper. He followed her lead, relieved she was as into kissing as he was. He liked kissing Lucy. He wanted to keep on kissing her.

Forever.

Ryland jerked back.

He didn't do forever.

She stared up at him with flushed cheeks and swollen lips. The passion in her eyes matched the desire rushing through his veins. Definitely a keeper. If he was looking for one...

Lucy grinned. "I like how you say hello."

He liked it, too. Especially with her.

But he had to remember to keep things light. No thoughts about forever. They had two weeks, if they were lucky. No reason to get carried away.

And he wouldn't. That wouldn't be fair to Lucy. Or her brother.

He owed Aaron that much, even if his old friend was wrong about Ryland breaking Lucy's heart. He wouldn't do that to her.

He inhaled. "Whatever you're cooking smells delicious."

"Macaroni and cheese." She turned on the oven light so he could see the casserole dish baking inside. "Dana marked her cookbooks with Connor's favorite recipes."

"I smell bacon."

Lucy smiled coyly. "That's one of the secret ingredients."

"I didn't know you were allowed to divulge secret ingredients."

She shrugged. "We shared our secrets last night so I figured why not."

The vase containing the iris he'd given her sat on the counter. Paintbrushes dried alongside it. "If we have nothing left to hide, show me your paintings."

Her lips quirked. "You really want to see them?"

She sounded surprised by his interest in her art. "I do, or I wouldn't keep asking."

"I—I don't show my work to a lot of people."

"It's just me."

Uncertainty flickered in her eyes. "Exactly."

Ryland didn't understand what she meant. "Show me one."

She raised a brow. "That'll be enough to appease your curiosity?"

He wasn't sure of anything when it came to Lucy. But he would take what he could get. "Yes. I'll leave it up to you if you want to show me more."

She glanced at the oven timer. "I suppose we have time now."

Not the most enthusiastic response, but better than a no. "Great."

Lucy led him down a hallway covered with framed photographs. One picture showed a large recreational vehicle that looked more like a bus.

"Is that your parents' RV?" he asked.

"Yes," she said. "How did you know about that?"

"Connor told me his grandparents were living in a camper and traveling all over the country."

"Yes, that's how they dreamed of spending their retirement. They finally managed to do it three months ago." She peeked in on Connor, who sat at his desk doing his homework. "They're in New Mexico right now."

Ryland wondered what Lucy dreamed of doing. He considered asking, but any of her dreams would be on hold until Aaron and his wife returned. Ryland admired Lucy's sacrifice. He'd thought watching Cupcake had been a big deal. Not even close. He followed her through another doorway.

The bedroom was spotless with nothing out of place. The queen-size bed, covered with a flower-print comforter and matching pillow shams, drew his attention. This was where Lucy slept. Alone, but the bed was big enough for two.

Don't even think about it. He looked away.

She went to the closet.

Ryland knew what to expect from a typical twenty-something woman's closet—overflowing with clothing, shoes and purses.

Lucy opened the door.

Only a few clothing items hung on the rack. A sheet of plastic covered the closet floor. Five pairs of shoes sat on top. Not a handbag in sight. Instead, the backsides of different-size canvases and boxes of art supplies filled the space.

Not typical at all.

Given this was Lucy he shouldn't have been surprised.

"This is something I painted when I was living in Chicago." As she reached for the closest painting, her hand trembled.

Ryland touched her shoulder. He wanted to see her work, but he didn't want to make her uncomfortable. Her bare skin felt soft and warm beneath his palm. "We can do this another time."

"Now is fine." She glanced back at him. "It's just a little hard..."

"To show this side of yourself."

She nodded.

The vulnerability in her eyes squeezed his heart. Her affect on him unnerved Ryland. He lowered his arm from her shoulder. "If it's any consolation, I know nothing about art. I'm about as far removed from an art critic as you can get."

"So if you like it, I'll remember not to get too excited."

He smiled.

She smiled back.

His heart stumbled over itself. His breath rushed from his lungs as if he'd played ninety minutes without a break at half-time.

What was going on?

All she'd done was smile. Something she'd done a hundred times before. But he could hardly breathe.

She pulled out the canvas. "Ready?"

No. Feeling unsteady, he sat on the bed.

"Sure." He forced the word from his tight throat.

Lucy turned the canvas around.

Ryland stared openmouthed and in awe. He'd expected to see a bowl of fruit or a bouquet of flowers. Not a vibrant, colorful portrait full of people having fun. The painting depicted a park with people picnicking, riding bicycles, pushing baby strollers and flying kites.

A good thing he was sitting or he would have fallen flat on his butt. The painting was incredible. Amazing. He felt transported, as if he were in the park seeing what she'd seen, feeling what she'd felt. Surreal.

He took a closer look. "Is that guy eating a hot dog?"

She nodded. "What's a day in the park without a hot dog from a vendor?"

Drops of yellow mustard dripped onto the guy's chin and shirt. The amount of detail amazed Ryland. He noticed a turtle painted next to the pond. An homage to Squiggy? "You're so talented."

"You know nothing about art," she reminded him.

"True, but I know quality when I see it," he said. "This is a thousand times better than any of the junk hanging on my walls in Phoenix."

She raised a brow. "I doubt those artists would consider their work junk."

He waved a hand. "You know what I mean."

"Thank you."

"No, thank you." This painting told him so much about Lucy. He could see her in each stroke, each character, each detail. Life exploded from the canvas. The importance of community, too. "I know a couple of people who own art galleries."

Her lips pursed. "Thanks, but I'm not ready to do that."

"You're ready," he encouraged. "Trust yourself. Your talent."

"I don't think I should do anything until Aaron and Dana get home."

Ryland hated to see Lucy holding back like this. "Think about it."

"I will. Would you like to see another one?" she asked to his surprise. "Not all of them are so cheery as this one. I went through a dark stage."

"Please." Looking at her work was like taking a peek inside her heart and her soul. He wanted to see more, as many paintings as she allowed him to see. "Show me."

Lucy would have never thought the best date ever would include mac and cheese, her nine-year-old nephew and a televised soccer game, but it had tonight. At first she'd been so nervous about showing Ryland her work, afraid of exposing herself like that and what he might think. He not only liked her paintings, but also understood them. Catching details most people overlooked.

She stood at the doorway to her nephew's bedroom while Ryland, by request, tucked Connor into bed.

The two talked about the game. Even though Fuego lost 0–1 to the Galaxy, both agreed it was a good game.

"They would have won if you'd been there," Connor said.

Ryland ruffled Connor's hair. "We'll never know."

"I can't wait to see you play."

As the soccer talk continued, Lucy leaned against the hallway wall.

Thanks to Ryland, her nephew was a happy kid again. Connor still missed his parents, but a certain professional soccer player had made a big difference. At least for now.

Lucy wondered if Connor realized when Ryland could play again he wouldn't be coaching. But if the Fuego played the Indianapolis Rage, maybe they could get tickets. She would have to check the match schedule.

Seeing Ryland play in person might be just the ticket to keep a smile on her nephew's face. Lucy had to admit she would like that, too.

"Good night, Connor." Ryland turned off the light in the bedroom. "I'll see you at practice tomorrow."

"'Night."

In the hallway, he laced his fingers with hers and led her into the living room. "I finally have you all to myself."

"We don't have to watch the post-match commentary?" she teased.

"I set the DVR so I wouldn't have to subject you to that." He pulled her against him. "But I will subject you to this."

Ryland's lips pressed against hers. His kiss was soft. Tender. Warm.

She leaned against him, only to find herself swept up in his arms. But his lips didn't leave hers.

He carried her to the couch and sat with her on his lap. Lucy wrapped her arms around him. Her breasts pressed against his hard chest.

As she ran her hands along his muscular shoulders and wove her fingers through his hair, she parted her lips. She wanted more of his kisses, more of him.

The pressure of his mouth against hers increased, full of hunger and heat. Her insides felt as if they were melting.

Ryland might be a world-class soccer player, but he was a world-class kisser, too.

Pleasurable sensations shot through her. Tingles exploded. If she'd been confused about the definition of chemistry, she understood it now.

Thank goodness he had his arms around her or she'd be falling to the floor, a mass of gooey warmth. Not that she was complaining. She clung to him, wanting even more of his kisses.

Slowly Ryland loosened his hold on her and drew the kiss to an end. "Told you this would be fun."

"You did." A good thing he wasn't going to be around long enough or this could become habit forming. Her chest tightened.

Lucy couldn't afford for anything about Ryland to become habit. She couldn't allow herself to get attached.

Neither of them was in a place to pursue a relationship. Neither of them could commit to anything long-term.

This was about spending time together in the short-term and having fun. And sharing some very hot kisses.

That had to be enough. Even if a part of her was wishing there could be…more.

CHAPTER ELEVEN

As THE DAYS PASSED, the temperature warmed. The sun stayed out longer. The Defeeters won more games than they lost. But Lucy wasn't looking forward to the end of spring. She didn't want Ryland to leave.

Being with him was exciting. Wicksburg no longer seemed like a boring, small town as they made the most of their time together. Practice twice a week. Dinner with Connor. Lunch when her work schedule or his physical therapy allowed. When she was alone, her painting flourished with heightened senses and overflowing creativity.

After Mr. and Mrs. James returned from their vacation, they became fixtures at games and invited everyone to dinner following a practice.

That Monday evening, a bird chirped in a nearby cherry tree in the Jameses' backyard. The cheery tune fit perfectly with the jubilant mood. The boys kicked a soccer ball on the grass while Cupcake chased after them barking.

Standing on the patio, Lucy watched the boys play.

"Connor reminds me of his father," Mrs. James said. She

wore her salt-and-pepper hair in a ponytail, a pair of jeans and a button-down blouse. "Though he's a little taller than Aaron was at this age."

"Connor's mom is tall." Lucy glanced at Mrs. James. "Thank you for having us over tonight."

"Our pleasure. It's so nice to have children here." She stared at the boys running around. "I've been telling Ryland to settle down so I can have grandchildren to spoil, but that boy has only one thing on his mind."

"Soccer," Lucy said at the same time as his mother.

Mrs. James eyed her curiously. "You know him well."

Lucy shifted her weight between her feet. "He's been helping me with the team."

"And going out with you." Mrs. James smiled. "Hard to keep things secret in a town Wicksburg's size."

They hadn't tried hiding anything. The more people who knew they were going out, the better. Lucy wanted nothing more than to enjoy her time with Ryland, but she felt as if she was trying to hold on to the wind. He would be blowing out of her life much too soon.

"It's so nice Ryland is with someone who knew him before he became famous," Mrs. James said.

"He was always a star player around here."

Ryland shouted something to the boys. Laughter filled the air.

"Yes, but he thinks of himself as a footballer, nothing else," Mrs. James explained. "Ryland needs to realize that there's a life for him off the pitch, too. I hope being here and getting reacquainted with you and others will help him see that."

"Soccer is his only priority." Lucy had been reminding herself that for days now. All the smiles, laughter and kisses they shared would be coming to an end. But she didn't want to turn into a sighing lump because he was leaving. "He's not interested in anything else."

"I wonder if soccer would be as important to him if he thought there was somewhere else he belonged."

I liked being part of a team. It didn't matter that I lived in a dumpy apartment on the wrong side of town or was poor or got beat up all the time. When I put on that jersey, I fit in.

Lucy remembered what he'd told her. "Belonging is important to him, but Ryland doesn't think he belongs in Wicksburg."

Mrs. James's eyes widened. "You've talked about this?"

Lucy hoped she wasn't opening a can of worms for Ryland, but his mother seemed genuinely concerned. "A little."

"That's a start." Mrs. James's green eyes twinkled with pleasure. "It's going to take Ryland time to realize where he belongs, and that he's more than he thinks he is."

"Maybe when he gets back to Phoenix." Lucy's chest tightened. "He doesn't have much time left here."

"He can always come back."

Lucy nodded. She hoped Ryland would return after the MLS season ended, but that was months away.

"Well, I'd better finish getting the taco bar ready," Mrs. James said. "The boys must be starving."

"What can I do to help?" Lucy asked.

"Enjoy yourself."

As Mrs. James walked away, Cheryl came up. She held an iPad. "Getting on the mother's good side is smart. I should have done that with my mother-in-law."

"It's not too late," Lucy said.

"Well, the divorce papers haven't been filed yet. But I don't want to talk about my sorry situation." Cheryl showed Lucy an article from a U.K. tabloid's website. "Guess this is what happens when you're with one of the hottest footballers around."

Lucy stared at the iPad screen full of pictures of her and Ryland. "Why would they do this?"

Cheryl sighed. "Because it's so romantic."

Romantic, perhaps. But not…real. The photos made it appear as if Lucy and Ryland were falling for each other. Falling hard.

The top photograph was from the Defeeters' first game when Ryland kneeled behind her and whispered in her ear, but it looked as if he were kissing her neck. The second showed them in a booth at the pizza parlor sitting close together and gazing into each other's eyes. The last one captured their quick congratulatory peck after the team's first win, but the photograph made it seem like a long, tongue shoved down each other's throats full-on make-out session. Okay, they'd had a couple of those, but not where anyone could see them let alone take a picture.

As Lucy read the article, the blood rushed from her head. The world spun. The pictures didn't imply a serious relationship. The words suggested an imminent engagement.

Oh, no. This was bad. "I can't believe this."

"I didn't realize things were so serious."

"Me, neither." Ryland wasn't going to like this. Lucy reread a paragraph. "They call me a WAG. Is that a British euphemism for hag or something?"

Cheryl laughed. "WAG stands for Wives and Girlfriends. Many women aspire to be one."

The acronym wasn't accurate. Surprisingly the thought of being Ryland's girlfriend didn't sound so bad. Unease slithered down Lucy's spine. She knew better to think that way. Dating Ryland didn't include being his girlfriend. Except everyone reading the article… "I hope people don't believe all this."

"You and Ryland care about each other. That's all that matters."

Care.

Yes, Lucy cared about Ryland. She cared…a lot.

As she stared at one of the photographs, a deeper attraction and affection for Ryland surfaced, accompanied by a sinking feeling in her stomach.

Oh, no. She'd been ignoring and pretending certain feelings didn't exist, but the article was bringing all that emotion out. She couldn't deny the truth any longer.

Lucy didn't just care about Ryland.

I love him.

The truth hit her like a gallon of paint dropped on her head.

She'd fallen in love with Ryland James. Even though she'd known all the reasons why she shouldn't.

Stupid, stupid, stupid.

"You look pale," Cheryl said. "Are you okay?"

"I don't know," Lucy admitted. "I really don't know."

Ryland had pursued her. She'd pretended she couldn't be caught, but she'd been swept up by his charm and heart the minute he'd turned them on her.

Lucy wanted people to be honest with her, but she'd lied to herself about how safe it was to date Ryland, to hang out with him, to kiss him.

"Don't let a gossip column bother you. Talk to Ryland about it," Cheryl suggested. "I'm sure he's dealt with this before."

Gossip, yes. But Lucy wasn't sure how many women had fallen in love with him. She couldn't imagine being the first, but she wasn't sure she wanted to know the number of women who had gone down this same path.

Talk to Ryland about it.

She'd experienced a change of heart about wanting a relationship. Maybe he'd had one, too. And if not…

No. This wasn't a crush. Her feelings weren't one-sided. His kisses were proof of that as was his wanting to spend time with her. He had feelings for her. She knew he did.

Lucy had shared her secrets and art with him. How hard could it be to tell him she'd lost her heart to him, too?

She would talk to Ryland and see where their feelings took them.

After dinner, Ryland carried in the leftovers from the taco bar while a soccer match between kids and adults was being fought to determine bragging rights.

In the kitchen, he set the pan of ground beef on the counter. "That's the last of it."

His mother handed him a plastic container. "I like Lucy."

"So do I."

"Good, because it's about time you got serious with a woman."

Ryland flinched. He stared at his mom in disbelief. "Who said anything about getting serious?"

"Your father and I aren't getting any younger. We'd like grandkids while we can still get around and play with them. You and Lucy would have cute babies."

"Whoa, Mom." Ryland held up his hands, as if that could stop a runaway train like his mom. "I like Lucy. That's a long way from having babies with her. I need to focus on my career."

His mom shrugged. "A soccer ball won't provide much comfort after you retire."

He spooned the meat into the container. "I'll settle down once I stop playing."

"That's years away."

Ryland covered the ground beef with a lid. "I hope so."

"That's not what your mother wants to hear."

"It's the truth," he admitted. "If I put down any kind of roots, I'm not going to be able to finish out my career the way I want to."

"A woman like Lucy won't wait around forever. She won't have to in a town like Wicksburg." His mom filled a plastic Ziploc baggie with the leftover shredded cheese. "While you're off playing football and partying with WAG wannabes, another man will sweep Lucy off her feet. She'll have a ring on her finger before Christmastime."

Ryland clenched his hands. Wait a minute. His mom had no idea what she was saying. "Lucy doesn't want a ring. Not from me or anyone else."

"You sound confident."

"I am," he admitted. "We talked about it."

"It?"

"Relationships. Lucy and I are on the same page." He wished his mom wasn't sticking her nose into his business. He kept his social life private so she wouldn't know what was going on. "I

can't be thinking about a relationship right now because of soccer. Lucy doesn't want to be entangled by any guy while she's
taking care of Connor."

His mom studied him. "So when you go back to Phoenix…"

"It's over."

"And when you come back?"

"You and Dad can visit me," Ryland said. "I've worked too
hard to get out of Wicksburg."

"You ran away."

"I left to play soccer."

His mother took a deep breath then exhaled slowly. "You're
an adult and capable of making your own decisions, but please,
honey, think about what you may be giving up if you leave town,
leave Lucy, and never look back."

He picked up the container of meat and placed it in the refrigerator. "You're way off base here, Mom."

"Maybe I am, but one of these days you're going to realize
soccer isn't the only thing in the world. I'd like for you to have
a life outside the game in place when that happens."

"You just want me back in Wicksburg raising a bunch of
kids."

"I want you to be happy."

"I am happy." So what if a lot of his happiness right now had
to do with Lucy? Their dating was only for the short-term. They
both agreed. His mother was wrong. This was for the best. "I
know what I'm doing. I know what I want."

And that didn't include Wicksburg or… Lucy.

Later that evening, after everyone had left, Lucy sat with Ryland on his parents' patio. Mr. James was showing Connor his
big-screen TV while Mrs. James gave Cupcake a bath after the
dog jumped into a garbage can.

Ryland leaned back in his chair. "The boys enjoyed themselves."

"Their parents, too." Lucy had thrown herself into playing soccer. A way to put a game face on, perhaps?

"Cheryl showed me an article from a U.K. tabloid tonight." Lucy held up the display screen of her smartphone. "It's about... us."

Heaven help her, but she liked saying the word "us." Ryland had to see how good they were together.

He took the phone and used his finger to scroll through the words. "This happens all the time. Don't let it bother you."

He sounded so nonchalant about the whole thing. "You don't mind that total strangers halfway across the globe are reading about us?"

"It's not about minding." As Ryland laced his fingers with hers, tingles shot up her arm. "Football is almost like a religion in other countries. Fans follow their favorite players' every move. If someone tweets that a star player is at the supermarket buying groceries, hundreds of people might show up in minutes. This article is no different than others they've published about me and other players."

"But you don't play over there anymore."

"I did," he said. "I could go back someday."

So far away. Lucy felt a pang in her heart. She didn't want him to leave. Not to Phoenix. Not anywhere.

She took a deep breath to calm her nerves. "The article makes it read like we're seriously dating, practically engaged."

"But we're not."

Ryland sounded so certain. No hesitation. No regret.

Lucy searched his face for a sign that he'd had a change of heart like her, but she saw nothing. Absolutely nothing to suggest he felt or wanted...more.

That frustrated her. She wanted him to be her boyfriend. The guy should want her to be his girlfriend.

Ryland put his arm around her. "This can be hard to deal with when you're not used to it. But it's how the game is played. You have to ignore it."

Lucy didn't want to ignore it. She wanted the article to be true. She wanted to be a WAG. Ryland's WAG. Not only his girlfriend, she realized with a start. But his…wife.

Mrs. Ryland James.

Lucy suppressed a groan. This was bad. Horrible. Tragic.

No promises. No guarantees. No sex.

"Hey, don't be sad." Ryland caressed her face with his hand. "It's just a stupid article full of gossip and lies. Nothing to worry about."

His words were like jabs with a pitchfork to Lucy's heart. The more he downplayed the article, the more it bothered her. And hurt.

Irritation burned. At Ryland. At herself.

Forget about telling him how she felt. She wasn't going to give him the satisfaction of knowing how much she cared about him when he didn't or wouldn't admit how he felt about her.

Annoyed at the situation and at him, she raised her chin. "I'm not worried. I just wanted to make sure this wouldn't damage the Ryland James brand."

The next day, Ryland took Cupcake on a walk around the neighborhood without the boot, per his doctor's orders. He'd chosen this time because he knew Lucy had a call with a client and wouldn't see him.

He didn't know what was going on with her. She'd given off mixed signals last night. Her good-night kiss suggested she was into him. But her attitude about the tabloid article made him think she might be getting tired of him and unsettled by that side of his fame.

Ryland didn't know what her reaction to his getting the boot off would be.

The little gray dog ran ahead, pulling against the leash.

"Are you ready for me to go back to Phoenix, Cupcake?"

The dog ignored him and sniffed a bush.

"I'm not." He had to leave, but what he and Lucy had to-gether was going to be hard to give up. More time with Lucy would be nice. More than nice. Too bad he couldn't go there or anywhere on the other side of nice. "But I'm not going to have a choice."

His cell phone rang. He pulled it from his pocket and glanced at the touch screen. Blake. About time. Ryland had left him a message last night.

"Did you plant the story about me and Lucy?" he asked.

"Hello to you, too." Blake sounded amused. "Yes, I'm doing well. Thanks for asking."

Ryland watched Cupcake sniff a patch of yellow and pink flowers. "Was it you?"

"No," Blake admitted. "That's not to say I didn't have a sug-gestion for the person who did."

Ryland knew it. The PR firm had to be involved. But Blake would never give him firm details. At least he hadn't in the past when something like this occurred. "Why?"

"Your future with Fuego isn't a sure thing," he said. "A seri-ous girlfriend will help your image. Bad Boy Ryland James get-ting serious with a hometown girl. It sends the message you're maturing and getting out of the party scene."

Ryland pulled Cupcake away from a rose bush with thorns. "You're reaching for something that isn't there."

"I spoke with both your coach and Fuego's owner," Blake said. "Settling down is the best thing you can do right now."

"You're sounding a lot like my mom."

"Your mom's a smart woman."

Ryland looked around to see if anyone was on the street. Empty. "Lucy and I aren't serious."

"A big, sparkling diamond engagement ring from Tiffany & Co. will change all that."

He felt a flash of something, almost a little thrill at the thought of proposing to Lucy. Must be a new form of nausea.

"Yeah, right. I'll catch a flight to Chicago tonight and go buy one."

"Indianapolis is closer," Blake said. "They have a store there according to their website."

"You're joking, right? Otherwise you've lost your mind."

"You said you wanted to play in the MLS," he said. "I'm making that happen for you."

"By lying."

"It's called stretching the truth," Blake said. "Let people see you buy an engagement ring. They can make their own assumptions."

"Lucy would never go for something like this."

"She'll be thrilled. Anyone who looks at those photographs can tell she's as crazy about you as you are about her."

"Crazy, maybe. But not in…" Ryland couldn't bring himself to say the word. "I like her." A lot. More than he'd ever thought possible. "But that doesn't mean I'm ready to get…serious."

Okay, so he'd thought about summer break and time off when he could be with Lucy and Connor. And Manny, the fat cat, too.

But Ryland had realized doing anything more than thinking about the future was stupid. He needed to focus, to prove himself, to play…

"Her life is in Wicksburg. At least as long as she's taking care of Connor," Ryland said. "My life is in Phoenix."

"You don't sound so excited about that anymore."

"I am." Wasn't he? Of course, he was. All this was messing with his head. "But Lucy can't spend the next year or so with us traveling back and forth between here and there, to see each other."

"You can afford it."

"Blake."

"Just playing devil's advocate."

"Be my advocate. That's what I pay you for."

"What do you want?"

Lucy. No, that wasn't possible. "I want to play again. Not the way I played last season with the Fuego, but the way I played over in the Premier League. When it…mattered to me. Working with the kids and Lucy reminded me how much I love the game. And how much I miss it."

"You don't sound the same as you did a month ago." Emotion filled Blake's voice. "For the first time in two years, it sounds like the real Ryland James is back."

"Damn straight, I am." But he couldn't get too excited. Thinking about leaving Lucy left a football-size hole in his chest.

But what could Ryland do? He had a team to play for, a job to do. His goal had always been to escape Wicksburg, not move back and marry a hometown girl.

Whoa. Where had that come from? Marriage had always been a four-letter word to him.

"The team's training staff is itching to work with you," Blake said. "They've been concerned about your training and conditioning."

"They'll be pleasantly surprised."

"Exactly what I hoped you'd say." Blake sounded like he was smiling. "My assistant can make your travel arrangements to Phoenix when you're ready."

Ryland's stomach knotted. He should be ready to leave now after weeks in Wicksburg, but Phoenix didn't hold the same appeal for some reason. "I see the orthopedist this afternoon."

"I hope we hear good news."

We. The only "we" that had come to matter to Ryland was him and Lucy. Uh, Lucy and the Defeeters, that is. They were a package. Emotion tightened his throat. "I'll let you know."

Face it. What could he do? No matter how wonderful Lucy might be, Ryland wasn't picket-fence material, even if he could now understand the appeal of a committed, monogamous relationship. Marriage wasn't a goal of his. He had a career to salvage. The longer he stuck around playing at having a relationship, the deeper things would get and he might end up hurting Lucy.

Ryland knew what he had to do. Get the hell out of Wicksburg. And get out fast before he did any more damage than he'd already done.

CHAPTER TWELVE

OUT ON THE field Wednesday afternoon, Lucy glanced at her watch. Fifteen minutes until the end of today's practice. Strange. Ryland had yet to show up or call. She glanced at the parking lot, but didn't see his father's blue truck.

Even though he'd annoyed her on Monday night, she still wanted to see him. She hoped nothing was wrong. He'd bowed out of dinner last night. After Connor went to bed, she'd used the time to paint.

Marco passed the ball to Tyler. Connor, playing defense, stole the ball and kicked it out of bounds.

Lucy blew the whistle. "Push-ups for the entire team if the ball goes out again."

The boys groaned.

She scooped up the ball and tossed it onto the field. Play continued.

"You're doing great, coach."

Her toes curled at the sound of Ryland's voice. She glanced over her shoulder. He walked toward her in a T-shirt and shorts and…

She stared in shock at the tennis shoe on his right foot. "Your boot. It's gone."

"I no longer need it."

"That's great." And then she realized what that meant. With his foot healed, he would return to Phoenix. Her heart sank, but she kept a smile on her face. Pride kept her from showing how much he'd gotten to her. "I'm happy for you."

"Thanks." He stared at her with a strange look in his eyes. "I want to talk to the boys."

Her muscles tensed. Lucy had a feeling this might not be his usual end-of-practice pep talk. She blew the whistle.

The boys stopped playing and looked her way. Smiles erupted on their faces when they saw Ryland.

He motioned to them. "Everyone gather around."

The boys sat on the grass in front of Ryland. So did Lucy.

"Sorry I was late for practice, but I like what I saw out there," Ryland said. "Keep talking to each other, passing the ball and listening to your coach."

He winked at Lucy.

Her tight shoulder muscles relaxed a little.

"I appreciate how hard you're working. I know the drills we do can be boring, but they work. If you do them enough times at practice, you won't have to think about doing the moves in a game. It'll just happen."

"I can't wait until Saturday's match," Connor said.

"Me, either," Jacob agreed.

The other boys nodded.

Ryland dragged his hand through his hair. "I know you guys are going to play hard on Saturday. But I won't be there. My foot's better. It's time for me to return to my team."

Frowns met his words. Sighs, too. The disappointment on the boys' faces was clear. The kids talked over one another. A few were visibly shaken by the news.

Tears stung Lucy's eyes. She blinked them away. She needed to be strong for Connor and the team. "Let Ryland finish."

The boys quieted.

"I'm sorry I won't be able to be with you during those last two games," he said. "But Coach Lucy will do a great job."

She cleared her dry throat. "Why don't we thank Ryland for all his help with the team?"

The boys shouted the Defeeters' cheer, but the words lacked the same enthusiasm shown on game day. Their hearts weren't in it.

Lucy didn't blame them. Her heart was having a tough time, too. She couldn't believe Ryland hadn't told her about leaving before he'd told the boys. He could have called if he hadn't had time. Even sent a text. But then she remembered the all-too-familiar words.

No promises. No guarantees.

Lucy couldn't be angry with him. Disappointed, yes. But Ryland hadn't played her. He hadn't lied. She'd known all along he was leaving. So did the boys and their parents. She just wasn't ready for the reality of it.

But this couldn't be goodbye. Even if he wasn't willing to admit it, they'd had too much fun, gotten to know each other too well for their dating to simply end. Of that, she was certain. They would stay in contact and see each other...somehow.

While Ryland said goodbye to each boy personally, she gathered up the equipment. As they finished, the boys ran off the field toward their parents.

Finally it was Connor's turn. He threw himself against Ryland and held on tight.

Her nephew's distress clogged Lucy's throat with emotion. She hoped this didn't put him back into a funk. He'd been handling his parents' deployment much better recently. Ryland might have been part of their lives for only a short time, but Connor had already gotten attached.

As Ryland spoke to her nephew, Connor wiped his eyes. This was one more difficult goodbye for the nine-year-old. But it wouldn't be a forever kind of goodbye. Ryland wouldn't do that to the kid, to his bud.

Someone touched Lucy's arm.

"Marco is in the car pouting. He told me Ryland is leaving," Suzy said. "I take it you didn't know."

"I knew he would be leaving. I just didn't know when," Lucy admitted.

"Cheryl showed me that article. His leaving won't change anything between you. You'll see each other. Every chance you can get."

Lucy nodded, hoping that was true.

"I'm going to take Marco to the pizza parlor for dinner. I'll take Connor with us," Suzy said. "You need some alone time with Ryland."

Yes, Lucy did. "I'll meet you there."

"If not, you can pick Connor up at my house."

She appreciated Suzy's thoughtfulness. "Thanks so much."

Suzy winked. "Don't do anything I wouldn't do."

Lucy could imagine what Suzy would want to do. If only she were that brave...

All Lucy could think about was how much she would miss Ryland, his company and his kisses. The memories would have to suffice until they saw each other again.

Ryland finished talking with Connor and sent him over to Lucy. She hugged her nephew and explained the plans for the evening.

Connor nodded, but the sadness in his eyes made her think he was simply going through the motions. Still, he hadn't said no. Being with Marco and having pizza, soda and video games might help Connor feel better.

Lucy watched Suzy walk off the field with an arm around Connor.

"He's upset," Ryland said, sounding almost surprised.

"He's had to say goodbye to his parents and now you," Lucy explained. "That's a lot for a nine-year-old boy to deal with."

"He'll rally."

Eventually. "So when are you leaving?"

"Tonight."

The air whooshed from her lungs. "That soon?"

"You knew I'd be leaving."

"Yes, I did." She kept her voice steady. Even though she was trembling inside, getting emotional would be bad. "But I thought I'd find out before everyone else."

She expected an apology or to hear him say this wasn't really goodbye because they would see each other soon.

"I have to go."

No apology. Okay. "You want to go."

A muscle twitched at his jaw. "Yeah, I do. I'm a soccer player. I want to play."

"I was thinking Connor and I could come and watch you play against the Rage when you come to Indianapolis."

"That would be—" Ryland dragged his hand through his hair "—not a good idea."

His words startled her. "Connor wants to see you play. So do I."

"I'm going to be busy."

"Too busy to say hello to us?"

"I need to focus on my career," Ryland said, his voice void of emotion. "I don't want a long-distance relationship or a girl-friend. I thought we were clear—"

"You can't tell me the time we spent together didn't mean anything to you." Hurt, raw and jagged, may have been ripping through her, but anger sounded in her voice. Lucy didn't care. She'd fallen in love with Ryland. She believed with her whole heart that he had feelings for her, too. "Or all those kisses."

"You know I like you," he said.

"Like." A far cry from love.

"Nothing more is possible."

Lucy stared down her nose. "Maybe not for you."

His gaze narrowed. "You said you weren't ready for a relationship or a boyfriend."

"I wasn't, but you showed me how good things could be. You opened me up to the possibility."

"I…" He stared at the grass. "I'm sorry, but I don't think something more between us would work out."

"It would." Her eyes didn't waver even though he wasn't looking at her. "I think you know it, too."

His gaze jerked up.

"You've admitted we're good together," she added.

"Chemistry."

"It's not just physical."

"We were never that physical."

"Sex is the easy part. Everything else is a lot harder."

"If we can't even manage the sex part, then we're not going to be able to handle anything else."

Ryland might like her. He might even care for her. But he would downplay whatever he felt because it would be too hard for him to deal with. Distancing himself rather than admitting how he felt would be much easier. He liked being a famous footballer. Soccer was safe. What he'd found here in Wicksburg with her wasn't.

Lucy took a deep breath. "You're scared."

"I'm not scared of you," he denied.

"You're scared of yourself and your feelings because there might be something more important in your life than soccer."

"That's crazy."

"No, it's not." Sympathy washed over her. "I've felt the same way myself. Not wanting to take any risks so I wouldn't get hurt."

He shook his head. "Did you take some headers with the boys during practice?"

Lucy wasn't about to be distracted. She pursed her lips. "I know you. Better than you realize. I'm not deluding myself. I'm finally being honest with you. But it's too late."

"I know you're upset. I have time before my flight. I can drive you home."

"No." The force of the word stunned her as much as Ryland. She almost backed down, but realized she couldn't. Dragging this out any longer wouldn't be good for either one of them. It was obvious he was pushing her away. Ryland wasn't ready to step onto the pitch and take the kickoff from her. She'd thought he was different, but he wasn't. Not really.

If he couldn't be honest with himself, how could he ever be honest with her? Bottom line, he couldn't. Even though her heart was splintering into tiny pieces, she needed to let him go.

"It's time we said goodbye." She would make this easy on him. Lucy took a deep breath. "Thank you your help with the team and Connor. You've taught me a lot. More than I expected to learn. Good luck. I hope you have a great career and a very nice life."

His nostrils flared. "That's it?"

That was all he wanted to hear from her. He wasn't about to say what she needed to hear. That he...cared. And even though she was positive he did, he couldn't say it.

Her heart pounded in her throat. Her lower lip quivered.

Hold it together. She didn't want him to see her break down. "Yeah, that's it."

Time to get out of here. Lucy gripped the equipment bag. She forced her feet to move across the field, but it wasn't easy. Her tennis shoes felt more like cement blocks. Each step took concentration. She wasn't sure she would make it all the way to her car.

Her insides trembled. Her hands shook. She thought nothing could match the heartache and betrayal of her husband and best friend. But the way she felt about Ryland...

I really do love him.

A sob wracked through her. Tears blurred her vision. She gripped the equipment bag until her knuckles turned white and her fingernails dug into her palms.

"Lucy," he called after her.

She forced her feet to keep walking.

Even though Lucy was tempted, she didn't look back. She couldn't. Not with the tears streaming down her face. And not when Ryland wasn't ready to admit the truth.

Saturday evening in Phoenix, Ryland stood next to the wall of floor-to-ceiling windows in his condominium. He rested his arm against the glass and stared at the city lights.

What a day.

He'd gotten an assist as an eighty-fourth-minute substitute. He hadn't expected any playing time his first game back, but was happy contributing to the 2–1 win. Mr. McElroy had greeted Ryland with a handshake when he came off the pitch. Coach Fritz had said to expect more playing time during a friendly scheduled for Wednesday and next Saturday's game.

Ryland James was back in a big way. Blake agreed. His teammates, however, were more subdued about Ryland's return. A few handshakes, some glares.

He didn't blame them. He was captain of the team and had missed the start of the season because he'd goofed off and injured himself. Really bad form. Irresponsible. Like much of his behavior last season and the one before that. At practice, he'd apologized, but it would take time to build that sense of camaraderie. He was okay with that.

On the coffee table behind him, his cell phone beeped and vibrated with each voice message and text that arrived. People, including the bevy of beauties he'd left behind, were more than happy to welcome him home with invitations to join them tonight at various clubs and parties, but he didn't feel like going out and being social. Not when that scene meant nothing to him now.

He kept thinking about Lucy and Connor and the rest of the boys. The Defeeters had played a match today. Ryland wondered how they did. He hoped they'd played well.

A part of him was tempted to call and find out. But appeasing his curiosity might only hurt Lucy more. She'd been angry with him. Hurting her hadn't been his intent, but he'd done it anyway and felt like a jerk.

Ryland missed Lucy, longed to see her, hear her voice, touch her, kiss her. But he needed to leave her alone. He needed to respect her decision to say goodbye the way she had. Respect her.

Aaron had warned her not to see him. Rightfully so. She deserved more than Ryland could give her. Not that he'd offered her anything. But he'd thought she was okay with that. Instead, she'd gotten upset at him. Told him he was scared.

Yeah, right.

All he'd tried to do was be honest with her. That had worked out real well.

Regret poked at Ryland. Maybe he could have done things better. Told her about his leaving differently. Said more… He shook it off.

What was he supposed to do? Give Lucy an engagement ring as Blake had suggested? Pretend he felt more for her than he did? She deserved better than that.

His cell phone rang. The ringtone told him it was his mother. "Hey, Mom. Did you watch the game?"

"No, we lost power."

Her voice sounded shaky. His shoulders tensed. "Is everything okay?"

"A tornado touched down near the elementary school. Your father and I are okay, so is the house, but we don't know the extent of the damage elsewhere," she said, her voice tight. "A tornado watch is still in effect. We're in the basement with Cupcake."

"Stay there. Keep me posted." Concern over Lucy and Connor overshadowed Ryland's relief at his parents being safe. A ball-size knot formed in his gut. "I love you, but I need to make a call right now."

"Lucy?"

"Yes."

"Let us know if she needs anything or a place to stay."

A potent mix of adrenaline and fear pulsed through him. He hit Lucy's cell-phone number on his contact list. Aaron's house was nowhere near the elementary school, but Ryland couldn't stop worrying. The Wicksburg soccer league played homes games at the elementary and middle schools. If the tornado touched down during match time...

There would have been sirens. No one would have been out at that point. Still he paced in front of the windows.

The phone rang.

Tornado warnings were all too common in the Midwest, especially in springtime. More than once he'd found himself in the bathroom of their apartment building in the tub with a mattress over him. But the twisters had always touched down on farmland, never in town.

On the fourth ring, Lucy's voice mail picked up. "I can't talk right now, but leave a message and I'll call you back."

The sound of her sweet voice twisted his insides. His chest hurt so badly he could barely breathe. He should be in Wicksburg, not here in Phoenix.

"Beep."

Ryland opened his mouth to speak, but no words came out. Not that he had a clue what he wanted to say if he could talk. He disconnected from the call.

Maybe she didn't have her cell phone with her. If she were at home...

He called the landline at Aaron's house. The phone rang. Again and again.

Ryland's frustration built; so did his fear. He clenched his hand. Why wasn't she answering? Where could she be?

"Hello?" a young voice answered.

He clutched the back of the couch. His fingers dug into the buttery leather. "Connor?"

"Ryland." The relief in the boy's voice reached across the

distance and squeezed Ryland's heart like a vise grip. "I knew you wouldn't forget about us."

"Never." The word came from somewhere deep inside him, spoken with a voice he didn't recognize. "My mom called me about the tornado."

"Aunt Lucy and I got inside the closet in the basement with pillows, a couple flashlights and the phone. It's one of those old dial ones." His voice trembled. "I have my DS, too."

"Extra playing time for you," Ryland teased, but his words fell flat. "Can I talk to your aunt?"

"She's looking for Manny."

The fat cat always tried to escape whenever the door opened. But if he'd gotten out today... "Where is he?"

"I don't know. Aunt Lucy moved the car into the garage and thinks he could have slipped out because she was in a hurry," Connor said. "We couldn't find him after the warning sounded. The siren might have scared him."

Sounded like Manny wasn't the only one frightened by the noise. Poor kid. "Your aunt will find him."

The alternative, for both Lucy and Manny, was unacceptable. Ryland glanced at the clock. If he caught a red-eye to Chicago and drove... But he had a team meeting tomorrow. And would Lucy want him to show up uninvited in the morning?

"Aunt Lucy said she would be back soon," Connor said finally. "She waited until the siren stopped to go outside. She didn't want to leave me alone if it wasn't safe."

Lucy would never put her nephew at risk, but Ryland didn't like the thought of her outside in that kind of weather with a tornado watch still in effect.

Silence filled the line.

"You hanging in there, bud?" he asked.

"Yeah," Connor said. "But the flashlight died. It's kind of dark."

Ryland grimaced. "See if your DS gives off some light."

"That helps a little."

Being thousands of miles away sucked. "I wish I were there."

"Me, too. But even if you were, you still wouldn't get to see our last game next Saturday," Connor said.

"Why not?"

"The field was destroyed so the season is over with. No more soccer until fall. If then."

"Because of the tornado?" Ryland asked.

"Yeah. Marco's mom called earlier," Connor explained. "My school is gone. The fields. The middle school. Some of the houses around there, too."

Gone. Stunned, Ryland tried to picture it. He couldn't. "Are Marco and his family, okay?"

"Yeah, but a tree landed on their car. Marco's dad is mad."

"Cars can be replaced." People couldn't.

Lucy.

Ryland wanted her in the basement with Connor, not out looking for Manny.

Damn. He hated not being able to do anything to help. Not that Lucy would want *his* help. Still… He gripped the phone.

Images of his weeks in Wicksburg flashed through his mind like a slideshow. Lucy handing him a container of cookies, teaching her how to do the warm-up routine and drills, watching her coach during the first match, drinking slushies with the team after games, kissing her.

You said you weren't ready for a relationship or a boyfriend. I wasn't, but you showed me how good things could be.

Things had been good. Great. If he could go back and do over his last day in Wicksburg…

But soccer had been the only thing on his mind. That and getting the hell out of town, running away as his mom had accused him of doing before.

A lump formed in his throat and burned like a flame.

"It's probably a good thing we can't play the last game." Connor's voice forced Ryland to focus on the present. "We got beat six–nothing today. Aunt Lucy said we were going through the motions and our hearts weren't in the game."

That was how Ryland had spent the last two years. He'd gotten tired of having to prove himself over and over again. He'd lost his hunger, his drive and his edge. He'd acted out without realizing it or the reasons behind his actions—anger, unhappiness and pressure. But he hadn't figured out how self-destructive his behavior had become until he'd returned to Wicksburg. Lucy and the boys had been his inspiration and let him rediscover the joy of the game. He'd connected with them in a way he hadn't since leaving town as a teenager.

And Lucy...

She showed him it wasn't about proving things to others, but to himself.

"The Strikers would have killed us anyway," Connor continued, talking about the game that wouldn't be. He sounded more like himself, less scared. "Ten–nothing or worse."

Ryland may have gotten his soccer career back on track here, but he still had things to take care of in Wicksburg. He wasn't about to drop the ball again. "No way. The entire team has improved since that first match. The Strikers won by three goals. You need to play that game if only to prove you can challenge them."

"There's no field to play on."

"Come on." Ryland couldn't let those boys down after all they'd given him. He pictured each of their faces. In a short time, he'd learned their strengths and discovered their weaknesses. Secrets were hard to keep when you were nine and ten. He'd watched their skills improve, but also saw other changes like limbs lengthening and faces thinning. "That's not the Defeeter attitude."

"It was a big tornado."

And a big loss with the game today. Ryland took responsibility for that. The way he'd left, as if he could ride into town and then just leave again without anyone noticing or being affected was selfish and stupid. "No worries, bud. I'll figure something out."

"Really?"

"Really." Ryland didn't hesitate. He would find the team a place to play next Saturday. "Is your aunt back?"

"No, but I don't know how to use call-waiting. I should get off the phone in case she needs to talk to me."

"Smart thinking. Tell your aunt to call me when she finds Manny." Ryland checked the time again. "I'll let you know where you're going to play against the Strikers."

"I wish you could be there if we get to play."

"So do I." A weight pressed down on Ryland. "There's no place I'd rather be than with you and the team and your aunt Lucy."

But it wasn't possible. Ryland had an away match next Saturday. He was supposed to get playing time. But he needed to be in Wicksburg with Lucy and the boys.

Just remember, actions speak louder than words.

Blake's words echoed through Ryland's mind. He straightened. He'd been so blind. What he wanted—needed—was right there in front of him. Not here in Phoenix, but in Wicksburg. He just hadn't wanted to see it.

But now...

Time to stop talking about what he wanted and make it happen.

For the boys.

And most importantly, with Lucy.

CHAPTER THIRTEEN

LUCY'S ARMS, scratched and sore after digging through tree limbs and debris to reach a howling Manny, struggled to carry the squirming, wet cat with a flashlight in her hand down to the basement. The warning siren remained silent, but they would sleep downstairs to be on the safe side. "You need to go on a diet, cat."

"Aunt Lucy?" Connor called from the closet. "Did you find Manny?"

"I found him." She opened the door, happy to see her nephew safe, dry and warm. "Why is it so dark in there?"

"The flashlight stopped working."

Yet Connor had stayed, as she asked, even in the pitch-black when he had to be scared. Her heart swelled with pride and love for her nephew. Aaron and Dana were raising a great kid. "Sorry about that. The batteries must have been low."

"It's okay." He held up his glowing DS console. "I had a little light."

Manny pawed trying to get away from her. The cat looked

like a drowned rat with his wet fur plastered against his body. "I think someone wants to see you."

Connor reached for the cat. "Where was he?"

"In the bushes across the street. I have a feeling he's had quite an adventure." Enough to last eight lives given the winds and flying debris the cat must have experienced. "I doubt he'll be so quick to dash outside again."

Connor cuddled Manny, who settled against her nephew's chest as if that were his rightful and only place of rest. At least until a better spot came along. "Oh, Ryland called."

Lucy's heart jolted. She hadn't expected to hear from him again. "When?"

"A little while ago." Connor rubbed his chin against the cat. Manny purred like a V-8 engine. "He wants you to call him back. He was worried about you finding Manny."

Lucy whipped out her cell phone. Service had been spotty due to the storm, but three bars appeared. She went to press Ryland's number.

Wait. Her finger hovered over the screen. Calling him back would be stupid. Okay, it was nice he was concerned enough to call and want to know about Manny. But this went beyond what was happening in Wicksburg today.

Lucy had been thinking about him constantly since he left town. She missed him terribly. She needed to get him off her mind and out of her heart. But she wouldn't ignore his request completely. That would be rude.

Lucy typed in a text message and hit Send. Now she could go back to trying to forget about him.

Early Monday morning, Ryland stood in the reception area of the Phoenix Fuego headquarters. He'd spent much of yesterday trying to figure how to help those affected by the tornado in Wicksburg. Money was easy to donate. But he wanted to do something for the team and Lucy.

Waiting, he reread the text she'd sent him.

Manny wet & hungry but fine.

Ryland had wanted to hear her voice to know she was okay. He'd received a six-word text, instead. Probably more than he deserved.

The attractive, young personal assistant, who was always cheering on the team during games, motioned to the door to her right. "Mr. McElroy will see you now."

"Thanks." Ryland entered the owner's office. The plush furnishings didn't surprise him. All the photos of children everywhere did. "I appreciate you seeing me on such short notice."

Mr. McElroy shook his hand. "You said it was important."

"Yes."

He pointed to a leather chair. "Have a seat."

Ryland sat. "A tornado rolled through my hometown on Saturday night."

"I heard about that on the news. No casualties."

"No, but homes, two schools and several soccer fields in town were destroyed," Ryland said. "The Defeeters, a U-9 Boys rec. team I worked with while I was home, has their final game of the season this Saturday, but nowhere to play. I want to find them, and all the teams affected by the tornado, fields so they can finish out their spring season. I'd also like to be on the sideline with the Defeeters when they play."

Mr. McElroy studied him. "This sounds important to you."

"Yes," Ryland said. "I'm who I am today because of the start I got in that soccer league. I owe them and the Defeeters."

Not to mention Lucy. He wanted a second chance with her. A do-over like young players sometimes received from refs when they made a bad throw-in or didn't quite get the ball over the line during kickoffs.

"That's thoughtful, but haven't you forgotten about the match against the Rage on Saturday night?"

Mr. McElroy's words echoed Blake's, but Ryland continued undeterred. "The Rage plays in Indianapolis. The stadium is a couple hours from Wicksburg. I know a way I can be at both games, but I'm going to need some help to pull it off. Your help, Mr. McElroy, and the owner of the Rage."

A tense silence enveloped the office. Ryland sat patiently waiting for the opportunity to say more.

"You've been nothing but a thorn in my side since I bought this team." Mr. McElroy leaned forward and rested his elbows on the desk. "Why should I help you?"

"Because it's the right thing to do."

"Right for the kids affected by the tornado?"

"And for us. Those kids are the future of soccer, both players and fans." Ryland spoke from his heart. The way Lucy would have wanted him to. "I know you don't want me on the team. I wasn't okay with that before. I am now. I don't care what team I'm on as long as I can play. But until the transfer window opens so you can loan me out across the pond, you need me as much as I need you."

Mr. McElroy's eyes widened. No doubt the truth had surprised him. "What kind of help are you talking about?"

Ryland explained his plan. "This is not only good for the players and the local soccer league, but it's also a smart PR move for the Fuego and Rage."

"Not smart. Brilliant. You can't buy that kind of publicity." Mr. McElroy studied him. "You're not the same player who left the club in March. What happened while you were away?"

"That U-9 team of boys taught me a few things about soccer I'd forgotten, and I met a girl who made me realize I'm more than just a footballer."

Smiling, Mr. McElroy leaned back in his chair. "You have my full support. I'll call the owner of the Rage this morning. Tell my assistant what you need to pull this off."

Satisfaction and relief loosened the knot in Ryland's gut. He stood. "Thank you, sir."

"I hope it all works out the way you planned," Mr. McElroy said.

"So do I."

Ryland had no doubt the soccer part would work, but he wasn't as confident about his plans for Lucy. He couldn't imagine his life without her.

She'd been right. Ryland had been scared. He still was. He just hoped it wasn't too late.

On Saturday, Lucy entered the training facility of the Indianapolis Rage. The MLS team had offered the use of their outdoor field for the final game of the Defeeters' spring soccer season against the Strikers.

Parents and players from both teams looked around in awe. The training field resembled a ministadium complete with lights, two benches and bleachers.

Lucy couldn't believe they were here.

When the soccer league president had offered the Defeeters an all-expenses-paid trip to Indianapolis to play their final game of the season, she thought Ryland was behind it because Fuego was playing the Rage that same day. But then she learned all youth soccer teams without fields to finish the spring season had been invited.

She hadn't known whether to feel relieved or disappointed.

Pathetic. No matter how hard she tried to push Ryland out of her mind and heart, he was still there. She wondered how long he would remain there—days, weeks, months...

Stop thinking about him.

Connor ran onto the field, his feet encased in bright yellow soccer shoes. The other kids followed, jumping and laughing, as if the damage back home was nothing more than a bad dream.

"This is just what we all needed after the tornado." Suzy took a picture of the boys standing on the center mark of the field. "A weekend getaway and a chance to end the soccer season in style."

"The hotel is so nice." Cheryl's house had been damaged by the tornado. They were staying with Dalton's father, who had traveled with them for today's game. Maybe something good would come from all of this and they could work out their differences before the separation led to a divorce. "I can't wait for tonight. I've never been to a professional soccer game before."

Tickets to the Rage vs. Fuego match had been provided to each family. Much to the delight of the boys, who couldn't wait to see Ryland play. Connor was beside himself with excitement, positive his favorite player would be in the game for the entire ninety minutes.

Lucy hoped not. Watching Ryland play for only few minutes would be difficult, let alone the entire match. Hearing his name mentioned hurt. Connor talked constantly about Ryland. That made it hard to forget him.

Thing would get better. Eventually. She'd been in this same place before with Jeff. Except with Ryland the hurt cut deeper. Her marriage had never been a true partnership, but she'd felt that way with Ryland, in spite of the short time they'd been together.

She shook off the thought. The match will be a nice way to cap off the day.

The boys screamed, the noise deafening. Only one thing— one person—could elicit that kind of response.

Her throat tightened.

Ryland was here.

Emotions churned inside her.

"That man gets hotter each time I see him." Cheryl whistled. "But who are all his buddies?"

"Yowza," Suzy said. "If it gets any hotter in here, I think I'm going to need to fan myself."

"Am I a bad mom if I'm jealous of a bunch of eight- and nine-year-olds?" Debbie asked.

"I hope not, because I feel the same way," Cheryl replied.

Lucy kept her back turned so she wouldn't be tempted to look at Ryland. But the women had piqued her curiosity. "What are you talking about?"

"Turn around." Cheryl winked. "Trust me, you won't be disappointed."

Reluctantly, Lucy turned. She stared in disbelief. Nearly a dozen professional soccer players with killer bodies and smiling faces worked with the Defeeters and the Strikers, helping the boys warm up and giving them pointers.

One Fuego player, however, stood out from all the others. *Ryland.*

His dark hair was neatly combed, his face clean shaven. He looked handsome in his Fuego uniform—blue, orange and white with red flames. But it was the man, not the athlete, who had stolen her heart. A weight pressed down on her chest, squeezing out what air remained in her lungs.

Suzy sent her a sympathetic smile. "This is a dream come true for the boys."

Cheryl nodded. "I think I've died and gone to heaven myself."

Lucy had gone straight to hell. Hurt splintered her already-aching heart. She struggled to breathe. She didn't even attempt to speak.

Everyone around her smiled and laughed. She wanted to cry. If only he could see how good the two of them would be together...

"Look at all the photographers and news crews," Suzy said.

Cheryl combed through her hair and pinched her cheeks. "No wonder the league had us sign those photo releases."

The media descended on the field, but their presence didn't distract the professional players from the kids. The boys, however, mugged for the cameras.

As the warm-up period drew to an end, the referee called over the Strikers. That was Lucy's cue to get ready. She had player cards to show the ref and her clipboard with the starting lineup and substitution schedule so each boy would play an equal amount of time.

"We're taping the game." Debbie motioned to the bleachers where her husband adjusted a tripod. "For Aaron and Dana."

"Thanks," Lucy said.

The referee called the Defeeters over.

Nerves threatened to get the best of Lucy. But in spite of all the hoopla and media, this was still a rec. soccer game. She had no reason to interact with Ryland and wouldn't.

With her resolve in place, Lucy lined up the boys for the ref. Ryland stood near the Defeeters' bench.

Her heart rate careened out of control.

Oh, no. He was planning to be there during the match.

The ref excused the Defeeters. As she walked to the bench, she looked everywhere, but at Ryland. Maybe if she didn't catch his eye or say—

"It's good to see you, Lucy," he said.

Darn. She cleared her dry throat. "The boys are so happy you're here."

"This is the only place I want to be."

The referee blew his whistle, saving her from having to speak with him.

The game was fast-paced with lots of action and scoring. At halftime with the score Defeeters two and Strikers three, Ryland talked to the boys about the game. With two minutes remaining in regulation time, Connor stole the ball from a defender and broke away up the left sideline. He crossed the ball in front of the goal. Dalton kicked the ball into the corner of the net.

Tie score!

The parents screamed. The boys gave each other high fives.

The Strikers pulled their goalie. A risky move, but they wanted an extra player in the game. The offense hit hard after the kickoff, took a shot on goal, but missed.

Defeeters' turn. Marco took the ball. His pass to Dalton was stolen. The Strikers' forward headed down the field, but Connor sprinted to steal the ball. He kicked the ball down the line to Dalton, who passed it to Marco. The goal was right in front of him. All he had to do was shoot at the empty goal.

"Shoot," Ryland yelled. So did everyone else.

The referee blew his whistle. The game was over.

The Defeeters had tied the Strikers.

"Great job, coach," Ryland said to her. "You've come a long way."

But she had so much further to go, especially when it came to getting over him. She didn't smile or look at him. "Thanks."

"You boys played a great game," Ryland said to the excited boys gathered around him. "The best all season."

Lucy knew they would rather hear from him than her. She didn't mind that one bit.

Connor beamed. "You said we could challenge them. We did."

Ryland messed up the kid's hair. "You did more than that, bud."

The two teams lined up with the coaches at the end, followed by the professional players, and shook hands. Ryland and the other players passed out T-shirts to both teams, posed for pictures and signed autographs. Talk about a dream come true. And there was still the match to attend tonight.

She gathered up the balls and equipment. "Come on, Connor. We can go back to the hotel for a swim before the game."

Connor looked at Ryland then back at her.

Lucy's heart lodged in her throat. She knew that conspiratorial look of his.

"I'm riding back to the hotel with Marco and his family," Connor said.

"I told the boys we could stop for an after-game treat on the way back to the hotel," Suzy said.

"Slushies, slushies," the boys chanted.

Those had become the new Defeeter tradition. Thanks to Ryland. But he wasn't offering to take the team out today.

Lucy remembered. He had to prepare for the match against the Rage tonight.

She thought about offering to drive the boys herself, but from the look on Connor's face, he had his heart set on going with

Marco. She couldn't ruin this magical day for him on the off chance Ryland might try to talk to her.

Time to act like an adult rather than a brokenhearted teenager. She raised her chin. "Sounds like fun. I'll meet you back at the hotel."

As the boys headed out, she followed them, eager to escape before Ryland—

"Lucy."

She kept walking, eyeing the exit.

"Please wait," Ryland said.

She stopped. Not because she wanted to talk to him, but because he'd helped her with the team. Five minutes. That was all the time he could have.

Ryland caught up to her. "You've been working hard with the boys."

"It's them, not me." She glanced back at the field. "I don't know what your part in making this happen was, but thank you. It meant a lot to the boys on both teams." She tried to sound nonchalant, but wasn't sure she was succeeding.

"I didn't do this only for them."

Her pulse accelerated.

"I'm sorry." His words came out in a rush. "The way I left was selfish. I was only thinking about myself. Not the boys. Definitely not you. I never meant to hurt anyone, but I did. I hope you can forgive me."

The sincerity in his eyes and voice tugged at her heart. She had to keep her heart immune. She had to get away from him. "You're forgiven."

His relief was palpable. "Thank you. You don't know what that means to me."

She didn't want to know. Just being this close to him was enough to make her want to bolt. The scent of him surrounded her. She wanted to bottle some up to take home with her. *Not a good idea.* "I need to get back to the hotel. Connor…"

Ryland took a step closer to her. "He's stopping for a snack on the way back."

Lucy stepped back. "I still should—"

"Stay."

The one word was a plea and a promise, full of anxiety and anticipation. She tried not to let that matter, but it wasn't easy. "Why?"

"There's more I want to say to you."

She glanced around the stadium. Everyone seemed to have left. "Make it quick."

He took a deep breath. "Soccer has been the only thing in my life for so long. I defined myself as a footballer. Playing made me feel worthy. But I lost the love for the game. The past couple of years, I made some bad decisions. I had no idea why I was acting out so badly until I got to Wicksburg. I realized how unhappy I'd been trying to keep proving myself with a new league, team and fans. Nothing satisfied me anymore. Working with the boys helped me discover what was missing. Soccer isn't only about scoring goals. I'd forgotten the value of teamwork. You made me realize I don't want soccer to be the only thing in my life. I want—I need—more than that. I need you, Lucy."

The wind whooshed from her lungs. She couldn't believe what he was saying.

"I know how important honesty is to you," he continued. "When I got to Phoenix, I realized you were right. I was scared. A coward. I wasn't being honest about my feelings. Not to you or myself. You mean so much to me. I'm finally able to admit it."

"I'm...touched. Really. But even if you're serious—"

"I am serious, Lucy." He took her hand in his. "More serious than I've ever been in my entire life. I was trapped by the expectations of others, the pressure, but you set me free. I'm more than just a soccer player. I don't want to lose you."

They way he looked at her, his gaze caressing her skin like a touch, brought tears to her eyes. She blinked them away. She couldn't lose sight of the truth.

Lucy took a deep breath. "We live in different worlds, different states. It would never work."

"I want to make it work."

"You know what happened with Jeff."

He nodded.

"Look at you," she said. "You're hot, wealthy, a superstar. Women want you. They fantasize about you. That's hard for me to handle."

"I know you've had some tough times in your life. We can't wash away everything that's happened before, but we can't dwell on it, either," he said. "Trust doesn't just happen. I can tell you all the right words you want to hear. That I'm not like Jeff. That I won't cheat. But what it really takes is a leap of faith. Are you willing to take that leap with me?"

Her heart screamed the answer it wanted her to say. Could she leap when her heart had been broken after spending only a few weeks with him? How could she not when Ryland was everything she'd dreamed about?

"When I was sick, people lied to me. The doctors, my parents, even Aaron. Maybe not outright lies, but untruths about the treatments, how I would feel and what I could do. I hated having to rely on people who couldn't be honest with me."

"So that's where your independent streak came from."

She nodded. "And then Jeff came along. He was honest with me, sometimes brutally so, but I liked that better than the alternative. I fell hard and fast only to find out he was nothing more than a lying, cheating jerk." She took a deep breath so she could keep going. "You've taught me so much and not only about soccer. Because of you I've learned I can accept help without feeling like a burden to someone. I've also learned I can forgive and trust again. I would love to take that leap with you. But I'm not sure I'm ready yet."

"I don't care how long it takes," he said. "I'll wait until you're ready."

"You're serious."

"Very." He kissed each of her fingers, sending pleasurable shivers up her arm. "I love you."

The air rushed from her lungs. She tried to speak, to question him, but couldn't.

Sincerity shone in his eyes. "I tried to pretend I didn't love you, but I'm no good at pretending when it comes to you."

Joy exploded inside her. She could tell they weren't just words. He meant them. Maybe taking the leap wouldn't be so hard. "I love you, too."

"That's the first step to taking the leap."

"Maybe the first two steps." Lucy kissed Ryland, a kiss full of hope and love and possibility. None of her dreams had come true so far, but maybe some...could.

Ryland pulled her against him. She went willingly, wrapping her arms around him. Her hand hit something tucked into the waistband of his shorts. It fell to the ground. She backed away.

A small blue box tied with a white ribbon lay on its side. She recognized the packaging from ads and the movies. The box was from Tiffany & Co.

Her mouth gaped. She closed it. He really was serious.

His cheeks reddened. "If I told you that's where I keep my lucky penny, I'm guessing you won't believe me."

Shock rendered her speechless.

"It's nothing." He took a breath. "Okay, I'll be honest. It's something, but it can wait. You're not ready right now."

She placed her hand on his. "Maybe I'm more ready than I realized."

As he handed her the box, hope filled his eyes. "This is for you. Today. A year from now. Whenever you're ready."

Lucy untied the ribbon and removed the top of the box. Inside was a midnight blue, almost black, suede ring box. Her hand trembled so much she couldn't get the smaller box out. She looked up at him.

"Allow me." Ryland pulled out the ring box and opened it. A Tiffany-cut diamond engagement ring sparkled against the dark navy fabric. The words Tiffany & Co. were embossed in gold foil on the lid. "Nothing matters except being with you. I love you. I want to marry you, Lucy, if you'll have me."

She couldn't believe this was happening. She forced herself to breathe. All her girlhood fantasies didn't compare to the reality of this moment. Ryland James had asked her to marry him. He'd been honest to himself and to her. He was fully committed to making it work. Lucy's heart and her mind agreed on the answer. Make the leap? She had no doubt at all. "Yes."

He placed the ring on her finger. A perfect fit, the way they were a perfect fit together. "There's no rush."

"No, there isn't." The love shining in his eyes matched her own. "Aaron and Dana won't be home until next year."

"It might take me that long to convince your brother I'm good enough for you."

"Probably," Lucy teased. "But with Connor in your corner, it might take only six months."

"Very funny."

She stared at the ring. A feeling of peace coursed through her. "So this officially makes me a WAG."

Ryland brushed his lips across hers. "A *G* who will eventually become a *W.* But you're already an *M.*"

"An *M*?" Lucy asked.

"Mine."

"I'll always be your *M.* As long as you're mine, too."

"Always," he said. "I think I may have always been yours without even realizing it."

"If you're trying to score…"

"No need. I already won." Ryland pulled her against him and kissed her again. "I love you, Lucy."

A warm glow flowed through her, making her heart sigh. "I love you."

* * * * *

The Soldier She Could Never Forget

Tina Beckett

Dear Reader,

Sometimes life gives us second chances: a dream job we passed up for something else, a return trip to a childhood home, a first love that was lost many years ago. And sometimes…sometimes we come to understand why things happened the way they did in the past.

Thank you for joining Jessi and Clint as they unexpectedly come face-to-face after years apart. As Jessi struggles to understand what went wrong between them Clint wrestles with the demons that haunt him. And maybe, through the power of forgiveness and with an approving nod from fate, they can rediscover a love they thought long dead.

Clint and Jessi's journey has a special place in my heart. I hope you enjoy reading their story as much as I loved writing it!

Much love

Tina Beckett

Books by Tina Beckett

Hot Brazilian Docs!
To Play with Fire
The Dangers of Dating Dr. Carvalho

One Night that Changed Everything
NYC Angels: Flirting with Danger
The Lone Wolf's Craving
Doctor's Guide to Dating in the Jungle
Her Hard to Resist Husband
His Girl From Nowhere
How to Find a Man in Five Dates

Visit the Author Profile page
at millsandboon.com.au for
more titles.

To my children. You bring me joy, every single day.

**Praise for
Tina Beckett**

"A tension-filled emotional story with just the right amount of drama. The author's vivid description of the Brazilian jungle and its people make this story something special."

—*RT Book Reviews* on
Doctor's Guide to Dating in the Jungle

"Medical Romance lovers will definitely like
NYC Angels: Flirting with Danger by Tina Beckett—
for who doesn't like a good forbidden romance?"

—*Harlequin Junkie*

PROLOGUE

Twenty-two years earlier

"JESS. DON'T CRY."

The low words came from behind her, the slight rasp to his tone giving away his identity immediately.

Jessi stiffened, but she didn't turn around. Oh, God. He'd followed her. She hadn't realized anyone had even seen her tearful flight out of the auditorium, much less come after her. But they had. And those low gravely tones didn't belong to Larry Riley, who'd had a crush on her for ages, or her father—*thank God!*—but Clinton Marks, the last person she would have expected to care about what she thought or felt.

"I—I'm not."

One scuffed motorcycle boot appeared on the other side of the log where she was seated, the footwear in stark contrast to the flowing green graduation gowns they both wore—and probably topping the school's list of banned attire for tonight's ceremony.

The gown made her smile. Clint, in what amounted to a dress. She hoped someone had gotten a picture of that.

He sat beside her as she hurried to scrub away the evidence of her anguish. Not soon enough, though, because cool fingers touched her chin, turning her head toward him. "You're a terrible liar, Jessi May."

Somehow hearing the pet name spoken in something other than his normal mocking tones caused hot tears to wash back into her eyes and spill over, trailing down her cheeks until one of them reached his thumb. He brushed it away, his touch light.

She'd never seen him like this. Maybe the reality of the night had struck him, as well. In a few short hours, her group of friends would all be flying off to start new lives. Larry and Clint would be headed for boot camp. And her best friend would be spending the next year in Spain on a college exchange program.

They were all leaving.

All except Jessi.

She was stuck here in Richmond—with an overly strict father who'd come down hard when he'd heard Larry was gearing up for a career in the army. The papers weren't signed yet, but they would be in a matter of days. She'd done her best to hide the news, but her dad had been bound to find out sooner or later. He didn't want her involved with a military man. Kind of unreasonable in a place where those kinds of men were a dime a dozen.

Maybe she should have picked an out-of-state college, rather than choosing to commute from home. But as an only child, she hadn't quite been able to bring herself to leave her mom alone in that huge house.

"What's going on, Jess?" Clint's voice came back to her, pulling her from her pity party.

She shrugged. "My dad, he… He just…" It sounded so stupid to complain about her father to someone who flouted authority every chance he got. If only she could be like that. But she'd always been a people pleaser. The trait had gotten worse once she'd been old enough to realize her mom's "vitamins" were actually antidepressants.

Instead of the flip attitude she'd expected from Clint, though, his eyes turned this cold shade of gunmetal gray that made her shiver. His fingers tightened slightly on her chin. "Your father what, Jess? What did he do?"

Her teeth came down on her lip when she realized what he was saying. There'd been rumors about Clint's family, that his father was the reason he was the way he was.

Her dad was nothing like that.

"He didn't do anything. He's just...unreasonable. He's against me being with people like you or Larry."

His head tilted. "Me...and Larry." His mouth turned up at the corners. "I see your dad's point. Larry and I are definitely cut from the same cloth."

They weren't. Not at all. Larry was like her. He was all about good grades and toeing the line. Clint, however, lived on the edge of trouble—his skull tattoo and pierced ear making teachers shake their heads, while all the girls swooned.

Including her.

His words made her smile, though. "You're both going into the army."

"Ah, I see. Your father wouldn't like me, though, in or out of the army."

Her smile widened. "He's protective."

He made a sound low in his throat that might have been a laugh. "The thing is..." his eyes found hers again and a warm hand cupped the back of her neck "...I didn't know I was even in the running. So I'm neck and neck with Larry *straight-A* Riley."

Something hot flared low in her belly. Clint had never, ever given the slightest hint he was interested in her. And yet here he was. Beside her. The only person to notice her walk off the stage and slip out the door after getting her diploma. The only one who'd followed her.

"I—I... Did you want to be?"

"No."

The word should have cut her to the quick, except the low pained tone was somehow at odds with his denial.

"Clint...?" Her fingertips moved to his cheek, her eyes meeting his with something akin to desperation.

Another sound rumbled up from his chest, coming out as a groan this time. Then, something she'd never dreamed possible—in all of her eighteen years—happened.

Clinton Marks—bad boy extraordinaire—whispered her name. Right before his mouth came down and covered hers.

CHAPTER ONE

"CHELSEA'S NEW DOCTOR arrived today." The nurse's matter-of-fact words stopped her in her tracks.

Jessica Marie Riley blinked and turned back to the main desk of the Richmond VA hospital, where her twenty-one-year-old daughter had spent the past two months of her life—a frail shell of the robust soldier who'd been so proud of toughing it out at army boot camp.

It had always been just her and Chelsea against the world. They'd supported each other, laughed together, told each other everything.

Until she'd returned from her very first tour of duty as a former POW...and a different person.

"He did?" Jessi's stomach lurched. Her daughter's last doctor had left unexpectedly and she'd been told there was a possibility she'd be shuffled between the other military psychiatrists until a replacement could be found.

Maria, the nurse who'd admitted Chelsea and had shown a huge amount of compassion toward both of them, hesitated. She knew what a sore spot this was. "Dr. Cordoba had some family issues and resigned his commission. It really wasn't his fault."

Jessi knew from experience how devastating some family issues could be. But with the hurricane that had just gouged its way up the coast, her work schedule at Scott's Memorial had been brutal. The shortage of ER doctors had never been more evident, and it had driven the medical staff to the brink of exhaustion. It also made her a little short on patience.

And now her daughter had lost the only doctor she'd seemed to bond with during her hospitalization.

Jess had hoped they'd finally get some answers about why Chelsea had spiraled into the depths of despair after coming home—and that she'd finally find a way to be at peace with whatever had happened in that squalid prison camp.

That tiny thread of hope had now been chopped in two. Anger flared at how easy it was for people like Dr. Cordoba to leave patients who counted on him.

Not fair, Jess. You're not walking in his shoes.

But the man wasn't walking in hers, either. He hadn't been there on that terrible day when her daughter had tried to take her own life.

She couldn't imagine how draining it was to deal with patients displaying symptoms of post-traumatic stress disorder on a daily basis, but Jessi had been handed some pretty awful cases herself. No one saw her throwing in the towel and moving on to some cushy private gig.

Maria came around the desk and touched her arm. "Her new doctor is one of the top in his field. He's dedicated his life to treating patients like your daughter—in fact, he transferred from California just to take over Dr. Cordoba's PTSD patients. At least until we can get a permanent replacement. He's already been to see Chelsea and reviewed her chart."

Top in his field. That had to be good, right? But if he was only temporary...

"What did he think?"

This time, the nurse wouldn't quite meet her eyes. "I'm not sure. He asked me to send you to his office as soon as you arrived. He's down the hall, first door on your left."

Dr. Cordoba's old office.

The thread of anger continued to wind through her veins, despite Maria's encouraging words. This was Chelsea's third doctor. That averaged out to more than one a month. How long did this newest guy plan on sticking around?

A sudden thought came to her. "How did the hospital find this doctor so quickly?"

"This is what he does. He rotates between military hospitals, filling in…" The sound of yelling came from down the hallway, stopping Maria's explanation in its tracks. A woman headed their way, pushing a wheelchair, while the older gentleman in the seat bellowed something unintelligible, his fist shaking in the air.

"Excuse me," said the nurse, quickly moving toward the pair. She threw over her shoulder, "Chelsea's doctor is in his office. He's expecting you. Just go on in." Her attention shifted toward the agitated patient. "Mr. Ballenger, what's wrong?"

Not wanting to stand there like a gawker, Jessi stiffened her shoulders and headed in the direction Maria had indicated.

First door on the left.

All she wanted to do was skip the requisite chit-chat and go straight to Chelsea's room. But that was evidently not going to happen. Not until she met with the newest member of Chelsea's treatment team.

Feeling helpless and out of control was rapidly becoming the norm for Jessi. And she didn't like it. At all.

She stopped in front of the door and glared at the nameplate. Dr. Cordoba's credentials were still prominently displayed in the cheap gold-colored frame. The new guy really was new.

Damn, and she'd forgotten to ask the nurse his name. It didn't really matter. He'd introduce himself. So would she, and then he'd ask her how she was. That's what they always did.

Tell the truth? Or nod and say, "Fine," just like she did every other time someone asked her?

She lifted her hand and rapped on the solid wood door.

"Come in." The masculine drawl coming from within was low and gruff.

The back of her neck prickled, the sensation sweeping across her shoulders and down her arms, lifting every fine hair in its path. If she had to pick a description to pair that voice with, she'd say impatient. Or sexy. Two words you didn't want associated with an army psychiatrist. Or any psychiatrist, for that matter. And certainly not one charged with her daughter's care.

He's probably fat and bald, Jess.

Comforted by that thought, she pushed the lever down and opened the door.

He wasn't fat. Or bald.

His head was turned to the side, obscuring most of his face, but the man seated behind the gray, military-issue desk had a full head of jet-black hair, the sides short in typical army fashion, while the longer top fell casually across his forehead. Jessi spied a few strands of gray woven through the hair at his temple.

He appeared to be intently studying his computer screen. Something about his profile tugged at her, just like his voice had. She shook off the sensation, rubbing her upper arms as she continued to stand there.

He had to be pushing forty, judging from the lines beside his eyes as well as the long crease down the side of his left cheek. The result of a dimple utilized far too many times?

Something in her mind swirled back to life as if some hazy image was trying to imprint itself on her consciousness.

"Feel free to sit," he said. "I'll be with you in a minute."

She swallowed, all thoughts of new doctors and balding men fading as worry nibbled at the pit of her stomach. Was something wrong with Chelsea? She tried to open her mouth to ask, but the words were suddenly stuck in her throat. Maybe that's why Maria wouldn't quite meet her eyes. Had Chelsea made another suicide attempt? Surely the nurse would have said something had that been the case.

Pulling one of the two chairs back a few inches, she eased into it, her gaze shuffling around the room, trying to find anything that would calm her nerves.

What it landed on was the nameplate on the doctor's desk. Not Dr. Cordoba's. Instead...

Jessi froze. She blinked rapidly to clear her vision and focused on the letters again, sliding across each one individually and hoping that an *a* would somehow morph into an *e*.

Her gaze flicked back to the portion of his face she could see. Recognition roared to life this time.

She should have realized that prickling sensation hadn't been a fluke when she'd heard his voice. But she would never have dreamed...

Images of heated kisses and stolen moments in the grass beside the creek near her high school flashed through her head.

God. Clinton Marks. A ghost from her past...a rite of passage.

That's all it had been. A moment in time. And yet here he was, sitting across from her in living color.

Worse, he was evidently her daughter's new doctor. How was that possible?

Maybe he wouldn't recognize her.

When his gray eyes finally swung her way, that hope dropped like a boulder from a cliff. A momentary burst of shock crossed his face, jaw squaring, lips tightening. Then the familiar mocking smile from school appeared, and his gaze dropped to her empty ring finger.

"I should have recognized his last name," he said. "Me and Larry. Neck and neck..."

His murmured words turned their shared past into a silly nursery rhyme. His next words shattered that illusion, however. "Still married to him?"

She swallowed. "Widowed."

Larry had died in a car accident a few months after their wedding. Right after he'd discovered from a mutual friend that she'd been seen returning to the auditorium with Clint the night of graduation. He'd asked her a question she'd refused to answer, and then he'd roared off into the night, never to come home.

"I'm sorry."

Was he? She couldn't tell by looking at him. The Clinton Marks of twenty-two years ago had worn this exact same mask during high school, not letting any kind of real emotion seep through. The earring was gone, and his tattoo was evidently hidden beneath the long sleeves of his shirt, but he still projected an attitude of blasé amusement. She'd seen that mask crack one time. And that memory now kept her glued to her chair instead of storming out and demanding that the "punk" who'd slept with her and then left without a word be removed from her daughter's case immediately and replaced with someone who actually cared.

Someone who had at least a modicum of empathy.

He did.

She'd seen it.

Experienced it.

Had felt gentle fingers tunnel through her hair, palms cupping her face and blotting her tears.

She sucked down a deep breath, realizing he was waiting for a response. "Thank you. He's been gone a long time."

And so have you. She kept that to herself, however.

His gaze shifted back to something on his monitor before fastening on her face once again. "Your daughter. There's no chance that...?"

"I'm sorry?" Her sluggish brain tried to sift through his words, but right now it seemed to be misfiring.

"Chelsea. Her chart says she's twenty-one."

It clicked. What he was saying. The same question Larry had asked her before storming off: *Is the kid even mine?* Pain slashed through her all over again. "She's my husband's."

His jaw hardened further. "You didn't waste much time marrying him after I left."

She was sure it would have seemed that way to him. But Clint had been already on his way out of town. Gone long before he'd actually left. There had never been any question of him staying, and he'd used protection that night, so surely he knew Chelsea couldn't be his. But, then, condoms had been known to fail.

"You weren't coming back. You said so yourself." The fact that there was a hint of accusation in her voice didn't seem to faze him.

"No. I wasn't."

And there you had it. Clinton Marks was the same old looking-out-for-number-one boy she remembered. Only now he was packed into a man's body.

A hard, masculine body with a face capable of breaking a million hearts.

He'd broken at least one.

Only she hadn't admitted it at the time. Instead, she'd moved on with her life the day he'd left, doing everything in her power to erase the memory of that devastating night. She'd thought she'd succeeded with Larry. And she *had* loved him, in her own way. He'd been everything Clint hadn't. Kind. Dependable. Permanent.

And willing to give up his career to be with her.

Three months later they'd married, and she'd become pregnant.

And Jessi certainly loved the child she'd made with him.

In fact, that was why she was here: Chelsea.

"It was a long time ago..." Her gaze flicked to the nameplate, and she made a quick decision about how to treat this unexpected meeting. And how to address him. "Dr. Marks, if you think that what happened between two kids—and that's all we were—will hinder your ability to help my daughter—"

"Are we really going to do this, Jessi May?" His brow cocked as the name slid effortlessly past his lips. "Pretend that night never happened? I'm interested in treating Chelsea, not in making a play for you, if that's what you're worried about."

Her face heated. "Of course I'm not."

And he was making it perfectly clear that he had no more interest in her now than he had all those years ago.

"I only asked about her parentage because I would need to remove myself from her case if it turned out she was…not Larry's."

In other words, if Chelsea were his.

What a relief it must be to him that she wasn't.

What a mess. Not quite a love triangle, but almost. There was one side missing, though. Larry had been infatuated with her. She'd been infatuated with Clint. And Clint had loved no one but himself.

Which brought her back to her current dilemma. "My daughter is sensitive. If she thinks you're treating her to work your way up some military ladder, you could damage her even more."

"I'm very good at what I do. And I'm not interested in going any further up the ladder."

The words weren't said with pride. In fact, there was an edge of strain behind them.

She believed him. The word *Colonel* in front of his name attested to decades of hard work. She knew from her father's days in the army that it took around twenty years to make that particular rank. Her dad had made it all the way up to general before his death five years ago.

In fact, her father was why she and Clint had wound up by the creek. When he'd realized Larry was headed for a military career her dad had gone off on her, using her mom's depression as ammunition for his position. The night of graduation had brought home all the changes that had been about to happen. Everyone she cared about had been on their way out of her life.

Only Larry had changed his mind at the last minute, inexplicably deciding to study at a local community college and take classes in agriculture instead.

Her glance went back to Clint, whose jaw still bore a hard edge of tension.

Me and Larry...neck and neck.

And Larry had stayed behind. With her.

The only one who knew about her dad besides her girlfriends was… "Oh, my God. You told him, didn't you? You told Larry about my father."

He didn't deny it. He didn't even blink. "How is he? Your father?"

"He's gone. He died five years ago." The pain in her chest grew. They may never have seen eye to eye about a lot of things, but she'd loved the man. And in spite of his shortcomings, he'd been a tower of strength after Larry had died and she'd been left alone, pregnant and grieving.

"I'm sorry." Clint reached across the desk to cover her hand with his. "Your mom?"

"She's okay. Worried about Chelsea. Just like I am."

He pulled back and nodded. "Let's discuss your daughter, then."

"The nurse said you've already seen her, and you've read her chart, so you know what she tried to do."

"Let's talk about that, and then we'll see her together." He pulled a yellow legal pad from a drawer of his desk and laid it in front of him. He was neat, she'd give him that, and it surprised her. Around ten pencils, all sharpened to fine points, were lined up side by side, and a single good-quality pen was at the end of the row. Nothing else adorned the stark surface of his desk, other than his nameplate and his computer monitor. So very different from the scruffy clothes and longish hair she remembered from their school days. And she'd bet those motorcycle boots were long gone, probably replaced by some kind of shiny dress shoes.

Maybe that had all been an act. Because the man she saw in front of her was every bit as disciplined as her father had been.

She shook herself, needing to gather her wits.

The only thing she should be thinking about was the here and now…and how the Clint of today could or couldn't help her daughter.

What had happened between them was in the past. It was over. And, as Clint had said, what they should be concentrating on was Chelsea.

So that's what Jessi was going to do.

If, for some reason, she judged that he couldn't help in her daughter's recovery, then she would call, write letters, parade in front of the hospital with picket signs, if necessary. And she would keep on doing it, until someone found her a doctor who could.

CHAPTER TWO

CLINT FORCED HIMSELF to stare over her shoulder rather than at the mouthwatering jiggle of her ass. The woman was no longer the stick-thin figure he'd known once upon a time. Instead, she boasted soft curves that flowed down her body like gentle ocean swells and made his hands itch to mold and explore.

Forget it, jerk. You're here for one thing only. To help Jessi's daughter and others like her.

No one had been more shocked than he'd been to realize the beautiful woman sitting across from him, worry misting her deep green eyes, was none other than the girl he'd lusted after in school.

The one he'd kissed in a rare moment of weakness, her tears triggering every protective instinct in his body.

The woman he'd handed off to the boy she'd really wanted—the one she'd married.

Unfortunately for Clint, he still didn't seem to be immune to her even after all these years.

He'd wanted to protect her.

Only he hadn't been able to back then. He couldn't now.

The only thing he could do was his job.

They reached Chelsea's room, and he shoved aside a new ache in his gut. The one that had struck when he'd realized the young woman's age was close enough to a certain deadly encounter to make him wonder whose she was.

Three months earlier and this story could have had a different ending.

No. It couldn't.

He'd done what he'd had to do back then—left—and he had no regrets.

Jessi glanced back and caught his look, her brows arching in question.

Okay, maybe he had one regret.

But it was too late to do anything about that now.

His fingers tightened on Chelsea's chart, and he started to push through the door, but Jessi stopped him. "I've been hearing things about the VA hospitals, Clint. You need to know up front that if I feel like she's not getting the treatment she needs here, I'll put her somewhere else."

His insides turned into a hard ball. He cared about his patients. All of them. No matter what the bean counters in Washington recommended or the hospital administration at whatever unit he was currently assigned to said or did, he treated his patients as if they were his comrades in arms...which they were. "It doesn't matter what you've heard. As long as I'm here, she'll get the best I have."

"But what if the hospital rules tell you to—?"

One side of his mouth went up. "Jessi May, always worried about something. Since when have you known me to play by anyone's rules?" A question they both knew the answer to, since he'd challenged almost every regulation their high school had been able to come up with.

"Would you please stop calling me that?"

His smile widened. "Is it a rule?"

"No." Her whole demeanor softened, and she actually laughed. "Because it'll just make you worse."

"I rest my case."

A nurse walked down the hallway, throwing them a curious look and reminding him of the serious issues Jessi was facing.

He took a step back. "Are you ready?"

"I think so."

Clint entered the room first, holding the door open for her.

Sitting in a chair by the window, his patient stared out across the lawn, not even acknowledging their presence. Hell, how could he not have seen the resemblance between the two women?

Chelsea had the same blond hair, the same pale, haunted features that her mother had once had. Only there was no way the young woman before him today could have survived basic training while maintaining that raw edge of vulnerability, so it was new. A result of her PTSD.

It affected people differently. Some became wounded and tortured, lashing out at themselves.

And some became impulsive and angry. Hitting out at others.

Clint wasn't sure which was worse, although as a teenager with a newly broken pinkie finger, he could have told you right off which he preferred.

Only he'd never told anyone about his finger. Or about his father.

And when he'd found Jessi crying outside the school building because of something her own father had done...he'd thought the worst. Only to have relief sweep through his system when it had been something completely different.

He drew a careful breath. "Hi, Chelsea. Do you remember me from earlier today?"

No reaction. The waif by the window continued to stare. He glanced at her chart again to remind himself of the medications Dr. Cordoba had prescribed.

He made a note to lower the dosage to see if it had any effect. He wanted to help Chelsea cope, not turn her into a zombie.

Jessi went over to her daughter and dropped to her knees, taking the young woman's hands in hers and looking up at her. "Hi, sweetheart. How are you?"

"I want to go home." The words were soft. So soft, Clint almost missed them.

Jessi hadn't, though. Her chin wobbled for a second, before she drew her spine up. "I want that, too, baby. More than anything. But you're not ready. You know you're not."

"I know." The response was just as soft. She turned to look back out the window, as if tuning out anything that didn't get her what she wanted.

Clint knew Chelsea's reaction was a defense mechanism, but having her own daughter shut her out had to shred Jessi's insides even though she was absolutely doing what was right for Chelsea.

He pulled up a chair and sat in front of the pair, forcing himself to keep his attention focused on his patient and not her mother. "I'm going to adjust some of your medications, Chelsea. Would that be okay?"

The girl sighed, but she did turn her head slightly to acknowledge she'd heard him. "Whatever you think is best."

He spent fifteen minutes watching the pair interact, making notes and comparing his observations with what he'd read of her past behavior.

She'd slashed her wrists. Jessi had found her bleeding in the bathtub and had fashioned tourniquets out of two scarves—quick thinking that had saved her daughter's life.

A couple of pints of blood later, they'd avoided permanent brain and organ damage.

Unfortunately, the infusion hadn't erased the emotional damage that had come about as a result of what her chart said was months spent in captivity.

Trauma—any trauma—had to be processed mentally and

emotionally. Some people seemed to escape unscathed, letting the memory of the event roll off their backs. Others were crushed beneath it.

And others pretended they didn't give a damn.

Even when they did.

Like him?

Jessi had coaxed Chelsea over to the bed and sat next to her, arm draped around her shoulders, still talking to her softly. He got up and laid a hand on her shoulder.

"I'll give you a few minutes. Stop in and talk to me before you leave the hospital." He didn't add the word *okay* or allow his voice to change tone at the end of the phrase, because he didn't want to make it seem like a request. Not because he wasn't sure she'd honor it, but part of him wondered if she'd head back to the front desk and demand to have another doctor assigned to the case.

Clint had to somehow break the tough news to Jessi that she was stuck with him for the next couple of months or for however long Chelsea was here. There just wasn't anyone else.

So it was up to him to convince her that he could help her daughter, if she gave him a chance. Not hard, since he believed it himself. Clint had dealt with all types of soldiers in crisis, both male and female, something Dr. Cordoba had not. It was part of the reason Clint had agreed to this assignment. His rotations didn't keep him anywhere for more than six months at a time. Surely that would be long enough to treat Chelsea or at least come up with a plan for how to proceed.

If he'd known one of Dr. Cordoba's toughest cases was Jessi Spencer's daughter, though, he wouldn't have been quite so quick to agree to return to his hometown.

Being here was dangerous on a number of levels.

Jessi's not the girl you once knew.

He sensed it. She was stronger than she'd been in school. She'd had to be after being widowed at a young age and raising a daughter on her own. And according to the listing on Chelsea's chart, Jessi was now an ER physician. You didn't deal with trauma cases all day long without having a cast-iron stomach and a tough emotional outlook.

He'd seen a touch of that toughness in his office. Her eyes had studied him, but had given nothing away, unlike the Jessi of his past, who'd worn her heart on her sleeve.

Just as well. He was here to treat the daughter, not take up where he'd left off with the mother. Not that he'd "left off" with her. He'd had a one-night stand and had then made sure her beau had known that to win her heart he had to be willing to give up his dreams for her.

Evidently he had.

That was one thing Clint wouldn't do. For anyone.

If he could just keep that in mind for the next couple of months, he'd be home free. And if he was able to help Chelsea get the help she needed while he was at it, that was icing on the cake.

He corrected himself. No, not just the icing. It was the whole damn cake. And that was what he needed to focus on.

Anything else would be a big mistake.

"And how long will that be?" Jessi's mouth opened, then snapped back shut, before trying again. "I don't want Chelsea's next doctor to give up on her like…"

Her voice faded away as the reality of what she'd been about to say swept through her: *Like Dr. Cordoba did. Like Chelsea's father did when he took off into the night.*

"Are you talking about Dr. Cordoba?"

She blinked. Had he read her mind? "Yes."

"He didn't give up on her." His voice softened. "His wife is very ill. He had to take a job that allows him to be home with her as much as possible. He couldn't do that and continue working long hours here. He knew his patients deserved more than that."

Oh, God. Her ire at the other doctor dissolved in a heartbeat. She'd been so caught up in her own problems that she hadn't even stopped to think that maybe he had been dealing with things that were every bit as bad as hers were. Maybe even worse. "I…" She swallowed. "I don't know what to say. I'm so sorry."

The events of the past months were suddenly too much for her, and her heart pounded, her stomach churned.

Please, no. Not now.

She'd had two panic attacks since Chelsea's hospitalization, so she recognized the signs.

Pressing a hand to her middle, she tried to force back the nausea and took a few careful breaths.

"I thought you should know." Clint leaned forward. "If you're worried about me suddenly taking off, don't be. I'll give you plenty of notice."

This time.

The words hung in the air between them, and for a horrible, soul-stealing second she thought he was hinting for her not to get her hopes up.

"I'm not expecting you to stay forever." The sensation in her chest and stomach grew, heat crawling up her neck and making her ears ring. Her vision narrowed to a pinpoint. And then it was too late to stop it. "I think I'm going…"

She lurched to her feet and somehow made it through the door and to the first stall in the restroom before her gut revolted in a violent spasm, and she threw up. She'd been running on coffee and pure adrenaline for the past several weeks, and she hadn't eaten breakfast that morning. The perfect setup for an attack.

That had to be the reason. Not finding Clint sitting behind that desk.

Again and again, her stomach heaved, mingling with tears of frustration.

When she finally regained control over herself, she flushed the toilet with shaking hands before going to the sink, bending down to rinse her mouth and splash water over her face.

She blindly reached for the paper-towel dispenser, only to have some kind of cloth pressed into her hand.

Holding the fabric tightly to her face and wishing she could blot away the past two months as easily as the moisture, she sucked down a couple more slow breaths, her heart rate finally slowing to some semblance of normality.

"Thank you." She lifted her head, already knowing who she'd find when she opened her eyes. "You shouldn't be in here."

"Why? Because it's against the rules? I thought we'd already sorted all that out." He added a smile. "Besides, I wanted to make sure you were okay."

The words swirled with bitter familiarity through her head. They were the same ones he'd said the night of their high-school graduation ceremony when she'd suddenly veered away from the rows of chairs and rushed out into the parking lot and then down to a nearby creek. Thankfully neither her dad nor mom had seen her. And an hour and a half later, when the ceremony had been over and the reception had been in full swing, she'd returned. With the lie that Clint had told her to use trembling on her tongue…that she'd been sick with nerves.

Her dad had bought it, just like Clint had said he would.

Only when she'd said it, it had no longer been a lie, because she had felt sick. Not because of nerves, but because the boy she'd always wanted—the boy she'd lost her virginity to—would soon be on his way to the airport, headed for boot camp. Leaving her behind forever.

"It's just the shock of everything."

"I know."

She shivered and wrapped her arms around herself. Clint made no effort to take off his jacket and drape it around her. It was a good thing, because she'd probably dissolve into a puddle all over again if he did.

"Have you eaten recently?"

"What?"

"I get the feeling you're running on fumes along with a

heaped dose of stress. Which is probably why—" he nodded at the closed stall "—that just happened."

Leave it to him to point out the obvious. "I can eat later."

He nodded. "Yes. Or you could eat while we go over some treatment options. I skipped breakfast this morning and could use something, as well. Besides, some carbs will help settle your stomach."

Before she knew it, she found herself in the hospital cafeteria with a toasted bagel and a cup of juice sitting in front of her.

A hint of compassion in his voice as he detailed the treatments he'd like to try told her this wasn't going to be an easy fix. It was something Chelsea would be dealing with for the rest of her life. He just wanted to give her the tools she needed to do that successfully.

It was what Jessie wanted, as well. More than anything. As a mom, she wanted to be able to make things better, to take away her daughter's pain. But she couldn't. She had to trust that Clint knew what he was doing.

He certainly sounded capable.

"And what if she tries to do something to herself?" She set the bagel back down on the plate, unable to leave the subject alone.

"I'll take steps to avoid the possibility." He steepled his fingers and met her gaze with a steadiness that unnerved her. The man was intimidating, even though she knew he wasn't trying to be. Despite his reassurances, she still wasn't convinced Clint was the man for the job. Especially considering their history—which, granted, wasn't much of one. On his side, anyway.

What other option did she have, though? An institution? Bring her home and hope Chelsea didn't try to take her life again?

No. She couldn't risk there being a next time.

She'd do anything it took to help bring her daughter back from wherever she was. That included seeing Clint every day for the rest of her life and reliving what they'd done by the bank of that creek.

Decision made.

"I want you to keep me informed of every move you make."

One brow quirked. Too late she realized he could have taken her words the wrong way. But he didn't throw a quick come-back, like he might have done in days gone by. Instead, he simply said the words she needed to hear most: "Don't worry, Jessi. Even if we have to break every rule in the book, we're going to pull her through this."

And as much as the word *we* made something inside her tingle to life, it was that other statement that reached out and grabbed her. The one that said the old Clint was still crouched inside that standard issue haircut and neat-as-a-pin desk. It was there in his eyes. The glowing intensity that said, despite outward appearances, he hadn't turned into a heartless bureaucrat after years of going through proper channels.

He was a rule-breaker. He always had been. And just like his bursting into the ladies' restroom unannounced, it gave her hope, along with a sliver of fear.

She knew from experience he wasn't afraid to break anything that got in the way of what he wanted. She just had to make sure one of those "things" wasn't her heart.

CHAPTER THREE

JESSI HAD JUST finished suturing an elbow laceration and was headed in to pick up her next chart when a cry of pain came from the double bay doors of the emergency entrance.

"Ow! It hurts!"

A man holding a little girl in his arms lurched into the waiting area, his face as white as the linoleum flooring beneath his feet. The child's frilly pink party dress had a smear of dirt along one side of it, as did her arm and one side of her face. That had Jessi moving toward the pair. The other cases in the waiting room at the moment were minor illnesses and injuries.

The man's wild eyes latched on to her, taking in the stethoscope around her neck. "Are you a doctor?"

"Yes. How can I help?"

"We were at a... She fell..." The words tumbled out of his mouth, nothing making sense. Especially since the girl's pained cries were making the already stricken expression on his face even worse.

She tried to steer him in the right direction. "She fell. Is this your daughter?"

"Yes. She fell off a trampoline at a friend's house. It's her leg."

Like with many fun things about childhood—climbing trees, swimming in the lake, riding a bike—danger lurked around every corner, ready to strike.

Jessi brushed a mass of blond curls off the girl's damp face and spoke to her. "What's your name?"

"Tammy," she said between sobs.

She maintained eye contact with her little charge. "Tammy, I know your leg must hurt terribly. We're going to take you back and help fix it." She motioned to one of the nurses behind the admission's desk. Gina immediately came toward them with a clipboard.

The girl nodded, the volume of her cries going down a notch.

"Let's take her into one of the exam rooms, while Nurse Stanley gets some information."

It wasn't standard protocol—they were supposed to register all admissions unless there was a life-threatening injury—but right now Jessi wanted to take away not only the child's pain but the father's, as well.

Maybe Clint wasn't the only one who knew how to break a few rules.

But she had to. She recognized that look of utter terror and helplessness on the dad's face. She'd felt the same paralyzing fear as she'd crouched in the bathtub with her daughter, blood pouring out of Chelsea's veins. She'd sent out that same cry for help. To God. To the universe. To anyone who would listen.

And like the distraught father following her to a treatment room, she'd been forced to place her child in the hands of a trained professional and pray they could fix whatever was wrong. Because it was something beyond her own capabilities.

But what if it was also beyond the abilities of the people you entrusted them to?

Raw fear pumped back into her chest, making her lungs ache. *Stop it.*

She banished Clint and Chelsea from her thoughts and concentrated on her job. This little girl needed her, and she had to have her head in the game if she wanted to help her.

"Which leg is it?" she asked the father.

"Her right. It's her shin."

"Did she fall on the ground? Or which part of the trampoline?"

She asked question after question, gathering as much information as she could in order to narrow the steps she'd need to take to determine the exact nature of the injury.

Gina followed them into the room and was already writing furiously, even though the nurse hadn't voiced a single question. That could come later.

"Set her on the table."

As soon as cold metal touched the girl's leg, she let out an ear-piercing shriek that quickly melted back into sobs.

As a mother, it wrenched at her heart, but Jessi couldn't let any of that affect what she did next. Things would get worse for Tammy before they got better, because Jessi had to make sure she knew what she was dealing with.

"Gina, can you stay and get the rest of the information from Mr...?" She paused and glanced at the girl's father.

"Lawrence. Jack Lawrence."

"Thank you." She turned back to her nurse. "Can you do that while I call Radiology?"

Once she'd made the call, she made short work of getting the girl's vitals, talking softly to her as she went about her job. When she slid the girl's dress up a little way, she spied a dark blue contusion forming along her shin and saw a definite deformation of the tibia. The bone had separated. Whether they could maneuver the ends back in place without surgery would depend on what the X-rays showed.

Within fifteen minutes, one of the radiology techs had whisked the five-year-old down the hall on a stretcher, her father following close behind. His expression had gone from one of fear to hope. Sometimes just knowing it wasn't all up to you as a parent, that there were others willing to pitch in, made a little of the weight roll off your shoulders.

So why did she still feel buried beneath tons of rubble?

Because Chelsea's injury went beyond the physical to the very heart of who she was. And Jessi wasn't sure Clint—or anyone else—could repair it. There was no splint or cast known to man that could heal a broken spirit.

A half hour later Tammy and her father were back in the exam room, and an orthopedist had arrived to take over the case. The urge to bend down and kiss the little girl's cheek came and went. She held back a little smile. She didn't need to break *all* the rules. Some of them were there for a reason.

Hopefully, Clint knew which ones to follow and which ones to break.

He did. She sensed it.

He wouldn't go beyond certain professional boundaries. Which meant he would try to keep their past in the past. If one of them stepped over the line, he'd remove himself from Chelsea's case.

Should she talk to Chelsea about what had happened down at the creek—tell her she'd gone to school with Clint? Not necessary. He appeared to have a plan. Besides, if she heaped anything else on her daughter, she might hunker further down into whatever foxhole she'd dug for herself. She needed to give Clint enough time to do his job.

"Jessi?" Gina, the nurse from the earlier, caught her just as she was leaving her patient's room. "You have a phone call on line two."

"Okay, thanks." It must be her mom, confirming their dinner date for tonight. She'd promised to update her on Chelsea's condition, something that made her feel ill. With her father gone, Jessi and Chelsea were all her mother had left. And though her mother was no longer taking antidepressants, she'd been forgetful lately, which Jessi hoped was just from the stress of her only granddaughter's illness.

Going to the reception desk, she picked up the phone and punched the lit button. "Hello?"

Instead of the bright, happy tones of her mother, she encountered something a couple of octaves lower. "Jess?"

She gulped. "Yes?"

"Clint here."

As if she hadn't already recognized the sound of his voice. Still, her heart leaped with fear. "Is something wrong with Chelsea?"

"No. Do you have a minute? I'd like to take care of some scheduling."

"Scheduling?"

A low, incredibly sexy-sounding hum came through the phone that made something curl in her belly.

"I want us to talk every day."

"Every day?"

About Chelsea, you idiot! And what was with repeating everything he said?

"Yes. Our schedules are probably both hectic, but we can do it by phone, if necessary."

"Oh. Okay." Was he saying he didn't want to meet with her in person? That he'd rather do all of this by phone? She had no idea, but she read off her schedule for the next five days.

A grunt of affirmation came back, along with, "I'll also want to meet with you and Chelsea together."

"Why?"

"Didn't Dr. Cordoba have family sessions with you?"

She shook her head, only realizing afterwards that he couldn't see it. "No, although he mentioned wanting to try that further down the road."

"I believe in getting the family involved as soon as possible, since you'll be the one working with her once she's discharged."

Discharged. The most beautiful word Chelsea had heard in

weeks. And Clint made it sound like a reality, rather than just a vague possibility. So he really was serious about doing everything he could to make sure treatment was successful.

A wave of gratitude came over her and a knot formed in her throat. "Thank you, Clint. For being willing to break the rules."

Was she talking about with Chelsea? Or about their time together all those years ago.

"You're welcome, Jess. For what it's worth, I think Chelsea is very lucky to have you."

Her next words came out before she was aware of them forming in her head. But she meant them with all her heart. "Ditto, Clint. I think Chelsea and I are the lucky ones."

"I'll call you."

With that intimate-sounding promise, he said goodbye, and the phone clicked in her ear, telling her he'd hung up. She gripped the receiver as tightly as she could, all the while praying she was doing the right thing. She was about to allow Clint back into her orbit—someone who'd once carried her to the peak of ecstasy and then tossed her into the pit of despair without a second glance. But what choice did she have, really?

She firmed her shoulders. No, there was always a choice. She may have made the wrong one when she'd been on the cusp of womanhood, but she was smarter now. Stronger. She could—and would—keep her emotions in check. If not for her own sake, then for her daughter's.

CHAPTER FOUR

THE FIRST FAMILY counseling session was gearing up to be a royal disaster.

Jessi came sliding into Clint's office thirty minutes late, out of breath, face flushed, wispy strands of hair escaping from her clip.

He swallowed back a rush of emotion. She'd looked just like this as she'd stood to her feet after they'd made love. He'd helped her brush her hair back into place, combing his fingers through the strands and wishing life could be different for him.

But it couldn't. Not then. And not now.

"Sorry. We had an emergency at the hospital, and I had to stay and help."

"No problem." He stood. "I have another patient in a half hour, so we'll need to make this a quick session."

"Poor Chelsea. I feel awful. I'm off tomorrow, though, so I'll come and spend the day with her."

When they walked into Chelsea's room, the first thing he noticed was that the lunch she'd been served an hour ago was still on a tray in front of her, untouched. At the sight of them, though, she seemed to perk up in her seat, shoveling a bite of mashed potatoes into her mouth and making a great show of chewing.

Manipulating. He'd seen signs of it earlier when he'd tried to coax her to talk about things that didn't involve the weather.

Her throat worked for a second with the food still pouched inside one cheek. She ended up having to wash the potatoes down with several gulps of water. She sat there, breathing as hard as her mother had been when she'd arrived a few moments ago.

"Enjoying your meal?" he asked, forcing his voice to remain blasé. So much for showing Jessi how good he was at his job.

As if this was even about him.

He ground his teeth as his frustration shifted to himself.

Chelsea shrugged. Another bite went in—albeit a much smaller one this time.

Not polite to talk with my mouth full, was the inference.

Well, she'd run out of the stuff eventually. And since she was pretty thin already, he was all for anything that would get food into her system. That was one of the comments on the sheet in her file. She didn't eat much, unless someone wanted to interact with her in some way. The staff had taken to coming to her room and loitering around, straightening things and making small talk. It was a surefire way to get that fork moving from plate to mouth.

He decided to give her a little more time.

Jessi stood there, looking a little lost by her daughter's lack of greeting. He sent her a nod of reassurance and motioned her to sit in one of the two nearby chairs and joined her.

"Let's go ahead and get started, if that's okay with you, Chelsea."

Chew, chew, chew.

She moved on to her green beans without a word. Okay, if that's the way she wanted to play it, he'd go right along with it.

He turned to Jessi, sorry for what he was about to do, but if anything could break through her daughter's wall it might be having to face some hard, unpleasant subjects. "Since Chelsea's busy, why don't you tell me what led her to being here."

Right on cue, Jessi's eyes widened. "You mean about the day I called…"

"Yes."

Her throat moved a couple of times, swallowing, probably her way of either building up the courage to talk about the suicide attempt or to refuse.

"Well, I—I called Chelsea's cell phone to let her know I was coming home early. It rang and rang before finally going over to voice mail. I was going to stop and pick up some Thai food—her favorite…" Jessi's eyes filled with tears. "I decided to go straight home instead, so we could go out to eat together. When I got there… Wh-when I got to the house, I—"

"Stop." Chelsea's voice broke through, though she was still staring down, a green bean halfway to her mouth. "Don't make her talk about it."

Whether the young woman wanted to spare her mother's feelings or her own, Clint wasn't sure. "What would you like to discuss instead, then?"

There was a long pause. Then she said, "What you hope to accomplish by keeping me here."

"It's not about us, Chelsea. It's about you."

"Where's Dr. Cordoba?" Her head finally came up, and her gaze settled on him.

"He went to work somewhere else."

"Because of me." The words came out as a whisper.

Clint shook his head. "No, of course not. He made the decision for personal reasons. It had nothing to do with you."

Jessi's chest rose and fell as she took a quick breath. "We all just want to help, honey."

"Everything I touch turns to ashes."

"No." Jessi glanced at him, then scooted closer to her daughter, reaching out to stroke her hair. "You've been through a lot in the past several months, but you're not alone."

"I am, Mom. You have no idea. You all think I'm suffering from PTSD, because of my time in that camp, don't you? Dr. Cordoba did. But I'm not."

Clint glanced at Jessi, a frown on his face. "You tried to take your life, Chelsea. Something made you think life wasn't worth living."

The girl's shoulders slumped.

"Does this have to do with your pregnancy?"

Two sets of female eyes settled on him in shock.

Hell. Jessi hadn't known?

It was right there in Chelsea's medical chart that her physical exam had revealed she'd given birth or had had a miscarriage at some point. He'd just assumed…

His patient went absolutely rigid. "I want her to leave. Now."

"But, Chelsea…" Jessi's voice contained a note of pleading.

"Now." The girl's voice rose in volume. "Now, now. *Now!*"

Jessi careened back off her chair and stumbled from the room as her daughter's wails turned to full-fledged screams of pain. She was tearing at her hair, her food flung across the room. Clint pressed the call button for the nurse and between the two of them they were able to administer a sedative, putting an end to Chelsea's hysterical shrieks. Her muscles finally went limp and her eyes closed. He stood staring down at her bed for a few moments, a feeling of unease settling over him as it had each time he'd met with Chelsea. There was something here. Something more than what was revealed in her records.

And it involved that pregnancy. She'd been calm until the moment the subject had come up.

It was time to do a little more digging. But for now he had to go out there and face Jessi. And somehow come up with something to say that wouldn't make things worse than they already were.

"I didn't know."

Clint came toward her as she leaned against the wall twenty

feet away from Chelsea's door. Her stomach had roiled within her as the nurse had rushed into the room and the screams had died down to moans, before finally fading away to nothing. All she wanted to do was throw up, just like she had during a previous visit, but she somehow held it together this time.

"I'm sorry, Jess." Clint scrubbed a hand through his hair, not touching her. "I'd assumed she told you."

"She hasn't told me anything. Could it have been while she was a prisoner?"

"I'm not sure. This is the most emotion I've seen from her in the past week. We hit a nerve, though. So that's a good thing."

"I can't imagine what she went through." She leaned her head against the wall and stared at the ceiling.

Chelsea's convoy had been ambushed during a night patrol by enemy forces disguised as police officers. The group had been held for four months. Chelsea had said they'd all been separated and interrogated, but she'd had no idea one of the prisoners had died until she and the rest of those rescued had been flown home.

Jessi sighed and turned back to look at him. "The army debriefed her, but I was never told what she said, and I—I was afraid to press her too much. She seemed to be doing fine. Maybe that in itself was a warning sign."

"There was no way you could have known what she was going to do." Clint pushed a strand of hair off her cheek.

She wasn't sure she could stand seeing her daughter in this much pain week after week. And a pregnancy…

Had her daughter been raped during her captivity? The army had said there was no evidence of that, but then again Chelsea wasn't exactly a fount of information. "I think I'm doing more harm than good by going in there with you."

"Let's see how it goes for the next week, okay? Chelsea was admitted under a suicide watch. That gives you permission to make decisions regarding her health care. She could still open up."

"She doesn't even want me here, Clint. You heard her." Jessi's head still reverberated with her daughter's cries for her to get out.

"That was the shock talking. She didn't expect me to ask that particular question. At least she's getting it out, rather than bottling it all up inside."

His eyes narrowed as he looked at her face. "How long's it been since you've done something that hasn't revolved around your job or Chelsea?"

She thought for a second. "I can't remember."

"The last thing she needs is for you to break down as well, which is where you're headed if you don't take some down time."

She knew he was right. She'd felt like she'd been standing on the edge of a precipice for weeks now, with no way to back away from it.

Before she could say anything, he went on. "You said you're off tomorrow. Why don't you go out and do something fun? Something you enjoy?"

"I need to spend the day here with Chelsea."

"No. You don't. She'll understand. It might not be a bad idea to give her a day to think through what just happened."

She hesitated. "I don't even know what I'd do." Chelsea might need a day to think, but the last thing Jessi wanted to do was sit at home and let her brain wander down dark paths.

"Tell you what. I don't have anything pressing tomorrow. Why don't we do something together? It's fair season. There's probably something going on in one of the nearby counties."

"Oh, but I couldn't. Chelsea—"

"Will be fine."

Conflicting emotions swept through her. The possibility of spending the day with Clint dangled before her in a way that was far too attractive. "I'm not sure…"

"Is it because I'm her doctor?"

"Yes." He'd given her the perfect excuse, and she grabbed at it with both hands.

"That can be remedied."

Panic sizzled through her. He'd hinted once before that he might drop her daughter's case.

"No. I want you."

He paused, then shook his head and dragged his fingertips across her cheek. "Then you have to take care of yourself."

She nodded, unable to look away from his eyes as they locked on her face. Several emotions flicked through them, none of them decipherable.

"I'll try."

"How about I check the local schedules and see if I can find something for us to do? Something that doesn't involve a hospital."

Guilt rose in her throat, but at a warning glance from him she forced it back down. "Okay."

He nodded and let his hand fall back to his side. "Are you going to be okay tonight?"

Was he asking her that as a psychiatrist or as a man?

It didn't matter. The last thing she wanted was to jeopardize her working relationship with the one man who might be able to get through to her daughter. She needed to keep this impersonal. Professional. Even though his touch brought back a whole lot of emotions she hadn't felt in twenty-two years.

But she had to keep them firmly locked away. Somehow.

"I'll be fine. Just call if there's any change, okay?" She was proud of the amount of conviction she'd inserted into her voice.

"I will. I'm off at ten, but the hospital knows how to reach me if there's a problem." He took a card from his desk and wrote something on the back of it, then handed it to her. "I'll give you a yell in the morning, but until then, here's my cell phone number. Call me if you need me."

If you need me.

Terrifying words, because she already did. More than she should. But she wouldn't call. No matter how much that little voice inside her said to do just that.

CHAPTER FIVE

CLINT STEPPED ONTO the first row of metal bleachers and held his hand out for her. Grasping his fingers, and letting him maneuver through the crowd of seated spectators, they went to the very top, where a metal brace across the end provided a place for their backs to rest.

She watched the next horse in line prance into the arena, ears pricked forward in anticipation. Three fifty-five-gallon drums had been laid out to form a familiar triangle.

Barrel racing.

The speed event looked deceptively easy, but if a horse knocked over a barrel as it went around it, the rider received a five-second penalty, enough to cost a winning ribbon.

"I used to do this, you know. Run barrels."

"I know you did."

Her head swiveled to look at the man sitting next to her, completely missing the horse's take-off.

"You did?"

He smiled. "I came to the fair on occasion. Watched a few of the 4-H events."

The thought of Clint sitting on one of these very bleachers, watching her compete, was unnerving. How would she have missed him with the way he'd dressed back then? He hadn't exactly looked the part of an emerging cowboy.

Exactly. She would have noticed him.

Which meant he'd never actually seen her race. She settled back into place.

"I didn't realize you were interested in 4-H."

His gaze went back to the arena. "I wasn't."

Something about the way he'd said that...

"Do you still have your trophy?" He was still looking straight ahead, thankfully, but her gasp sounded like a gunshot to her ears, despite the noise going on around her.

The metal brace behind her groaned as more people leaned against it. Jessi eased some of her weight off it.

"How did you know I...?" She'd only won one trophy in all, her years of entering the event.

"I happened to be in the vicinity that day."

How did one *happen* to be in the vicinity of the fair? It spanned a large area. And the horse arena wasn't exactly next to the carnival rides or food.

"You saw me run?"

"I saw a lot of people compete."

Okay, that explained it. "So you came out to all the horse events?"

"Not all of them. I had a few friends who did different things."

Like run barrels? She didn't think so. Neither did she re-member him hanging out with any of her 4-H friends. And the only year she'd won the event had been as a high school senior.

The next horse—a splashy brown and white paint—came in, and she fixed her attention on it, although her mind was going at a million miles an hour. The rider directed the horse in a tight circle near the starting area and then let him go. The animal's neck stretched forward as he raced toward the first barrel, tail streaming out behind him.

"Here!" the rider called as they reached the drum, using her voice along with her hands and legs to guide the horse around the turn. She did the same for the second and third barrels and then the pair raced back in a straight line until they crossed where the automatic timer was set up. Nineteen point two three seconds.

The announcer repeated the time, adding that it put the horse and rider into second place.

Clint leaned closer, his scent washing over her at almost exactly the same time as his arm brushed hers. The dual assault made her mind blank out for a second. So much so that she almost missed his question. "I always wondered. Why do some of them start with the left barrel rather than the one on the right?"

Play it cool, Jessi.

"B-because horses have a dominant side, kind of like being right- or left-handed."

"Interesting. So your horse was right-handed?"

She swallowed. So he *had* seen her. She'd hoped maybe he'd heard that she'd won from a friend, rather than having been there in the flesh. What did it matter? So he'd seen her race. No big deal.

But it was. And she had no idea why.

"Yes, she was."

Neither of the next two horses beat the time of the leader. Despite her wariness at coming out today, and her horror at realizing he'd watched her the day of her win, she could feel the muscles in her body relaxing. He'd been right to suggest she take a day off.

A *real* day off.

"Do you think Chelsea—?"

"The hospital will call me if they need me. We're both off duty today."

She frowned. "She's my daughter, Clint. I can't help but worry about her."

"I'm not asking you to put her from your mind. I'm asking you to enjoy your day. It's what she would want."

She sighed. "She did seem happy when I told her where I was going." Jessi had insisted on stopping to see Chelsea before they'd left, although she hadn't told her that she and Clint were going together.

"Exactly." He bumped her with his shoulder again. "And she's probably going to ask what you did. So let's make it good."

Jessi's eyes widened. How was she supposed to respond to that?

She was still trying to figure it out when she heard a weird screech of metal, then Clint's arm was suddenly behind her, crushing her tightly against him.

"Hold on!"

She thought at first it was because a new horse had started the course, but then she sensed something falling, followed by screams.

When she glanced back, she saw that the metal support had broken free—probably from the weight of everyone leaning against it—and was dangling from the far side of the bleachers. And on the ground...

Oh, Lord. Fifteen feet below them were five people who'd evidently tumbled backward off the top seat when the structure had given way. Others were now on their feet in a panic, trying to rush down the stands to get to the ground. One person tripped and landed on another spectator a few rows down.

"Stay here," Clint muttered.

Like hell. "I'm coming with you. I'm a doctor, too, remember?"

Someone in the judges' booth called over the loudspeakers, asking for everyone to remain calm. And also asking for medical assistance.

Clint cautiously made his way down, trying to make sure

he didn't trample on anyone, and again holding her hand as he took one step at a time.

By the time they reached the bottom they could hear a siren that cut off just as it reached the wide dirt aisle that separated the main arena from campers and horse trailers. The crowd opened a path to let it through.

One of the victims was now on her feet and waving away offers for help. Another person had disappeared, evidently also unhurt. But the remaining three were still on the ground, although one was sitting up, holding his leg.

"I'm a doctor," Clint said to him. "Can you hold on for a minute while we check the others?"

"Go," the man said, his thin, wiry frame and rugged clothing suggesting he was a farmer or someone who worked with livestock.

Jessi motioned that she'd take the far patient, a woman who was on her side, moaning, while Clint took the last remaining patient, a child, who was writhing on the ground and crying. They pushed through layers of people who wanted to help.

"I'm a doctor, let me through," she said to a man who was kneeling next to the woman. The man backed up to make room in the tight circle.

The EMT vehicle stopped and two medical workers jumped from the back just as Jessi crouched near her patient. The woman was conscious but obviously in a lot of pain.

"Where does it hurt?"

"Brandi," she gasped, ignoring the question and trying to roll onto her back, only to stop with a moan. "My daughter. Where's Brandi?"

Jessi glanced to the side, but couldn't see Clint through the bodies of onlookers, but his patient had looked to be a little girl.

"How old is your daughter?"

"She…she's five. Pink shorts." Talking was an obvious struggle for her.

That had to be Clint's patient.

"Someone's helping her right now. Where does it hurt?"

"M-My ribs. It hurts to breathe."

Jessi did a quick rundown of the woman's vitals. Everything seemed good, except for a marked tenderness on her right side. "Did you hit your head at all?"

"No. Just landed flat on my side. I couldn't get up."

One of the emergency services workers knelt beside her. "What have you got?"

Jessi glanced at the man, who looked to be almost as young as Chelsea. "Possible rib fractures." She read off the woman's vitals. "How's the little girl next to us?"

"Fractured wrist, but she looks good to go."

Jessi's patient broke down in tears. "Is that her? My daughter?"

It was amazing someone hadn't been more seriously injured or even killed in that fall. But luckily the bleachers had been built on dirt rather than a harder surface like concrete or asphalt.

She turned to the EMT. "Can you ask Dr. Marks if his patient's name is Brandi? It's her daughter, if so."

"Sure. I'll be right back."

Asking everyone to move back as he did so, she finally had a clear line of sight to Clint. He gave her a reassuring wink that made her smile.

God, how familiar that was. And it still made a jolt of electricity go through her system.

The girl was indeed Brandi, and within minutes everyone had been bundled up into two ambulances, which were creeping back between the throngs of horses and people, and soon disappeared. The sirens were off this time, probably trying not to spook the horses and risk more accidents.

Clint grasped her elbow and eased her over to the side. "They're taping off the bleachers."

Her adrenaline was just beginning to dissipate from her system. "I felt the piece of metal give a little bit earlier, but it's been here for ages. I had no idea it could come loose."

"Just an accident."

"Thank God it wasn't worse. How about the person who fell, trying to get down?"

"Evidently they were all okay, since we didn't have any other patients."

With the excitement dying down, people were moving over to the rail next to the arena as the remaining barrel racers moved back into position.

"Do you want something to eat?"

She glanced up at him. "You can eat, after all that?"

He tweaked her chin. "They're all fine, Jess. Let's enjoy the rest of the day."

Their patients may have been fine, but Jessi wasn't so sure about herself. The memory of his hand grasping hers as he'd hauled her up the steps wound around her senses. She missed his touch. Wanted to reach over and…

The cell phone on Clint's hip buzzed. The hospital? Her whole body stiffened as dread rose up to fill her being.

Clint's system went on high alert as he put the phone to his ear.

"Marks here."

"Clinton? Clinton Marks?"

Frowning, he tried to place the feminine voice on the other end of the line. While the light Southern drawl was familiar, it definitely wasn't anyone from the hospital, because they would have called him "Doctor." If this was some telemarketer, they were about to get an earful for scaring Jessi.

And she was scared. He could read it in her stiff posture and the hands clenched at her sides.

He decided to go ultra-formal. "This is Dr. Marks."

"Well, *Dr.* Marks—" there was an air of amusement to the voice now "—this is Abigail Spencer, Jessi's mom. Chelsea's grandmother. You remember me, don't you?"

Hell. That's why she sounded familiar.

He mouthed "Your mom" to relieve Jessi's fears, wondering why she was calling him instead of Jessi.

Jessi evidently had the same idea as he did, because she frowned and checked her phone. Maybe it was dead or something.

Clint and Jessi's dads had both been stationed at the same base, so he'd seen her parents quite a bit during his school years. His memories of Mrs. Spencer were of a kind woman with blond curls very like her daughter's and a quiet smile. So very different from his own mother's tense and fearful posture that had cropped up anytime she'd heard that front door open. Or how she would place her body in front of her son's until she had gauged what mood her husband had brought home with him. He rubbed a thumb across his pinky. His mother hadn't always been able to protect him, though.

Which was why the Spencer household had seemed so strange and alien to him. He'd never been able to shake the feeling that Jessi's mom had seen right through to the hurting kid hidden beneath a rebellious leather jacket and spiked hair. He brought his attention back to Jessi's mom as the silence over the phone grew awkward. He cleared his throat. "Of course I remember you. How are you?"

"Anxious to see my granddaughter. But Jessi told me that's not a good idea right now. I want to ask why. It's been over two months."

He didn't understand what that had to do with him, unless Jessi had used him as an excuse to deflect her visits. But whatever it was, that was between the two of them as far as he was concerned.

"I'm sorry, Mrs. Spencer. I really think you should talk to your daughter about that, because I can't discuss Chelsea's treatment. Jessi would have to give written authorization to—"

A poke to his arm made him look at the woman beside him. She shook her head.

Mrs. Spencer's voice came back down the line. "I can do better than that. Why don't you come over for dinner tonight? Jessi will be here, and we can hash all this out between the three of us." There was a pause. When her voice came back it was on the shaky side. "I'm her grandmother. Don't you think I'm entitled to know what's going on?"

"Again, that's not up to me." He felt like an utter jackass for saying those words to a woman who'd been nothing but nice to him during his time in Richmond, but Jess was staring holes right through him. "Jessi has medical power of attorney at the moment."

"She's trying to protect me, but I don't need protecting." An audible breath came through the receiver. "Won't you please come to dinner?"

There was no way he was going to walk into a situation like that without Jessi being fully aware of what was coming, and he wasn't willing to admit her daughter was standing right next to him. Not without Jess's approval. "Tell you what. Call your daughter and talk to her. If she's in agreement with me coming over tonight, I'll be glad to." How was that for admitting he had no other plans for a Friday evening?

Another poke to the arm, harder this time. "What are you doing?" she whispered.

He gave her a helpless shrug.

Unlike Jessi, he'd never married, instead throwing his whole life into helping others who were dealing with traumatic events stemming from their military service. It had been the least he could do for his dad, who, like Chelsea, had felt all alone.

"Okay, I'll do that." A quick laugh made a warning system go off in his head. "Do you still like corned-beef brisket?"

She remembered that? He'd eaten over at their house exactly once, which was when he'd discovered how overprotective her dad was—the polar opposite of his. And he hadn't liked Clint. At all. Clint had never been invited back to the house again.

"I love brisket." Not that he thought there was a snowball's chance in hell that Jessi would agree to him coming over and talking about Chelsea's condition. If she'd wanted her mom to know how treatment was going, surely she would have told her by now.

"See you around seven, then."

Not quite sure how to answer that, he settled for a noncommittal reply. "Thank you for the invitation, Mrs. Spencer."

The phone clicked off.

He met Jessi's accusing eyes. "Why did you let her invite you to dinner?"

As if he'd had any choice in the matter. One eyebrow went up. "I think the more important question is how did she get my number and why is she calling me, instead of you?"

"I don't know what you—"

Her phone started playing some samba beat that made him smile. Jessi groaned. "Oh, Lord. How am I going to get you out of this?"

"Don't worry about trying. I can come, if it's okay with you." Why he'd said that he had no idea.

"Hi, Mom. No, I'm...out at the fair." She licked her lips, while Clint handed money to the man in the funnel cake booth. "I know, I'm sorry. It was a spur-of-the-minute thing. A friend invited me."

She listened again, her face turning pink. "No, it's not a *guy* friend."

Pretend feathers all over his body began to ruffle and quiver in outrage as he accepted two plates from the vender. Uh...he could show her he was a guy, if she needed proof. Scratch that. She'd already seen the proof.

"Don't sound so disappointed, Mother." She rolled her eyes and glanced back at him. "You did what? How did you get his number?"

Her lips tightened, and she plopped down on a nearby bench, shutting her eyes for a second. "That's right. I forgot I left his card on the refrigerator. What were you doing at my house, anyway?"

Clint shifted beside her, uneasy about listening in on the conversation.

"Mom, you are going to spoil Cooper rotten. You know he has a weigh-in coming up."

Cooper? He set one of the plates on her lap and kept the other for himself. Did Jessi have another boyfriend? Visions of some muscle-bound hunk lounging in her bed came to mind.

No, she would have said something to him.

And exactly when had he given her the chance? He'd asked about Larry, but not about any other man who might be waiting in the wings.

"What? Clint *already* agreed to come? Wow, he sounds a little desperate, doesn't he?"

She stuck her tongue out at him, just as he took a bite of his fried cake, making him relax in his seat. "Okay, I'm about done here, so I'll start heading back that way. Love you."

He hadn't exactly agreed to go, and he was glad Jessi had heard for herself his side of the conversation. His smile widened. It would seem Mrs. Spencer could play loose and easy with rules, too.

She got off the phone and picked her cake up with a napkin he held out to her.

"Desperate, am I?" He didn't try to hide the wry tone to his voice.

"What could I do? If I said you couldn't come to dinner, she'd make up her own conclusions. And I couldn't exactly admit that you were sitting right next to me, eating funnel cake, could I?"

That part was his fault. He'd been the one to pretend they weren't together.

"So who's Cooper?" He dropped the question as if it were no big deal. Which it wasn't.

"A communal beagle," she said, as she swallowed. "Mmm… that's good stuff."

Also good was the dot of powdered sugar on her lower lip. One he was just able to refrain from licking off.

"A communal...beagle?"

Her tongue sailed across her lip, whisking away the sugar. "Okay, I guess that does sound weird. He adopted me about a year ago...came waddling up to the door and scratched on it. No one ever claimed him, so Mom and I have been caring for him between the two of us. He's on a diet. Supposedly." Stretching her legs out in front of her, she went on, "When I have to work late, Mom takes him to her house. You'll probably meet him tonight. Since you're evidently coming to dinner."

She munched down on another piece of cake, moaning in enjoyment. "That is if you still have room for food after this."

"You haven't asked me if I had plans for the evening."

Her eyes widened. "Oh, God. I'm sorry. Do you?"

"No. But I don't want to make things any harder for you than they already are." The tortured look when she'd discovered her daughter's pregnancy came back to haunt him. "I know this isn't easy, Jess."

"No, it's not." She paused, setting her food back on her plate. "Can you let me set the tone of the conversation? Mom will just worry herself sick if she knew the extent of what Chelsea is facing. And she hasn't seemed herself recently either. She was on antidepressants for several years, so it has me worried."

He frowned, surprised by the information. But people sometimes hid their problems well. "Does she know about the suicide attempt?"

"Yes. But she wasn't there when it happened. She only knew...afterwards."

He touched her hand. "You sure you want me to come?"

"I'm not sure of anything right now. But Mom is right. Chelsea is her granddaughter. One she hasn't seen in over two months. It's time to start letting her know what's going on. I—I just want to feed her the information in bits she can process. She's been through a lot in the past five years."

Since her husband's death.

"I understand." He withdrew his hand and sat up straighter.

"I'll let you answer specific questions, and I can fill in any of the medical gaps. How does that sound?"

"Perfect. Thanks so much, Clint."

Well, at least she hadn't thrown his card away. Then again, she hadn't kept it in her wallet either. "If you're done, I'll take you back to the house. I'm pretty sure you don't want us arriving in the same car."

She handed him her plate and waited until he'd thrown them both in a nearby trash receptacle to answer.

"Probably not a good idea." She smiled and stood to her feet. As they made their way back to the parking area, Clint had one thought. He hoped tonight went a whole lot better than his day had.

Jessi's plans for a relaxing evening at home looked like they were shot to hell. Between helping her mom set the table and dragging her makeup bag from her purse to touch up the dark circles under her eyes, she was getting more and more antsy. It was one thing to spend a few relaxing hours at the fair. It was another thing entirely to eat a meal with him while her mother grilled them about Chelsea's condition, which of course she would.

She'd just put the last swipe of mascara on her lashes when the doorbell rang and Cooper started up with the baying his breed was famous for. She froze, the makeup wand still in her right hand. Sucking down a breath, she quickly shoved it back in the tube, blinked at herself in the bathroom mirror and headed to get the door.

By the time she got halfway down the stairs she saw her mother had beaten her to it, apron wrapped around her waist. The door opened, and Cooper bumbled forward to greet the newcomer.

As Clint bent to pet the dog, Jessi couldn't help but stare. He'd evidently showered as well, because his hair was still damp. Dressed in a red polo shirt that hugged his shoulders and snug black jeans that hugged other—more dangerous—parts, he looked better than any funnel cake she'd ever had. He straightened and went over to kiss her mother's cheek, while Cooper continued to snuffle and groan at his ankles.

His eyes came up. Met hers across the room.

A sting of awareness rippled through her as his gaze slid over her white peasant shirt and dark-wash jeans before coming back up to her face. One side of his mouth pulled up into something that might have been a smile. Then again, it could have just as easily been classified as a modified grimace. Either way, the action caused that crease in his cheek to deepen and her heart rate to shoot through the roof.

Sexy man. Sexy smile. Stupid girl.

Hurrying the rest of the way down the stairs, she grabbed Cooper's collar and tugged him back into the house, while greeting Clint with as much nonchalance as she could muster under the circumstances. "Glad you could make it."

Not that there'd been much choice on either of their parts. Her mom had made sure of that. And right now the woman was the perfect hostess, ushering Clint in and offering him a drink, which he declined. That surprised her. He'd been such a rebel in high school that everyone had assumed that he'd played it loose and easy with alcohol, although she'd never actually seen him touch the stuff.

Her mom glanced at her in question, but Jessi shook her head. She needed all her wits about her if this evening was going to go according to plan. If she could help it, they were going to avoid talking about Chelsea as much as possible, and when her mom pressed for information, she would be honest but gloss over some of the more depressing aspects of her granddaughter's present situation. Like the fact that she either didn't want to talk about what had precipitated her suicide attempt, or she had simply blocked out that portion of her life. Who knew which it was? And it wasn't like Clint had had much time to get to the bottom of things. He'd been her doctor for, what…a little under a week?

"You look lovely," Clint said to her once her mom had gone to the kitchen to put the finishing touches on their meal. Cooper, obviously hoping for a few dropped morsels, puttered along behind her.

"Thank you." She bit her lip. "I'm really, really sorry you got caught in the middle of this."

"It's fine. I haven't had a homemade meal in…" He paused. "Well, it's been a while."

A while since someone had cooked for him? Jessi found that hard to believe. A man like Clint wouldn't have any trouble finding dates. He was even better looking now than he'd been in high school, although she never would have believed that possible. Gangly and rebellious as a teenager, he had filled out, not only physically—which was impressive enough—but he now had a maturity about him that had been lacking all those years ago. Oh, he'd made all the girls, including her, nervous wrecks back then. But as a man—well, she'd be hard pressed to say he wasn't breathtaking in a totally masculine way. From the self-assured smile to the confidence he exuded, he gave her more than a glimmer of hope that this was a man who could help her daughter.

"Have a seat," she told him. "Mom will be back any minute, and I'd like to set some quick ground rules. Like I said earlier, I haven't told her much about Chelsea's behavior—she knows about the suicide attempt, but not much about her time at the hospital. I wanted to keep it simple until I felt like there was some ho—"

Her voice cracked as an unexpected wave of emotion splashed over her, blocking the one word she wanted to believe in.

"Until you felt like there was some hope?" He finished the sentence for her. "There's always hope, Jess. I think we'll start seeing a little more progress in the coming weeks."

He shifted to face her. "Exactly what do you want me to say to your mom? I'm not comfortable with lying."

And yet he'd been the one to suggest she lie to her father about what happened after she'd run out of the gym during graduation all those years ago. To protect himself from her dad's wrath? Or to protect her?

Maybe it had been a little of both.

"I don't expect you to lie. You said there's always hope. If you could just keep that as a running theme when you talk about Chelsea, it would help Mom feel better."

"She's going to ask to see her, you know. Is there a reason you don't want her to?"

"I'm worried about her, like I told you earlier. I want to…be there when she sees Chelsea."

And I want you to have time to work your magic first. She didn't say the words, but she wanted them to be true. She trusted him. Why that was she couldn't say. She hadn't seen them interact that much. But he'd said he'd do his very best for Chelsea and she believed him. She just hoped it was enough.

Five minutes later, they were called into dinner. Cooper settled under the table with his head propped on Clint's right foot, despite all her efforts to deter him.

"He's fine," Clint said. "As long as he doesn't expect me to share any of that delicious-looking brisket."

They all laughed, and Jessi gave a quick sigh of relief. She'd half expected her mom to grill Clint on Chelsea's prognosis from the moment they sat down, but it was mostly small talk as Jessi munched lettuce leaves with nerves that were as crackly as the salad. The feared topic didn't hit until they were halfway through her mom's famed brisket, which, despite being as succulent as ever, was getting tougher and tougher for her to force down.

"Jessi tells me that she thinks Chelsea is dealing with PTSD. Is that what you're seeing, as well?"

Clint dabbed his mouth with his napkin and nodded. "We

see quite a number of veterans who come back with issues related to what they've seen and done."

"Does that mean you have some ideas on how to proceed?"

Jessi's eyes jerked to his and found him watching her. She put her fork on the table as she waited for him to answer.

"We're keeping our options open at the moment. I'm still working through the notes from her previous doctor."

"That's right. I forgot you'd just moved home. What perfect timing. Or were you just so homesick that you couldn't bear to stay away any longer?"

Jessi sucked down too much of the water she'd been sipping and choked for a second, but Clint didn't miss a beat. "Doctors are transferred to other locations on a regular basis, just like any other member of the armed forces." He gave a rueful twist of the mouth. "We both know about that, don't we?"

Way to go, Clint. Find something you have in common and use it to evade the real question.

Kind of like he'd done when she'd asked him why he had to leave the day after graduation. "I've already signed the papers, and that's when they told me to show up" had been his answer. She'd bought it at the time. But now? She had a feeling he'd just wanted to avoid her making any demands on him after their shared time together.

Which stung even more now than it had when he'd said the words.

Jessi's mom smiled back. "I'm sure you've done your share of moving, just like we did when Jessi was little." She paused then said, "I'm really glad you're back, though, and that you'll be the one treating Chelsea."

Clint's face registered surprise. "Why is that?"

Cutting into another section of her meat, her mom glanced up with a hint of sadness mixed with what looked like relief. "Because you, more than anyone, know what it's like to live with the effects of PTSD."

CHAPTER SIX

THE ROOM WAS silent for five long seconds.

Clint knew, because he counted every damn tick of the clock. He hadn't told Jessi or anyone else about his dad and the problems he'd had. Could his mom have mentioned it to Abigail or someone else from their past?

Worse, did Jessi know?

Even as the questions ducked through his cerebral cortex, looking for a believable response, he thought he saw pity flit through Jessi's eyes, although right now her mouth was hanging open in shock.

But, eventually, he had to say something. The ache in his pinky finger sprang to life, reminding him of all the reasons he'd decided to join the military and leave Jessi far behind. He clenched his fist to rid himself of the sensation and made a decision.

He was going to tell the truth. Air his dirty laundry—at least about his father. After all these years.

"Yes. I do know."

Jessi's fork clattered to her plate, and her mouth snapped

shut. "Mom, I don't think that's an appropriate thing to blurt out at the dinner table."

Wounded green eyes, so like her daughter's, widened. "Oh, I'm sorry. I didn't realize. I just assumed that everyone knew—"

"It's okay," Clint said, his thumb scrubbing across the crooked joint, a habit he used as a daily reminder of why his job was so crucial. Because PTSD didn't affect just the individual soldier…it affected everyone around them, as well. "I didn't talk about my problems much. And for a long time I didn't realize that something could be done."

Jessi finally spoke up. "*You* had PTSD?"

"No. My dad did. It was back when I was in high school."

Differing emotions flickered through her eyes. Sadness. Shock. Then finally the one he'd hoped never to see: guilt.

"Clint, I—" Her tongue flicked across her lips. "You never told any of us."

"Would *you* have?"

He knew she'd catch the inference. That her father—a tough army boot-camp instructor—had been vehement in his opposition to her being involved with anyone in the military. After Mrs. Spencer's words, he now wondered if it was because Jessi's dad and the entire base had witnessed the hell his mom had gone through because of his dad. Because of the way he'd used the bottle to blot out the demons related to his war deployment. It hadn't worked. He'd just created a living hell for everyone around him. Clint wouldn't want any daughter of his to go through what his mom had on a daily basis.

Whatever Mr. Spencer's reasons, it had ended up saving Clint's hide down at that creek. It—and his enlistment papers—had given him the perfect out for leaving Richmond. He'd jumped at the excuse, although he now realized that's all it had been. An excuse. He'd been afraid *of* his dad and *for* his dad. Had run away from the possibility that he might turn out to be just like him. But most of all, he hadn't wanted anyone to know the shame he'd felt.

The irony was, they had known, according to Abigail.

"No," Jessi said. "I wouldn't have shared my secrets with just anyone."

The hint of accusation in her voice was unmistakable. Because she had shared *her* secret with someone: him. But he hadn't returned the favor by telling her his. Maybe because he hadn't wanted to add any more to her plate. Maybe because the only thing he'd wanted at the time had been to erase the pain in her eyes.

Instead, he'd ended up making love to her and adding to his long list of sins. Which included leaving her the very next day. He'd thought it was to protect her.

Not that it had done any good. Jessi's own daughter was now struggling with trauma related to her military service, so he hadn't ended up protecting her from anything. Just his own ugly past and uncertain future.

Little had she known back then that he had harbored a secret crush on her. Maybe it had been part of the whole badass, wanting-to-redeem-himself syndrome. The same reason he'd enlisted. A need to redeem himself and maybe even his father— or at least to make peace with what had happened.

Clint's job, though, had turned into a passion he just couldn't shake. In some small measure he *had* redeemed himself. Each time he was able to help an emotionally wounded soldier have a shot at a normal life, he was somehow giving his father the help he'd never received when he'd been alive. And in doing that—Clint flexed his damaged finger again—he helped protect their sons and daughters.

Abigail broke into his thoughts. "I really am sorry. I just assumed that Jessi knew, since you went to school together."

They'd done more than just that. Which was something he could not—would not—think about right now. Not with her mom sitting there, looking more than a little mortified.

"It's fine…"

"Don't worry…"

He and Jessi spoke at exactly the same time, which caused everyone to laugh and broke the tension instantly. Even Cooper gave a quick *woof* of approval.

And although he'd been the one to say, "Don't worry," he was worried. More than a little. Because every time he caught Jessi watching him, his gut slid sideways.

"I have some peach ice cream for dessert," Abigail said, "if anyone wants some."

He glanced down at his watch. Almost nine. He could safely take off and claim to have survived the evening. "Thank you, but I probably should be heading home. I have an early morning tomorrow."

He pushed his chair back, dislodging Cooper from his foot in the process. The dog's nails clicked on the hardwood floor as he slid from beneath the table and pressed his cheek against Clint's calf. Reaching down, he scratched behind the animal's ears.

"Are you sure?" Abigail asked.

"Yes, unless there's something I can do to help clean up."

She smiled. "Not a thing." A quick frown puckered her brow. "I almost forgot. When can I see Chelsea? I don't want to set her treatment back, but if I can just spend a minute or two with her to assure myself that she's really—"

"Of course." He glanced at Jessi for confirmation. "How about if we make it for the next time Jessi and I meet with her? Friday at three?"

Jessi nodded her approval. "It's okay with me. I want to talk to you a little bit about her condition first, though, okay, Mama? I don't want you to be shocked by what she might say... or not say."

"I wasn't born yesterday. I know it's bad. I just want to see her."

"I'll pick you up on my way home from work, then. We can go together." She kissed her mother on the cheek, something that made Clint's chest tighten. Despite Mr. Spencer's heavy-handed ways, this had been a house of love. It was obvious the two women were close. And he was glad. Glad that her teenage angst hadn't left any lasting scars.

His arthritic pinky creaked out a warning shot when he curled his hand around the chair to push it back in.

"Thanks again for dinner, Mrs. Spencer."

"You're very welcome, and I'm glad you came. I already feel better."

As he started for the door, he was surprised to find Jessi right behind him. "I'll walk you to your car."

He opened the door, forgetting about Cooper. The dog bounded out before he could stop him.

"It's okay," Jessi said. "He does it to everyone. He won't go far."

The walk down the driveway was filled with the scent of magnolia blossoms, a smell he remembered well. Unbeknownst to Jessi, he'd sat in front of her house for hours the night of graduation, listening for any sounds of fighting, or worse. It had been hard back then to remember that not every father struck out with his fists.

But there'd been nothing that night. Just the muggy heat and that rich floral scent—something he connected to Jessi every time he smelled it. Even now, memories of the soft carpet of moss he'd felt beneath his hands as he'd supported his weight swirled around him. Of her face, soft and flushed, tilting back as he'd trailed his mouth down her neck.

Damn. He never should have come here.

He quickened his steps, only to have her hand touch his arm as they reached his car. He turned to face her, keys in hand, ready to get the hell out of there. The faster he left, the sooner he could regain his sanity.

Which right now was nowhere to be found. Because all he wanted to do was kiss her. Right in front of her house. To relive a little of the magic he'd experienced all those years ago.

"Why didn't you tell me...back then?" she asked.

He might have known this was why she'd wanted to come

with him. "I thought I'd explained that. It was my problem, there was no reason to involve anyone else."

"God, Clint. I bawled my eyes out about my dad's stupid rules without even knowing what you—"

"I didn't tell you because I didn't want anyone to know. Besides, it doesn't matter anymore. It's all in the past."

"And your dad is gone."

His jaw clenched. His father's liver cancer, brought on by years of alcohol abuse, didn't mitigate the fact that Clint wished he'd known sooner how to help him. "So is yours."

"Yes. I'm just glad he's not suffering. The strokes came faster at the end…"

"I'm sorry." He put his arm around her, meaning to give her a quick squeeze and release her. Instead, somehow she wound up against his chest, palms splayed against his shirt, staring up at him with those huge eyes.

The same eyes that did something to his insides every damn time she looked at him. It had happened in high school. And it was still happening now. He leaned back against the car door, still holding on to her.

She bit her lip for a second. "For what it's worth, I'm glad you were the one—back then. And I'm glad it's you now."

Whoa. If that wasn't a kick in the gut, he didn't know what was. She was glad he'd been the one who'd taken her virginity and not Larry? He'd beaten himself up about that for years afterwards.

And what did she mean, she was happy it was him now? She had to be talking about Chelsea.

"I had no idea who she was, Jess, until you stepped into that room. I swear."

"I didn't know it was you either. Until I saw the nameplate on your desk."

Her fingers came up and touched the line of his jaw, and she smiled. "I never believed that rebel freedom air you put on back in school."

He cocked a brow. "Oh, no? And why was that?"

"Because you looked so lost at times. I just never understood what caused it back then."

Before he had time to tense up, she continued. "Mama is right, you know."

"How's that?"

"You are the absolute best person to be treating Chelsea." She closed her eyes for a second before looking up at him again. "I'm so glad you're here, Clint. So glad you came home."

The squeezing sensation in his chest grew. The tightrope he was toeing his way across was thinner than he'd realized... harder to balance on than he'd expected.

"Promise me you won't drop the case," she added.

That's exactly what he *should* do. Especially now. Bow out and ask someone else to step in. Transfer the hell out of that hospital and go back to California.

A thought came to him. Was this why Jessi was in his arms, staring all doe-eyed at him? "I can't make you that promise. I have to do what I think is in the best interests of your daughter."

"I know. Just promise me that tomorrow, when you walk into that office, you'll still be the one treating her."

He was suddenly aware of her fingers. They were still on his skin, only now they'd moved slightly backward, putting his senses on high alert—along with certain parts of his body. "I'll be there for her."

"Good. Because I think I'm about to do something very, very stupid."

He didn't need to ask what it was. Because he was on the verge of doing something just as stupid.

But it didn't stop him from tugging her closer, neither did it stop his lips from closing over hers in a sudden crazy burst of need.

And once their mouths fused together, he was transported to the past. Twenty-two years, to be exact. He'd been unable to get enough of her. Her taste. The faint scent of her shampoo or body wash, or magnolias—whatever the hell it had been that had filled his senses, intoxicating him more than the booze he'd been offered earlier ever could have.

A faint sound came from her throat. He was fairly certain it wasn't a gasp of protest, since her arms had wound around his neck and her body had slid up his as she'd gone up on tiptoe. He buried his fingers in the hair at her nape, the slight dampness probably due to the Virginia humidity, but it brought back memories of perspiration and bodies that moved together in perfect harmony. Of...

The sound of Cooper's plaintive howl split the air a short distance away, followed by the sound of the front door opening. Abigail's voice called out the dog's name.

Cursing everything under the sun, he let Jessi pull free from his lips, even though the last thing he wanted to do was let her go. He wanted to drag her into the car and drive right to the creek to see if that night had been everything he'd remembered it being.

Abigail's voice called the dog's name again. The bushes shielded them from view, so Clint didn't look. Besides, his gaze was glued to Jessi's pale features.

Even when Cooper decided to lumber over to them, instead of going to the house, he didn't break eye contact.

"Sorry. I'm sorry." The gutted apology as she backed up one step, then two, made his lungs burn. The back of her hand went to her mouth, and she pressed hard. Her feet separated them by another pace, then she reached down to capture Cooper's collar. "Please, don't dump her. This was my fault. Not hers."

As she led the dog back to the front door, Clint gave his head a silent shake. There was no one else. He couldn't leave. Not yet.

Chelsea couldn't afford to lose two doctors in the space of two weeks.

Which meant Clint couldn't afford to start something he would never be able to finish. He'd made love to Jessi once and had barely been able to find the strength to walk away. If it happened twice, there was no hope for him.

So, from now on, he would tread carefully. And keep his distance from Jessi and her mom as much as possible.

CHAPTER SEVEN

CHELSEA WAS TALKING.

Not a lot, but Clint had noticed a subtle shift in her demeanor over the past several days as they met for their sessions. She was more interested and less withdrawn. He wasn't sure what had caused the change, but he was all for it.

Besides, it kept him from having to deal with the devastating consequences of that kiss he and Jessi had shared beside his car. And the suspicious thoughts that had crept into his mind in the meantime.

Had she tried to manipulate him into staying?

No. Jessi wasn't like that. When he'd left all those years ago, she'd never said a word to try to make him change his mind. Yes, she'd made him promise that he'd remain on her daughter's case—right before she'd locked her lips to his, but it wasn't as if she was the only one who'd been thinking along those lines. He'd been just as guilty. And she'd been very careful to maintain her distance ever since. Their consultations were now over the phone—despite their earlier agreement to meet with Chelsea together—and her voice during those calls was brisk and businesslike.

Just like the doctor she was.

And she was smart. She knew exactly the right questions to ask regarding her daughter's state of mind. According to the nurses, her visits to Chelsea occurred during his off hours. He had no doubt she'd somehow found out his schedule and was purposely coming when he wasn't around.

As grateful as he should be for the breathing space, he found himself irritated at the way he missed her presence.

What else could he do, though? He'd always prided himself on his self-control, because it was something his dad had never had much of. And yet Clint lost it every time he was around Jessi.

Every. Damn. Time.

It had been true twenty-two years ago, and it was still true today. He just couldn't resist her. The good girl that he'd had a secret crush on in high school had turned him into an impulsive, reckless creature. One he feared, because he recognized the beast all too well. He'd looked into impulsive, reckless eyes so like his own during his teenage years.

That raw, angry kid had morphed into a cool, rational man somewhere along the way, and in doing so had found himself. Had found an antidote that worked. But it only functioned if he didn't let anyone get too close.

Today would be the test. Jessi was due here with her mom in a little over an hour. He'd warned himself. Scolded himself. Immersed himself in work. All to no avail.

His heart was already pounding in anticipation of seeing her—trying to justify being with her one more time.

Just one kiss. He could stop anytime he wanted.

Sound familiar, Clint?

Substitute *drink* for the word *kiss* and you had his dad in all his lying glory.

Not good.

His assistant pushed open the door. "Dr. Marks? Miles Branson is here for his appointment. Are you ready for him?"

"Yes, send him in. Thanks, Maria."

As hectic as his morning had been, with two new patients and a flurry of consultations, he shouldn't have had time to think about Jessi at all. But she'd found her way into every nook and cranny of his brain and surged to the forefront whenever he had a free moment.

Like now.

Miles came in and, after shaking Clint's hand, lowered himself into one of the chairs across from him. Another PTSD patient, this particular man had made great strides in his treatment over the past couple of weeks. It could be because of that new baby girl he had waiting at home for him.

"How're Maggie and the baby?" he asked.

"Both beautiful." The smile the man gave him was genuine, and the furrows between his brows seemed less pronounced than they'd been when Clint had arrived. He scrolled through his phone for a second and then handed it over.

Miles's wife and a baby swaddled in a pink blanket lay on a hospital bed. She looked exhausted but happy, while it was obvious their daughter was trying out her new set of lungs, if the open mouth and red, angry-looking face were anything to go by.

"Beautiful. You've got a great pair of girls there." Clint pushed the phone across his desk.

"I'm a lucky man." He smiled again, glancing down at his wife and daughter. "You know, for the first time in a long time I actually believe that."

"I know you do. Are you ready to try for a reduction of your medication?"

"Can I do away with it altogether?"

Clint paused for a second. While his superiors were very conscious of time and money, his only concern was for his patients. He'd been known to ruffle a few feathers along the way, but had still somehow made it up the chain of command.

While paroxetine wasn't addictive, like the benzodiazepine family of medications, he still felt it was safer to reduce the dosage gradually while maintaining a regular therapy schedule as they progressed.

In the two years since Miles had first been seen by other doctors, the man had gotten engaged and then married to a wonderful woman who knew exactly what he was battling. And, thank heavens, this man hadn't shown the agitation and anger issues that Clint's dad had.

"Let's knock it down from sixty milligrams a day to twenty and go from there." He grabbed his prescription pad and wrote out a new dosage recommendation. "We'll maintain our sessions, and in a couple of weeks, if all goes well, we'll reduce them even more. How does that sound?"

Miles sat back in his chair, his posture relaxed and open. "It sounds like living. Thanks, Doc."

For the next forty-five minutes they went through the new father's moods and actions, detailing where he'd struggled, while Clint made notes he would transcribe later. Together they made a plan on how to deal with the next several weeks, when having a new baby at home would put more stress on both him and the family.

When they finally parted, he opened the office door to let Miles out and his glance immediately connected with Jessi and her mom, who'd arrived fifteen minutes early for their session with Chelsea. He nodded at the pair, walking Miles over to his assistant's desk and giving a few last-minute instructions on scheduling.

Taking a deep breath, he finally turned and made his way over to the pair in his waiting area. Jessi, dressed in a casual white-flowered dress that stretched snugly across her top and waist, stood to her feet. Flat, strappy sandals showed off pink toenails and dainty feet. He swallowed when he realized he'd been staring. All his misgivings from earlier came roaring back. He shoved them aside.

"Sorry to keep you waiting," he muttered, his voice a little gruffer than he'd expected. But seeing Jessi up close and personal created this choking sensation that closed off the upper part of his throat.

Her mom was the one to break the stare-fest. "We were a little early, at my insistence. I'm anxious to see my granddaughter."

"I'm sure you are."

Abigail was in a pair of jeans with a white button-down shirt. At almost sixty, she was still a beautiful woman, with high cheekbones and eyes very like her daughter's. And her granddaughter's, for that matter.

"Do you want to meet in my office or head down to Chelsea's room? Jessi gave a little shrug, no longer attempting to look directly at him. Maybe she felt as uncomfortable as he was about this meeting. "Wherever you feel is best."

Her mom spoke up again. "I haven't seen Chelsea's room. Do you think she would mind if we met her there? I'm curious about where she's been staying." She blinked a couple of times. "Not that I'm saying there's anything wrong with the hospital. It looks modern and well cared for."

Not what she'd expected. She didn't say the words, but he could imagine her thoughts.

The VA's reputation had taken a beating in the press over the last year. And not without reason, but the corruption was slowly being weeded out, and Clint hoped the end result would be a system of hospitals the country's servicemen and women could be proud of.

Clint had done his best to make sure his patients received the best treatment possible. And he knew there were a lot of other dedicated doctors who also cared deeply about their patients. The waiting lists were staggering, and, yes, it would probably be much easier to find work in the civilian sector for better pay and a lighter workload. But that wasn't why he did what he did.

"You're fine," he assured Abigail. He turned to his assistant. "Could you call down to Chelsea's room and let her know we're on our way?"

"Of course, Doctor." She picked up her phone and dialed as Clint nodded toward the hallway to their right. "Jessi, you know the way."

She stood and slung the strap of her purse over her arm, making sure her mother was following her. She glanced back at him. "Any last-minute instructions?"

"No. Chelsea's been more open, as I told you over the phone. I think that's an encouraging sign." Not that they'd made definitive steps in her treatment. The new class of antidepressants he'd prescribed was kicking in, though, so he had hopes that as the fog of despair continued to lift, she would start looking to the future, instead of crouching in the past. They had yet to talk about the specifics surrounding her months in captivity. She'd reiterated that she hadn't been tortured or assaulted, but as to what exactly had happened during that time, there was still a large swath of information that was missing. Clint had even tried going through channels and seeing if her superior officers knew anything more. But they were what Clint would label as "careful" with their words. It hadn't been anything in particular that was or wasn't said. It had just been the way the information had been delivered. And every story had been told in an identical fashion.

For Clint, that fact alone raised a huge red flag.

"Nana!" he heard the greeting even before he reached the room. And the happiness in that one word was apparent. As was the sight of the two women embracing, while Jessi stood back to allow the reunion to happen.

"How's she really doing?" she asked him in a low voice as Abigail sat on the edge of the bed, her arm around her granddaughter.

"Just like I said. She's talking more."

"Any idea yet on the why?"

The why of the suicide attempt.

"We haven't made it that far, yet."

The exchange ended when Abigail waved her daughter over. "Doesn't she look wonderful?"

She didn't, and they all knew it. Still pale and frighteningly thin, Chelsea did not have the appearance of a soldier who'd been through the worst that boot camp had to offer...who had survived a stint as a POW. She looked like a fragile piece of china that might shatter at the slightest tap.

While they talked, Clint grabbed two chairs from an empty room that adjoined Chelsea's and added them to the two that were already against the pale gray walls—Clint had learned how important equalizing the setting was, which was why his office had three identical chairs. One for him and two for those who met him there. His rank was above that of many of his patients, but that didn't mean he had to act the part.

"Dr. Marks?" Jessi's voice interrupted his thoughts.

Although it rankled at some level, he knew it was better for them to address each other in a formal manner in public, although he'd told Chelsea—in vague terms—that he and Jessi had known each other in the past. It was easier to be as truthful as possible, while holding back information that could be deemed harmful to her treatment.

"Sorry," he murmured. He turned to Chelsea. "Do you feel up to sitting with us?"

"Yes." She swung her legs over the side of the bed, waving off her mom, who'd immediately moved to help her. "It's okay. I can do it."

She was in a set of flannel pajamas that Jessi had evidently brought in during one of her other visits. Ideally, he would have liked her to be dressed in normal clothes for their meetings. And in recent days she'd made more of an effort.

So why was today different?

Was she trying to appear fragile, warning away any talk that crept toward painful subjects?

It was too late now to ask her to change, and he didn't want to do anything that would upset Jessi's mom in the process. Besides, he had another client in an hour and a half and he wanted to make sure that Chelsea wouldn't be cut off in the middle of anything important.

They sat in a circle. Chelsea and Abigail glanced at him expectantly, while Jessi's gaze was centered on the folded hands she held in her lap.

"Chelsea, it's been a while since your grandmother has seen you, am I correct?"

The young woman's hand snaked out and grabbed Abigail's. "I'm glad she's here."

"So am I."

He wasn't going to push hard this session, he just wanted to reintroduce the family and make sure everyone knew that their old ways of interacting might not work in this new and different world. Chelsea had gone to war as one person and had come back another. They all had yet to see where exactly that left her mom and grandmother, although the reunion had gone much more smoothly than he would have expected.

Even as he thought it, Abigail pressed her fingertips to her eyes and wiped away moisture that had gathered beneath them. "Oh, no, Nana. Don't cry." Chelsea wrapped her arms around the older woman. "Mom, there's a box of tissues in my top drawer. Would you mind getting me one?"

Jessi jumped up and headed toward the small end table beside the bed. She drew out the top drawer, found the box and withdrew it. Then she stopped. Chelsea was facing away from her mother and couldn't see her, but Clint could. A strange look crossed her face as she peered at something inside that drawer. She started to reach for it then withdrew her hand.

Chelsea, as if realizing something was wrong, swiveled around in her chair. "Can't you find...? Oh, no, Mom. Please don't."

But it was already too late, because Jessi had reached back into the drawer and withdrawn what looked like a wad of tissues. Glancing at Chelsea and seeing the horror in her eyes, he realized that's not what that was. Not at all.

Even as he looked, Jess smoothed down the bottom edge of the thin paper and came forward a couple of steps, only to stop halfway. It was a doll of some sort.

No. Not a doll. A baby. Painstakingly crafted from the tissues in the box in her drawer.

"Chelsea, honey." Jessi's voice dropped away for a second before coming back again. "What is this?"

CHAPTER EIGHT

JESSI SLUMPED IN a chair in Clint's office. "I don't understand. What could it mean?"

Her daughter had refused to talk about the strange item, withdrawing back into her shell until Clint called a halt to the session and let Chelsea crawl back into her bed. She'd silently held out her hand for the doll and laid it carefully back inside the drawer.

The act made Jessi shiver.

She'd sent her mom home with a promise to stop by later, and Clint had ordered the nurse to call him immediately if there was any change.

"I don't know what it means. Maybe she miscarried while she was overseas. Maybe it's something she made as a coping mechanism. There could be any number of explanations, but until she tells us we won't know for sure."

"Will you ask her again tomorrow?"

"I'll see how she is. We may have to work our way toward it slowly." He dragged his fingers through his hair and leaned back in his chair. "It could just be a dead end."

"Who makes a doll out of a box of tissues? It just doesn't seem...normal."

When he stared at her, she closed her eyes. "Sorry. That didn't come out right. It's just that everything seemed to explode out of nowhere two months ago."

"I know. It just takes time."

"What if she never gets better? What if she's like this for the rest of her life?"

He reached across and covered her hand with his. "Thoughts like that aren't going to help anyone."

"Did you struggle with those kinds of thoughts during high school? About your dad? Did *he* ever get better?"

When he went to withdraw his hand with a frown, she grabbed at his fingers, holding him in place.

"Oh, God, Clint, I'm so sorry," she whispered. "I'm just worried about Chelsea."

"I know." He laced his fingers through hers. "I gave her a sedative, so she should sleep through the night. We'll start fresh in the morning."

"I want to be there when she wakes up."

He studied her for a minute or two, before shaking his head with what looked like regret. "I don't think that's a good idea, Jess. When you and your mom left, she was agitated and withdrawn. I don't want those memories to be the ones that resurface when she opens her eyes. Give her a day."

"A day?" She couldn't believe he was asking her to stay away from the hospital for an entire day. "I'm not the only one worried. Mom is, as well."

"I'll call you as soon as I see her. Are you working tomorrow?" He let go of her hand and reached for one of his pencils, jiggling it between his fingers as if he needed something to keep him busy. Or maybe it was a hint that he needed to get back to work.

"I'm on the afternoon shift, starting at three. I'd better get out of your hair." She stood to her feet, then thought of something. "What if you get a call in the middle of the night?"

"If something serious happens, I'll be in touch."

"Promise?"

"Promise." He must have read her dubious smile, because one side of his mouth curved into that familiar half smile. "Would you like me to pinkie-swear, as well?"

Despite her worry, she found her own lips twitching. "Would you, if I asked you to?"

"Yes."

Something icy hot nipped the air between them. She held her breath and then released it in a long stream. "Or you could come and spend the night at the house. Just in case."

Why on earth had she asked that? It was too late to take back the offer, although she could clarify it. "On the couch, of course."

His eyes softened, but he shook his head. "I have to work for a couple more hours. Besides, I don't think my staying with you would be a good idea, Jess. Things never quite remain that simple between us. And I meant what I said about taking myself off the case if I think my objectivity has been compromised."

Oh, Lord, that's right. He'd intimated that he'd hand Chelsea over to someone else if things got too personal between them. "I wasn't asking you to sleep with me. Not this time."

She'd gone that route once before, asking him to make love to her by the creek, desperately needing a few minutes out from beneath her father's thumb.

"I don't remember complaining the last time you did."

No. But then again she hadn't seen him volunteering to hang around the next day—although it had probably been too late for him to back out of boot camp by that time. And who was to say he would stick around in Richmond now? Some servicemen loved the adventure of a new place every couple of years. Not Jessi. Once she'd gotten to high school, her father had finally seemed willing to settle down and stay until she graduated. Then she'd married Larry, who hadn't known she'd had a dalliance with his friend. Not until that last day of his life.

She blocked out the thought and concentrated on the here and now as Clint got up and opened the door to his office.

She walked through it and then hesitated on the other side. "So you'll call me tomorrow."

"As soon as I have some news. Yes."

They said their goodbyes, and already his manner was more aloof. Businesslike.

Once she got to the front door of the hospital she lifted her chin and made a decision. If Clint could keep his personal life separate from what happened at the hospital, then she could, too. For everyone's sakes, she was going to have to learn to take her cues from Clint, adopting that same professional demeanor whenever she was here.

No matter how hard it was starting to be.

The suicide had come out of nowhere, and while it hadn't been one of Clint's patients it brought home the thin line he was walking with Chelsea and Jessi. The entire hospital was on edge because of it.

It wasn't easy for any doctor to lose a patient, no matter what anyone said. True impartiality was hard to come by at the best of times…and with Jessi it seemed to border on the impossible.

He'd felt the anguish radiating from every pore of her body when she'd lifted that macabre paper figure out of her daughter's drawer. And it had taken a lot of self-restraint to remain in his seat, observing Chelsea's reactions, and not rush over to make sure the woman who wasn't his patient was okay.

While he and Jessi hadn't been involved emotionally in the past—a thought he stubbornly clung to, no matter what his gut said—there could be nothing at all between them now.

Not just because of his patient. Not just because of his and Jessi's past. But because of his job and his own personal baggage.

Once they found a replacement for him, he was headed back

to San Diego. It was either that or request that his transfer to Richmond be made permanent, something he couldn't see happening. He was the one they called on for temporary assignments. It's what he wanted. Moving around a lot kept his mind on the job at hand, rather than highlighting his lack of a personal life. And the unlikelihood that he'd ever have much of one.

Not that he hadn't tried. He'd been in serious relationships. Twice. But both times the woman had left, saying she felt he was withholding himself emotionally.

He had been. Somehow he could never quite let his guard all the way down. His every move was calculated. Controlled. And that's the way he liked it.

He was very aware that wasn't what most women looked for in a man. He was just not husband material.

Because of his dad?

Hell, the second Jessi had mentioned his father in his office he'd tried to yank his hand away, very aware that his crooked finger was right there for her to see. And ask about. The last thing he wanted to talk about was his past. Jessi's father might have been a pain-in-the-ass drill sergeant—but at least he'd loved her enough to care about who she saw. What she did.

His cell phone beeped. When he glanced at the caller ID, he winced. Jessi. The very person presently haunting his every thought. And it was already midmorning. He was supposed to have called her to let her know how Chelsea was.

He pressed the answer button and bit out an apology. "Sorry, Jess. We've been swamped and I hadn't had a chance to call you yet."

She brushed aside his apology with a cleared throat. "Was she okay when she woke up?"

Despite the worry in her tone, her voice flowed over him, soothing away some of the worst parts of his morning. A few muscles in his jaw relaxed.

"I haven't had an in-depth conversation with her. Just a few minutes of small talk as she ate breakfast. We're due to have a therapy session at two."

"But she's okay."

He realized what she was looking for, and all the day's heartache came roaring back. "She doesn't seem to be obsessing over what happened yesterday. I'll call you when I've talked to her again."

"Hmm." She didn't say anything more.

"I know I promised. I'm sorry." He gritted his teeth.

"No, it's just that I have to be at work at three, and I'll probably be just as swamped with patients as you seem to be, since it's a holiday."

Ah, yes. Father's Day. Something he tried to forget every year. He glanced down at his left hand, where the crook in his finger reminded him of a whole childhood of fear and unhappiness. That wasn't the only reason he wasn't crazy about this particular day. At this point in his life, he didn't see himself ever carrying the title of father, even if he found someone and married her. He was close to forty, and had never really given kids much of a thought.

Maybe he should ask Jessi if the day held any special significance for Chelsea, though…good or bad. He should be prepared for any eventuality.

"Will Father's Day add to Chelsea's stress levels?"

There was silence over the line for a long minute. "No. Larry died before she was born. She only knows him through pictures." There was something sad about the way she said it.

He forced the next words out even as his insides tightened. "You didn't have much time together."

"No, we didn't. The worst thing is he might still be alive if someone hadn't…" The words ended on a strangled note.

Something burned in his gut. "If someone hadn't what, Jess?

"It doesn't matter. What does is that I have a wonderful daughter from our union. That's what made the hard times after his death bearable."

The image of Jessi mourning her husband was enough to make that burning sensation tickle the back of his throat. She'd had a daughter with the man. And as much as he told himself he didn't care, the cold reality was that part of him did—the same part that had leaped when he'd first realized who Jessi was and had wondered if Chelsea might be his.

But she wasn't. And if he was going to do his job, he had to remember that and keep on remembering it.

"About my session with her. How about if I send you a text, rather than trying to call? That way you can check in when you've got a free moment."

"That would be fantastic. Thank you, Clint. But please do call if something changes. I'll set my ringer to vibrate just for your number. If it does, I'll know it's important, and I'll find a way to answer, or I'll call you right back."

The tension in his gut eased and something warm and dangerous took its place. She was going to be listening for his call and his call only.

Okay, idiot. It's in case of an emergency. It's not like she's putting your number on speed dial or anything.

"So you have the number here, if you have any questions or need something, right? I remember you said my card was on your refrigerator." He glanced at the business card on his desk, since he hadn't quite memorized his Richmond number yet. "Or do you need me to read it off to you again?"

"Nope. I've already programmed it into my phone. In fact, I have you on speed dial," she said. "Just in case."

CHAPTER NINE

FATHER'S DAY SHOULD be outlawed.

Or at least the giving of gifts involving any type of motor should be banned. So far that afternoon, Jessi had treated a leg that been kissed by a chain saw, a back injury from an ATV accident and a lawn mower that had collided with a lamppost before bouncing back and knocking its new owner unconscious. Not to mention assorted other minor injuries. And she still had two hours to go until the end of her shift. The one thing she hadn't seen had been the screen on her cell phone lighting up or feeling its vibration coming from the pocket of her scrubs.

All was silent with Clint and her daughter.

Sighing, she grabbed the next chart and headed for the curtained exam room. Patient name: William Tuppele. Complaint: the words *fishing hook* and *earlobe* ran through her head before she blinked and forced her eyes to read back over that part.

Okay. So it wasn't just things with motors that should be banned from this particular holiday.

When she entered the room, a man dressed in hip waders

with a camo T-shirt tucked into them sat on the exam table. And, yep, he was sporting a shiny new piece of jewelry.

She looked closer and gulped. Had something behind his ear just moved?

Stepping farther in the room, she glanced again at his chart. "Mr. Tuppele." She omitted the words *How are you?* because it was pretty obvious this was the last place the man wanted to be. Instead, she aimed for cheeky. "Catch anything interesting today?"

Instead of smiling, the man scowled. "Great, I get a nurse who thinks she's a comedienne."

She bristled, but held out her hand anyway. "I'm Dr. Riley. How long have you been like this?"

"About an hour." His gaze skipped away from hers, his words slurring the slightest bit. "My son caught me with his hook. It was his first fishing trip."

"Hmm." She kept the sound as noncommittal as possible, but from the way his face had turned scarlet and—she tried not to fan herself openly—the alcohol fumes that bathed every word the man spoke, she would almost bet there was no "son" involved in this particular party. Rather, she suspected a male-bonding episode that had gone terribly wrong.

Hip waders and booze. Not a good combination. They were lucky no one had drowned. "Did someone drive you to the hospital?"

She certainly didn't want to let a drunk loose on the roads.

"One of my buddies. He's down in the waiting room."

Jessi could only hope the *buddy* had been less generous when it came to doling out those cans of beer to himself. She made a mental note to have someone check on his friend's sobriety level.

She sat on her stool just as the worm—and, yes, it was indeed a piece of live bait—gave a couple of frantic wiggles. Lord, she did not want to touch that thing, much less have to handle it. But the best way to remove a fishing hook was to cut off the end opposite the barb and push the shank on through, rather than risk more damage by pulling it back out the way it had gone in. That barb acted like a one-way door. They went in, but they didn't want to come out.

The worm moved again.

"Hell," said the man. "Can you please get this damned thing off me? It stinks."

And it's creeping me out.

Mr. Tuppele didn't say the words, but she could well imagine him thinking them, because the same thoughts were circling around in her head, too. Maybe this was the worm's way of exacting revenge on anglers everywhere.

And maybe she could call one of the male nurses.

Ha! And give her patient a reason for his earlier sexist remark. Hardly. "When was your last tetanus shot?"

"Haven't been to a doctor in twenty years. Wouldn't be here now if one of my…er, my son hadn't been so squeamish about taking it out himself. "Is my ear going to be permanently pierced? I don't cotton to men with earrings and such."

She smiled despite herself, tempted to match his it-was-my-son fib and tell him that, yes, he would be permanently disfigured and might as well go out and buy a couple of nice dangly pieces of jewelry. But she restrained herself. "No. I knew a man who had his ear pierced in high school but had to stop wearing an earring when he went into the military. It's all healed up now."

At least she assumed that's when Clint had stopped wearing the single hoop in his ear, because there was no sign of it now. And how was it that she had even noticed that? Or remembered what he'd worn back then?

She'd kind of liked his earring, back in the day.

"Good. Don't need anyone getting any strange ideas about me."

Too late for that, Mr. Tuppele. She already had a few ideas about him. And they went much deeper than men sporting earrings. "Let me set up. I'm going to call in a nurse to give you a shot to numb your ear."

"I don't need it numbed. I just need that damned thing out."

"Are you sure?" The rest of the staff was going to thank her patient for sparing them the need to get close to that wriggler.

"Just do it."

"Okay." Trying not to shudder, she got her equipment together, praying the worm died before she had to deal with it. As disgusting as she found it, she felt a twinge of pity for the creature. It hadn't been its choice to be cast into a river for the first hungry fish to gulp.

Gloves in place, she squirted some alcohol on the wound in back of his ear, waiting for the string of cuss words to die down before continuing. She grabbed her locking forceps and clamped the instrument right behind the worm. If the barb had gone all the way through his ear, she could have just cut it off and backed the hook out, worm and all. But while there was a tiny bit of metal showing in the front of the lobe, the barb was still embedded in the man's flesh. It was going to hurt, pushing it the rest of the way through. She got a pair of wire cutters and took a deep breath, then moved in and cut the eye, leaving as much shank as possible behind that worm.

"Okay, I'm going to have to push the barb through the front, are you sure you're okay?"

"Fine."

Holding the front of the man's earlobe with her gloved fingers, she used the forceps to push hard, until the barb popped through.

The man yelled out a few more choice words, but he'd held remarkably steady. Having a hook shoved through your ear was evidently a surefire way to sober up. Fast.

"All right, the worst part is over. I just need to pull the hook the rest of the way out." Holding a tray beneath his ear so she wouldn't have to touch the worm, she removed the forceps and used them to grasp the barb in front. Then she pulled steadily, until the worm plonked onto the instrument tray and the hook was the rest of the way through his ear.

Praying the creature didn't find his way off the counter and onto the floor, she set the tray down and used a piece of antiseptic soaked gauze to sponge away the blood and dirt from the front and the back of the man's ear and then took a piece of dry gauze and applied pressure to stop the bleeding. "Can you hold this here? We'll need to get you a tetanus shot as well as some antibiotics, just in case."

Mr. Tuppele did as she asked and squeezed his earlobe between the two sides of gauze. But when she carried the worm over to the garbage can, the man stopped her with a yelled "Hey!"

She turned toward him, still holding the tray. "Yes?"

"That thing dead?"

She glanced down. It wasn't moving any more, thank God. "I think so."

"Touch it to make sure."

Horror filled her to the core. She hated fishing. Hated bugs. Broken bones, bullet wounds, she could whiz through with ease, but anything that wiggled or crawled or stared with cold-blooded eyes she was just not into. "I'll let you do the honors." She held out the tray and let the man jab the worm with a finger while she cringed. Thankfully it remained limp, even after two more pokes.

"Damn. I was hoping to use that one again."

Again? Hooking himself once hadn't been enough?

She gave a mental eye roll. "Sorry about that. It was probably the alcohol."

"There ain't that much in my blood."

And... Okay.

Dumping the worm and the cleaning gauze into the trash bin, she turned back to face him. "I'll have the nurse come in with the shot and your prescription. Make sure you see your doctor if that ear puffs up or doesn't seem to be healing after a couple of days. Or if you develop a fever."

She took the gauze from him and checked his ear, before pressing tiny round bandages over the front and back of the puncture wound. "You can take those off in a couple of hours."

The man managed to mumble out a "Thank you."

Her phone buzzed, making her jump.

Clint. It had to be.

Patting the man on the back and telling him to take care, she went out and gave instructions to the nurse and asked her to send someone out to check on his buddy. By that time her phone had stopped ringing. "Anyone else waiting for me?"

The nurse grinned. "Not at the moment. But the new barbecue grills are probably being fired up even as we speak."

"Heaven help us all."

Hopefully, that wave of patients would come through after she was off duty. She forced out a laugh, even though she was dying to grab her phone and call Clint back. He knew she was on duty. Knew she'd get back to him as soon as she could.

The nurse got the injection ready and carried it into the room, leaving Jessi alone in the hallway. She took out her phone and glanced at the readout, even though she knew who it was.

C. Marks.

Hitting the redial button, she leaned a shoulder against the wall, an ache settling in her back at all the bending she'd done today.

"Marks here."

"Clint? It's Jessi. What's up?"

"Just calling to see how much longer you were on duty."

Jessi glanced at her watch. "I have another half hour, why?"

"I thought we might get together and talk about Chelsea."

"Is something wrong?"

"No, she's fine. No major developments, but no setbacks either. I just haven't eaten, and I assume you haven't either. Would you like to go somewhere? Or I could come to the hospital and eat with you in the cafeteria."

She grimaced, glancing at the room she'd just come from. "No. The food here isn't the best, and I'm not really hungry. I could do with a shake, though, while you get something else."

She was still puzzling over his sudden change of heart.

"A shake sounds fine. How about we get it to go?"

Okay, she hadn't thought this far ahead. "And go where?"

"We could go to the park on the east side."

The park? She glanced out at the streetlights that were already visible in the darkening sky. "Sounds like a plan."

"Good. I'll meet you at the front entrance of the hospital, okay?"

"I'll be there."

Maybe somehow in that period of time she could shake off all thoughts of sitting inside Clint's car in a dark park, sipping on a milk shake. Or the fleeting images of what they could do once they finished their drinks and had said all they needed to say.

A warning came up from the depths of her soul, reminding her of days gone by and how badly he'd broken her heart. But only because she'd let him.

You can't head down that road again, Jess.

No, she couldn't.

Well, if her heart could make that decree, then she could somehow abide by it.

So she would have to make one thing very clear to herself before he came to pick her up. She would not kiss Clinton Marks again. Not in the dark. Not in a park.

The impromptu rhyme made her smile.

And if *he* kissed her instead?

As much as she might wish otherwise, if that ever happened, then all bets were off.

Because she might just have to kiss him back.

CHAPTER TEN

"You used to have an earring in high school."

A swallow of his milk shake went down the wrong way, and Clint gave a couple of rough coughs before turning in his seat to stare at her. In the dim light of the parking lot at a nearby burger joint, he could just make out her questioning gaze. He'd decided against going to the park, worried about being *too* alone with her.

This was more public, although he wasn't exactly sure what he was worried about. Surely they could both handle this situation like adults. Running into each other from time to time was part of adult behavior.

And going to the fair and having dinner with her and her mother?

All part of being back in his hometown. It meant nothing. At least, he'd better make sure it didn't.

And what about her asking about his earring?

Jessi must have changed clothes before leaving the hospital, because she wasn't wearing a lab jacket or rubber-soled shoes but a pair of slim, dark jeans, lime-green T-shirt and a pair of shoes that had a wedged heel. Not what he would consider doctor gear at all. In fact, she looked much more like the teenager he'd known in high school than a mom with a grown daughter.

He felt like an old fuddy-duddy in comparison, still in his shirt and tie. He could have sworn the kid at the drive-through window had eyed Jessi with interest. Clint had thrown the teen a glare in return, which had felt like something Jessi's actual father might have done.

When had he turned into such a square?

Maybe when he'd seen the emotional wounds of those returning from battle. And how they reminded him of his own.

"I did have an earring. I took it out the night before I reported for boot camp."

The night of their graduation. The night he'd made love to Jessi. It had marked the end of an era for him, a journey from childhood to becoming a man. Removing the earring that night had been something the old Clint wouldn't have done. He'd have reported to boot camp and waited until someone ordered him to take it out. But he hadn't. After watching Jessi's house for a while that night, he'd gone home—avoiding the after parties and festivities that had gone along with graduation—and stared at himself in the bathroom mirror. God, he'd wanted to stay in Richmond that night. For the first time he'd thought of doing something other than running away. And it had been all because of Jessi.

Instead, he'd unhooked the small gold hoop and pulled it from his ear. As if that one act would give him the courage to walk away when everything inside him had been yelling at him to stay and fight for her, shoving aside his fears about what might happen if he did. What kind of life he might drag her into, if he stayed.

But, even if he'd decided to risk it all for her, Jessi was already spoken for, at least according to Larry and all their friends.

The image in the mirror that night had told him which of them had had a better shot of giving Jess a good life. The choice had been obvious—at least to him. He had just been a screwup from a dysfunctional family, his finger a constant reminder of what that brought.

He hadn't wanted that for her.

So he'd let her go. An act his teenage self had decided was the mature thing to do. He still had that old hoop in a box somewhere.

Jessi unexpectedly reached up, her fingers cool from holding her frozen drink as they touched his chin. Using gentle pressure, she turned his head to the right, leaning over to look. Her breath washed across his skin, the scent of vanilla catching hold of his senses and making him want to sneak a taste of her mouth.

"Is there still a hole where your earring used to be?"

What was with all the questions? And why had he ever thought sitting in a car—or anywhere else—with her was a good idea?

Just being an adult. Proving he could control his impulses.

He swallowed. "I haven't really looked in a while. Why?"

"We had a guy come into the ER tonight who'd hooked himself while fishing and I had to push the barb all the way through his ear. He was worried his family would think he'd pierced it." She gave a soft laugh. "He wanted to know how long it would take to heal. I told him he should be more worried about the risk of tetanus than a tiny hole."

Her nose wrinkled. "The worst thing was there was still a live worm attached to the end of that hook."

"Well, that had to be an interesting scenario."

"I almost couldn't do it." She let go of him and leaned back in her seat. "Did you ever have to do something and wonder if you'd be able to get through it?" She made a sound in her throat. "Never mind. Of course you have."

He could think of two at the moment. One was leaving her behind twenty-two years ago. And the other was not touching her now, when everything inside him was straining to do just that. "I think everyone eventually gets a case like that. Or at least wonders if the patient would be better off with another doctor."

Jessi suddenly bent to get her milk shake. In the process the lid came off, dumping the cup, and half of its contents, right onto her lap.

He moved to grab it just as her cry of dismay went up. "Oh, no. Clint, I'm so sorry. Your car."

"I'm more worried about you turning into a block of ice." He sent her a half grin as he tried to scoop some of the shake back into the cup. It only ended up sloshing more onto her shirt and jeans.

"Don't move." He got out of the car, cup in hand, and strode into the restaurant to throw it away, exiting a few seconds later with a fresh empty cup and a handful of napkins.

Together they corralled most of the spillage between the paper cup and a spare lid, and then sopped up the remainder with the pile of napkins.

"I always was the clumsiest girl in high school."

"Don't do that."

"What?"

"You used to cut yourself down for things, even when they weren't your fault."

He could always remember some self-deprecating comment or other she would throw out there in school, making everyone laugh and passing it off as a big joke. But there had always been a ring of conviction to the jibes that had made him wonder if she didn't actually believe all the "I'm such a klutzo" and "Wow, am I ever a nerd" statements.

She glanced up at him, her hand full of napkins. "Everyone did that. Even you."

Yes, he had. And he knew for a fact that he'd believed most of what he'd said. Maybe that's why it bothered him so much when she did it.

"Let's get you home."

"I'll pay for whatever it costs to clean your seats."

He shook his head. "They're leather. I'll just wipe them down with a damp rag. They'll be fine. You, however, might need to be hosed off." He said it with a grin to show he was joking.

"Thanks for being so understanding," she said, as he gathered up the rest of the trash and got out of the car once more to throw it all away.

Understanding? Hell, he was barely holding it together. He put the car in Drive and followed her directions to her house. "Come on in while I change. We can talk about Chelsea over coffee, if that's okay?"

"Sounds good."

No, it didn't. It sounded idiotic. Impulsive. And he should leave. Now. But something drove him to open his car door and follow her up the steps to her house.

It's just coffee. She hasn't propositioned you. You're her daughter's doctor, for God's sake.

He was the one who'd called to arrange this meeting in the first place.

Which meant he should have asked her to come to his office, not a fast-food joint.

But surely Jessi had patients who were acquaintances or the children of acquaintances during her years of working in the ER. And it would make sense that she might meet them in the hospital cafeteria or a coffee joint to catch up later. It was kind of hard to work in a town where you grew up—no matter how large—and never expect to run into anyone you knew.

Only Jessi was more than an acquaintance.

And what they'd had was more than a quick hello and goodbye.

That was years ago. They'd spent a little over an hour down by a creek, hopped up on hormones and the thrill of graduating from high school. And she'd been distraught by her father's unbending rules.

It was in the past. All of it.

And that kiss beside his car at her mother's house a week ago?

Fueled by memories of that shared past. It wouldn't happen again. Not if he could help it.

She unlocked the door, glancing behind her as if to make sure he was still coming. "I'll get you that rag if you want to wipe the seat down while I change. I'll leave the front door open."

"Sounds good." And if he were smart, he'd leave the rag just outside the door afterwards and take off in his car before she could come back out of her bedroom.

And that would be just as unprofessional as kissing her had been.

At least that was his mental excuse, because after wiping up the few drops of milk shake from his seat he found himself back inside her house, calling up the stairs to her and asking her what she wanted him to do with the rag.

"Just put it in the sink and have a seat in the living room. I'll be down in a few minutes."

Instead of doing as she asked, he rinsed out the rag and hung it over a towel bar he found in her utility room. Then he spotted the coffee machine on one of the counters and a huge glass jar filled with those single-serving coffee filters that seemed to be all the rage nowadays. He had one of the machines at home himself. The least he could do was make the coffee while he waited. He'd just found the mugs when Jessi came traipsing back into the kitchen, this time dressed in a white floral sundress similar to the one she'd worn during dinner at her mom's, her feet bare, hair damp as if she'd showered.

He tensed, before forcing himself to relax again.

Of course she'd had to rinse off. She'd had a sticky drink spilled in her lap. It meant nothing.

"Sorry, Clint. I didn't intend you to get the coffee ready, too."

"No problem. I just thought I'd save you a step." He realized something. "Where's Cooper?"

"At Mom's. He's a communal pet, remember? I get him tomorrow."

"Ah, right."

She reached in a cabinet. "What do you take in your coffee?"

"Just sugar."

She set a crystal bowl down and then went over to the refrigerator and pulled out a container of milk. "Help yourself."

"Thanks."

They worked in silence until the coffee was done and they'd moved into Jessi's living room, which was furnished with a huge sectional and a center ottoman. Pictures lined the fireplace mantel and as he took a sip of his coffee he wandered over to them. There were several snapshots of Chelsea doing various activities and one of a more formal military pose. She was soft and natural in every photo except the last one, since official portraits were supposed to be done sans smile. But even in that one there was a spark of humor lighting her eyes that the woman back at the VA hospital lacked.

There was one picture of Jessi and Larry in their wedding attire. Both of them looked so young. Larry would be forever ageless, never having had a chance to really grow up and become a man.

He might still be alive if someone hadn't...

Her earlier words came back to mind. If he *were* still alive, Clint would probably not be standing here in her living room right now.

He probably shouldn't be, regardless.

And the sight of the two of them smiling up at each other sent something kicking at his innards. A slight jabbing sensation that could have been jealousy but that made no sense. He'd been the one who'd left. What had he expected Jessi to do? Dump Larry and wait for him to come back for her?

He hadn't. He'd never set foot in Virginia again until now. And if he'd known who Chelsea was before he'd agreed to come, he doubted very seriously he would be standing here now.

"Clint?"

Her voice reminded him that he was still staring at the picture. "Sorry. Just seeing how Chelsea was before she deployed."

He turned and sat on the shorter leg of the sofa perpendicular to her. "She smiled a lot."

"Yes. She was happy. Always. Which is why it's so hard to see her like this and not know how to help her."

"I'm sure it is." He took another sip of his coffee, wishing he hadn't added quite so much sugar.

"Did she talk at all today?" Jessi tucked her legs up under her, smoothing her hemline to cover her bare knees.

"She shared a little about what her days in captivity had been like. What she did to pass the time."

"You said on the phone there weren't any breakthroughs. You don't consider that one?"

That was a tricky question to answer. Because while it was technically more than Chelsea had told him in the past, she'd spoken without emotion, as if she were using the information itself as one more blockade against questions that might venture too close to painful subjects. Like that macabre tissue paper baby she kept in her nightstand.

"It does help to know a little about what went on. But she's not talking about her captors or about her rescue. Just about what she did. Reciting her ABCs and having conversations inside her head."

Jessi slumped. "It's been almost two and a half months."

He didn't mention that sometimes the effects of PTSD lasted a lifetime. His dad, instead of getting better, had slowly sunk into a pit filled with alcohol, drawing away from those he'd known and loved. And when he or his mom had tried to force the issue... Yeah, that was something he didn't want to talk to Jessi about.

"I know it seems like forever. But she was held for four months. It takes time. Sometimes lots of it."

She stared down at her cup for several long seconds before glancing up with eyes that held a wealth of pain. "It sounds so terrible for me to say this out loud, but I'm afraid to have her home again. Afraid the next time she tries something I won't get there in time to stop her."

Clint set his coffee cup down on a tray that was perched on an ottoman between the two seating areas. He went over to sit beside her, setting her coffee aside as he draped his arm around her shoulder and drew her close. "Jess, you're dealing with some aftereffects yourself. Maybe you should talk to someone."

She lifted her head. "I'm talking to you."

"I mean someone objective." The second the words came out of his mouth he wished he could haul them back and swallow them whole. He tried to clarify his meaning. "It would be a conflict of interest for me to treat you both."

He realized that explanation wasn't any better when she tried to pull away from him. He squeezed slightly, keeping her where she was. "I'm not explaining myself very well." Hell, some psychiatrist he was. He couldn't even have a coherent conversation with this woman.

"No, it's okay." She relaxed, and her arm snaked around his waist with a sigh. "I'm being overly sensitive."

No, she wasn't. And Clint was drawing closer and closer to a line he'd sworn he wasn't going to cross with her. But with her head against his chest and her hand curled around his side, her scent surrounded him. *She* surrounded him.

Her fingers went to his left hand and her head lifted slightly, staring at something. Then she touched his damaged finger. She bent a little closer. "What happened?"

Damn. He tried to laugh it off. "An old war wound."

"You never mentioned going to war."

He hadn't. That particular war had been fought here on American soil. Not even his father had known what he'd done to his son with that hard, angry squeeze.

"I was making a joke. A bad one." He shrugged. "It's not important."

Her head went back to his chest, but her finger continued to stroke his crooked pinkie, the sensation strangely intimate and disturbing on a level that was primal.

He needed to get up and move before either of them did something they would regret.

Then she lifted his hand to her mouth and kissed his finger, the delicate touch ramming through his chest and driving the air from his lungs.

Her tongue trailed across the skin, and his hand tightened slightly on her shoulder. He wasn't sure whether or not it was in warning. And if it was, was he warning her not to stop? Or not to continue? His body responded to the former, rejecting the latter. Because he did want her to continue. To keep on kissing him with those featherlight brushes. And not just there. Everywhere.

"Jess," he murmured. "I think I should move back to the other seat."

She stopped, still holding his hand. "Does that mean you're going to?" Her whispered words were as much a caress as her touch had been.

Heat swirled through him.

"Not if you keep talking to me in that tone of voice."

She let go of his hand and moved hers a little bit higher, smoothing over his biceps until her palm rested on his shoulder. And when she looked up at him, he was lost.

Decision made.

He was going to kiss her. Just like she'd kissed him. Softly. Gently. And with just enough contact to drive her wild.

CHAPTER ELEVEN

IT WAS AS if the past twenty-two years had rewound themselves.

The second his lips touched hers, Jessi was back by the creek, her only worries her father's strict rules and getting to school on time. And it felt so good. So carefree.

If only she'd known how free she'd been back then.

But she could experience it again. With the same man. Just for a little while.

She'd always thought Clint had been invincible all those years ago. But her mom's comment about his father and discovering that crooked little finger showed her he wasn't. He was just as human as she was. Back then...and maybe even now.

Jessi threaded her fingers through his hair, hearing Clint's low groan as he moved to deepen the kiss, shifting her until she lay half across his lap, one of his hands beneath her shoulders, his other splayed flat on her stomach. It was that hand that made her go all liquid inside. It wasn't doing anything special but it was between two very sensitive areas of her body, both of which were doing their damnedest to coax his fingers to slide their way.

A gentle touch of his tongue was enough to get her full attention.

Yes!

Surely he wouldn't stop this time. It had been ages since she'd been with someone. So long that the slightest movement of his body had her eagerly lapping up the sensations like a person deprived of food and water, and desperate for any sign of relief.

She was ready for that kind of relief. For him.

Clint.

And here he was, in her house. And there was absolutely no one around. Not her mom. Not Chelsea.

Just the two of them.

So she pressed closer to him, deepening their kiss, his soft lips making her feel dizzy with need.

And finally...finally, the hand at her waist woke up, his thumb drawing little circles on her belly that had her moaning with anticipation, arching up into it with a mental plea that he evidently heard. Because with a single movement it slid up and over her right breast, that circling thumb finding her nipple without hesitation. Her sundress had a built-in bra, but it was thin, just a shelf of netting with a piece of elastic beneath it, so his touch was heady and intimate, arcing straight down to her toes and then back up again.

When his fingers moved away, she whimpered in protest. His mouth slid from hers, depriving her of another point of contact.

"Clint..."

His hand moved to the back of her head, supporting it as the scrape of his chin along her cheek put him at her ear. "I don't want to stop."

The moment of truth. She sensed he was giving her time to compose herself, to give her a chance to put an end to things even while telling her he didn't want to.

She made a dangerous decision.

"Then don't."

His fingers tightened on the back of her head. Then his other hand went to the thin strap on her sundress and tugged it down her arm, leaving one shoulder bare.

There was a slight hesitation, then that wicked thumb went to work, brushing the joint where her shoulder met her arm. "Is this what you want?"

"More." The word came out as a shaky whisper. She hardly dared to believe she was goading him to continue. But this was exactly what she needed. To have someone just sweep aside her normal code of conduct and make her...*feel* again.

"How about this?" His fingertips moved higher, trailing from beneath her jaw down the side of her neck and along her collarbone. Light ticklish touches that made her ache and squirm.

She wanted him everywhere at once, kissing her mouth, cupping her breast, filling her with his heat where it counted the most. So she took his hand and placed it on her breast, where she wanted it.

"You read my mind, Jess." The words came out in a half growl that made her shiver.

He ducked beneath the edge of her sundress and found her bare skin. He paused then curved his palm over her, the light friction on her nipple sending a low sound up her throat.

"Hell, woman. You need to warn a man before you go braless."

Encouraged by the rough words, she bit her way up his jaw and then smiled against his mouth. "My dress has a bra. You just missed it."

"Could have fooled me." His thumb and forefinger captured the tight bead and gave a gentle squeeze that made her squirm again. "But in that case..."

He removed his hand and urged her off the couch and onto her feet, while he sat, legs splayed.

"Wh-what are you doing?"

"I want to see you—all of you—but at the rate I'm going, I'm not going to make it that far." A quick flash of teeth accompanied the words.

She smiled back at him, his meaning giving her a shot of courage and daring her to tease him back. "I think I can help with that. What would you like to see first?" Balling the skirt portion of her dress, she slid the hem part way up her thighs, keeping her attention focused on his face.

A muscle worked in his jaw, and he placed his hands flat on his thighs. "Let's start from the top. And work our way down. Just like we did in school."

The reminder of how his hands had trailed from her face to her breasts and finally down to that last forbidden place made hot need spurt through her. And the way his knuckles turned white as his long fingers dug into his thighs told her that need wasn't one-sided.

"Okay, let's do that." She let go of her skirt and trailed the back of her right hand down her neck, like he'd done moments earlier, only she didn't stop at her collarbone. Instead, she dragged her fingers along the edge of her bodice—one strap still draped over her arm. The second strap flipped down.

"Next?" she asked, waiting for direction.

"Peel it down. Slowly." The low words weren't abrupt and bossy, rather they coaxed her to do his bidding. Dared her to cross a threshold to a room she'd never entered before. Her times with Larry had been good, but they'd been to the point. Vanilla sex that had been a sharing of hearts and minds, even if it hadn't been superimaginative. Then again, they'd had such a short amount of time together, there hadn't been a chance to venture much further than that.

And that wasn't something she was going to think about.

Not when Clint was right here, holding the door open and asking her to step through it.

This was what she wanted—what she expected from Clint. Wild and raw and real...echoes of the rebellious boy he'd once been. The one who had whispered to a matching defiance within her, drawing it out and fulfilling her in ways she never would have imagined.

So she crossed her arms and took a strap in each hand and pulled with slow, steady pressure that made the fabric of her dress roll back on itself, revealing the upper swell of her breasts. She kept going until she got to the most crucial part, then hesitated.

"Jess." The whispered word shifted her eyes back to his. But he wasn't looking at her face. He was staring at the half-exposed portion of her body, the heat in his expression taking away the last of her inhibitions. She tugged, and he swallowed.

"You have no idea how much I want to drag you down here and finish this."

"Then do it." She let her arms go to her sides, making no attempt to hide herself from him.

He reached behind him and retrieved his wallet from his pants. Her mouth watered, thinking he was going to pull a condom out and do exactly what she'd suggested. And a packet did appear, but he made no move to haul her down onto the couch.

"Here or in your bedroom?"

"It doesn't matter." It was the truth. She wanted him. Badly, and she didn't care where it happened, as long as it happened. And soon.

He smiled again and set the condom on his thigh, making her tighten inside. Because six inches north of that packet was a bulge that left no question as to whether or not he wanted her.

"Does that dress have a zipper?"

It took a second for the question to register, and when she glanced up at him she saw that he knew exactly where she'd been looking. That he'd meant for her to measure the distance between possibility and reality. Because nothing was for sure until he slipped that protection over himself and thrust into her.

"Yes."

"Can you reach it?"

She nodded, her now shaking fingers going to the side of her dress, finding the pull tab then sliding it down to her hips, her other hand holding the rest of the garment in place.

"Let it go," he murmured, his meaning clear.

Releasing her grip, the fabric slid to the floor, leaving her standing in front of him clad only in her panties.

She expected him to tell her to remove those as well, but instead his fingers went to the button of his slacks and undid it.

"Once those come off, honey, it's all over." His bald words made the breath stall in her chest. As did the fact that he was sliding his own zipper down and ripping the condom open.

She wanted to do that. "Wait."

Wary eyes moved to her face. Oh! He thought she was stopping him.

Hurrying to correct him, she said, "Let me."

He took the condom from the packet. "Next time."

Next time!

Her lips parted as he drew the waistband to his briefs down and exposed himself. And unlike her, Clint had no inhibitions. None. Not the last time they'd been together. Not this time. His eyes burned into hers as he sat there. He toyed with the open condom.

The nub at the apex of her thighs tightened, making her squeeze her legs together, aching for some kind of relief.

She licked her lips. "Put it on."

"First your panties."

Hurrying to do as he asked, she hooked her thumbs into the elastic and started to bend over to slide them down, only to have him interrupt her. "Watch me as you do it."

Shifting her focus back to his face, she finished, stepping out of her underwear and standing back upright.

"Beautiful," he murmured. "Even more now than then."

He finally rolled the condom down his length, and took himself in hand. "Now come here, honey."

She moved between his still splayed legs and shuddered when the fingers of his free hand slid in a smooth move up her thigh and found the heart of her. Just the process of removing her clothing while he'd watched had made her body moist and ready.

"Hell. Just like I remember."

By the time he'd finally touched her by the creek, she'd been shaking with desire. One flick of his finger had sent her over the edge. She'd been so embarrassed, only to have him shush her and tell her how much he liked it. When he'd finally entered her, she had already been riding the crest of that same wave, shattering right along with him.

The Clint of today slid one finger inside her, wringing a moan from her. He stayed there, just like that, not moving. She shuddered, needing him so badly she couldn't speak.

"Spread your legs for me."

Somehow, she shuffled her legs farther apart.

"Perfect." He sat up straight, the pressure of his finger inside her holding her right where she was, putting his face dangerously close. Too late, she realized that was what he'd been aiming for all along. "How much will it take this time, Jess?"

Another reference to their first time together.

He added a second finger and pushed deep, using the pair to edge her hips closer. Suddenly off balance, she was forced to clutch his shoulders. "How much, Jess?" he repeated.

Then, as she watched, he moved his mouth until it was pressed against her…and let his tongue slide right across her.

It was as if he'd lit a fuse inside her. Her nails dug into his shoulders and every muscle in her body stiffened as what he was doing blotted out everything except the sensation of his tongue moving backward along her in a slow, drawn-out motion. The fuse ran out of line in a millisecond, and she detonated, crying out as his fingers finally moved, pumping inside her while she convulsed around them.

Then she was in his lap, his hands gripping her butt as he thrust hard into her, filling her beyond belief. She wrapped her hands around his neck, her mouth going to his ear as she rode him furiously, whimpering as her climax continued to crash all around her. He gave a muttered oath and then jerked his hips forward, holding her tight against his body as he strained upward for long seconds, the pressure inside her causing a new wave of convulsions.

When his muscles finally went limp, his arms encircled her back, thumb gliding along her spine.

She drew a deep, careful breath, registered Clint's heavy breathing and smiled, the problems of the day melting as his scent mixed with her own and filled her head. She nuzzled his cheek and then went back to his ear.

"I guess I'm not the only one who went up pretty fast."

His fingers tightened around her, although his voice was light. "Is that a complaint?"

"No. It was sexy, watching you lose control."

He drew her mouth back to his and kissed her long and deep. "Is that so? In that case, maybe we should find out which one of us holds out longer...the second time around."

CHAPTER TWELVE

"IT'S JUST BEEN a long time, and I was upset."

Not the first words a man wanted to hear when he woke up after a night of passionate lovemaking. But there they were, and Clint was at an obvious disadvantage, since he was lying on her couch, an afghan draped over his privates, while Jessi hovered above him, already dressed, looking both worried and...

Hungry.

It was there in her eyes as they slid over his body and then darted back to his face, as if she was doing her damnedest not to look at him.

They'd never even made it back to her bedroom last night, instead using the long L-shaped couch to its full advantage.

Well, if she thought he was going to make it easy for her...

He slid up and propped himself up one of the throw pillows as he eyed her right back.

"Well, that's a hell of a good morning."

She took a step closer. "Sorry. I just don't want you to think..."

"That last night meant something other than great sex?"

Her eyes widened. "That's not what I was going to say."

"So it did mean something," he said, not sure which he preferred.

"No." She held out a hand to stop him from saying anything else. All that did, though, was give him a way to reach out grab her wrist.

She half laughed, half screamed. "Clint, stop. I'm trying to be serious."

"Oh, honey, so am I."

She let him drag her to the sofa and haul her down on top of him, where a certain area of his body was already displaying its delight at this turn of events.

"Wait. Let me finish my thought."

Leaving his fingers threaded in her hair, he looked at her, knowing his next words were not what he wanted to say at all. Hell, he didn't want her to say *anything* except what she wanted him to do to her. But he forced the words out. "Okay, so talk."

She drew an audible breath. "I just didn't want you to think last night had anything to do with Chelsea."

Her eyes trailed away from him, but the words themselves hit him in the chest like a bucket of ice water, sluicing away any hint of desire and leaving a cold trail of suspicion in its wake.

A sour taste rose up in his throat.

"I hadn't thought that at all, Jess." He rolled until she was wedged between him and the back of the couch as he stared at her. "Until just this very second. Did last night have something to do with her?"

"No! Yes. There are just things that you don't know. About how her father...about how Larry died. Not even Chelsea knows. But if someone from our past sees you, I'm afraid she could find out."

"I think you'd better tell me, then."

Jessi's eyes filled with tears. "A few months after we got married he told one of his friends I was pregnant. Well, the friend had seen us—you and me—leave graduation together and come back within minutes of each other. It got him thinking. He suggested Larry ask me whose child I was carrying." There was a pause before she continued. "We had a huge fight, and he accused me of sleeping with you. When I wouldn't deny it, he said Chelsea probably wasn't even his."

She shifted against the couch, and he eased back to give her some breathing space.

Clint could barely open his mouth. "His death?"

"He stormed off...so very angry. He went to a bar, and then a few hours later his car hit an embankment. He died instantly."

Hell. He felt like the biggest ass in history.

He leaned his forehead against hers, guilt causing his muscles to cramp. One more thing destroyed by his lack of control all those years ago. "Dammit. I'm sorry, Jessi. I had no idea."

So many mistakes: if he hadn't impulsively raced after her that night. If he hadn't stayed there with her and done the unthinkable... If he hadn't left her to deal with it all afterwards.

The small box of baggage from the past morphed into a shiny new trunk of regret.

They remained like that for a minute or two until Jessi gave a little sniff.

He scooted back some more, giving her a chance to compose herself, trying to ignore the quick swipe of palms across damp cheeks. The last thing he wanted to do was hurt her.

Then...or now. But it would seem he'd done both.

And he knew what he had to do to keep from hurting her further.

He sat up and slid off the sofa, conscious of her eyes following his movements as he gathered his clothing and headed for the bathroom just down her hallway. After he'd flushed and washed his hands, he dressed quickly, avoiding his image in the mirror as much as he possibly could, because whenever his eyes met those in the reflection, angry accusations stared right back at him.

How had he let this happen again?

When he was around her, his common sense went out the window, and he let his emotions rule.

Just like his father. He didn't hit, but his actions caused just as much damage. Dammit, they'd culminated in a young man's death. Someone Jessi had loved.

He had to take himself off Chelsea's case. It was no longer about remaining objective but about doing what had served him—and everyone around him—well for the last twenty-two years: staying away from emotionally charged situations.

If he'd known the details about Larry's death, he would have taken himself off Chelsea's case that very first day. This time, though, he wasn't going to let Jessi carry any of the blame for what just had happened between them. Nope, he was going to stuff it into his own bag of blame. One that seemed to swell larger every time he laid eyes on her. When he returned to the living room, Jessi was still there, seated on the sofa, only this time she had a phone to her ear.

"Of course, honey," Jessi said to whoever was on the line. "I'll check with Dr. Marks and see how soon we can arrange it." Her glance met his and she mouthed, "Chelsea."

Jessi's daughter was calling her? Right now?

He sat beside her, suddenly very aware of all inappropriate things they'd done in this house last night.

The second she clicked off the phone, she finally looked at him. Really looked at him. "Chelsea wants to talk about something." She licked her lips as if afraid of saying the next words. "She wants us both to be there."

Please, don't quit yet.

The words chanted through her skull as Clint dropped her off at Scott's Memorial to pick up her car and then waited for her to follow him back to the VA hospital.

They hadn't said much once she'd got off the phone, and the interior of his car had been filled with awkward silence and a sense of dread that had blocked her stomach and clogged her throat.

How could she have been so stupid to think last night wouldn't have any serious repercussions? Her only excuse was that it had felt so good to be in his arms. So right.

Only it wasn't right.

The timing had always been lousy when it came to her and Clint. If he'd stayed all those years ago, she never would have married Larry. But she never would have had Chelsea either.

And just like last time Clint wouldn't be there for the long haul. As soon as they'd found a replacement for him, he'd be gone.

He would waltz out of her life once again.

It's just not meant to be. It never was.

The words trailed through her head as if dragged on a banner behind a plane for all the world to see.

Her subconscious rejected them, though, cutting the line and watching as the lettering fell to the ground in a swirl of white canvas and belching smoke.

Before she had a chance to come to any conclusions, Clint pulled to a stop in one of the few parking spaces that had another spot beside it. She slid her car next to his and took a couple of deep breaths before she got out and went to where he stood, waiting. "You won't say anything, will you?"

Clint looked at her as if she had two heads. "About what? Larry? Or about us having a second one-night stand?"

A flash of intense hurt zinged through her chest, making her gasp for air.

As if realizing what he'd done, he hooked his index finger around hers. "Sorry, Jess." He gave a squeeze before letting her go. "I seem to spend a lot of time issuing apologies nowadays."

She tipped her chin back. "Let's just see what she wants." The words came out sharper than she'd meant them to, but maybe that was a good thing. She could put her armor back in place and pretend last night had meant nothing. "We can discuss everything else later. If we could avoid arriving at her room at the same time, that would make me feel more comfortable."

"So you want me to hide out in my office for a few minutes before joining you."

Saying it like that made Jessi realize how cheesy and paranoid the idea sounded. "You're right. Let's just go together."

Once they got to Chelsea's room, they found her seated on the bed, that eerie tissue-paper baby on top of the nightstand. Jessi tensed. That had to be what she wanted to talk about.

She leaned down and kissed her cheek. "Hi, sweetheart."

Chelsea grabbed her around the shoulders, wordlessly hugging her tight for a minute or two. Then she whispered, "I'm sorry for putting you through what I have for the past couple of months. I love you, Mom. Always remember that."

A chill went over her at the solemn words. She stood up and glanced at Clint. "All that matters is that you start feeling better."

"I think I will as soon as I get something off my chest."

Once they were all seated, Clint started things off with some light conversation, never even hinting that he'd been with Jessi in anything other than a professional capacity. Instead, he asked about Jessi's day at work yesterday, subtly guiding her to tell the fishhook-in-the-ear story. Chelsea actually laughed right on cue.

"You hate worms," her daughter said.

"I do. I still remember you bringing in a jar of dirt for me on Mother's Day. Little did I know that that you and Grandpa had spent hours digging up earthworms to put in it."

Chelsea grinned again. "You screamed when one of them dug through the dirt and slithered along the inside of the jar. Grandpa laughed and laughed."

Jessi smiled at the memory of Chelsea and her dad's conspiratorial glances at each other as they'd handed her their "gift."

"You always were the fearless one."

"Not always." Chelsea's smile faded. "I need to tell you something. Something about when I was held in Afghanistan."

"Okay." She glanced at Clint, but he simply nodded at her.

Setting the doll in her lap, Chelsea took a deep breath. "You were right about my pregnancy. I was expecting when I was captured. I hadn't told anyone because it meant a ticket straight home—and I didn't want that. The whole thing was so stupid. It was an accident. I kept meaning to do something—say something—but I put things off...and put things off." Her eyes came up. "And then we were ambushed."

Jessi's heart contracted. "Did they...did they do something to you, honey?"

"No." Chelsea glanced up at the ceiling her eyes filling with tears and spilling over. "I mean, they didn't hurt me physically. They isolated me and made me change into a long, loose tunic. Then they wrote a script and forced me to read it in front of a camera."

Jessi had never heard about any message, but she didn't say anything, just let Chelsea continue talking.

"As one month turned into two, the isolation started to get to me, and I began talking to the baby. Every day. I went from just wanting her to go away to needing her for my own survival."

Her?

Oh, God, had they made Chelsea deliver the baby and then stolen it from her? Was that what the doll was all about?

When Chelsea's words stopped, Clint voiced the question that Jessi couldn't bring herself to ask.

"What happened to the baby?" The line of his jaw was tight, as if he too was struggling with his emotions right now.

"She died."

"Oh, Chelsea..." Her mind went blank as she tried to find the words to say. But there was nothing.

"She died, and I couldn't do anything to save her."

"Your captors didn't help?"

She shook her head. "I didn't want them to know I was pregnant, because I wasn't sure how they'd react to an unmarried woman carrying a child. So I hid my condition. It wasn't hard under the robes. I was in my cell most of the time, and I figured once I delivered, they'd let me keep her, or maybe even let us go."

Clint spoke up. "How far along were you when you were captured?"

"Around three months." She turned to glance at him. "I lost track of time after a while, but I think she was born around four months into my captivity."

Too small. Without the help of modern medicine the baby wouldn't have had much chance to survive.

Chelsea continued. "She came in the middle of the night. She was so tiny. And absolutely perfect." Her fingers caressed the doll. "She never even cried. I held her for a long, long time, praying for her to take a breath." Her voice broke for a second, but then she continued. "After a while, I knew she was dead, and I was afraid if anyone found out, I'd be killed, too—and I didn't want anyone other than me touching her. So I tore off a piece of my robe and wrapped her in it, then I scratched a hole in the dirt floor of my cell with my fingernails and buried her. I was rescued less than a week later."

A couple more tears trickled free, and Jessi reached over and held her hand, her own vision blurry.

"I'm so, so sorry, Chelsea." Her daughter had dealt with all of this by herself. There'd been no one there to help her...no one to comfort her. Her own heart felt ready to shatter in two.

A box of tissues appeared on the tiny table in front of them. Chelsea took several of them and wiped her eyes and then blew her nose before turning to look at her.

"Once she was gone, I realized just how alone I was. I couldn't even mark my baby's grave. And if I died there, I would be just like her. Dumped in a shallow grave somewhere. No one would even know I existed. After I got home, I started thinking maybe that would be for the best. That the baby should have survived. Not me. That I should be the one forgotten, instead of her."

Clint leaned forward. "You wouldn't have been forgotten, Chelsea. People would have grieved deeply, just like you grieved for your baby. You have a mother who loves you. A grandmother. Comrades in your unit. And you're right where you should be. You're here. Alive. Everything you did while in that cell had to be done. It gave you a chance to survive. Gave you a chance to make sure your baby would never be forgotten.

"If you had died, her memory would have died with you." He paused, keeping his gaze focused on her. "And yet look at what's happened. Your mom now knows about her. I know about her. You'll probably talk to more people about her as you live your life. She won't be forgotten. Your very survival makes that a certainty."

Chelsea seemed to consider his words for a minute, and then nodded as if coming to a decision. "I'd like her to have a grave here in the States. A marker with her name on it."

"Of course we'll do that." Jessi wondered if the ache in her heart would ever stop. She'd been about to be a grandmother of a baby girl who might have survived, given access to modern medical facilities. But those were things she could never say to Chelsea—*would* never say to her. They would decide together whether to tell Chelsea's paternal grandparents. Larry's parents were still alive, and Jessi and Chelsea kept in touch with them regularly. As for her mother...

They could think through all that later. The important thing was that Chelsea was talking. Working through things she hadn't told another soul.

She had to ask. "Does the father know?"

"No. I never told him, and there seems to be no point now." She licked her lips. "And he could get in serious trouble if the truth were made known."

"Why?"

"He's an officer, and I'm not. We weren't supposed to get involved with each other to begin with."

Jessi shot Clint a glance that was probably just as guilt-filled as she feared. But he wasn't looking at her. At all.

"Did you love him?"

"No. And he didn't love me. It just happened. Neither of us meant for it to, and we've never gotten together again. It was just the one time."

God. Chelsea could have been describing exactly what had happened years ago, only with different players. And Chelsea was right about one thing. Larry had found out and the consequences had been disastrous. And so very permanent.

Her stomach clenched and clenched.

And unlike Chelsea, she hadn't learned from that mistake all those years ago. She'd gone right back and done it again.

Jessi hadn't been able to resist Clint.

She never had. He'd been just as taboo as that officer Chelsea had spoken of.

Chelsea glanced at Clint. "You told me during our first meeting that you were here to help me get through this. So I'm ready to try. I promise to work really hard."

Clint stiffened visibly in his seat.

Chelsea, totally unaware of the strained dynamics in the room, kept on talking. "Did you go through boot camp, Dr. Marks?"

"I did." Nothing in his voice betrayed his feelings, but Jessi knew. She knew exactly the struggle going on inside him right now.

"Then you know a soldier agrees never to leave a wounded comrade behind."

He gave a quick nod.

"I may not be missing a limb or have any visible external injuries except these..." she held out her wrists, showing the scars "...but I am wounded. So please, please don't leave me behind."

CHAPTER THIRTEEN

They were making progress.

It came in fits and starts, but the past week had seen Chelsea come further than she had since she'd been at the hospital.

And Clint was still on her case, even though in his heart of hearts he knew he shouldn't be. But Chelsea's words had reached to the heart of who he was as a soldier, and he knew that he would have wished more than anything that someone had been there for his father. But they hadn't. He'd dealt with his demons alone. That's not what he wanted for Chelsea.

Besides, since that session, Jessi had been careful to keep her distance, speaking to him only when he asked her something during joint sessions or when he saw her in the halls at the VA hospital. It was like she was walking on eggshells around him.

Well, so was he, around her. And the edges of those shells were beginning to feel damn uncomfortable beneath his feet.

But as long as he could maintain things for another few weeks, they should be fine. Chelsea had gotten her wish not to be abandoned "like her baby." And she was gradually starting to believe that none of what had happened had been her fault. She'd soon be discharged and start doing her sessions on a weekly outpatient basis—which meant he'd be seeing even less of Jessi.

And that made his chest tighten in ways he'd never thought possible. In fact, he hadn't felt this way since...

Since the day he'd left her twenty-two years ago.

Just like he'd leave her again once his transfer papers went through.

And, yes, he was prepared to put in for one, even though a little voice inside of him whispered that when this was all over—when Chelsea was no longer his patient—he could ask Jessi out on a real date and woo her the way he'd once dreamed about.

Except nothing had changed. Not really.

He was still not the right man for her. He was still too cautious—too afraid to let himself be with any one woman.

Besides, Jessi had already experienced the worst parts of coming from a military family, having a daughter who'd served and come back with serious issues. Did she really need to be involved with a man who dealt with wounded soldiers day after day? Wouldn't it just remind her of all she'd gone through with Chelsea?

Never had he felt the weight of responsibility more than he did right now.

"Dr. Marks?" One of the nurses popped her head into the room. "Peter Summers just called. He's asking for a refill of his methadone prescription."

Another complicated case.

He sighed. Peter's maintenance dosage of the drug was dependent on his showing up for his sessions, the last two of which he'd missed. A longtime addict, methadone was meant to replace cravings. The treatment regimen was highly regulated and required sticking to a precise schedule. That meant outpatient sessions and progress reports. Clint would have followed those guidelines even without the corresponding laws, just because it was the right thing to do.

Hell, it didn't seem like he'd been too worried about doing the right thing when he'd been rolling around on Jessi's couch.

And thoughts like that would get him nowhere.

"Would you mind calling him and setting up a new appointment? Tell him he can't have a refill without coming in."

Consequences. Larry's tragic death came to mind. The consequences of his fling with Jessi.

Well, someone else besides him might as well learn the meaning of the word.

"Will do." The nurse jotted something down onto the paper in her hand. "Oh, and I didn't know if you knew, but there's someone waiting to see you. At least, I think she is. She's come down the hallway and almost knocked on your door twice before going back to the waiting room and just sitting there."

He glanced at his planner. He wasn't scheduled to see anyone for another couple of hours. "Any idea who it is?"

"It's Chelsea Riley's mother."

His throat tightened. Jessi was here to see him? Had almost knocked on his door twice?

"Is she still here?"

The nurse nodded. "She's in the main waiting area."

He pushed his chair back and climbed to his feet. "Has she been to see Chelsea yet?"

"No, that was the strange thing. She came straight here without asking anyone anything." She shrugged. "I thought you might like to know."

"Thank you." He shoved his arms into his sports jacket. "If I'm not in my office when you get hold of Peter Summers, could you leave me note with his next session date? Or let me know what he said?"

"Sure thing."

With that, the nurse popped back out of the room, leaving him to struggle with whether to go down to the waiting area and talk to Jessi or to pretend he knew nothing about it and either wait for her to come to him or to leave, whichever she decided.

Consequences, Clint. You have to do more than talk the talk—you have to be willing to walk the walk. Even if it means walking away.

Despite his inner lecture, he wandered down the hallway—like the idiot he was—and found her in the waiting area, just like Maria had said.

Jessi's head was down, her hands clasped loosely between her jeans-clad knees. She could have been praying. Hell, maybe that's what he should be doing right now. Because just seeing her was like a fist to the stomach. A hard one. Hard enough to leave him breathless and off balance.

And all those emotions he'd worked so hard to suppress boiled up to the surface.

The waiting room was full, only five or six seats empty in the whole place and neither of them next to where Jessi was perched. He moved in, catching the eye of an older man, who, although gaunt, still sat at stiff attention. Clint nodded to him, receiving the same in return. He finally got to where Jessi was seated.

"Jess?"

She glanced up, the worry in her green eyes immediately apparent. She popped to her feet. "I was just coming to see you."

"I know. One of the nurses told me."

Her teeth came down on her lower lip. "I figured it must look weird. I just couldn't get up the nerve to…" She glanced around, bringing back the fact that the room was full and now more than one or two sets of eyes were following their exchange with interest.

"I'll take you back to the office," he said. "And I'll run down to the cafeteria and get us some coffee." He wasn't sure how smart it was to be alone with her. But as long as he kept the door unlocked, they'd be fine. At least, Clint hoped so.

He went to the cafeteria and ordered their coffees. She liked hers with milk, something he shouldn't remember, but did. He dumped a packet of sugar into his own brew and headed back to his office.

When he pushed through the door, he noted she still wore the same haunted expression she'd had earlier. Setting her coffee on the desk in front of her, he went around to the other side and slid into his office chair. "What's going on, Jess?"

"It's Mom. I—I felt like I had to tell her about…about Chelsea's baby, since she and my mom are close." She blinked, maybe seeing something in his face that made her explain further. "I'd already talked to Chelsea about it. She knew I was going to tell her."

"And how did your mom react?"

Her clenched fingers pressed against her chin. "That's just it. She's in the hospital. And I don't know what to tell Chelsea. I know she's going to ask as soon as I go in there."

Shock spurted through his system. "What happened?"

"I think I told you, she hasn't been quite herself lately. Anyway, when she heard the story, she seemed to be handling it okay, then she suddenly started feeling a weird pressure in her chest." Jessi blew out a breath. "It turns out one of her arteries is 90 percent blocked. She needs bypass surgery. She'd been having symptoms for about a month, but didn't want to worry me."

He immediately went to reach for her hand then stopped when Jessi slid hers off the top of the desk and into her lap.

Keeping her distance. Asking for his professional opinion.

Of course that's what it was. She'd already told him what she needed to. She wanted to know whether or not she should tell her daughter about what had happened. She hadn't come to him for comfort or anything else.

Just medical advice about her daughter…his patient.

Right now, though, the last thing he wanted to do was think this thing through. What he wanted was to get out of his chair, walk around the desk and grab her to his chest, holding her while she poured out her heart.

Impulse control.

With his recent track record, holding her was exactly what he shouldn't do.

He took a sip of his coffee and let the heat wash down his throat and pool in his stomach, adding to the acid already there. "I think you should tell her the truth about your mom's condition. Maybe not the events preceding the attack but that her doctor found a blockage in an artery and has decided it needs to be addressed as quickly as possible."

"So you don't think I should tell her about Mom knowing what happened with the baby?"

"Not unless she asks you point-blank. The truth might eventually come out, but I don't think you need to hurry into any kind of explanation right now. That can wait until after the surgery. When your mom—and Chelsea—are better."

The truth might eventually come out.

Great advice, Marks, considering your and Jessi's current situation. And what had happened to her late husband once that truth had indeed come out.

None of that mattered at the moment. "When is the procedure scheduled?"

"They want to do it as soon as possible. This afternoon, in fact."

He sat back in his seat. "Maybe it's good that this happened when it did. At least you were with your mom at the time and knew what to do."

"Did I, Clint? What was I thinking, just blurting something like that out?"

"You said she'd been having symptoms for a while. Besides, I'm sure you didn't 'blurt it out.' You were doing what you thought was best for your mom and for Chelsea."

Like he was doing, by continuing to treat Jessi's daughter? Actually, yes. Nothing had happened to suggest that this couldn't all work out for the best as far as Chelsea was concerned.

"I just never dreamed it might lead to—"

"I know." He paused. "Do you want me to be there when they do the procedure?"

"Don't you have patients?"

Not a direct refusal. More like a hesitation…trying to feel him out, maybe?

"I have one more to see in about an hour and a half. What time is her surgery scheduled for?"

"Five." Her hands came back onto the table and wrapped around her mug.

"I'll be done in plenty of time to get to the hospital." He waited until her eyes came up and met his. "Unless you don't want me there."

There, if she wanted reassurance, he would give it to her. And he had a feeling she could use a friend right now, even if they could never be anything more than that.

"I'd actually like you to be there, if it's not too much trouble."

"Of course it's not."

This time her fingers crept across the desk and touched the top of his hand. He turned his over so it was palm up and curled his fingers around hers.

"Thank you so much, Clint. I know it's hard after everything that went on between us."

"Not hard at all."

They sat there in silence for a few long seconds, hands still gripping each other's. Only now he'd laced his fingers through hers, his thumb stroking over her skin.

A few minutes later she left—with his promise to be at the hospital before her mom's procedure.

And somehow in that period of time he was going to give himself a stern pep talk about what he should and shouldn't do as he sat with her in the waiting room.

And all he could do was hope that—for once—his heart decided to cooperate.

CHAPTER FOURTEEN

JESSI PACED THE waiting room of the hospital an hour into her mom's surgery, her chaotic thoughts charging from one subject to another. Her daughter had been so upset by the news that she hadn't asked if Jessi had told her about the baby.

Or asked any deeper questions about why Jessi had told Clint before she'd told her.

That was good, because the last thing she needed to do was heap one more tricky situation onto the pile.

And tricky was the best way she could think of to characterize her and Clint's relationship.

There was no way she could be falling for Clint all over again. They hadn't seen each other in over twenty years. But as they'd worked together, treating patients at the fair, there'd been a feeling of rightness. A rightness that had continued when they'd made love at her house a week later.

Except feelings didn't always mean anything, at least where she was concerned, because she'd always had a thing for Clint. Even back in high school.

It didn't make a difference then, Jessi, and it's not going to make a difference now. He's going to leave. Just you wait and see.

All those confused feelings had to do with Clint being her first. After all, you never really forgot your first love, right? And she *had* loved Chelsea's father. Very much. If it hadn't been for their argument, Larry would still be alive. Would she even be giving Clint a second glance if he were?

Something else she didn't want to think about because it just made her feel that much worse.

The man in question was seated in one of the cushioned chairs in the hospital waiting room, elbows on his knees, watching her pace. She went over to him. "How do you think it's going?"

One corner of his mouth turned up. "You mean since the last time you asked me? All of five minutes ago?" He patted the chair next to him. "Why don't you sit down? Wearing a hole in the linoleum isn't going to help anyone right now."

She blew out a breath, worry squeezing into every available brain cell and wiping away any other thoughts. Plopping down in the chair, she leaned back and closed her eyes. "What if Mom or Chelsea finds out what we've done?"

"Where did that come from?" His arm went around her shoulders and eased her closer.

"I just don't want to make anything worse for either of them."

"No one's going to find out."

"Larry did." She was immediately sorry she'd said it when his body stiffened.

"Sorry, Clint. I'm just worried."

"I know." He sighed. "You need to stop pacing."

Her eyes opened, and she cranked her head to the right to look at him. "I already did."

"Not there." He nodded at the floor, then his fingers went to her temple and rubbed in slow circles. "I mean up here. You're driving yourself crazy. Nobody's going to find out, unless one of us tells them. And I don't see that happening."

"Thank you," she murmured. "You've been a lot cooler about all of this than I have any right to expect."

He chuckled. "Cool, huh? I don't know if I would call it that, exactly."

She wasn't sure what he meant by that, and she was too nervous to try to figure it out right now. All she knew was that she was glad he was there with her.

Jessi leaned into Clint a little bit more, allowing herself to absorb a little of the confident energy he exuded. That energy was something that had drawn her to him as a high school student, and it wasn't any less potent now.

"How long are they going to be?"

"Jess, it takes time. The doctors felt pretty sure going in that everything was going to run according to plan."

"Yes, but anything could happen." Even as she said it, she allowed her eyelids to slide together, letting his clean scent wash through her, canceling out the sharp bite of disinfectant and illness that came with being at a hospital. She was used to those smells, for the most part, but right now, when she was worried about her mother, they were reminders that sometimes things went wrong, and people died.

"It could, but it probably won't. I think she's going to be just fine."

His words were so inviting, offering up a reality that was in stark contrast to the gloomy paths her own thoughts were circling.

"I hope you're right."

This time when her eyelids slid closed, she allowed them to stay like that, lulled by his easy assurances.

Maybe because that's what she wanted to believe.

Either way, she found herself emptying her mind of anything that didn't revolve around the man beside her. And of how right, and good, and...restful it felt to be with him right now.

Dangerous to let him know that, though.

A hand squeezing hers brought her back. She blinked, the harsh glare of the overhead lights flooding her system.

Heavens, she'd fallen asleep. While her mom was undergoing bypass surgery.

"Jess, the doctor is heading this way."

She jerked her head off his shoulder so fast she thought it was going to bounce to the floor and roll down the hall. Dragging her attention to the present, she glanced past the wide door of the waiting room to see that her mom's doctor was indeed striding toward them, no longer wearing his scrubs.

Standing, she waited for him to reach her, vaguely aware that Clint had climbed to his feet beside her, his fingers at the small of her back as if knowing she still needed that connection.

Even before the doctor reached them, he flashed a thumbs-up sign and a smile. "Everything went really well, better than we could have hoped for, actually," he said. "The harvested vein went in without a hitch and her heart is going strong. She should feel better than she's felt in quite a while. Her other arteries still look pretty good. With a change in diet and exercise, hopefully they'll stay that way for a long time to come."

Relief rushed through her system. "So she's going to be okay?"

The doctor nodded. "Absolutely. Barring anything unforeseen, we'll release her in the next few days. She'll need someone home with her for about a week after that. We checked her insurance, and it'll cover a home nurse."

"Thank you so much. When can I see her?"

He smiled. "She's in Recovery at the moment. You know the routine. Once she's moved into a room, we'll let you see her." For the first time his glance slid smoothly to Clint. "But just you right now."

The touch at her back moved away.

Chelsea hurried to make the introductions, but left out why Clint was there, waiting with her.

The surgeon held out a hand. "Dr. Marks, good to meet you.

I served as an army doc before moving over to private practice. I appreciate all you do for our military."

She tensed, wondering if Clint would question why he'd moved when there was so much need—much like she'd done when she'd heard about Dr. Cordoba resigning his commission. All Clint said, though, was, "I'm happy to do it. The country needs both civilian and military doctors. I'm glad you were there for Jessi's mom."

If Dr. Leonard thought it was strange that Clint was there with her or that he'd called her by her first name, he gave no hint of it. He simply nodded and let them know he'd send a nurse out to get Jessi when her mother was settled in. Then he turned around and headed back the way he'd come.

She glanced up at Clint. "Thanks for waiting with me. If you need to get back to the hospital, I understand."

"I already told you, I'm done for the day. I'll stay and make sure everything is okay."

"Thanks again." She bit the side of her lip. "Sorry for falling asleep on you. I can't believe I did that."

His fingers touched her back again. "You've been carrying a lot of weight around on those strong shoulders, Dr. Riley. Maybe it's time you let someone else help with the load from time to time."

Was he offering his services in that regard? And if he was, did she dare let him?

Maybe she already had just by accepting his offer to be here during the surgery.

"I'm sorry you've gotten dragged into my family's problems. Both in high school and now."

He turned her and laid his hands on her shoulders—ignoring everyone else in the room. "No one 'dragged' me." He squeezed softly before letting her go. "Either then or now. I'm here because I want to be."

And later, after Chelsea was better. Would he still be there?

Something she didn't dare even think about at the moment.

Because who knew when that would be. It could be years before Chelsea was well enough to function without the help of someone like Clint. Although she imagined the emphasis would be on counseling later, if there came a time that she didn't need medication to help her cope.

And Jessi knew how things worked in the military. Clint would be transferred out of here, either sooner or later, whereas she had settled her life in Richmond for the long haul. Her mom and daughter were here—not to mention Cooper—and she couldn't imagine leaving them.

Not even for Clint?

She stepped back a pace, not willing to face that question quite yet. Besides, there was nothing between them other than what boiled down to a couple of one-night stands.

One-night stands.

Why did that explanation make her throat ache in a way it hadn't all those years ago?

Hadn't it? Her subconscious whispered the question into her ear, but Jessi raised a hand and swished it away, making Clint frown.

"You okay?" he asked.

"Yes. Just relieved." She took another step back. "Seriously, you don't have to sit here with me. I'm sure you've got other things to do."

His frown grew deeper. "If you're worried about Chelsea or your mom finding out, don't. I won't tell them I was here unless you want me to."

"No!" She cleared her throat and lowered her voice when she realized a couple of pairs of eyes in the waiting room had shifted their way. "I don't want to have to explain why."

Because she wasn't even sure of the answer, and she was afraid to look too closely at the possibilities. She might just discover something she was better off not knowing.

She'd already had her heart broken. Not once. But twice.

Once by Clint and once by her husband's accusations. She didn't want to risk another crack in an already fragile organ.

Clint's voice was also low when he responded. "I already said I wouldn't say anything. So don't worry about it."

But he sounded a little less confident than he had a few minutes ago, when he'd assured her that her mother would be just fine.

"Thanks."

They both sat down, but this time without talking, and Clint didn't put his arm back around her. She tried to tell herself she was glad. But deep inside it made her feel lonely, yearning for something she was never going to have.

And what was that exactly?

A relationship with Clint?

Those four words caused a shudder to ripple through her. Her arms went around her waist, even though the waiting room wasn't chilly.

God, she hoped that's not what she was looking for. Because that wasn't on the cards for her or for Clint. Going down that road would be a recipe for disaster.

She would do better on that front, starting now. Despite her earlier thoughts, she needed to start relying on Clint less than she currently was.

The problem was, Jessi honestly didn't know how she was going to back away when the time came.

Because that crack in her heart was just waiting for an excuse to widen. And she had a feeling it was already far too late to stop that from happening. The crowbar was there in hand, poised and ready.

Or maybe it wasn't her hand that wielded that power at all.

What if, in the end, Clint was the one to decide if her heart came apart in jagged pieces or remained intact?

When the nurse finally came down to tell her her mom was awake and ready to see her, Jessi was relieved to be able to walk away from her spinning, panicked thoughts…and to put her attention firmly where it should have been all along: on her mom and Chelsea…and off Clint.

CHAPTER FIFTEEN

THE SUN WAS peeking out from between heavy storm clouds. Both figuratively and literally. At least as far as Chelsea was concerned. A good omen.

Jessi's mom was home and recovering after her bypass surgery. Clint had seen Jessi in passing, but she had her hands full at the moment with her job, her mom and her daughter.

Which brought him back to the item on his desk.

Transfer papers.

Or rather a request to terminate his temporary assignment in Richmond and head back to Cali, where, from what he'd read on the internet that morning, all was sunny and bright. Not a cloud in sight.

And, hell, he could use a little more light right now to clear his head.

To sign or not to sign, that was the question.

No, it wasn't. He'd eventually put in that request. It was only a matter of time. And willpower.

Willpower he'd been sorely lacking in the past several weeks.

To stay would be a mistake. Something he'd convinced himself of time and time again.

His presence here in Richmond brought back memories of not-so-happy times for all of them.

How many times had Jessi mentioned Larry's name? Hell, he hadn't even known the man had died when he'd arrived here, much less the reason for it. And Jessi had been carrying that around for all these years.

And being here with her was a definite reminder of his own bitter childhood. People from his past knew more than he'd realized—judging from Mrs. Spencer's comments at dinner. They'd evidently talked amongst themselves about his father's problems.

And Clint's explosive reactions when he was around Jessi? Also reminders of what a lack of control could cause—had caused. He might have enjoyed it at the time, but there were consequences for everything in this life.

He'd have to leave some time or other. Why not now? Chelsea was scheduled to be released from the hospital next week. She'd continue her sessions as an outpatient…a victory he should be cheering, instead of acting like he was about to be shot off to the moon, never to be heard from again.

Maybe he'd request deployment instead. That should take him far enough away. Or he could just let the army decide where he was needed, rather than ask to return to San Diego.

Chelsea popped her head in, as if she'd heard his thoughts. "Have you heard anything about my grandmother yet?"

He slid the transfer papers beneath a file folder, not willing to let her see it. No need to cause a panic. It would take time for the orders to go through, anyway.

"No, just that she's been released." He smiled at her. "And you really should learn to knock, young lady. I could have been with a patient."

He motioned at the chair across from his desk.

Her lips twisted. "You're right. Sorry."

"No problem." He tapped the eraser end of his pencil on the smooth gray surface of the desk, the hidden papers glaring at him from their hiding place. "As I was saying, your grandmother seems to be doing pretty well, according to your mom. She just has to take it easy for a few weeks."

Just like he did. He'd seen firsthand the problems that jumping into something with both feet could bring.

"Hmm…"

"And what does that sound mean?" He forced a light smile, although it felt like the corners of his mouth were weighted down with chunks of concrete.

Chelsea's own light attitude vanished. "I was hoping to do something, but I guess it can wait until Nana's feeling better."

"Anything I can help with?"

"I'm not sure. Maybe. I was telling Paul that I'd like to hold a memorial service for my…for the baby. He said he'd like to come. So did some of the others in our group."

Paul Ivers, a young man who'd moved over to sit by Chelsea during one of their group sessions. When had this particular conversation taken place?

"I don't see why that couldn't happen at some point."

"I'd want you there as well, if that's okay. You've helped me so much."

"I haven't done anything, Chelsea. You've come this far under your own power. I've just been here to listen and facilitate."

"Maybe you don't think you've done much, but I do. And you said you knew each other before. I asked Mom about that, and she said you, she and my dad were all in school together. My dad's not here anymore, so it would mean a lot if someone who knew him came."

Me and Larry, neck and neck.

He'd been a stand-in for the man back then. The last thing he wanted was to be one now.

Was that what he'd been when he'd made love to Jessi back

at her house? A stand-in for a man who was dead and gone? A man whose death he'd helped cause?

"Please, Dr. Marks?" Chelsea's voice came back again.

Clint sat there, conflicted. He believed in keeping his word whenever possible, something his father had never seen fit to do.

In fact, a lot of the strict rules governing his life had come about because of his dad's poor judgment. Maybe that wasn't such a bad thing. Those rules had served him well, until he'd come back to Richmond. "I can't promise anything, Chelsea, but if I'm still here, I'd love to come."

Her eyes widened then darkened with fear. "You're thinking of leaving?"

He hurried to put her mind at ease. "I simply meant if you hold the service five years from now, there are no guarantees I won't have been transferred somewhere else by then."

His buzzer went off before he had time to think.

When he answered, his assistant said, "Mrs. Riley is here."

His already tense muscles tightened further. Hearing Jessi referred to as Mrs. anything stuck in his craw.

Jessi Marks. Now, that had a nice ring to it.

No, it didn't.

Hell. This day was turning out to be anything but the good omen he'd hoped for fifteen minutes earlier. It was morphing into a damned nightmare.

"Oh, good," said Chelsea. "We can ask her what she thinks."

Perfect. He had a feeling Jessi was going to love this almost as much as he did.

He responded to his assistant, rather than to his patient. "Send her in."

Jessi scooted through the door, her face turning pink when she spied her daughter sitting in one of the chairs. Then her eyes crinkled in the corners. "Hi, sweetheart. I was just headed down to see you."

"Were you?" Chelsea's lips slid into a smile. "Guess you decided to stop by and see my doctor first."

Pink turned to bright red that swept up high cheekbones like twin beacons of guilt.

Chelsea waved away her mother's discomfiture and stood up to catch her hand. "Anyway, I'm glad you did, because we have something to tell you."

"We do?"

"You do?"

He and Jessi both spoke at once, then their eyes met. Hers faintly accusing as she met him stare for stare. She was the first to look away, though.

Chelsea blinked as she glanced from one to the other. "I don't actually mean 'we' because I kind of sprang this on Dr. Marks."

That was one way of putting it.

She glanced at him again. "Is it okay if I tell her?"

"That's completely up to you." He had to force the words out as invisible walls began to close in around him. So much for his quick, silent escape. What a damn mess. No matter which way he spun, seeking the nearest exit, he only dug himself in deeper and deeper.

Pulling her mom over to the chairs, they both sat down, then Chelsea told Jessi what she'd told him, in almost exactly the same way. As if she'd been rehearsing the words over and over until she'd got them perfect.

His insides coiled tighter.

Once her voice died away there was silence in the room, except for Clint's phone, which gave a faint pinging sound as it received a message of some type.

Jessi licked her lips, her gaze flicking to Clint for a mere second before going to rest on her daughter. "I think that's a lovely idea."

"I asked Dr. Marks about letting the group come…and I invited him, as well. He said he'd be there, if he was still in Richmond."

"'Still in Richmond'?"

The words curled around a note of hurt, the sound splashing over him in a bitter wave.

This wasn't how he'd wanted her to hear the news.

Chelsea's hand covered her mother's. "No, I mean he said that if I had the service five years from now, he might have been transferred somewhere else by then."

Jessi's body relaxed slightly.

Did she care that he might move away?

Of course not. She had to know as well as he did how utterly foolish it would be for them to go any further than they already had. And she'd withdrawn a little over the past week, changing their working relationship into one of professionals who were collaborating on a patient they had in common. Only to Jessi she was no patient. She was her daughter—someone she loved with all her heart and soul. He saw the truth of it each time the women looked at each other and in the way Chelsea touched her mom, as if needing the reassurance of her presence.

To be loved like that would be...

Impossible. For him, anyway.

And he needed to pull himself together before someone realized how jumbled his emotions had become.

"Of course I'll be there." The words came out before he had time to fully vet them. So he added, "If I can."

"When do you want to do this?" Jessi's voice became stronger, as if she saw this as a way for her daughter to close this chapter in her life and move on to the next one. One that Clint hoped with all his being would be full of laughter and happiness. This family deserved nothing less, they'd been through so much over the years.

He did not need to add more junk to the pile. They both had enough to deal with right now. He decided to change the subject. "How's your mom?"

"Good. The home nurse is with her this morning. She's getting stronger every day. In fact, she said today that finding out...er...finding out about her blockage might have been one of the most positive, life-affirming experiences she'd ever gone through. She feels tons better and is raring to get out of bed and go back to work on her garden and play with Cooper." Jessi shook her head and squeezed Chelsea's hand. "I think I know where you got your stubbornness from."

"Mine?"

Laughing, Jessi said, "Okay, mine, too."

That was one thing Clint could attest to. This was one strong trio of women, despite the momentary flashes of pain that manifested themselves in physical reactions: Abigail's heart blockage. Chelsea's suicide attempt. Jessi's reaching out to an old flame during a crisis?

Yes. That was exactly it.

It should have made him feel better—set his mind at ease about leaving in the months ahead. Instead, a cold draft slid through his body and circled, looking for a place to land. He cleared his throat to chase it away. It didn't work. It lay over him in a gray haze that clung to everything in sight, just like the morning dew. What it touched, it marked.

And that mark was...

Love.

He reeled back in his seat for a second, trying to process and conceal all at the same time.

He loved her? Heaven help him.

How could he have let this happen? Any of it? All of it?

He had screwed up badly. Had let his emotions get the best of him, just like he always had when he was around this woman.

The transfer papers seemed to pulse at him from beneath the binder with new urgency. The sooner he did this the better.

And his promise to Chelsea?

"What do you think Nana would want me to do?" Even as his own thoughts were in shambles, Chelsea's were on the brink of closing old wounds and letting them heal.

"I think Nana would want you to be happy, honey."

"Can we have the service next week, then? I don't know

how long the members of the group will keep coming to sessions. We can have a private memorial for just our family later, if Nana feels up to it."

"We can have it anytime you want."

And in that moment he knew he had to see this through. He had to be there for Jessi, just as she had to be there for Chelsea. Abigail wasn't up to taking on that role yet. And Larry was no longer there.

And he wanted to. Wasn't that what love was about? Sacrificing your own comfort and well-being for someone else's?

Like he'd done once upon a time?

He peered into the past with new eyes. Eyes that saw the truth.

He'd loved her even then. Even as he'd been preparing to hand her over to another man. One whose father didn't drink himself into a rage and let his fists do the talking.

A normal, mundane life.

Something Clint hadn't been able to give her. Because back then he'd had anger issues, too. Toward his father, who'd dished it out. Toward his mom, who'd sat there and taken it. Toward the world in general, for turning a blind eye toward what had been going on in homes like his.

The military had helped him conquer most of his anger, but only because it had instilled discipline in its place, and had channeled his negative energy into positive areas.

But his life still wasn't peaceful. It was filled with patients like Chelsea, who scrabbled and clawed to find some kind of normalcy.

Jessi had been through enough. She'd deserved better than him back then, and she still did today.

She deserved a professor or architect or poet. A man who brought beauty into her life. Not memories of days gone by.

I'm going to have to give her up all over again.

And he was going to have a few more scars to show for it.

He realized both pairs of female eyes were on his face, both wearing identical expressions of confusion. One of them had said something.

"I'm sorry?"

Chelsea bit her lip. "I asked if next Sunday would work for you? Or do you have other plans?"

"No. No plans." Once he'd said it, he realized he could have come up with an excuse. Like what? A date? That would go over really well with Jessi. Besides, he'd meant what he'd thought earlier. He wanted to be there for her...and for Chelsea. Like the family he'd never had?

Maybe. Maybe it was okay to pretend just for a few hours—to soak up something he'd never be able to have in real life.

Like a wife and daughter?

Yes.

Even if they both belonged to a man who could no longer be there for them.

So he would act as a stand-in once again. For an hour. Maybe two. And he could pray that somehow it was enough to get him through the rest of his life.

CHAPTER SIXTEEN

SHE WANTED TO hold Clint's hand, but she couldn't.

Not in a cemetery, while mourning a tiny life that had been snuffed out before its time. Standing next to him would have to be enough.

Only it was so hard. Hard to remain there without touching him.

Curling her fingers into her palms, she forced them to stay by her sides as a chaplain she'd never met talked about life and death...commemorating a granddaughter she'd also never met.

A hand touched hers. Not Clint's, but Chelsea's. Her daughter's fingers were icy cold, her expression grim, eyes moist with grief as the minister continued to speak.

"In the same way this marker serves as a reminder that a tiny life was placed into Your loving arms, we, like Marie Elizabeth Riley, need to place our trust and hope in You, the Author and Finisher of our faith, that we will one day see her as she was meant to be. Whole and full of life..."

The sudden rush of tears to eyes that had been dry took Jessi by surprise, overriding whatever else the chaplain was saying.

She fumbled in her purse, letting go of Chelsea's hand for a second as she searched for a tissue.

Clint, still, solemn and heartbreakingly handsome in a dark blue suit, pressed a handkerchief into her trembling hands. She glanced up at him to find him watching her, something dark and inscrutable in his gray eyes. Was he irritated at her for blubbering? But this baby would have been her first grandchild...would have probably survived if Chelsea had had access to health care.

And that was another thing that had driven her daughter crazy with guilt. All those what-ifs. *If* she had just spoken up... *if* she'd admitted she was pregnant, instead of fearing a reprimand or, worse, of being sent home in flurry of paperwork and inner shame... *if* she'd told her captors the truth. The baby's father had never been notified. Chelsea saw no reason to cause trouble for a man with whom she'd had a one-night stand.

Jessi knew what that was like. She'd had two of them. Both with the same man.

The chaplain asked everyone to bow their heads, so Jessi closed her eyes. And felt a hand to her right clasp hers once again. Chelsea.

And then, out of nowhere, warm fingers enveloped her other hand, lacing between hers.

Clint.

Oh, God. The tears flowed all over again. She'd wanted to hold his hand, and he'd not only read her mind, he'd found a way to accomplish the impossible.

A flicker of hope came to life in her chest.

Maybe it wasn't impossible. He had certainly made love to her like she'd meant something to him.

Then again, he'd done the same thing all those years ago. Maybe it was different now. They were both older. Wiser. They'd both lived through things many people never had to experience.

She tightened her grip around both hands, allowing herself to feel connected to him in a way that had nothing to do with sex. Or need. But was something deeper. More profound.

No.

Not happening.

And yet he'd made the impossible possible.

As the prayer went on, Clint gave her hand a quick squeeze, then released it.

When she peeked between her lashes, she saw that she wasn't the only one who had a male hand linked with hers. The young man next to Chelsea stood so close their shoulders and arms touched. And his index finger was twined around her daughter's.

She swallowed. Maybe, just maybe, she could let herself believe. Just like the chaplain said.

The seed took root and spread throughout her being, twisting around her heart and lungs until she wasn't sure where they started and the belief ended. Maybe that was the way it was meant to be.

She could talk to Clint. Somehow find out if he felt the same way. Surely he did. Otherwise why would he have held her hand?

Because she'd been crying? Maybe. That was why it was important to talk to him. And she would. Just as soon as the service was over, and she'd made sure her daughter was okay. Her mom was at home. They still hadn't told Chelsea about the circumstances behind the heart episode, and they'd both agreed to keep that quiet. Her mom also felt it was best for her to stay at home for this particular event. Neither of them wanted anything to mar the service. And although Jessi trusted Clint not to say anything, one of them could inadvertently let something slip without realizing it.

The prayer ended, and Chelsea took the white rose in her hand and gently kissed the bloom, then placed it across the bronze marker that had been set in the lush grass beside Larry's grave. Grass that hadn't needed to be turned up, since there was no body to bury this time. The back of Jessi's throat burned. Larry would have loved his daughter. And his granddaughter, if he'd been able to see past his own hurt and pride. Two lives, needlessly lost.

But at least there was now a place where Chelsea could come and remember—along with a concrete bench that had been placed at the foot of the graves, a gift from her mother. She hoped they could come here each year and remember.

The service ended with a flautist from their church playing "Amazing Grace," the light, bright sound of the instrument giving the hymn a sense of hope and peace. It's what Chelsea had wanted, and as her daughter moved to stand beside the same young man as before, a quick glance was shared between the two of them. Jessi looked at him a little more closely. Surely it was a good thing that her daughter was beginning to look past the pain in her heart and see a future that was brimming with possibilities.

Like Jessi herself was?

When she gave Clint a sideways look, she saw that his attention was also on the pair. She could have sworn a flash of envy crossed his expression before disappearing. His gaze met hers, and he nodded to show her he had noticed, then he leaned close, his breath brushing across her ear as he murmured, "Try not to worry. Paul's a good man."

Words hung on the tip of her tongue, then spilled past her lips. "So are you, Clinton Marks."

His intake of breath was probably not audible to anyone except him, but even so he froze for several seconds at her comment, while his brain played it over and over in that same breathy little whisper.

She thought he was a good man?

Emotion swelled in his throat, and he forced himself to stand up straight before he did something rash right in front of her late husband's grave. Like crush her in his arms and kiss her like there was no tomorrow. Tell her that he loved her and would always be there for her.

As the last notes of the song died away, people began to filter out of the cemetery. Chelsea leaned over to Jessi and said, "I'll see you later on at Nana's?"

"I probably won't be there for a few hours, okay? There's something I need to do first," said Jess.

"Okay." The two women embraced for several long seconds then broke apart. Paul walked her daughter over to her car and held the door open, leaning over to tell her something before closing it.

"What do you have to do?" Clint asked.

If he was smart, he'd say his goodbyes right now before he got caught up in some kind of sentimental voyage that would end with him dragging her back to his place.

"I thought we might go back to my house for a little while."

He waited for her to tack a valid reason on to the end of that phrase. But she didn't. Instead, she simply waited for him to respond to the request. One that had come right on the heels of her other shocking comment.

He should end it right now. Cut her short before she could say anything else with a brusque, "Not a good idea and you know it."

Right. He could no more bring himself to say something like that than the moon could grow an oxygen-rich atmosphere. Or maybe it could, because right now he was having trouble catching his breath and his head felt like it was ready shut down.

He glanced back at the markers, Larry's name biting deep into his senses and grinding them into something he no longer recognized. Needing to get away before it took another chunk from him, he said, "Sounds good. Are you ready?"

"Do you want to follow me back?"

Honey, I'd follow you anywhere, if I could.

Maybe things weren't as dire as he'd painted them. Would it be so bad if he and Jessi somehow tried to make a go of things?

That paper on his desk came to mind. He could just tear it up and dump it in his waste can, and no one would be the wiser.

The thought grew as they walked to the parking lot together. With no one else around, Clint took her hand again, gripping it with an almost desperate sense of reverence. This woman did it for him. She met him right at his point of deepest need. And she had no idea.

And if she wanted to go back to her place and discuss Chelsea's case, he was going to be crushed with disappointment. Because he wanted her. In the past. Right now in the present. And in the days that stretched far into the future.

Whether or not any of that was possible was another matter. But maybe he shouldn't worry about leaping right to the end of this particular book. Maybe he should turn one page at a time and savor each moment as it came.

Because who knew how long anything in this life was going to last? Wasn't today a reminder of that?

He saw her to her car and smiled when he did the exact same thing young Paul had done. Opened her door for her and then leaned across it. Only instead of saying something, he kissed her. Right on the mouth. Right in the middle of a public parking lot.

And he didn't give a rip who saw him.

One page at a time. And he was loving the current chapter because, instead of a quick peck and retreat, Jessi's lips clung to his for several long seconds. When he finally forced himself to pull back, she gave him a brilliant smile. "I think we're on the same page."

A roll of shock swished through him. Coincidence. It had to be. Unless Jessi had suddenly become a mind-reader.

Then again, he found it pretty damned hard to hide his feelings from this particular woman. They bubbled up and out before he could contain them. That's what had gotten him into trouble when they'd been in high school and again a couple of weeks ago. It was impossible to be near her and not want to touch her. Hold her. Make love to her.

He didn't respond to her words, just said, "I'll meet you at your house." Because if he was wrong, if she wasn't feeling the same deep-seated need that he was, he'd end up eating his words and feeling like a fool.

The fifteen-minute drive seemed to take forever, but finally she pulled into the driveway of her house. They got out of their cars and stared at each other for a minute before coming together.

Then he was reaching for her and dragging her into his arms, kissing her with a fervor he had no business feeling. But she kissed him back just as hard, her hands winding around his neck, going up on tiptoe so she could get closer.

Her tongue found his, leaving no doubt in his mind where her thoughts were headed. And that was fine by him, because his had been there for hours...weeks.

"Keys." His muttered words were met with a jingle, then he swept her up in his arms and strode to the front door. "Unlock it."

It gave him a thrill to note that her hands shook as she twisted around to do as he asked, because he knew his were trembling just as hard, along with every other part of his body. Half in anticipation of what was to come and half in fear that somehow it was all going to fall apart before they got inside...before he got the chance to strip her clothes from her body—in her bedroom this time—and drive her to the point of no return.

Because he was already there. There was no turning back from the emotions that were throbbing to life within him. He couldn't bring himself to say them, so he would show her instead. With his mouth. With his hands.

With his heart.

And hope that somehow she'd be able to decipher their meaning.

He kicked the door closed, trying not to trip when Cooper suddenly appeared, barking wildly and winding around him. He let Jessi down long enough for her to let the dog out into the backyard before hauling her back up into his arms. This time he lifted her higher so that his mouth could slant back over hers, his fingers digging into the soft flesh of her thighs, her waist. Right on cue, her arms went back around his neck and she held on tight.

Clung as if she were drowning.

Well, so was he.

"Bedroom," he muttered against her mouth. Could he not get anything out other than one- and two-word sentences?

Evidently not.

And if she was going to stop this parade, she had the perfect opportunity to drag her lips from his and tell him to put her down, that they were going to sit on that long sofa and talk.

She didn't. "Down the hallway, first door on the right."

Then she was kissing him again, her eyes flickering shut even as his had to remain open to avoid tripping over furniture or running into a wall as he made his way down the hallway and arrived at her bedroom. He paused in the doorway and eyed the space, noting the frilly pillows on the bed and the hinged frame that held two pictures on the nightstand. One of Jessi with another man. And one of her holding that man's baby.

Larry.

His chest tightened, and he pulled back slightly, rethinking this idea.

"What's wrong?" Her breathless reply washed over him.

He nodded at the nightstand, and she glanced in that direction and then tensed before looking back up at him. She shook her head. "It's okay, Clint. He's been gone a very long time."

She didn't say that she didn't love him, or that Larry wouldn't mind if he could see them.

Just that the man had been gone a long time.

He stood there, undecided. Could he lie in that bed and thrust inside her, while her dead husband watched them?

"Take me over there," she murmured.

He didn't want to. Wanted to suggest they go back to the familiar sofa in the living room. But his feet had ideas of their own. He carried her over to the small table and watched as she tipped the frame over onto its front so that the pictures were no longer visible.

"Better?" she asked, one corner of her mouth curling.

It was. A little, anyway. "Yes."

"Okay, now put me on the bed—" her fingers sifted through the hair at the back of his neck, sending a shiver over him "—and take off all my clothes."

"Your wish—" he wiped Larry from his mind and dropped her from where he stood, then smiled at the squeal she gave as she bounced on the mattress and lay there staring up at him "—is my command."

She licked her lips. "Then come down here and start commanding me."

CHAPTER SEVENTEEN

BEFORE HE COULD do as she asked, Jessi sat up and scooted to the edge of the bed, allowing her legs to hit the floor. Then she grabbed him behind the knees and dragged him forward a step or two, parting her legs until he stood between them.

"I thought I was doing the commanding," he said.

"Changed my mind," she said with a laugh, removing his keys and wallet from his pockets and putting them on the bed. "Because you'll end up having all the fun, like last time."

His brows went up. "I don't remember hearing any complaints."

"That's because there weren't any." Reaching for his belt buckle, she slid the loop out in one smooth move that made his mouth water. "And I don't think you'll be hearing any complaints now. At least, not from me."

With the buckle undone, she moved to the button of his dress slacks.

Hell, she wasn't going to hear any complaints from him either. Although his ideas for maneuvering her to the point of no return were not going according to plan.

Or maybe she'd had the very same thoughts about him.

His flesh twitched.

And he was already too far gone to back out now.

Down went his zipper. "Wait."

She stopped and met his eyes. "Am I doing something wrong?"

No, she was doing everything exactly right. And that was the problem. He really *was* too far gone. His body was pumping with anticipation. Too much too soon and he was going to have trouble not letting go in a rush. It was why he hadn't let her touch him last time.

"No, honey." His hand tangled in her hair, resisting the urge to drag her forward and show her exactly what he meant. "I just don't want you to do anything you don't want to do."

One perfectly arched brow went up an inch, and she licked her lips. "And if I want to?"

Even as she said it, she peeled apart the edges of his slacks and pushed them down his hips, until they sat at midthigh.

No trying to hide what she did to him at this point, because it was right there in front of her. Her hands moved around to the backs of his thighs, sliding over his butt and grabbing the elastic waistband of his briefs. "Are you ready?"

Oh, he was ready all right. But he wasn't so sure he was ready for what she wanted.

Dammit, who was he kidding? He was a man. He wanted it. Wanted every last thing she could think of doing to him.

And he wanted it now.

"Do it."

That was all it took. She dragged his underwear down in one quick tug, her nails scraping over his butt in a sensual move that set all his nerve endings on high alert.

He bobbed free, inches from her face. Her thumbs brushed along the outsides of his legs as her hands curled around the backs of his thighs, holding him in place. Then she leaned forward without hesitation, her mouth engulfing him in a hot, wet rush that made him grunt with ecstasy.

She remained like that for several seconds, completely still, her eyes closed, nostrils flaring as if the sensation was heavenly.

Hell, lady, you should be standing in my shoes.

He struggled like a wild man to contain the warning tingle, using every bit of ammunition in his bag of tricks to keep from erupting right then and there. Tangling his hand in her hair, he dragged her backward until he popped free. "Damn, woman. You're going to get more than you bargained for if you keep that up."

She laughed. "Haven't I told you? I love bargains. Especially when I get more bang for my…buck."

The pointed hesitation before she said that last word made his flesh tighten in anticipation. A silent promise to give her exactly what she wanted: a hard, fast bang that was, oh, so good.

Just like last time.

But this time he wanted to draw out his pleasure. And hers.

So, keeping his fingers buried in her hair, he drew her forward again, watching as she slowly opened her mouth.

Yes!

He edged closer, dying to feel her on him, then pulled away at the last second. He repeated the parry and feint several times with a slow undulation of hips that was a blending of obscene torture—emphasis on the torture. At least for him.

She clenched the backs of his thighs, trying to tug him closer, while he remained just out of reach. "Clint. Please…"

"What do you want, Jess?"

"Right now? I want you."

That was all it took. He pushed her backwards on the bed, knocking the frame off the end table in the process, and shoved her full skirt up around her hips. Black satin panties met his hungry eyes. He jerked them down and then kicked his way out of the rest of his clothes, cursing when one foot got hung up in the waistband of his briefs. Once free, he tossed a condom packet onto the bed and lay down, hauling her on top of him, until she was straddling him, her skirt pooling around her hips.

"You wanted to be in control, Jess? You've got it."

Her eyes trailed from the straining flesh outlined beneath the fabric of her skirt up his bare chest, until her eyes met his. "In that case, do you want me clothed? Or unclothed?"

Unclothed. His mind screamed the word, mouth going dry. He had to force himself to say, "Your game. Your rules."

She gave him a slow smile. "Mmm. I like the idea of making my own rules." Taking her skirt in hand, she pulled the black silk up his erection in a long, slow move that made him rethink his assessment. Then she let it slip back down the way it had come.

Okay, clothed was pretty hot, too. Especially when she continued to hold his gaze, and he knew she could spot every muscle twitch in his cheek, discern every time he had to hold himself in check. Like now, when myriad sensations began to gather in his chest. In his gut...

"Jess..." It was meant to be a warning, but her name came out as a low hum of air.

One of her hands crawled beneath her skirt and found him. And the tactile awareness of being able to feel what she was doing but not see it made the act seem secretive and forbidden. An exotic ritual that defied time and space.

She slid forward and shifted her hips up and over his ready flesh. He braced himself, but she didn't come down on him in a rush, as he'd expected. Instead, she brushed him across her skin, back and forth, her eyes closing, lips parting. He swallowed hard when he realized what she was doing—using him on her body, giving herself pleasure, rocking her hips in time with her hand.

Holy hell. This was as hot as her mouth had been.

Worse.

Because then she'd only been pleasuring him. Now she was bringing both of them to new heights of throbbing awareness.

Every cell in his body wanted to thrust home and end the torment. He could just slide up and inside her in one fast move, and she would probably let him…probably welcome him. But the shifting expressions on her face were too entrancing to do anything but lie there and take whatever she wanted to dish out.

"God, Jess. You're killing me here."

"What do you want?" She turned his earlier words around and pushed them back at him.

Only he knew exactly what he wanted. "I want you to make yourself come."

Her fingers tightened, and her movements became quicker, bolder, her breasts straining beneath her shirt as she brushed herself against him—or brushed him against herself—he didn't know which it was and didn't care. He was dying to cup her, to scrape his thumb across those hard nipples now visible even through her blouse and bra, but he wanted this round to be all hers.

All around him, he felt her slick heat. Lust spiraled through him, growing stronger with each stroke, even as her movements became more purposeful. Reaching sideways, Clint found his wallet and the condom just inside it. He wrapped his fingers around the plastic wrapper, gripping it tight, hoping he'd still have the sanity to use it when the time came.

Jessi's breathing quickened, her teeth coming down on her lip as her body continued to feign the motions of sex. Good sex. The kind of sex that didn't come along every day, with every woman.

No, there was only one woman he'd ever shared this kind of connection with.

Her body stiffened suddenly, pressing hard against him. Then she went off with a cry, her body pulsing against the tight need of his erection. Tearing into the packet, he reached beneath her skirt and sheathed himself in a rush before plunging into her and losing himself in the continued contractions of her orgasm.

Using her hips, he pulled her down onto himself as hard as

he could, already too far gone to try to last any longer. Instead, he pressed upwards in greedy thrusting motions as he allowed himself to plummet mindlessly over the cliff of his own release, falling, falling, until there was nowhere else to go.

Nothing registered for several seconds—or it might have been minutes. Hours, even.

When he could finally breathe again, finally think, he gathered her to his chest, his fingers sliding up through the damp strands of her hair and holding her close.

"Remind me not to put you in charge ever again."

"So you *are* complaining." She snuggled closer.

"Never."

He kissed her brow, her taste salty with perspiration, and allowed his eyelids to finally swing shut…no longer afraid he was going to miss something crucial.

With one last sigh, he propped his chin on her head and allowed his body to relax completely.

Something tickled the side of her arm.

There it was again. It wasn't Cooper, because he was in the living room, and the bedroom door was shut.

Her mind reached out to grasp something, only to have it shift away uneasily. The sensation returned. A light rhythmic stroke trailing up toward her shoulder now.

Her eyes opened to find someone standing beside the bed, watching her.

Clint.

"Hello, sleepyhead. I fed Cooper and let him out. Hope that was okay."

"Mmm…"

Since his voice sounded as rough as hers felt, she wasn't the only one who had fallen asleep after the second time they'd made love.

In her bed. In her house. And the second time he'd undressed her slowly. Carefully. Kissing his way down her body in a way that had made her heart melt, even while her senses had been kicking into high gear.

Like now. Only it was her heart that was soaring, rather than her libido. Because Clint was still here. He hadn't hightailed it out of here like she'd half expected. The hope she'd grasped earlier continued to grow, picking up speed as she finally acknowledged the possibilities that this might just work out between them.

"Hey, yourself. What time is it?" She rolled onto her back to look at him fully.

"About five in the afternoon." A hand reached up to scrub the stubble on his jaw. "Do you have to work?"

Work? At a time like this?

"Have you been walking around the house like that?" The man had fed Cooper and let him out...stark naked?

He smiled. "Why? Does it bother you?"

"Define bother."

He laughed. "So, about work..."

"No. No work, but I need to check on Chelsea and my mom, like I told them I would."

"I thought you might. Otherwise I would have let you sleep. As it was, if Cooper hadn't scratched at the door, I was going to wake you in a completely different way." He found one of her hands and linked his fingers through hers.

She closed her eyes, happiness flowing over her. "Wow. You're up for a third round?"

"Believe me, I'm up for all kinds of things. Round or otherwise." A quick glance down showed he was already up and ready.

"Mmm." She let out a sigh as a thought came to her. Talk. That's what she'd meant to do at some point, only she'd gotten sidetracked. She dipped a toe into the water. "Do you think Chelsea and Paul are going to start seeing each other?"

"I think it's a possibility. Why? Is that a problem?"

"Do you think it's a good idea?"

"Don't know. They've both been through some tough times. They'll either be able to support each other, or they'll drag each other down."

A shiver went over her. "I hope I never have to live through anything like the past couple of months ever again. How do you deal with patients who are in such pain on a daily basis? I think it would eat at my heart." She hesitated before continuing. "And after what happened with your dad…"

Lifting his hand to kiss it, his crooked little finger caught her attention. She changed her aim and kissed that knuckle instead.

He stiffened at her act. "My dad is the reason I'm in this line of work."

Pulling away, he reached down and picked something up off the floor. She frowned, and then saw it was the picture frame he'd knocked off. Flipping it over, he went to put it on the nightstand then stopped, his jaw tightening as he stared at it.

"Clint?"

He shook his head, throat moving for a second. Jessi swiveled her eyes to look at the frame.

The glass on Larry's side had broken, a series of jagged, cobweb-looking cracks distorting his features and obscuring half of his face.

When she glanced back at Clint he looked…stricken. That was the only word she could think to describe it.

She reached out a hand. "Hey, it's okay. It's only a cheap frame. I can get another one."

He set it on the table but wouldn't quite meet her eyes.

Something was wrong. Very wrong.

"Jessi, I need to tell you something."

A wave of foreboding licked at her toes, then her ankles. Soon it was waist deep and rising.

She reached out to touch him, but the second she did, he backed away and found his trousers, sliding into them and fastening them before he looked at her again.

"I was going to wait and tell you later, but this seems as

good a time as any." A muscle worked in his jaw. "They've found a permanent replacement for Dr. Cordoba. He arrives in two weeks."

She wasn't sure what this had to do with them. "Chelsea will continue her sessions with him, then."

"Yes." He scooped his dress shirt from the floor and pushed his arms through the sleeves.

Why was he getting dressed? This was good news. They wouldn't have to hide their relationship anymore.

Right?

"So that means we'll be able to see each other without—"

"No." His lean fingers moved quickly to button up his shirt. "We won't. I'm putting in my transfer papers. You knew this was only a temporary assignment. Just until they found another doctor. I'm going back to San Diego."

What? Her mind screamed that word over and over and over until it was hoarse with grief and confusion.

He'd made love to her last night as if he couldn't get enough. As if she really meant something to him. And now he was leaving?

Shades of the past came back to haunt her. Hadn't he already done this once before? Screwed her and then taken off without a backward glance?

The ominous wave was still rising, faster than ever, splashing up her neck and cresting over her head until she couldn't breathe. Horror washed through her at all she'd done with him last night, at how truly and freely she'd given herself to him.

In. Love.

And he'd felt nothing. *Nothing.*

As the silence drew out, he finally broke it by saying, "I should have told you before…" He motioned at the bed.

He hadn't been willing to change his life for her twenty-odd years ago so why had she thought he would now?

Sitting up and not bothering to cover her nakedness, she glared at him, welcoming the anger—because it kept away the tears. "Yes, you should have. But, then, you wouldn't have had one last trip down memory lane, would you? Treating patients isn't the only thing you're good at, Dr. Marks. You're also an expert at using people, and then ditching them when you've had what you wanted."

She climbed to her feet and stood there. Refusing to be vulnerable. Refusing to care what he did.

Only she knew deep inside it was a lie. The cracks in the picture frame now mirrored the ones in her heart, splitting wide open and spilling everything inside her into the dust that had become her life.

"Jess, that's not the way this—"

"No!" If he said one more word she was either going to burst into tears or slap him across the face with all her might. "Just go. Have Chelsea's new doctor call us when he arrives."

He grabbed the rest of his clothes and shoved his bare feet into his dress shoes. "I'm sorry, Jess."

Tossing her head, she bit out a quick reply. "Don't be. It was a blast from the past. We had our own mini high school reunion right here in my bedroom, but now it's time to pack up and get back to our own lives, in our own cities."

She didn't ask him exactly when he was leaving. She didn't want to know.

Clint's throat moved as he looked at her for another minute. Then he said, "Goodbye, Jessi."

With that, he turned around and walked out of the bedroom, his receding footsteps on the hardwood floor marking his location and searing the message into her brain. There was no slowing of his pace, no hesitation as the front door opened and then closed.

Clint was leaving. And this time he wasn't coming back.

CHAPTER EIGHTEEN

A WEEK WAS all it took to change his life forever.

He'd filed expedited transfer papers, asking them to put him wherever they needed him, preferably deployed overseas. He wound up at the VA hospital in New Mexico instead.

It might as well have been the other side of the world.

He sat at a desk that looked exactly like his previous one and wondered how he'd gotten here. Aimless. Rootless. And, thus far, patientless. They were letting him get settled in.

Right. Like that's what he needed. More time to think about what had happened that night in Jessi's bedroom.

He'd been all set to tell her how he felt, and then he'd picked up that frame and seen the damage he'd caused.

To her marriage. To her life.

At that moment he'd felt as shattered as that glass.

Being with Jessi again had wreaked havoc with his insides, turning him back into that impulsive screwup he'd been in high school.

He couldn't risk messing up her life a second time. Neither could he ask her to pick up and move away the next time he got his transfer papers. Jessi's life was in Richmond. With Chelsea and her mom—and those two graves.

Clint's place was with his patients. The one thing he knew he was good at.

She'd be okay without him. Seeing Chelsea get better would give her hope for a new beginning. He'd soon be relegated to the past again—where he belonged.

His phone rang. He glanced at the readout and his mouth went dry, his blood pressure spiking.

A Richmond area code.

Only it wasn't Jessi's number. He didn't recognize it.

Damn it!

When would the hope finally die? It was over. He'd ended it himself—and she hadn't been sorry to see him go. She'd not said one word to discourage him. Instead, she'd practically shoved him out the door.

Checking the door to his office to make sure it was closed, he pressed the speakerphone button and stared at the open case file in front of him. So much for trying to get up to speed.

"Hello?"

"Dr. Marks?"

He recognized the voice immediately. "Chelsea? Is everything okay?"

"I don't know. I mean, everything's fine with me. It's Mom."

His heart plummeted. "Is she all right?"

"No." There was a pause, and then her voice came through. Stronger. With just a hint of accusation. "I saw you holding hands at the memorial service. How could you just…leave like that?"

"I was transferred. You know how it works."

A curse word split the air, and Clint picked the phone up and put it to his ear, even though he knew his assistant wouldn't be able to hear their conversation through the thick walls.

Chelsea's voice came back through. "You're right. I do know how it works. And there's no way you'd be able to get the okay for a transfer that fast unless you asked for it to be expedited. Or unless you'd been sitting on it this whole time."

"What does it matter? The Richmond hospital was a temporary assignment."

"Did I say something? Do something?"

"No." He hurried to set her mind at ease. "This had nothing to do with you, Chelsea. I'm proud of how hard you've worked on your recovery. You've faced the past head-on and now you're ready to move into the future."

A laugh came over the phone, but it was without humor. "That's what you always told us during group, wasn't it? That we had to face the past and see it for what it was without running or hiding from the truth. But in the end that's not what you did, is it?"

Hell, how had a tiny slip of a girl managed to read him so well? He had run. He'd taken one look at that broken glass, and instead of facing his fears, instead of talking to Jessi about everything that had happened, he'd turned tail and run.

Because he was afraid to face the future. Afraid his past would somehow catch up to him and splash its ugliness on to Jessi.

In reality, he'd been looking for an excuse to flee ever since he'd seen her sitting in his office that first day.

Why? Because he loved her, and just like back in high school he'd hightailed it out of town rather than having the courage to tell her how he felt and let her decide what to do with that information.

"What happened between me and your mother isn't any of your business."

"Sure it is. She's. My. Mother." She took an audible breath. "When I was in trouble, you never hesitated to bleed every detail of my therapy to her, because…she had a right to know the truth. She's listed as my next of kin. Well, guess what, Doctor, that works both ways. I'm her next of kin. I have a right to know. Did you even care about her at all?"

He swallowed. "Yes."

"Well, she cares for you, too. She's been smiling and saying all the right things, but she's not okay. She looks awful."

"I'm sorry."

"Not good enough. You might outrank me, but I'm going to tell you straight up what I think."

He smiled despite himself. "There's no question you and your mom are related."

"Yeah? Well, here it is. You're no better than a common deserter."

Shock rolled through him. "Excuse me?"

"You heard me. When the battle inside your head got tough, you turned around and walked away, instead of acting like a soldier and facing it, the way you told us to do. She's not the enemy, Dr. Marks. I don't know what it is you're fighting, but I suggest you figure it out and come back and face it. Otherwise you'll regret it for the rest of your life."

She looks awful.

He'd rushed off so sure that he was doing the right thing and saving the woman he loved a whole lot of pain.

What if he'd ended up *causing* her pain instead?

Hell. He was an idiot. "Reprimand noted and accepted."

"Good. You said you cared about her. Do you love her?"

He smiled, making a decision he should have made twenty-two years ago. "I think your mom deserves to hear that from the source, don't you?"

"Then get back here and tell her. Because I'm pretty sure she loves you, too."

Jessi pulled her sticky scrubs away from her midsection, fanning the fabric against herself as she headed into the parking lot. It was an hour past the end of her shift, and she was only now able to leave the hospital.

A gang war had seen her dealing with multiple gunshot wounds. Two had died en route to the hospital and another three had needed surgery. One of them had a broken finger in addition to other more serious wounds, but that small injury had been the one that had made her finally break down and admit the truth. That she missed Clint. Terribly.

She had a feeling Chelsea knew something was wrong, and her mom—almost completely recovered from her surgery a month ago—had also cast some worried looks her way. She had no idea why. She'd been acting cheerful, even if that's all it was. An act.

Straightening her back, she quickened her pace. This was ridiculous. How long was she going to keep mooning over something that was never going to happen? She needed to pull herself together and forget about…

Keys in hand, she paused halfway across the parking lot. Someone in uniform stood near where she'd parked her car, the tall military bearing painfully familiar. How many times had she seen that stance?

Her dad. Her daughter. In a military town, it was impossible not to recognize the proud upright posture. Only this went beyond that. This was…

Clint.

Oh, God. Something inside her urged her to turn around and dash back to the safety of the hospital.

No. She was not going to let what that man did or didn't do dictate her actions and emotions any longer. So she walked toward him, trying not to look directly at him as she did so, afraid he'd see the misery in her eyes.

When she reached her car she saw that she was right, he was standing right next to it. She'd have to pass in front of him to get to the driver's door.

"I thought you'd left," she said, her voice sounding as chipper as ever.

"I did." He didn't move. Didn't crack a smile at her tone. "I came back."

Her heart took a swan dive. What? Had he decided he hadn't tortured her enough?

She swallowed. "Why?"

"Because I'm done running. When you told me about Larry and his death, it was like a hole opened up and swallowed me whole. If I hadn't followed you that day…if I'd let him chase you outside instead, you'd still be one big happy family."

He drew in an audible breath. "And then I broke that frame, Larry's frame, and it was as if the universe was sending me a message. That I'd screwed up your life once before, and I could very well do it again if I stayed."

Her own breath caught in her lungs before whooshing back out. "Why didn't you say something?"

"I thought I was doing you a favor."

"Well, you didn't. I—" He cut her off with a finger pressed across her lips.

"Let me finish, while I still have the nerve. I came back to tell you I love you. I have since high school when I found you crying beside the creek." He paused. "I gave you up once, thinking it was for your own good, but I'm not going to do it again. Unless you tell me to go."

She pushed his hand away.

"Twice." The correction came out before she could stop it. "You gave me up twice. Why should I believe you this time?"

"Because it's the truth, Jess. I swear it." He took a step forward.

She tried to force herself to move back, but she couldn't. She just stood there, staring up at him. Maybe the summer heat had gone to her head and he was a mirage. After all, he didn't look hot at all.

Okay, so he looked superhot in that uniform, but not in the way she'd meant it.

"So what changed your mind this time?"

She had to know he hadn't just come back on a whim. That he was here for the long haul this time.

"That's a complicated question. I've never been truly terrified of anything—not even my father. But you scare me, Jess. The fear that I might not be good enough for you because of my past. Larry's death just seemed to echo that fear. It took a wise young woman to set me straight."

She frowned, until something clicked. "Chelsea."

He nodded. "Yes. She challenged me to come back and face my fears. So here I am. This is my battleground, and I'm not going to retreat. Not this time. Unless you tell me to."

He was handing her the power. Just like the last time they made love. Only this time it wasn't a game, and she had to be very sure of her heart. Trust that he wasn't going to leave, this time. That he wasn't going to take off like Larry and do something crazy, instead of sitting down and talking out their problems.

Did she trust him?

Yes. If he had the guts to face his fears, then she owed it to herself—and him—to do the same.

"Well, I guess we're at an impasse, then," she said in as serious a voice as she could manage, when all she wanted to do was throw herself into his arms and kiss him until neither of them could breathe. "Because I'm not going to tell you to leave. And you're evidently not going to leave on your own."

His eyes clouded for a second, but he stood firm. "No, I'm not."

"Then you'll just have to stay." She thought of something. "Wait. What about your transfer?"

"It hasn't been officially approved, it was still in the works, but they let me move early. My current contract is almost up, so I can resign my commission—go into private practice—if that tilts the odds in my favor. We wouldn't have to move. Ever. We could stay right here in Richmond."

This time she did throw herself at him, wrapping her arms around his neck. "Those odds were already tilted once I saw you standing here. I love you, too, Clint, no matter what you decide to do. You do so much good for people like Chelsea. And if the paperwork on your transfer goes through before you can cancel it, I'm coming with you."

He grabbed her up and held her tight—so tight that she felt the air rush from her lungs. She didn't care.

She loved this man. More than she ever had.

Leaning down, he caught her mouth in a kiss that held a wealth of love and longing. "There's only one thing I want to do right now."

She laughed. "Really? Can it wait until I've had something to eat?"

"It could, but…" He withdrew and reached inside the jacket of his uniform, pulling out a small jeweler's box.

Her hands went over her mouth, afraid the sun and heat were still playing tricks on her. "Clint?"

He snapped the box open to reveal a ring. Small and twinkling and perfect. "It was my grandmother's. Mom gave it to me before I went into the service. She said I might need it one day. She was right." He smiled. "I'd get down on one knee, but I'm afraid I'd be seared permanently to the pavement if I did. Damn, I'm screwing this all up. I should have waited to ask you to marry me until dinner, when we could have champagne, or until I had the ring resized—"

"No. This is the perfect place. The perfect ring. And you're the perfect man for me." Tears gathered in her eyes. "And I accept your proposal, Colonel Clinton Marks."

He kissed her again. Then Jessi unhooked the chain from her necklace and let him slide the slender ring onto it, where it dangled in the hollow of her collarbone. Fingering it while heat waves danced over the black tar surface of the parking lot, she blinked. "Where's your car?"

"Someone offered me a lift."

She could guess who that might be. "Chelsea again?"

"Yes."

"So you've been standing in the parking lot for over an hour?"

"Not quite. I had a little help tracking your movements."

Ahh…so that's why Chelsea's text—asking her to let her know the second she got off work—had been waiting for her when she'd switched her phone back on.

She clicked the button to unlock her car. "I guess we should put her out of her misery, then."

"Already done. I told her if you weren't home in an hour to assume we were out celebrating somewhere."

"Oh? You were that sure of yourself, were you?"

He grinned. "You have no idea what I've been through over the past month. I wasn't sure of anything, least of all myself."

"So what kind of celebration were you thinking of?"

He slid into the passenger seat and waited for her to join him. "I was thinking of something small and private."

"Interesting." Her pulse rate sped up, despite her earlier words about eating something. "So whose turn is it to be in charge this time?"

He eased his fingers deep into her hair and turned her face toward him. "How about if from now on we make sure it's an equal partnership?"

"Yes," she breathed as he leaned down to kiss her again, allowing her senses to begin that familiar climb. "That's the perfect solution."

EPILOGUE

"Do you, Jessica Marie Riley, take Clinton Shane Marks to be your lawfully wedded husband?"

Clint faced Jessi as she said the words that would legally bind her to him. Only they were already bound by cords much stronger than anything the minister could say.

Jessi had convinced him that the broken frame didn't represent what he'd done to her life all those years ago. Instead, it symbolized a breaking free from the mistakes of the past in order to face a future that was clean and new. They were getting a second chance, and Clint didn't intend to waste one second of it.

After they'd repeated the rest of the vows, he gripped her hands and let the emotion of doing so pour over him in a flood. And it was okay. No more shoving them behind a wall and hoping they'd stay there. He wasn't his father. He knew how to control those unhealthy feelings, while giving himself over to the ones that made two people into one.

"You may kiss the bride."

"Gladly." He wrapped his arms around Jessi's waist and reeled her in. "Love you," he whispered against her lips.

"Love you, too," she mouthed back.

Only then did he allow himself to really kiss her, putting his heart and soul into the joining of their lips.

"Whooo..." The sound came from the seats behind them, growing in volume the longer the kiss went on.

Clint smiled and leaned back, allowing his hands to slide down her arms until he was clasping her fingers once again. His grandmother's small diamond glittered up at him, a promise of the future. A promise further evidenced by the ultrasound in a drawer in his office desk. Jessi was expecting. A surprise to both of them. And for someone who'd thought he'd never be a father, it was another emotional first. A good one, though.

Jessi squeezed his hands and then turned to motion Chelsea and her new fiancé up to the front.

Paul had proposed just a week ago, and Chelsea had accepted, so there would be more wedding bells in the future. And probably more births along this crazy path they were all on. Her daughter hugged her long and hard, while Paul shook Clint's hand and wished him well.

Then Clint wrapped his arm around his new bride, while the minister introduced them as Mr. Clint and Mrs. Jessica Marks.

Smiles and cheers from some army buddies and their families and friends came from all around them.

This was where he belonged. He'd faced his deepest fears and they hadn't destroyed him. They'd given him hope.

Hope for a future filled with happiness as well as trials, but, most important, love.

"Shall we?"

Jessi grasped his hand and ran down the aisle, half dragging him along with her.

"What's the rush, Mrs. Marks," he asked.

They reached the door and pushed through it. "I've been

waiting all morning for the chance to smash a piece of wedding cake all over your face."

"That's more exciting to you than us getting married?"

"No." She threw him a happy grin. "It's what comes after that has me all worked up."

"Dare I ask what that is?"

"You could, but you might not want me to explain in a public venue."

He laughed, his heart lighter than the frothy layers of his bride's cream-colored dress that fluttered around her knees.

"Then lead on, woman. We've got a cake to cut."

* * * * *